A disturbing occurrence

Her eyes were wide now; his words calm and clear. She realized that she was lying on the ground and that he was kneeling over her, one arm cradling her head, his other hand patting her cheek. Full night was falling around them. The whole world teemed with shadows.

"I must have tripped," she murmured. "Can't . . . remember."

"Don't talk yet. Just keep breathing."

"No, I *have* to talk. What are you doing here? Did I yell or something?"

Etienne shook his head. "If you did, nobody heard you. They're pretty busy upstairs, taking the tour."

"Then how did you—"

"I just had me this . . . feeling."

"You came to find me? How long have you been here?"

"Not long. Just keep yourself quiet now, and—"

"And you didn't see anything? Not that you *could* have seen anything . . . and I don't even know how long I was—" She broke off, biting her lower lip. "What *was* I, anyway? Unconscious? Asleep?"

"I'm thinking you probably fainted. But you were trying to talk the whole time . . . somewhere way back in your head. Things I sure wasn't understanding."

Miranda had no chance to respond. From out of nowhere, a chill stabbed through her, worming along her spine and into her limbs, leaving her trembling and light-headed. At once, Etienne eased her into a sitting position. He wrapped both arms around her and held her close.

"It's like summer out here," he mumbled, "and you're ice cold."

Books by
RICHIE TANKERSLEY CUSICK

Walk of the Spirits
Shadow Mirror

THE UNSEEN
Part One: *It Begins*
Part Two: *Rest in Peace*
Part Three: *Blood Brothers*
Part Four: *Sin and Salvation*

RICHIE TANKERSLEY CUSICK

SPIRIT WALK

WALK OF THE SPIRITS • SHADOW MIRROR

speak

An Imprint of Penguin Group (USA) Inc.

SPIRIT WALK

WALK OF THE SPIRITS

SPEAK

Published by the Penguin Group

Penguin Group (USA) Inc., 345 Hudson Street, New York, New York 10014, U.S.A.

Penguin Group (Canada), 90 Eglinton Avenue East, Suite 700, Toronto, Ontario, Canada M4P 2Y3
(a division of Pearson Penguin Canada Inc.)

Penguin Books Ltd, 80 Strand, London WC2R 0RL, England

Penguin Ireland, 25 St Stephen's Green, Dublin 2, Ireland (a division of Penguin Books Ltd)

Penguin Group (Australia), 250 Camberwell Road, Camberwell, Victoria 3124, Australia
(a division of Pearson Australia Group Pty Ltd)

Penguin Books India Pvt Ltd, 11 Community Centre, Panchsheel Park, New Delhi – 110 017, India

Penguin Group (NZ), 67 Apollo Drive, Rosedale, Auckland 0632, New Zealand
(a division of Pearson New Zealand Ltd.)

Penguin Books (South Africa) (Pty) Ltd, 24 Sturdee Avenue, Rosebank, Johannesburg 2196, South Africa

Penguin Books Ltd, Registered Offices: 80 Strand, London WC2R 0RL, England

First published in the United States of America by Speak, an imprint of Penguin Group (USA) Inc., 2008
This omnibus edition published by Speak, an imprint of Penguin Group (USA) Inc., 2012

1 3 5 7 9 10 8 6 4 2

THE LIBRARY OF CONGRESS CATALOGING-IN-PUBLICATION DATA:
Cusick, Richie Tankersley.
Walk of the spirits / by Richie Tankersley Cusick.
p. cm.
Summary: After losing everything in a Florida hurricane, seventeen-year-old Miranda and her mother
move to her grandfather's home in Louisiana, where she falls in with an interesting group of students,
and discovers that she can communicate with spirits like her grandfather did.
ISBN: 978-0-14-241050-9 (pbk. : alk. paper)
[1. Ghosts—Fiction. 2. Space and time—Fiction. 3. Louisiana—Fiction. 4. Mystery and detective stories.]
I. Title.

PZ7.C9646Wal 2008
[Fic]—dc22
2007036073

Speak ISBN 978-0-14-242791-0

Printed in the United States of America

ALWAYS LEARNING   PEARSON

For Aunt Deanie and Uncle Jim—because your love, support, and laughter through the years have inspired me more than you could ever know. I love you.

1

SHE WAS TIRED TODAY BECAUSE OF THE SCREAMING.

That horrible screaming that had woken her up last night, just like it had the night before. Screams out of the darkness that cut into her heart like razor blades; distant, muffled screams that trapped her and dangled her precariously between consciousness and full-blown nightmares.

"Miranda?"

At first she'd thought it was the hurricane all over again. Shrieking wind, screeches and groans of the roof and walls splitting and exploding around her. Or maybe her mother's cries of terror. Or her own hysterical weeping...

But then, of course, she'd realized where she was. In a different bed, in a different house—far from Florida, far from the home where she'd slept and felt safe. And those screams were so *real*. Much more real than *any* dream could ever be.

She hadn't had a decent night's sleep since they'd moved here to St. Yvette.

Naturally, Mom didn't believe her about the screams; Mom just kept telling her she was imagining it. And the harder Miranda tried to sleep, and the harder Mom tried to rationalize, the worse everything got. Miranda's energy was sapped. Her thoughts strayed down a hundred dark paths. It was impossible for her to concentrate on anything anymore.

"Miranda Barnes?"

"Huh?" Snapping back to attention, Miranda saw Miss Dupree paused beside the chalkboard, fixing her with a benevolent gaze. The whole class turned in Miranda's direction.

For a split second, Miranda wondered what they saw. A slight, not-very-tall girl with short brown hair pushed nervously behind her ears? A nice-enough girl with hazel eyes and a heart-shaped face and a light sprinkling of freckles across her nose?

Or the silent girl, the sullen girl, who, in her three days at St. Yvette High School, had yet to meet their eyes when they passed her in the hall? Who never spoke, never smiled, never bothered to be friendly?

They couldn't see the fear—that much she was sure of. The shock, the anguish, the grief, the emotions that choked her every time she let her guard down.

So she *wouldn't* let her guard down. Not with these kids, not in this school, not in this town. Not now. Not ever.

"Oh. Yes. I'm here," she mumbled. As her cheeks flushed, Miranda's hands clenched tightly in her lap.

"I know you're here, dear," Miss Dupree went on sweetly. "I was just explaining this little assignment we're all going to be working on."

"*Little* assignment?" a voice complained from the front row. "Come on, Miss Dupree, it counts for half our grade!"

"I'm well aware of that, Parker. And just think how much it would count for if it were a *big* assignment!"

The room erupted in laughter while the young man lounged back in his desk and grinned. *Parker Wilmington,* Miranda was already familiar with *that* name. She was sure she'd heard it uttered longingly from the lips of every girl in St. Yvette High, from giggly freshmen all the way up through her senior class. Tall and blond, sea-green eyes, those gorgeous, unruly strands of hair framing his handsome face, no matter how many times he shook them back. Star quarterback, not a single game lost last season. Self-confident swagger, cocky smile, and . . . taken. *Very and most definitely taken.* By the beautiful girl who was sitting next to Miranda at this very minute.

Miranda glanced quickly across the aisle. *Ashley.* Ashley . . . something, she couldn't remember. Ashley Something-or-Other with the long golden hair and the petite figure and the sexy little cheerleader uniform she was wearing today. One of those picture-perfect girls who would always be drooled over and sought after and passionately admired. *So of course she's with Parker Wilmington. Who else?*

Miranda didn't realize she was staring. Not until Ashley turned and beamed her a perfect white smile.

"Miss Dupree's broken us up into study groups," Ashley leaned toward her and whispered. "I asked her if you could be in ours."

It caught Miranda completely off guard. Study group? Oh, God, the *last* thing she wanted to do was be trapped in a group of strangers, especially curious ones. She'd felt the stares in the hallways, in the classrooms, across campus. She was all too aware of her novelty status here at St. Yvette High School as the Girl Who Lost Everything in the Hurricane. And soon, she knew, the questions would come—questions she couldn't handle, traumatic memories she didn't want to relive. So she'd tried her best to keep a low profile. Kept to herself and stayed invisible. Better that way, she'd decided, much better that way. She wasn't ready for socializing yet—not of any kind. She wanted to be alone—*needed* to be alone—to process all that had happened in the last few weeks, to sort everything out. What she didn't want or need right now were people feeling sorry for her or asking those painful questions or trying to butt into her life—

"I'm Ashley."

Again Miranda jolted back to the present. She was getting used to everyone's southern accents, but Ashley's still managed to fascinate her. Extra thick, extra rich, like warm, melted honey. She saw now that Ashley's hand was taking her own and giving it a firm, friendly shake. Conjuring a tight smile, Miranda kept the handshake brief.

"All right, class!" Miss Dupree motioned for silence. "You've had several weeks now to come up with your topics. Just a reminder: I want these projects to be socially oriented. Something that will get you involved in this town. Something to help you learn more about your community and the neighbors you share it with. I want to see some original ideas, people. Something creative and—"

"Gage wants to know more about *his* neighbor, Miss Dupree." On Miranda's left, a girl in black clothes and heavy black eye makeup stretched languidly in her seat. "The one who keeps getting undressed at night with the curtains open and the lights on."

In mock horror, Parker swung around in his chair. "Hey! *You and Ashley* are Gage's neighbors!"

"I *meant* the house behind him," the girl said calmly.

Clutching his chest, Parker gasped. "Gage! You pervert! That's Mrs. Falconi—she's ninety-six years old!"

This time the laughter reached hysteria. Miranda saw the girl give a slow, catlike smile, while a boy near the window—Gage, she supposed—blushed furiously and shook his head.

"Roo, stop it!" Ashley hissed, but she couldn't quite hold back a delighted grin. "Why do you always have to embarrass him?"

The other girl shrugged, obviously pleased with herself. "Because it's so easy. And he's so cute when he's embarrassed."

"All right, people, all right!" Clearing her throat, Miss Dupree struggled to keep her own amusement in check. "Thank you, Roo, for that fascinating bit of information. And should any of us notice a pervert lurking outside our windows tonight, we can all rest easily now, knowing it's only Gage."

The class went wild. Poor Gage went redder.

"Time to break into your study groups." Miss Dupree moved to her desk, then gestured toward the back of the room. "Oh . . . Miranda?"

"I told her she's with us, Miss Dupree!" Ashley spoke up quickly, while Roo regarded Miranda with undisguised boredom.

Miss Dupree smiled. "Then she's in good hands."

As the rest of the kids reassembled themselves, Parker sauntered back and eased himself down beside Ashley, giving her a quick kiss on the lips. Roo pulled her desk in closer. And Gage, flashing Roo an I-can't-believe-you-did-that look, made his way across the room and promptly smacked her on the head with his notebook.

Roo was right, Miranda decided: Gage *was* cute, embarrassed or not. The same height as Parker, but more slender, his shoulders not as broad. Soft brown hair, a little shaggy, big brown eyes, long dark lashes, and sensitive features, despite the huge frown he was currently leveling at Roo.

Gracing each of them with her smile, Ashley picked up a blue sequined pen. "Well, we're all here, I guess. Except for Etienne. Is he working today—do any of y'all know?"

"An alligator probably ate him." Roo yawned.

Trying not to be obvious, Miranda cast her a sideways glance. She could see now that Roo was short—not much over five feet—with a solid body, more curvy than plump. The girl seemed entirely unself-conscious in her long black Victorian dress and black combat boots. A silver crescent moon hung from a narrow black ribbon around her neck; silvery moons and stars dangled from her multipierced ears. Her bangs were long and thick and partially obscured her brows. And she had purple streaks—the same shade of purple as the heavy gloss on her lips—in several strands of her overdyed black hair.

As Roo's dark eyes shifted toward her, Miranda looked away. There'd been a few kids like Roo in her own high school at home, but she'd never gotten to know them. Never even spoken to them, really. In fact, she and her friends had jokingly called them the Zombie Rejects and avoided them at all costs.

"We definitely need his input." Once more, Ashley's voice drew Miranda back. "Etienne always has good ideas." She sat up straighter, pen poised over paper. "Oh, and Miss Dupree said Miranda can be in our group, okay?"

There were nods all around and mumbles of agreement. Parker winked. Gage shot Miranda a quick glance, while Roo still seemed bored. As Ashley made introductions, Miranda did her best to sound polite, but offered no more than that.

"So!" Ashley began cheerfully. "Out of all those ideas we had last time, which one are we going to do for the project?"

Parker shrugged. "They all sucked, and you know it."

"No, they didn't." Gage's voice was soft, gentle, like his eyes, just as Miranda had expected it to be. "I think the Symbolism of Cemetery Art is pretty good—"

"Good why? 'Cause you thought of it?" Roo asked.

"Good because it's . . . you know . . . interesting."

"Yeah, if you're a maggot."

"Well, it's better than Southern Belle Rock Bands."

Roo looked mildly annoyed. "The Development and Liberation of Women Musicians During the Antebellum Era, excuse me very much."

Ashley waved her paper at them. "Come on, we don't have much time. Maybe Miranda has some ideas."

"What?" Instantly Miranda felt four pairs of eyes on her. "Um, no. Sorry."

The truth was, she hadn't been paying much attention these last few seconds. It was something she was beginning to get used to—this zoning in and out of memories when she least expected it, when she was least prepared—but that didn't make it any easier. It still managed to catch her by surprise. *Sad surprise, lonely surprise.* Like just now, when Gage had mentioned something about art and cemeteries, a picture had snapped into Miranda's mind. She and Marge and Joanie in New Orleans over summer vacation, traveling there for a week with Joanie's parents. Shopping; flirting with those cute bellmen at the hotel; sightseeing around town—old buildings, museums, mansions, graveyards. *Was that only two months ago?* It seemed like years. The last really fun thing they'd done together before everything changed—

"What's this?" Leaning over Miranda's shoulder, Gage pointed to some scribbles on the front of her notebook. "Ghost Walk?"

Miranda looked down at the words. Yes, definitely her own handwriting, though she didn't remember putting them down just now.

"What the hell's a Ghost Walk?" Parker asked. His grin widened as he nudged Ashley in the ribs, and Miranda quickly turned her notebook over.

"It's . . . nothing."

"No, really," Ashley urged her. "Really—what is it?"

Don't make me talk about this—I had so much fun then— now it hurts too much to remember . . .

"Miranda?"

"It's . . . like a tour." Miranda kept her eyes on her desk, wishing they'd all just go away and leave her alone. "A haunted tour. My friends and I went on one in New Orleans. A guide takes you around to all these different places and tells you about their history. Except each place has some scary story connected to it—like some horrible tragedy or unsolved mystery."

"I've heard of those," Roo mumbled, far from impressed.

"Of course you have, O Queen of Darkness," Parker shot back at her.

Gage, however, was intrigued. "Do all the places actually have ghosts?"

"Well . . ." *Oh great. How did I get myself into this?* Meeting their gazes now, Miranda stumbled on. "Well, I don't know if *all* of them do—"

"Then why do they call it a Ghost Walk?" Parker challenged, even as Ashley clapped a hand over his mouth.

Miranda couldn't help sounding defensive. "People *have* seen ghosts there. But there's also local legends and superstitions—all kinds of weird supernatural things that have happened in the city."

"So it really is historical, right?" Ashley was squirming excitedly in her seat. "Not just made up?"

"That's what the guide told us—that all the stories are documented. So yes, it's all historical—just more of a *dark* history."

"Miranda, that's *perfect!*" As Ashley squealed, the whole class turned to see what was happening. Ashley immediately told them to mind their own business, then lowered her voice while Parker wrestled her hand from his face. "Oh my God, that's so perfect! That's *the* most perfect idea for *the* most perfect project! You're a genius!"

"What project?" Looking confused, Parker bent toward them. "Our project?"

"Not one single person's had an idea as good as this. And it'll be fun, too! Miss Dupree is going to *love* it!"

One corner of Parker's mouth twitched. He shifted in his desk, stretching his long legs out in front of him. "A ghost tour. Here. In St. Yvette."

"It's socially oriented, right? It involves historical research . . . we'll have to learn more about the community . . ."

Gage nodded. "I like it." He glanced over at Roo, who merely shrugged. A shrug that could have been either pro or con, Miranda couldn't tell.

Ashley, however, was still bubbling over. "Miranda, this is so wonderful! You'll have to tell us more about it! How to get organized, what we need to do, where we need to start—"

"Whoa! Hold on!" Backing up a step, Gage lifted both hands. "Give her a chance to breathe, why don't you?"

"I'm sorry. I'm sorry, you're right. Miranda, do you want us to explain the project to you some more? I mean, maybe we haven't filled you in enough on the details? Or the schedule or how it's graded and stuff? Or maybe you have some questions?"

"I have a question," Roo announced, before Miranda could even open her mouth.

The girl draped herself over her desk. Frowning slightly, she fixed Miranda with a solemn, dark-ringed stare.

"So," Roo said. "How does it feel living with a lunatic?"

2

"**What?**"

At first Miranda thought it was a joke. Some private, inside joke the group had decided to play on her, just to see how she'd react.

Except she didn't *get* the joke. She didn't *understand* the joke. And slowly it began to dawn on her that Roo's stare wasn't wavering, that Roo wasn't smiling. And that the others had gone silent, that they were watching Roo with strange expressions on their faces, and there was an undercurrent in the air, like cold electricity.

"What?" she managed to say again. "I don't understand."

She wanted to say more, but her voice stuck in her throat. She wanted to walk away from them, but her stomach had gone queasy.

"Roo," Ashley whispered.

"What's wrong?" Seemingly puzzled, Roo glanced at each of them in turn, then back again at Miranda. "You know," she said matter-of-factly, "Jonas Hayes—your *grandfather*. I mean . . . what's it like? Aren't you scared?"

Parker snorted a laugh. "Jesus, Roo."

Gage said nothing, only folded his arms across his chest. He leaned back against the wall and focused on something outside the classroom window.

"Scared?" Miranda's mind was whirling. Her head was beginning to pound. "What are you talking about?"

"Nothing!" Ashley broke in. Reaching for Miranda's hand, she gave it a quick squeeze. "Look, Roo gets everything mixed up. Don't pay any attention to her."

Miranda's head pounded harder. *Lunatic? My grandpa? Why are they all watching me like that? I can't stand it—*

"Miranda," Ashley sounded alarmed. "Are you okay?"

But Miranda couldn't answer. It was Roo's voice that answered instead, toneless, coming from some far-off place. "I thought she knew about her grandfather. I thought she knew, or I wouldn't have said anything."

"You're so pale." Ashley's hands were on Miranda's shoulders now, patting gently. "Do you want some water?"

"Maybe she's going to pass out," Parker said. "Maybe you should slap her or something."

"Oh, for heaven's sake, Parker!"

"Well, I didn't mean hit her hard—"

"This isn't the football field. Nobody's going to hit anybody."

"I'm fine." Miranda nodded. "Honest. I'm fine." But her stomach was churning, dry heaves almost, at the back of her throat. She should have had something for lunch, should have eaten breakfast like Mom told her to do. "*What* about my grandfather?"

But it was as if she hadn't spoken.

"She *is* pale," Gage insisted. "Do you think she's gonna be sick?"

Parker was instantly on his feet. "Turn her the other way!"

"I told you I'm fine," Miranda snapped back at him, at all of them. Why couldn't they just mind their own business? Wasn't she already going through enough without adding more people and problems to her train wreck of a life?

The classroom, the study group, everything blurred in a hot rush of anger. She wanted to escape, but she couldn't see the door.

And if only it were that easy, Miranda thought. *If only there were some magical door I could just escape through, and be happy again . . .*

Not enough that the hurricane had struck. Everything lost, everything gone.

No house anymore, no possessions. Mom's business completely wiped out. Old friends, dear friends, never-seen-again friends. Some hopefully relocated to places unknown. Others left behind, helpless victims and heartbreaking fatalities of the storm.

"We'll go home again someday," Mom had promised her, trying to sound both brave and comforting. "This is a temporary situation, Miranda."

Miranda had wanted so much to believe her. But deep down, she'd wondered if Mom really believed it herself.

"Just till we get back on our feet," Mom kept insisting. "Just till then. It's not like we'll have to live in St. Yvette forever."

St. Yvette. St. Yvette, Louisiana. To Miranda, who'd spent her whole life on the sparkling white beaches of Florida, they might just as well have been moving to the darkest end of the earth.

"So why can't we just get our own place?" she'd begged her mother. "Why do we have to live with relatives I don't even know?"

"Because." And for just a heartbeat, she'd seen true panic in her mother's expression, a look so foreign that it scared her. "Because," Mom had repeated as the look vanished and her voice calmed. "We don't have anywhere else to go."

Just hearing Mom say it made Miranda want to cry—and she hadn't let herself do that since the disaster. Not since the brutal hurricane had ravaged the Florida coastline and their warm, sunny beach house and the only world she'd ever known. Not since they'd been forced to leave everything—and everyone—behind.

She'd felt sick as they'd driven the rented car into St. Yvette five days ago. The sticky heat choking her breath away, squeezing sweat from every single pore. They'd had to stop at a drawbridge, where she'd caught a glimpse of shrimp boats in the murky water. And on the opposite shore, an old Catholic cemetery, its aboveground tombs rotting away between moss-draped trees. The air so thick and heavy, like being wrapped in wet gauze. The stench of dirty water. A cloying sweetness of flowers. An undercurrent of fresh oil and sweat, raw meat and fish guts.

ST. YVETTE WELCOMES YOU.

She'd stared at the weathered sign on the side of the road.

She'd clenched her arms around her chest to keep from getting hysterical.

I've survived everything else. But I'll never survive this. Never. Not in a million years.

"Well," Mom had said cheerfully. *Way* too cheerfully, Miranda had been quick to note. "So here we are, huh? At last. And actually, it doesn't seem that different from when I left."

That was a million years ago, and do I even care? Miranda's shrug was equally grim. "How old is this place, anyway?"

"It predates the Civil War. There's a lot of history in this area."

"So where are all the plantations and stuff?"

"There're a few nearby. We'll go see them, I promise—"

"And what's that weird smoke?"

Mom had frowned at her, sniffed the air, frowned again. "I don't smell any smoke. You mean, like an actual fire?"

"No, never mind. It's gone now."

The truth was, it had vanished almost as soon as she'd noticed it—more like a thought, really, than an actual smell. And not like a cigarette either, or charcoal, or burning leaves, or any other smoke Miranda was familiar with. Pungent and faint and at the same time . . . acrid and damp . . .

"Don't recognize it?" Mom had pressed her.

"No." *But I* should *recognize it,* Miranda had thought uneasily, without knowing why. *I* should *recognize that smell . . .*

"Hey." Mom was talking again. "Don't be fooled by this side of town. The rest of it's really beautiful."

"You don't know that."

"Well . . . I remember that."

"Things change."

It was like an accusation hanging between them. Mom had been quick to try to dispel it.

"But some things don't. Like mystery. And romance. History and legends and old, old secrets—"

"What secrets?"

"I wasn't being specific, honey. I just meant that *all* small towns have secrets. That's part of their charm."

Miranda had watched more scenery go past the car window. Old neighborhoods. Old houses. Gardens. Civil War statues. Antique shops. Old churches. An elementary school. Another cemetery. An old train depot. A park. An old fountain. Another cemetery.

"Charm's not exactly the word I'd use," she'd muttered. "Try dead. God, it can't get any worse than this."

"Yes," Mom answered quietly. "Yes, it can always get worse."

"Oh. Thank you, Mom. I really needed that positive outlook."

"I *am* being positive, honey. I'm just trying to show you how lucky we are. It could be worse. For lots of people, it's worse. We didn't have to be separated, you and I. We didn't have to go into a shelter. We have each other. We have a home to go to."

"You call this a home?"

"We have family here."

"But you don't even love Grandpa."

"No, Miranda, that's not true—"

"The two of you haven't seen each other or talked to each other in . . . how long? My whole life?"

"It has nothing to do with you. It's—"

"I know, I know. Complicated. Why won't you ever tell me?"

Mom's hands had gripped the steering wheel. "It's nothing for you to worry about. Nothing for you to even think about. This is between Grandpa and me, okay?"

"Fine, Mom. Just fine."

And then the long pause. That long anger-hurt pause before Mom finally spoke again.

"Honey . . . for what it's worth . . . our lives really will be happy again."

"It's not worth much. And how can you even believe that?" Miranda shot back, then instantly felt bad at the flinch of pain on her mother's face.

"I have to believe that, honey," her mother whispered. "I have to . . ."

"—have to hand in your project ideas before you leave," Miss Dupree was saying. "And I expect a rough outline on Monday."

Miranda snapped back to attention How long had she been zoned out just now? Seconds? Minutes? Noting the four intense stares aimed in her direction, she remembered her rude little outburst and felt her cheeks go hot.

"Miranda, are you really, truly okay?" Ashley fretted.

"Of course I am." Trying to avoid Ashley's gaze, Miranda focused on the front of the classroom.

"You scared me," Ashley went on. "I thought for a minute we might have to take you to the nurse."

"It's nothing. I'm just—" As Miranda's brain scrambled, she heard the sound of the bell, Miss Dupree shouting last-minute reminders, the chaos of students spilling out into the halls. Thank God it was last period. Thank God it was the weekend. Thank God she wouldn't have to deal with any more people or conversations for a few days.

Grabbing her things, she bolted for the door. She kept her head down, pushing her way along the noisy corridor, but Roo's words echoed even louder in her mind.

"How does it feel living with a lunatic?"

So what haven't you told me, Mom? And what haven't you been telling me all these years?

"Miranda, wait up!"

Miranda walked faster. As a group of kids jostled her to one side, a hand closed around her elbow, steering her over to the wall and away from the Friday-afternoon stampede.

"You passed your locker," a voice said, and she found herself looking up into kind, brown eyes. Gage pointed in the opposite direction from where she'd been going. "Or . . . maybe you knew that."

"Look," Miranda answered irritably. "I just want to get home, okay?" Then, as Gage quickly stepped back, she took a deep breath and started over. "I'm sorry. And I'm sorry for how I acted before. I'm having a terrible life right now."

"I understand. I've had a terrible life myself more than once."

"Yeah, well . . . you've probably never felt like throwing up in the middle of class."

Gage considered this a moment. "No . . . but Roo threw up on *me* once in second grade."

She noticed his dimples now, as he smiled. A totally melt-your-heart smile, shy but sincere.

"—didn't mean it," he was saying, and Miranda focused back on their discussion.

"Didn't mean what?"

"Roo." He sounded apologetic. "What she said back there. About your grandfather."

"Look, I don't know anything about my grandfather, okay? If you want to know something about him, I'm the *last* person you should ask."

"I'm not asking."

"We're living in his garage apartment, but—thanks to my mom—I'm not allowed to meet him." Miranda didn't know why she was telling Gage all this. She certainly didn't want to, but there was something so unthreatening about him that her words kept tumbling out. "I've never talked to my grandfather. I've been here in town five whole days, and I still haven't seen him. Now I guess I know why."

Slowly, Gage shook his head. "I don't understand."

"Well, that makes us even."

Gage didn't seem to mind her bad mood. "The thing is, Roo doesn't mean to hurt anybody. She's just . . . honest."

"That's a tactful way of putting it."

"She says things out loud before she thinks them through."

"Well, she obviously knows more about my family than I do. So what's the story? Why don't *you* tell me?"

Hesitating, he lowered his eyes. "I don't think it's my place—"

"Here's the deal. I was ten years old before I even *knew* I had a grandfather. Alive, I mean. I always thought all my grandparents were dead, because that's what my parents told me. Then one day I was going through my mom's closet, and I accidentally knocked this box off a shelf. And this picture fell out—some man I didn't recognize, with his arm around my aunt Teeta."

"Everyone around here loves your aunt." Gage's soft eyes lifted again to Miranda's face. "In fact, she's about the best person I've ever known."

"I've always loved her, too. I've talked to her on the phone since I was little; she's never forgotten my birthday or Christmas. But the date on that picture I found? It was taken just two weeks before, and Aunt Teeta had written on the back: 'Love from your family.'"

"Wow. What'd you do?"

"I confronted my mother, and that's when she admitted I really *did* have a grandfather. Not only that, but I'd *always* had a grandfather, and not only that, but he *lives* with *Aunt Teeta*."

"And?"

"And nothing. She said they'd been out of each other's lives for years, and that's the way it would always be, and I should let it go."

"You never talked about your grandfather again?"

"I tried to. But Mom just wouldn't."

"What about your dad?"

Miranda's heart clenched. "My dad died before I could ask him. In fact, his funeral was that day—the day I found my grandfather's picture."

"I'm . . . sorry—"

"Don't be. You didn't know."

"So what about now?" Shifting his books, Gage leaned one shoulder against the wall. "Maybe your aunt Teeta could help you meet your grandfather. I bet she wouldn't tell your mom."

"I've almost asked her a couple times."

"But . . . ?"

But what if I finally meet Grandpa, and it all turns out wrong? She couldn't tell Gage what her biggest wish had been since she was ten years old, what she'd hoped and prayed for so desperately. That someday, somehow, maybe she really *could* get to know her grandfather. That maybe Mom and Grandpa would settle their differences, whatever they were. *And that maybe having Grandpa in my life could be like having a dad again . . .*

But before she could answer, voices shouted at the end of the corridor, and Parker, Ashley, and Roo came walking toward them.

"They're calling you," Gage warned her.

Flustered, Miranda started backing away. "Look, I don't know what got into me just now. I never do things like this, I never act like this, I swear. So if you could forget it ever happened—"

"Don't worry." Though his lips showed a trace of amusement, his eyes were warm and sympathetic. "Don't be so hard on yourself. And if it helps any—that stuff about your grandfather is just town gossip."

She wished she knew what he meant. Wished he'd say more, elaborate, explain. But the others were here now—Ashley chattering, Parker arguing, Roo watching Miranda and Gage with sly curiosity.

Squealing, Ashley threw her arms around Miranda, while Gage ducked swiftly out of the way.

"You'll get used to her, Miranda," Parker sighed, pulling Ashley back.

But Ashley broke free at once. "Miss Dupree loved your idea! She can't wait to see how we put it all together. She says it's the most original and creative topic in the whole class!"

"Make that the most ridiculous," Parker muttered.

Miranda tried valiantly to resist Ashley's hug. "Hey. It *wasn't* my idea—"

"Don't be so modest! Of course it was!" Giving Miranda one last squeeze, Ashley got down to business. "Okay. So we'll all meet at the library later and start our planning. You can come, can't you, Miranda?"

"Well, I—"

Parker's loud groan cut her off. "Oh please, not the library. All that whispering gives me a headache."

"You *are* a headache." Roo yawned.

"Let's just go to The Tavern. I need background music."

"Too crowded. Too noisy." Shaking his head, Gage leaned in toward Miranda. "It's a restaurant," he explained. "Not much to look at, but the food's great. Everybody hangs out there."

Roo did a thumbs-down. "Two no votes for The Tavern. It won't get dark for a while—why don't we just go to the Falls?"

Looks passed from one to another, followed by nods all around.

"Have you seen the bayou yet, Miranda?" Gage asked, while she fumbled for an excuse.

"Not exactly. I mean, sort of, from a distance. But really, I don't think I can—"

"Then this'll be a first for you!" Ashley was delighted. "We'll be right *on* the bayou."

Parker nodded, deadpan. "Alligators and water moccasins, up close and personal."

"Oh, Parker, for heaven's sake. Don't listen to him, Miranda. I've never seen any nasty things around there."

"Except for Roo," Parker added. "She can be pretty nasty."

Roo pointedly ignored him. The boys grinned, and Ashley chattered on.

"It's pretty at the Falls, but it has atmosphere, too—kind of spooky. Anyway, the *perfect* place to plan your Ghost Walk."

"It's not *my* Ghost Walk," Miranda said again, frustrated. "And I hadn't planned on going—"

"We'll pick you up at your grandpa's in a couple hours."

"Y'all are serious." As the reality of their project seemed to hit him at last, Parker burst out laughing. "A Ghost Walk in St. Yvette? There's not even twelve hundred people in this stupid town, and most of them are boring as hell. How much—what did you call it . . . dark history?—can there be?"

"Oh, stop whining." Losing patience, Ashley glared at him. "There's bound to be lots of old secrets buried around here."

Secrets, Miranda thought wryly. And what was it Mom had told her that day? *All small towns have secrets . . . that's part of their charm . . .*

She realized Gage was looking at her. She deliberately turned away.

Yes, you're so right, Ashley. There must *be lots of old secrets buried around here.*

Especially the ones in my own family.

3

"WHAT'S GOING ON, MOM?"

Miranda stopped in the doorway and glared at her mother, who was standing in the middle of the room, rummaging frantically through her purse. The upstairs garage apartment was small and stuffy—way too cramped for the two twin beds and antique sofa, the table and chairs, and the oversize armoire that had been brought over from the main house.

Oh, God, how depressing.

Her eyes made a quick sweep of the room, taking in the corner kitchen space with its tiny stove, microwave, mini-refrigerator, and narrow pantry; the old-fashioned lace curtains at the windows; the framed sepia-toned photographs on the pale pink walls. A vase of red carnations sat on the lemon-oiled coffee table, and though Aunt Teeta had done her best to make the place homey and comfortable, even those loving touches couldn't disguise the faint odor of age and mildew, or the relentless heat.

"Hi, honey, how was school?" Still digging in her purse, Mom didn't bother to look up. "Can you believe I have a job interview in about five minutes, and I can't find the keys to Teeta's car?"

"Mom—"

"I know, I know—the heat's terrible. Of all the days for the air conditioner to go out, but I think she's already called someone to fix it, and I've got this little fan running, so—"

"How *could* you, Mom?"

Loose change and crumpled tissues spilled from the purse onto the floor. Miranda's mother gave a cry of frustration and bent to retrieve them.

"How could I *what,* honey? Let the air conditioner break? Since when have I known the first thing about air conditioners? Okay, be honest—do you think this blouse is okay? Professional enough? I had to borrow it from Teeta, so it's a little big and— Oh, I almost forgot. She picked up a few things for you on her lunch hour today . . . wasn't that nice? Some shorts and T-shirts she thought you'd like—"

"How could you not have told me?"

"About the clothes? Because she wanted it to be a surprise!"

"I'm not talking about Aunt Teeta! I'm talking about how you lied to me!"

"Lied?" Mom was all attention now. Straightening, she fixed Miranda with a puzzled frown. "When? About what?"

"You know what. *Grandpa.*"

The change was immediate on her mother's face. A pretty face, Miranda had always thought—and still so incredibly young-looking, despite the lines of both laughter and pain around those wide, violet eyes; in spite of the gray highlights accenting that dark, shoulder-length hair. But as Miranda continued to stare, her mother's lips tightened, and those beautiful eyes sparked with anger.

"What *about* your grandpa?" Mom's voice had gone cold, yet Miranda pushed on.

"Everyone in school knows about him! Everyone in *town* knows about him! Everyone but me! How could you? How could you have kept—"

"Miranda, calm down. I just . . ." Taking a deep breath, Mom glanced at the clock beside the kitchen sink. "Look, I don't have time to talk about this right now. Your aunt Teeta went to a lot of trouble to get me this job interview, and I have to go."

"This is important!"

"Well, at the moment, *this* is *more* important. We need money so we can pay our own way. Get our own place."

"How can a stupid job interview—or a new house—be more important than my grandfather being a *mental case*?"

Miranda was shouting now, but her mother's tone was emotionless. "I'm sorry you had to hear those rumors. And I'm sure you . . . probably have questions—"

"Gosh, Mom, do you *think*?"

"But I can't go into it now. There's a lot to be said, and we'll need time. Maybe when I get back—"

"I don't know if I'll be here. I have a big school project. I have to meet some kids to study."

"Tomorrow, then. Another day won't make any difference."

"Of course not. I mean, what's one more day compared to seventeen years?"

She watched her mother's lips open, then close again.

Watched as her mother walked toward her and reached out, even though Miranda immediately jerked away.

"I didn't mean for you to find out like this—" Mom began, but Miranda cut her off.

"How *else* was I going to find out?"

There was a long pause. Then Mom said firmly, "I don't want you discussing this with anyone. No matter what people ask you, no matter what people say. This is a private family matter, and it's no one else's business. Understand?"

Miranda didn't answer. The lump in her throat was like dry cotton, and she closed her eyes against a furious sting of tears. Even when the screen door banged shut, she refused to turn around—not till Mom had driven completely away.

I'll never trust her again. Never, as long as I live.

She latched the screen door, then sank slowly onto the couch. She could hear the soft whir of the fan, but not a single breeze stirred the air around her. She felt trapped, her heart broken. When something wet trickled down her cheek, she couldn't be sure if it was sweat or tears or both.

There's no way I can stay here. I'll die if I have to stay here.

Here, with all the lies and shame and questions and secrets surrounding her. Here, with everyone pointing and whispering and gossiping behind her back. Bad enough to be the new kid in town, the hurricane refugee, the outsider—but the granddaughter of the town crazy, too?

I'm more than a freak. I'm a total alien.

Back home, before the hurricane, she'd had so many friends—Marge and Joanie, especially. The three of them had been invincible and totally inseparable. They'd been popular and smart—all of them honor roll students. They'd joined the same clubs, volunteered on the same committees, won awards for the yearbook and school paper, even triple-dated whenever they could. They'd studied together, shopped together, spent hours on the beach, talking and wishing and planning their futures.

And now it's like they never existed. Like it was all just a dream . . .

Of the three of them, Joanie's house had been the only one left standing after the hurricane. There were some shingles gone, and some windows blown out, but the floodwaters had risen only over the front porch and into one small section of their living room. Nobody had expected the storm to be so fierce, so destructive, so deadly. People had done the usual sandbagging, the usual boarding up of windows and doors, the usual hoarding of groceries and water. They'd felt confident to stay at home and ride out this hurricane as they had so many others in the past.

Only this hurricane was different.

And by the time people realized just *how* different, it was already too late.

The beaches, of course, were the first to go. Houses and businesses, docks and boats, hotels full of tourists—everything tossed like confetti, everything split like kindling. Huddled with her mother under a mattress, Miranda felt their whole house fall to pieces around her.

Later, she wondered how they'd managed to survive at all.

Many hadn't.

Friends . . . neighbors . . . loved ones . . . pets—in the aftermath of the storm, as the death toll rose, the shock and grief became unbearable. Without homes or utilities, without the most basic of necessities, thousands of people turned helplessly to overcramped shelters, and their once-beautiful community became a wasteland.

Miranda still couldn't remember everything that happened after the storm. Only that Joanie's father had rescued them, coming in his boat and hauling them out of the rubble. For a week Miranda and her mother and Marge's family stayed together at Joanie's house, discussing their options and what to do. While the grown-ups decided their fate, Miranda and her two best friends clung to one another and cried.

God, how she missed them.

Joanie was still in Florida. Miranda had called her that very first day in St. Yvette, and both of them had cried all over again. Marge's family was staying with friends in Wisconsin, Joanie told her, and gave Miranda the address and phone number.

"Mom says I can't run up Aunt Teeta's long-distance bill." Miranda had forced back a fresh wave of tears. "And you know I don't have my cell phone or computer anymore. I don't know how much I'll be able to call."

Joanie's voice was heavy and sad. "So many people have moved away already. So many of our friends. We're not going to graduate together, but, Miranda, you've *got* to keep in touch. We *all* do. Promise me. Promise me we'll always stay close."

"I promise." Yet even as she said it, Miranda knew in her heart that things would never be the same.

That she and Marge and Joanie would never be the same. *I wonder what you two are doing right now? Thinking of me? Missing me as much as I miss you?*

It hurt too much, remembering. Every time she did, her heart felt broken all over again. *Nobody understands how unhappy I am . . . how alone. Nobody cares.* She hated feeling sorry for herself, but she didn't even know who she was anymore.

Worse, though, was the shame. This shabby apartment over a garage, this nothing little town. Handouts and charity and having to ask for every single thing. And now this . . .

My grandfather. The lunatic.

No . . . as much as she loved and missed her best friends, she doubted she'd be calling them again anytime soon. *Not till I have something to be happy about, not till my life gets better. Which means* never. Pushing those thoughts firmly from her mind, Miranda got up from the couch. She'd taken only a couple steps when suddenly she stopped, frowning, sniffing the air.

Smoke?

That faraway hint of smoke again . . . the same thing she'd smelled that day as she and Mom drove into town. Just like before, no more than a thought—here and then gone again. Puzzled, she crossed the room and peered out the open window above her bed.

No smoke there . . .

The garage stood quite a distance behind Hayes House—

the main house where her grandfather and Aunt Teeta lived. Miranda could see only part of it across the sprawling expanse of lawn and the moss-covered oak trees that shadowed the grass. Of course, she had no idea what the inside of that house might look like—she'd been forbidden even to step through the door. But outside there were gnarled old trees all around, and wrought-iron benches for sitting, and a shady veranda with tall, brick columns. There were azaleas in front, and an herb garden in back, and at night the perfume from all those lovely plants soaked the hot, humid air, floating all the way up to her bed, almost sickeningly sweet. Behind the house, the yard stretched for nearly half an acre, before finally sloping down to a tall stone wall and the park that lay beyond.

Miranda had heard all about Rebel Park. It was the sacred resting place of southern soldiers—not only from the Civil War, but from every war since—and St. Yvette's consummate pride and joy. A tasteful blend of memorial and family recreation, open seven days a week but securely gated at night, a place where people could make use of the walking path, as well as pay their respects.

From here, Miranda's view consisted of lush grass; a large, tranquil pond; the oversize statue of a Confederate drummer boy; and towering magnolia trees. She was glad the actual graveyard was on the opposite end of the park. She couldn't imagine looking out her window and seeing it there, so close, every single day.

From somewhere in the distance, faint voices rose and shouted, many voices together, yet too muffled to understand.

She thought she heard a car backfire—once . . . twice . . . five times. She decided it might be kids setting off firecrackers instead.

She felt uneasy all of a sudden. Nervous to be here alone, though she wasn't sure why. She'd never been afraid to stay alone before, but she couldn't stop thinking about that mysterious odor of smoke. Heavy yet faint; disturbingly real, yet with no more substance than a dream.

"I'm being ridiculous." It made her angry to feel so unsettled. Angry and vulnerable and fiercely defensive. "I must have imagined it."

A cold breath touched the back of her neck.

"No," a voice whispered. *"No . . . you're wrong."*

4

"**WHO'S THERE?**" Panicked, Miranda whirled around. "Mom, is that you?"

From where she stood, she could see the entire room, even the tiny bathroom through its open doorway. She could see her lone reflection in the full-length antique mirror near the corner. She could see that the whole apartment was empty.

And yet . . . something was here.

Slowly . . . steadily . . . the temperature seemed to be dropping. The air hung heavy and still. She wanted to scream, to run, but her own voice was paralyzed, and her feet stayed rooted to the floor.

"No . . . you're wrong . . ."

It spoke again, that voice. Coming from a place she couldn't find, from a person she couldn't see. A whisper she heard perfectly, though the room was deathly silent.

A distinctly male voice. The voice of a stranger. A voice so hollow, so hopeless, it sent chills down to the very pit of her soul.

Miranda choked out a cry. She didn't realize she'd been holding her breath; she had no idea how long she'd been standing here, transfixed by the empty apartment around her.

But now she could feel the sticky heat, hear the whir of the fan and the buzz of a housefly at the window screen.

Had she slipped into a daydream? How much time had passed? She remembered now: she was supposed to go with her study group; they were stopping by to pick her up. Had she missed them? Had they come and gone without her even hearing? Maybe they'd assumed she wasn't home. Or maybe . . .

A prank?

Her cheeks burned at the thought of it. Maybe they'd played a trick on her—hey, let's scare the new girl with her Ghost Walk idea! Maybe they were down there even now, with their tape recorder and spooky voices, waiting for her to come out so they could all have their big laugh. Or maybe they'd run off already— this'll freak her out, make her *really* think she's crazy!

Miranda flung open the door. She couldn't see a car outside, but that didn't mean the group wasn't hiding somewhere. And though she wasn't exactly sure whether she was trying to get *away* from the source of the voice, or get *to* the source of the voice, she stumbled out onto the landing and down the steps at breakneck speed.

Too late, she saw the figure at the bottom of the stairs—the figure starting up as she was running down. Caught by the momentum, she didn't even have time to shout a warning before the two of them collided full force.

"Whoa! You trying to kill *me* or just *yourself* ?"

Miranda reeled from the blow. As a pair of arms steadied her, she staggered back and gazed up at the young man blocking her way.

He was easily six feet tall—long and lean in his muddy workboots, worn T-shirt, and jeans low on his hips. The curved hollows of his cheeks were accentuated by strong, high cheekbones, and she could see taut ridges of sinewy muscle along the length of both arms. His skin looked naturally tan. He had thick waves of jet-black hair tousled almost to his shoulders, and his sensuous lips were pressed hard into a frown.

He reminded her of some wild gypsy.

Once her initial shock had passed, Miranda was furiously annoyed. "What's wrong with you? It's not like you didn't see me coming. Why didn't you get out of my way?"

"And let you fall?" His eyes reflected mock horror. They were the blackest eyes she'd ever seen. "But I'm so much more comfortable to land on than the driveway, yeah?"

The driveway, like so many back roads around town, was a narrow, rutted path of crushed oyster shells. Miranda's anger turned down a notch.

"You could've warned me," she muttered. Her heart had stopped pounding, though she still felt seriously shaken. "How long have you been out here?"

He wasn't frowning at her now. His face was calm and expressionless, which was almost more unnerving. "I'm not stalking you, if that's what you mean."

"Was someone just out here with you?"

"No."

"Are you sure? You weren't talking to anyone a minute ago?"

"There's nobody here but me. And I'm pretty sure I'd know if I was talking to myself."

"Look . . . I *know* I heard a voice."

This time he raised an eyebrow, his gaze sweeping over the empty yard. "And just how long you been *hearing* this voice?"

Was he teasing her? Being sarcastic? Whatever it was, Miranda didn't appreciate it. "Who are you, anyway? What are you doing here?"

"Miss Teeta sent me to fix the air conditioner."

Miss Teeta. Miranda still wasn't used to all this old-fashioned southern courtesy, so ripe with tradition and respect—the yes ma'ams and no sirs and gentle obsession with good manners. The conclusion she'd finally reached was that adults and old people were treated with the utmost politeness, but if you were friends with them, you could preface their first name with Miss or Mr. *Miss Teeta, the real estate lady. Miss Wanda, at the beauty shop. Mr. Louie, who brings the mail each day.* Even Mom had already lapsed into the etiquette of her upbringing—Miranda had heard her referring to the neighbors down the street as Miss Emmeline and Mr. Henry.

"So . . . you gonna let me in?" the young man asked. His voice was deep and slightly husky. Definitely a southern accent, but with something else—*a trace of French, maybe?*—mixed in. Sort of musical and mysterious. *Sexy, even . . .*

"How do I know you're telling the truth?" Miranda stood her ground. "You could be a burglar."

Cocking his head, he jerked his chin toward the apartment. "Me, I'd have to be pretty desperate to rob this place. Not much profit these days in lace doilies and gumbo pots."

So he *had* been in the apartment before. Still trying to

maintain her dignity, Miranda conceded with a curt nod and led the way upstairs.

"Mmmm . . . bet you're really hot," she heard him mumble behind her.

"Excuse me?"

"With the air-conditioning broken"—his tone was all innocence—"it's gotta be over a hundred degrees in here."

As the screen door closed behind them, he strode over to the window unit and immediately began an inspection. Miranda stood watching a moment, then took a seat on the couch. There was no whispery voice in here now.

Could I have imagined it?

"I've told Miss Teeta a thousand times, it's no good to keep fixing this ole piece of junk. Everything's gotta die sometime." The young man seemed to be talking more to himself than to her. As Miranda watched, he wrestled the air conditioner off the sill and set it carefully on the floor.

The prospect of spending even one more minute in this heat was unthinkable. "You mean you can't fix it?"

"I can fix anything, *cher.*"

"That's not my name," she corrected him. *And aren't you just pretty impressed with yourself, Mr. Repair Guy.*

For a split second he looked almost amused, but then his features went unreadable once more. While he knelt down to resume his work, she gave him another curious appraisal. She hadn't noticed those scars on his arms before—faint impressions, some straight, some jagged, some strangely crisscrossed. She wondered briefly if he'd been in an accident when he was younger.

Her eyes moved over the rest of his body. He was busy unscrewing the back off the air conditioner, his movements quick and fluid. She saw him glance at her, and she quickly looked away.

"Sorry about what happened," he said. There was an awkward pause before he added, "To you and your mama—the hurricane and all. Must be tough, what y'all are going through."

Miranda stared at him as he bent forward, his hair falling down around his face, shielding it from view. "How do you know about that?"

"Everybody knows about that. And if they didn't already know before you came, I'm sure they knew five minutes after you got here." He shrugged, but didn't look up. "Small town. You'll get used to it."

No, you're wrong. I'll never get used to it. I'll never get used to people knowing my business or invading my privacy. Only Marge and Joanie shared those things with me. Only them.

"I hate it here." The words were out, bitter and angry, before Miranda could stop them. Embarrassed, she turned her attention to the floor. *Great. Now I'll probably be quoted on the six o'clock news . . .*

Repair Guy, however, didn't seem at all offended. "You'll change your mind."

"What do you mean, I'll change my mind?" Another flash of anger went through her. "You don't even know me."

"The town, it has a way of pulling you in." He squatted back on his heels. He wiped his face across one sleeve of his T-shirt, leaving a smear of dirt on his forehead and down his left cheek. "And maybe I know you a whole lot better than you think."

Flustered, Miranda groped uselessly for a comeback.

"You really did hear someone before, didn't you?" He fixed her with a calm, deliberate stare. "And what about the screams? Have you heard those, too?"

5

MIRANDA COULDN'T MOVE. It was as if every muscle had frozen in place and her mind had gone completely blank.

She had a sense of his scrutiny, a sense of her own confusion, an endless silence—but it wasn't till the screen door burst open that she was finally able to stumble up from the couch.

"Why, here y'all are!" With a delighted laugh, Aunt Teeta hurried in, her plump arms spread wide, her blue eyes sparkling. "I didn't see your truck outside, Etienne! I was afraid maybe you wouldn't have time for me today."

Etienne? Miranda shot him a startled glance just as Aunt Teeta caught him up in a hug. Hadn't those kids in class been talking about someone named Etienne?

"Hey, Miss Teeta," he said. "Uncle Frank had to borrow it—he'll be passing by in a minute to get me." He still hadn't smiled, Miranda noted, but he didn't seem to mind Aunt Teeta's enthusiastic show of affection.

"All right now, tell me." Releasing him, Aunt Teeta cast a hopeful look at the air conditioner. "Can you fix it—one more time?"

"You know I can."

Another hug. Another laugh. It was always that way with Aunt Teeta. Arms open wide to hug everybody in sight, and that big, warm, contagious laugh that made everyone within earshot laugh right along with her.

Except Miranda didn't feel much like laughing.

"So how do you like my handyman?" Aunt Teeta greeted her, pulling Miranda close. "Isn't he a genius?"

Miranda managed a nod.

"I wasn't sure your mama told you he was coming," Aunt Teeta went on. "But I see you two have already met."

Repair Guy answered smoothly. "We sort of . . . ran into each other."

"Well, I'm so glad. Etienne, this is my niece, Miranda. I wasn't exaggerating now, was I? About how beautiful she is?"

"No, ma'am, you weren't exaggerating at all."

With a silent groan, Miranda glanced longingly at the door while her aunt bustled back across the room.

"And Miranda, this is Etienne Boucher. I'm surprised y'all don't know each other from school."

"I've been working the last few days," Etienne said.

"It's one of those special programs, Miranda." Aunt Teeta's voice lowered, as though sharing some great secret. "He goes to school part-time, and the rest of the time he works. And he *still* manages to charm all the ladies in town."

For the first time, Etienne seemed almost embarrassed.

"And my, but he cleans up good—I've seen him." Winking at Miranda, Aunt Teeta was perfectly deadpan. "It just goes to show you—you can't judge a greasy ole book by its cover."

Hooting with laughter, she gave Etienne one last hug, then headed outside. "I've got some houses to show this afternoon," she called over her shoulder. "But the door's open, and there's iced tea and pecan pie. You know where to find them."

"Thanks." Etienne hoisted the air conditioner into his arms. "Another time, maybe."

"Whenever you can, hon. You know you're always welcome. Oh, and about the heat in here—"

"I'll make sure Uncle Frank brings a unit by and gets it running. Y'all can use it till this one's fixed."

"Darlin', you are my hero of the day!"

"Wait up—I'll walk out with you."

Miranda could only stand there and watch them go. She couldn't believe it. *"And what about the screams?"* he'd said. And now he was acting as if nothing had happened. He'd totally blindsided her, and now he was leaving. *"Have you heard those, too?"*

She started after him, but suddenly noticed the clock. Those kids from her class would be here any second to pick her up, and she wasn't halfway ready.

Damn. Why did I ever agree to study with them? She'd never be able to concentrate. She'd never be able to come up with any ideas. Not now. Not after what had happened to her today, not after what Etienne had just said.

Who is *this guy?*

She barely managed to change clothes before a horn blared from the driveway, sending her reluctantly downstairs.

"Hey!" Parker exclaimed. "A woman who's actually on time. You paying attention, Ash?"

Parker sat behind the wheel of a gleaming red convertible—a

BMW, Miranda recognized at once—with Ashley perched next to him, and Roo smoking a cigarette in the backseat. Etienne was leaning against the car, head lowered, arms crossed on Parker's door. As Miranda got closer, he reached casually for Roo's cigarette, took a drag, then handed it back again. Gage was nowhere to be seen.

"Mosquito bait." Scooting over, Roo stared at Miranda's bare legs. "You should've worn jeans."

"Her shorts are fine," Ashley argued. "I brought bug spray."

Roo had added more makeup, Miranda noticed—more black around the eyes, a black outline around the lips—and the black hair with its purple streaks was now gathered into a strange, twisted configuration on top of her head. Miranda tried not to stare, but she couldn't help it. As Roo slid over to make room, Miranda was taken with the girl's exotic eyes—their pale color of soft, smoky green. Heavy-lidded eyes, daunting in their boldness, yet, at the same time, distant . . . almost dreamy. It was unsettling to look into those eyes. Miranda wondered if it was unsettling for everyone.

"—we'll see y'all there!"

Startled, Miranda realized that Ashley was talking to Etienne, who'd pulled back from the car. In the next second, Parker had revved the engine and shot onto the road, making conversation next to impossible.

"Parker, for heaven's sake, *slow down*!"

The BMW decelerated smoothly into the speed limit. Parker grinned as Ashley glared at him.

"Quit showing off," she scolded, then turned her attention to

Miranda. "I don't know how much of St. Yvette you've seen so far, but I really think you'll like the Falls. It's a ways out of town though, so people sort of forget about it."

"I don't." Roo frowned. "I go there a lot."

"And that way we sort of forget about you, too." Parker spoke up. "So it works out great."

Determined, Ashley kept on. "There's hardly ever anybody out there. That's why we like it so much."

"Well, that and the poisonous swamp. And the man-eating diamondback water snakes. Don't forget those." In the rearview mirror, Parker's eyes widened dramatically. "And then one day . . . the new girl in town went off to the Falls with her friends." His voice deepened, horror-movie style. "And she was never seen again."

"Parker, will you stop? That's not funny."

Though Parker was laughing, Miranda didn't think it was funny either—especially since she'd just suspected them of trying to terrorize her. Not that she suspected them anymore—not after Etienne's disturbing comment—but then again, what did she really know about these kids? What did she really know about Etienne?

Her thoughts grew darker and anxious. *Mom said we'd be safe here in St. Yvette; Mom said our lives would be normal. But that was before I knew about Grandpa, before I heard that voice and those screams in the night—*

"—the Falls," Ashley was explaining once more. "Closer to the water than it used to be. I wish they'd fix it so it wouldn't flood."

This time Miranda did her best to focus. "So . . . it's like, a waterfall?"

"No." Roo exhaled a stream of smoke. "It's like, a cemetery."

"A *real* cemetery?"

"I told you this was a bad idea." Taking a last puff, Roo tossed the cigarette. "I told you it would freak her out too much."

"I didn't say I was freaked out. I just asked if it was a real cemetery."

"Actually, it's a park *and* a cemetery—" Ashley began, but Roo cut her off.

"There was a big battle here during the Civil War. And afterward, there were lots of dead Yankee soldiers who couldn't be identified. So when nobody claimed their bodies, the town built a cemetery for them." She paused, chewed thoughtfully on a short, black fingernail. "Originally, it was called Site of the Fallen Union. But over the years, it got shortened to just the Falls."

"And therein lies the irony!" Parker grinned. "Because, as we all know, it wasn't the *Union* that ended up falling."

Straining forward, Roo tilted the rearview mirror so that Parker's face disappeared from view. He calmly readjusted it.

"There's so much Civil War stuff here in St. Yvette," Ashley said. "Especially on the Brickway. Did you know that practically everything on the Brickway is over two hundred years old?"

Miranda swept windblown hair from her eyes. "I think Aunt Teeta mentioned something about that."

Aunt Teeta had mentioned quite a lot of things about St. Yvette, but Miranda had paid little attention. She'd never been particularly interested in history—not of where she'd lived before, or anyplace else. But one thing she'd learned in her short time here was that these townspeople were fiercely proud and protective of their heritage. And they never seemed to grow tired of talking about it.

"The Brickway goes in a circle," Ashley explained. "About a mile long from start to finish, with—how many buildings?" Glancing at Roo but getting no help, she guessed. "Fifteen? Twenty?"

Miranda made a supreme effort to be polite. "All I know is that it's a street made out of bricks, and it's about a block away from Aunt Teeta's house."

"Oh, that's right!" Ashley remembered. "Hayes House is your family's house! Well, it isn't actually *on* the Brickway, but it's still considered part of the Historic District. We have a really nice museum here—it's run by the Historical Society. And it has guidebooks and brochures and all kinds of information. And Roo and I were thinking—"

"*You* were thinking," Roo corrected, though Ashley ignored her.

"—we were thinking the Brickway might be the perfect place to put your Ghost Walk."

"It's not *my*—" Miranda began once again, but Ashley didn't even slow down.

"So if each of us took a few buildings and did some research on them, I'm sure we could find lots of great scary stories, right?"

"The Falls is supposed to be haunted," Roo said, though she couldn't have sounded more indifferent about it.

"So much for folklore," Parker added. "Have any of us ever seen one single ghost in all the times we've been there?"

"Not all those bodies at the Falls got buried in tombs," Roo explained. "A lot of Union soldiers were dumped in shallow graves, or mass graves—and there's no telling how many ended up in the bayou. There were probably hundreds never even found at all. I mean, they couldn't have picked up every body part lying around."

"So be careful, Miranda," Parker warned. "You might hear a whole lot of little phantom feet marching around there."

"Ewww!" Ashley jerked back in alarm.

"Ah, don't worry," Parker soothed her. "That's why we always bring Roo along. To scare creepy things away."

Roo shot him a glance. "Then how come *you're* still here?"

Without warning the car swerved into the oncoming lane. As the girls screamed, Parker veered back on course and looked immensely pleased with himself.

"Will you quit doing that!" Ashley was furious. "I *hate* when you do that! Don't you realize how dangerous it is?"

"Oh, no, Parker. Please. Do it again." Roo stared grimly at the back of his head. "I just love that sensation of flying through the air and splattering into a tree."

Parker didn't seem the least bit contrite. "*As* I was saying—"

"You've said enough. Now quit being a jerk, and keep your eyes on the road." Still visibly shaken, Ashley twisted around to face the backseat. "The Falls has really gone downhill. It's not nearly as nice as it used to be. Not at all like the Confederate cemetery in town."

Roo grimaced. "Hard to believe Rebel Park was once a battlefield. All that suffering and death."

"I thought you liked suffering and death," Parker threw back. "I mean . . . you always *look* like suffering and death."

"Parker, *watch where you're going*!" Ashley's voice went shrill. "For God's sake!"

As the speedometer dropped down again, Miranda shut her eyes and clutched the edge of her seat. "So Rebel Park, the one behind Hayes House, was the actual battlefield?"

"I'm not sure." Ashley considered a moment. "I mean, it was a huge battle. So the park was probably only part of the battlefield."

Once more, Parker looked in the rearview mirror. "Back then, all this area was farmland and woods and swamps. That's where most of the fighting happened. The town was pretty much spared—mainly because the Union army used it for their headquarters."

"Parker's mom works at the Historical Society." Roo glanced at Miranda. "He really isn't that smart."

Though Miranda had opened her eyes again, she felt edgy and distracted. Something was tugging at the corners of her mind, something vaguely familiar that she couldn't quite identify.

"—slaughter," a voice said.

Miranda jumped. She looked at Roo, who was gazing levelly back at her.

"The battle of St. Yvette was a complete slaughter," Roo said again. "The Confederates never had a chance. You can read about it—all the accounts are equally gruesome."

Parker winced. "Can you tell by now that she's really *into* gruesome?"

"There was so much smoke, it was like nighttime. They couldn't even see the sun."

"Guns and cannons," Parker clarified, while Ashley threw each of them a pleading glance.

Feeling more anxious by the minute, Miranda tried her best not to show it. Roo's eyes were still fixed on hers in a bold, unwavering stare. Almost as though the girl sensed her sudden vulnerability and was closing in for the kill.

"They said the air was actually wet." Roo's tone was somber. "Wet and red. From all the blood spraying everywhere."

Reaching back, Ashley pounded Roo on the knees. "You are *making* that up! Just to be disgusting! Now *stop* it right—"

"Actually, she's not," Parker broke in. "Making it up, I mean. She *is* disgusting."

From the look on his face, it was obvious how much this pained him, taking Roo's side. "The battle of St. Yvette was one of the bloodiest ever recorded around this area. But then, the Civil War was also the bloodiest war up to that time."

And the nag was still there, that persistent little nag in Miranda's head, refusing to be ignored. It pushed her to the edge of her seat and leaned her in close to Parker.

"Why was it the bloodiest?" she asked him.

Nodding, Parker spoke louder. "Partly because of the bullets. Up till then, bullets were round—they didn't hit their targets that well, and they tended to bounce off bone. But during the

Civil War, there were these new conical bullets that were heavier and more pointed. A lot more accurate. A whole lot more blood. Bad infections, too. When a bullet like that tore through a guy's skin, it took dirt and parts of his clothes and who knows what else with it. It was pretty much a death sentence."

"Bet you're glad you asked." Roo slanted a look at Miranda.

But Miranda had sunk back into her own uneasy thoughts. She knew what it was now, that restlessness in her mind— the memory of that strange, familiar smell. And while Parker had been talking, she could *swear* that smell had come to her again—a faint odor of smoke mingled with . . . *what? Sulfur? Flesh? Blood?*

"Oh my God," Miranda murmured.

"Oh, Miranda, I know." Ashley was quick to sympathize. "I can't stand to hear about blood either. I can't stand to look at blood. I can't even stand to think about it! So y'all talk about something else, okay?"

As Ashley went on to scold Roo and Parker, Miranda scarcely listened. What she'd heard and smelled earlier had seemed so totally real. And now this—this Civil War battle— was it related somehow? She'd never even heard of the battle of St. Yvette. Never studied a single detail about it, never read a single historical account. Didn't have the slightest knowledge about artillery smoke or bullets.

So how could this be possible, when it all sounded crazy, even to herself? *Because I can't be sure, can I? How can I be absolutely* sure *that I've smelled the battle smoke—that I've heard the cries of the wounded and dying?*

Once again she felt overwhelmed with uncertainty. *I must have seen something about that battle—on TV maybe, or in a magazine. Because the other can't be true, it's too* impossible *to be true.*

And what on earth had ever possessed her to think it?

6

RESTLESSLY, Miranda tried to concentrate on the scenery flying past. It occurred to her that she hadn't noticed any buildings for a while—other than an abandoned gas station and a couple of rotted barns. Trees closed in from both sides of the road, and the road itself had begun to narrow, winding on beneath scattered canopies of moss. When Parker made a sudden left turn into the woods, Miranda felt as if they were all being swallowed alive.

What have I gotten myself into?

The paved road began to disappear. Soon it was nothing more than a trail of mud and crushed oyster shells rutted deep with tire tracks, and barely wide enough for the car. Trees grew even thicker here, shutting out the light. Moss brushed over the top of her head, and she slid lower in her seat.

Even the air had changed. Heavy and wet and overly ripe with smells, and a promise of water close by. These smells were different from the wind-and-surf beach she was used to. These smells were secret and primal and dark.

"Here we are," Parker announced, and the car lurched to a sudden stop. As he killed the engine, a wave of silence engulfed them.

Miranda sat there, eyes and ears straining to adjust. Straight ahead of her, among moss-shrouded trees, was the Union cemetery they'd told her about, and beyond that, the murky waters of Bayou St. Yvette.

"Come on!" Ashley called, and Miranda realized everyone else was out of the car. "This way!"

But Miranda didn't move. She couldn't stop staring at the cemetery.

In a halfhearted attempt at maintenance, someone had recently clipped back weeds and underbrush, leaving a few stone urns holding plastic flowers. But the old tombs—no more than a dozen and built aboveground—lay scattered at odd angles with no hint of order. Some resembled low-lying slabs, suggesting only one or two occupants; others stood nearly as tall as Parker, indicating several inner burial compartments, stacked one upon another. None were marked with names. No grass grew between them. Peeling whitewash hung like scabs, leaving gaps in the powdery brick and rotted plaster. Some tombs had actually sunk into the ground; others were partially washed away, victims of too many floodwaters, she guessed.

Hundreds dead and only these few pitiful graves.

Remembering what Roo had said earlier, Miranda wondered just how many abandoned soldiers had lain in mass graves all these many years, or in the overgrown tangle of the woods, or at the bottom of the bayou.

Despite the sweltering heat, she rubbed a chill from her arms. That heaviness in the air was growing worse—oppressive almost—the way a room could feel when it held too many people.

With a sheer effort of will, she climbed out of the car and

caught up with the others. They were sitting at an old picnic table in a small, concrete shelter.

"Oh, there you are!" Ashley motioned Miranda down beside her. "Wasn't I right? Isn't it nice here?"

Miranda thought fast. "Well . . . there's atmosphere, that's for sure."

"I could never come here all by myself. But when Roo's mad or sad or worried about something, this is where she always runs away to."

"Yeah." Parker sighed. "Too bad she always runs back home again."

"And thank you so much, Ash." Roo forced a saccharine smile. "For sharing my secret place with everybody in the whole entire universe."

"Oh, Roo, I didn't—Look, there's Etienne. I hope he remembered to pick up Gage."

Miranda craned her neck for a better view. What she saw was an old muddy pickup truck lurching slowly along the road, then coming to a stop about thirty feet behind Parker's BMW. There was a half trailer hitched to the back—both it and the truckbed were full. Among the cargo, Miranda could pick out lawn mowers, ladders, chain saws, and a generator.

Jumping casually to his feet, Parker flashed an endearing smile. "Just stay put now, ladies—I'll see if they need any help. I have to get the cooler out of my car, anyway."

Miranda caught the quick glance Roo shot him—something between curiosity and outright suspicion. "Don't bother," Roo said, just as casually. "I'll do it."

Before Parker had a chance to respond, Roo turned and started walking. Parker's expression tightened for a second, then went carefully neutral as he headed for Etienne's truck.

"Wait, Roo, we'll go with you." Ashley gestured to Miranda. "There's some blankets in the trunk, and I forgot the darn bug spray."

Miranda was only too glad to join them—any distraction to keep her mind off the day's unsettling events.

Reaching the convertible, Ashley popped the trunk and started digging inside. Roo immediately hauled out a small ice chest and opened the lid.

For a moment Roo stood there, staring down into the cooler. Then, pulling out a beer, she turned to Ashley and held up the can.

"Nice, Ash. Star quarterback busted for drinking. *Again.*"

"He's not getting busted. And he's *not* drinking—not like before. Especially not since our last fight."

"So what's this?" Roo's glance moved between Ashley and Etienne's truck, where the three guys were deep in conversation. "A root beer in disguise?"

"It's not like he's the only guy at school who has a beer once in a while. It's no big deal."

"It will be when his coach finds out."

"Well, Coach doesn't ever have to *find* out." The implication was clear. "Unless *somebody* tells him."

"Nobody has to tell Coach anything, Ashley. It's amazing all the things you can find out about a guy when he pees in a cup."

Roo gave a mock wave. "Surprise! Good-bye, Parker! Good-bye, scholarship! Good-bye, multimillion-dollar career!"

"He's not even playing right now—not till his shoulder's completely healed. And anyway, one little beer won't make any difference."

"He's scary enough when he's driving and *hasn't* been drinking." Roo's tone was mildly chastising. "Or haven't you noticed?"

Ignoring the comment, Ashley reached back into the trunk, grabbing some blankets and the bug repellent.

"You're not helping him, you know," Roo persisted. "You're enabling him. You're just afraid he'll dump you if you don't go along with what he wants."

Ashley tossed her things at Roo. "Here. You bring these. I'll take the cooler."

It was obvious to Miranda that the argument was over—though she seriously doubted if either side had won. Unsure what to do, she watched Ashley hoist the cooler and march away.

"Love really is blind." Roo let out a gloomy sigh. "Love is also dangerous, insane, and highly overrated."

There was a long pause before Miranda finally asked, "Are you speaking from personal experience?"

"No, from *Ashley's* personal experience. Sisters are *also* highly overrated."

"You two are sisters?" Miranda hadn't meant to sound so shocked, but Roo took it in stride.

"Why are people always so surprised by that? Yeah, we're

sisters. Stepsisters, actually. But our parents got together when we were both three years old—so we've never *felt* like stepsisters. We're not anything alike though."

No kidding. Miranda almost smiled.

At the sound of approaching voices, she turned to see Parker, Gage, and Etienne walking past. Etienne mumbled something she couldn't quite catch. Parker kept his eyes straight ahead, while Gage shot them a quick glance.

Roo tossed the blankets into the backseat, then reached for Miranda's arm. "Stand here and hold your breath."

Miranda felt the first cold squirt of bug spray. Before she could move, Roo had doused her from top to bottom, and she was choking on fumes.

"There. That should do it." After pitching the can into the trunk again, Roo slammed down the lid and leaned back against the car. She fished a cigarette and matches from her jeans pocket. Then she lit up and inhaled a slow, satisfied breath. "So what do you think of Etienne?"

The abrupt question caught Miranda completely off guard. She said the first thing that popped into her mind. "He came to fix our air conditioner."

"Yeah, everybody calls Etienne when something breaks or doesn't work right. He can fix anything. He's got the touch."

"So he said," Miranda recalled.

"Besides, he really needs the money."

Miranda felt suddenly awkward. It wasn't her business to discuss Etienne's private life—yet she couldn't help being a little curious.

"He and his mama run swamp tours back in the bayou." Roo flicked ashes into the trampled weeds. "Tourists really like that kind of thing, don't ask me why. He works construction jobs, too. Mows lawns, cuts trees, takes fishermen out in his boat. Stuff like that."

"Quite a résumé."

"And not bad to look at either." Roo arched an eyebrow. "Or haven't you noticed?"

"I don't even know him."

"You don't have to know him to notice."

Miranda hedged. "Well . . . sure. I guess he's kind of cute."

"Cute? Kind of? I'd say *that's* the understatement of the century."

"Does he have a girlfriend or something?" As Roo flicked her an inquisitive glance, she added quickly, "He keeps calling me Cher."

Clearly amused, Roo shook her head. "It's not a name, it's a . . ." She thought a minute. "It's like a nickname . . . like what you call somebody when you like them. Like 'hey, love' or 'hey, honey' or 'hey, darlin'. It's sort of a Cajun thing."

Miranda felt like a total fool. No wonder Etienne had gotten that look on his face when she'd corrected him about her name.

"His dad's side is Cajun," Roo explained. "That's where Etienne gets that great accent."

Miranda's curiosity was now bordering on fascination. She knew very little about Cajuns—only the few facts Aunt Teeta had given her. Something about the original Acadians being expelled from Nova Scotia in the eighteenth century, and how they'd finally ended up settling all over south Louisiana. And how they'd come to be so well known for their hardy French pioneer stock, tight family bonds, strong faith, and the best food this side of heaven.

"Before?" Roo went on. "When he walked by? He was talking to you in French. Well . . . Cajun French, actually."

"He was?" Miranda wanted to let it go, but the temptation was just too great. "What'd he say?"

"He said, 'Let's get to know each other.'"

A hot flush crept up Miranda's cheeks. It was the last thing she'd expected to hear, and she was totally flustered. Maybe Roo was making it up, just poking fun at her—after all, she didn't quite know *what* to make of Roo.

"Oh," was the only response Miranda could think of.

"He and Gage are cousins, you know."

This was even more shocking than Roo and Ashley being stepsisters. "I had no idea."

"First cousins. Their mothers are sisters—twins. Etienne's mama got cancer a few years ago. She was so sick for a while, we were all scared. She's better now though. They're a really close family—Gage always says it's like he and Etienne each have two moms. And Gage's daddy helps them out a lot—he owns a fleet of trawlers—he hires Etienne on with his crews during shrimp season."

"What about Etienne's father?"

"Dead."

"I'm so sorry."

"Don't be." Roo shrugged. "Didn't you notice those scars on Etienne's arms? His daddy beat him—and his mama—on a regular basis."

Miranda looked away. The unexpected reality of it sickened her. This was something that happened on crime shows, not to people she knew.

"We better get back," Miranda said, not wanting to hear any more. Gathering up the blankets, she tried to switch gears. "So, are you . . . and Gage . . . together?"

"What? Gage and me?" Wryly amused, Roo took another puff of nicotine. "Here's the thing about Gage and me. We've lived next door to each other since kindergarten. There's not much about each other we don't know."

"So . . . best friends forever? That sort of thing?"

"We did have sex once." Roo was matter-of-fact. "But then we decided—why ruin a perfect friendship?" Holding her cigarette at arm's length, she casually studied the black and purple lipstick smudges around its filter. "He was *amazing*."

"I . . . see." Miranda couldn't tell if she was being teased, shocked, or confided in. "Thanks very much for sharing."

"Of course, he'd be completely mortified if he knew I'd told you. He has this real problem about sharing personal stuff."

Roo pushed herself away from the car, dropped her cigarette butt, and ground it underfoot. Then she walked off without a word, leaving Miranda to trail behind. By the time the two of them reached the cemetery, the others were already engaged in a lively discussion.

"There's always the Historical Society. And the Ladies of the Southland." Lounging back on top of the picnic table, Gage drew up one knee and draped his arm across it. "Parker's mom could help with that."

Parker recoiled in mock horror. Taking the blankets from Miranda, he spread them on the ground, plopped down, and pulled Ashley down beside him, not bothering to hide the beer he was drinking. "No! No way! Leave my mom out of this."

"Just see if she'll talk to us, Parker," Ashley insisted. "Think of it as investigative reporting."

"Hey. Lois Lane. Mom and I don't like seeing each other any more than we have to. What part of *no way* don't you understand?"

Etienne was leaning against a tree, arms folded over his chest. Now that Miranda knew his family background, it was all she could do not to stare at those faded, telltale marks over his skin.

"What's up, Boucher?" Roo greeted him. "Is that your screwdriver, or are you just glad to see me?"

While everyone groaned, Etienne spread his arms wide. "You just have that effect on me, *cher.*"

Roo grabbed a soda from the cooler, then settled herself comfortably on a low-lying tomb. She motioned Miranda to sit with her.

"We have to decide how to start our research," Ashley said. "Like, should we look for information on the whole town, or just one specific area. Roo and I decided we should all focus on the Brickway."

"*You* decided we should all focus on the Brickway," Roo mumbled, popping the tab on her can.

Gage nodded. "Ashley's right. If this is a walking tour, some kids in our class might not want to walk very far."

"If, in fact, anybody wants to walk on this tour at all," Parker couldn't help adding. "Come on . . . we're not *really* going to do this ghost stuff, are we?"

Ashley rolled her eyes. "Well then, maybe we should have transportation. Maybe we could use our cars?"

"*Our* cars? Etienne and I are the only ones with wheels."

"What a perfectly brilliant idea, Ash." Roo shot her sister a bland look. "Ghost BMW. No . . . wait. Ghost Truck. I'm all tingly with dread."

"Or Ghost SUV?" Despite Ashley's wounded expression, Parker clasped his hands beseechingly at Gage. "Oh, pretty please, can we use your mom's minivan?"

Ashley's lips tightened. "Parker, this is serious!"

"Look, I know it's half our grade." Easing back down, he took a swig of beer and tried to reason with her. "But let's face it—the whole thing's pretty stupid. And impossible."

"It's not stupid. And why is it impossible? All we have to do is research old places that might be haunted."

"And just how do you propose we do that? Oh wait, I know— let's just knock on people's doors. Excuse me, we're doing a survey—are there any creepy ghosts living in your house? Ash, come on. We can't force things to be haunted just so they can be close enough to walk to."

A disappointed silence fell. For several minutes everyone seemed lost in thought, till Etienne unfolded himself from the tree.

"Don't y'all know anything about your own town?" He walked over to the cooler and pulled out a beer. To Miranda, who watched him, he moved with all the grace and stealth of a predatory cat.

"Well, I'm not going to flunk this project," Ashley said crossly, "just because Parker's an idiot."

Roo promptly frowned. "Where's your compassion? Parker can't help being an idiot."

"Okay now, listen." Holding up both hands, Etienne motioned for quiet. "I think Ashley's idea is the way to go. Say we start at the Battlefield Inn. Follow the Brickway going east, past the park. We got us all those old buildings to pick from—there's gotta be plenty dark stories there, yeah? So if we do the whole mile circle of the Brickway with our little tour stops, I'm guessing it should take about an hour."

Ashley gazed at him admiringly. "Which is exactly how long Miss Dupree said our presentations should be!"

Approving looks passed back and forth. After a brief pause, Etienne continued.

"That Ghost Walk in New Orleans." He turned to Miranda. "A lotta atmosphere, yeah?"

Miranda did her best to remember. "Sort of a winding route—I mean, it was easy to lose all sense of direction, and a couple times the guide swore we were lost."

"For effect."

"Definitely for effect. There were alleys and backstreets and little courtyards. Lots of closed-in places, lots of shadows and dead ends. Low doorways we had to duck under, things like that. And sometimes ghosts came out of the dark and scared us."

"Right there on the tour?" Ashley's eyes widened. "The ghosts actually let you see them in person?"

"No," Parker said. "Only in spirit."

"Actors, Ashley." While the others laughed, Miranda tried to hold back a smile. "Just people *pretending* to be ghosts."

Ashley looked immensely relieved. "Oh, I get it! Like a big outdoor haunted house!"

"Come on, y'all. This has gotta be about more than just scaring people," Etienne reminded them.

The laughter died down. All attention shifted back to his face.

"It's about the town," he went on. "Finding out about the history of St. Yvette and—"

"Okay, we get it," Parker broke in impatiently. "The history of the town. All its evil secrets and unsolved mysteries; and the skeletons in its closets; and the curses; and the big, bad, bloody murders; and the crazy weirdos—"

There was a brief, uncomfortable silence as all eyes focused on Miranda. Even Parker had the grace to look embarrassed.

"No offense," he mumbled.

"Okay! Great!" Ashley did her best to divert attention. "Miss Dupree wants a rough outline Monday. So let's start working on ideas and meet again tomorrow." Jumping up from the blanket, she chattered just a little too brightly. "Outside the inn, ten o'clock. Oh, Etienne—you can come, right?"

"Sure." Slowly he ran a hand back through his hair. "As long as I'm at work by one."

"Perfect! We can walk the route and time it. And pick out which buildings are . . . historic."

"They're all historic," Roo said.

"Well . . . scarily historic."

"If each of us looks up just one or two buildings, it shouldn't be that hard." Gage slid lightly to his feet. "I don't mind doing some research tonight."

Parker stretched and stood, wrapping his arms around Ashley and nuzzling her neck. "Yeah, that's exactly what we had in mind, too. Right, Ash? Some good, basic, investigative research."

"Forget it." Pushing him off, Ashley tried to keep a straight face. "Only if you're a ghost."

Roo raised her hand. "No problem there. I'll be glad to kill him."

It didn't take long to pack up. They gathered their things, and made one last survey of the area. Miranda was still wondering how she could approach Etienne, get him alone, ask him to explain those strange comments he'd made back at the apartment. Puzzling over this, she noticed Parker gulping the last of his beer. In true quarterback style, he drew back his arm and let the can fly toward one of the tombs.

It hit its mark, bounced off, and ricocheted across several more graves. Foam splattered onto the nameless markers and ran down into the weeds.

"Touchdown!" he roared. "And the crowd goes *wild*!"

But it wasn't a crowd that came bursting through the trees just then. Wide-eyed and stumbling and gasping for breath.

The old man stopped just a few feet away. At first glance, he could have been a corpse risen from some lost grave, his stringy white hair matted with leaves and twigs, his torn clothes a muddy shroud, his gaunt face and bony arms smeared with dirt and blood. He swayed to one side, shaking violently from head to toe. And then, as the others stood paralyzed, he gestured frantically toward the woods.

"Can't you hear him?" the old man mumbled. "He won't stop. He won't rest. And God forgive me . . . I'm so tired . . ."

Miranda felt a slight movement behind her.

She heard Roo whisper in her ear.

"Well, Miranda . . . meet your grandfather."

MIRANDA COULDN'T BELIEVE IT.

Jonas Hayes? This scary old man babbling incoherently in front of her? With the terrified face and snarled, scraggly beard? And looking nothing at all like the grandfather in her photograph?

Because she *knew* what her grandfather looked like; she'd *kept* that photograph.

Even though Mom had taken it away from her that first time and put it back in the box on that high shelf in the closet. And even though Mom had forbidden her ever to snoop through that closet again.

Miranda had done it anyway.

She'd waited for Mom to leave the house, and the very next chance she got, she'd taken the photograph and hidden it in a brand-*new* secret place, among her most cherished treasures.

She'd looked at it so many times.

And on that fateful day of the hurricane—for some strange reason she still didn't understand—she'd suddenly had an overwhelming urge to pull the photo out from the loose floorboard under her bed and stuff it deep down inside one pocket of her jeans.

She loved that picture. When she and Mom moved into the garage apartment, she'd slipped it, all crumpled and dog-eared, beneath her mattress for safekeeping. She didn't even have to look at it anymore to recall her grandfather's face—she'd memorized that face perfectly through the years.

That kind-looking, quiet-looking scarecrow of a man. Craggy and rail-thin, with a thick mop of graying brown hair. With the neatly trimmed beard and the long arms and those sad, sunken eyes—eyes as pale blue and faded as his summer linen suit.

And now *this*?

This total raving lunatic, scarcely able to stand on his own two feet?

No, this was *not* her grandfather.

"That's not him," she murmured to Roo.

"Yes, it is."

"You're crazy."

"No," Roo whispered back. "*He* is."

"Why can't I see it?" The old man's voice was almost pleading. "I'm his only chance . . ."

As he glanced back through the trees, Miranda could swear that his skin turned pale beneath its layers of grime. She realized that Etienne was walking toward him. And now that the initial shock had passed, everyone else began to stir cautiously behind her, their voices low and muffled.

" . . . the hell's he doing here?"

" . . . belongs in a straitjacket—"

"Ssh, don't let Miranda hear you . . ."

But Miranda had already heard. Her heart was beating so fast, she thought it might explode.

"It's okay, Jonas. You know me. Calm yourself down."

Etienne's voice was low, but firm. He held up both hands in a nonthreatening appeal.

Confused, the old man darted his eyes from side to side, before settling his gaze once more on Etienne.

"I'm tired," Jonas murmured again.

"I know you are. That's why we're gonna take you on home—"

"Then who'll watch out for him? For *all* of them? After I'm gone?"

"Don't you be worrying about that. You and me, we'll figure something out."

Etienne had reached the old man's side. For a second it seemed as if Jonas might bolt, but then a deep breath shuddered through his entire body.

"I never told you about him." His head lowered; both arms hung limply at his sides. "I should have . . . but I never did . . ."

"There's a lotta time for that," Etienne assured him. "Whatever it is, you can tell me about it later, yeah?"

With a strange sense of detachment, Miranda watched the bizarre scene playing out. It took several moments to realize that her classmates had crowded in around her. Wary glances were being traded back and forth. Ashley looked scared to death; Parker's expression hovered somewhere between disbelief and outright laughter. And though Gage and Roo had their heads bent together, Miranda could still make out whispered snatches of conversation.

"Who's he talking about?"

"I don't know."

"Well, who do you *think*?" Roo persisted.

"I think he's scared and confused." Abruptly, Gage cut her off. "I think *he* doesn't know what he's talking about. Just let it go, Roo."

Miranda blocked out as much as she could. *I don't believe it. I won't believe it. He can't be my grandpa.* And yet she heard herself asking, "Is that really my grandfather? What's wrong with him?"

"I told you," Roo said. "He's crazy."

Parker jabbed Roo hard in the ribs. "Roo, shut up."

"Well, it's true. How come nobody wants to say what's true?"

"Not now," Gage murmured, but more firmly this time. "Parker's right—just be quiet."

Roo's reply was a grunt and a shrug. Miranda felt someone squeeze her hand, and realized it was Ashley.

Then, without warning, the old man staggered and hit the ground. Before anyone could grasp what was happening, Etienne knelt beside him and eased him carefully onto his back.

"Call 911!" Etienne shouted.

Parker automatically began patting himself down, searching through all his pockets. "Shit. Where's my cell?"

"I have mine—" Gage began, but Ashley's voice stopped him.

"It won't do any good. We're out of range here, remember? There's no signal!"

Emotions battled in Miranda's heart. She wanted to run *to* her grandfather—she wanted to run *away* from him. She couldn't do either one. She couldn't even move.

"Get him in the car!" Etienne ordered. And then, when

nobody volunteered, his tone sharpened. "Why are y'all just standing there? *Allez!* Hurry up!"

Everyone scrambled except Miranda. As Parker, Roo, and Gage raced forward to help, Ashley began tugging her away.

"Come on." Urging Miranda into a run, Ashley headed for the BMW. "Do you know your aunt's phone number? Your mom's?"

Numbly, Miranda shook her head. "Aunt Teeta's working." *And Mom won't come.*

She climbed in the back of the convertible where she'd sat before. To her surprise, Etienne and Gage lowered the old man into the seat and rested his head awkwardly across her lap. Ashley had buckled herself into the front. With some hasty and expert maneuvering, Etienne managed to squeeze in beside Miranda, while Parker jumped behind the wheel and fired up the engine. Etienne tossed his keys to Gage, who immediately ran to the truck with Roo.

"My seats," Parker moaned. "Who's going to clean all that?"

Ashley was not amused. "Your family has a maid and a gardener. And enough money to replace your car every time it gets a speck of dust on it. Now *drive!*"

The car lunged forward. Before Miranda knew it, they were already halfway to the main road.

All she could do now was stare down at this stranger's face— this slack, rawboned face with its age lines crusted in dirt, and the blood already dried in those deep, wrinkled creases of . . .

Sorrow? Pain?

No, it's something worse than pain, isn't it, Grandpa? Some-thing much worse than pain ...

For a split second, her mind filled with shadows.

"What happened to him back there?" she finally asked. "Who was he talking about? What was he running from?"

Ashley offered Miranda a sympathetic smile, then shook her head in bewilderment.

Straining forward, Etienne tapped Parker on the shoulder. "Take the bayou road. It'll be faster."

"Where we going?" Parker called back to him. "The clinic or the hospital?"

"Too far to the hospital—it'll have to be the clinic for now. They can always move him later if they need to."

"No!" As cold fingers clamped onto Miranda's wrist, she tried desperately to pull away. She heard Ashley's cry and the squeal of tires as Parker struggled to free himself from Ashley's flailing arms.

"No . . . no clinic." Still clinging to Miranda, Jonas Hayes fixed her with a gaze so pleading it nearly broke her heart. Then his fingers began to relax. And the words he spoke next were choked with emotion.

"Why . . . you're Miranda," he whispered. "You're my grand-daughter."

An icy current surged through her. As she returned his gaze in shocked silence, it was as if they were the only two people in the car.

"I'm begging you." His eyes closed now, wearily. "No

emergency room. Too many questions . . . too many stares. Please . . . just take me home."

Miranda glanced helplessly at the others. Etienne looked grim; Ashley was as close to her door as she could get; Parker watched uncertainly in the rearview mirror.

Not even sure why she was doing it, Miranda leaned toward Etienne. "Maybe we *should* take him home. Maybe he'd be more comfortable there, with Aunt Teeta."

"We don't know what's wrong with him or how bad he's hurt," Etienne answered. "He needs a doctor. You can call your aunt from the clinic."

Miranda hesitated. Her grandfather had lapsed back into unconsciousness, his grip loosened, his hand still covering hers. *This hand of a stranger,* she thought again. *And yet . . . he recognized me. He knows who I am.*

"Take him home." Miranda's voice was loud and firm. "I'll stay with him."

The mood in the car changed instantly. Miranda could almost swear she heard a collective sigh of relief from the front seat.

But not from Etienne.

He was staring at her, his expression unclear. She wasn't sure if she should feel noble or guilty about the decision she'd just made.

"Aunt Teeta will be back soon." For some reason, she felt the need to defend herself. "I'd rather not do anything till then. I mean, maybe this has happened before. She'll know how to handle it better than we can."

Etienne started to say something. His lips parted, then settled into a thin line. Miranda deliberately peered out the back windshield at Roo and Gage in Etienne's truck.

No one spoke the rest of the trip. It was only when Parker sped into the driveway of Hayes House that Miranda's grandfather stirred again.

"You'll help him, won't you?" He wasn't talking to Miranda this time; he seemed to be talking to no one. "Find what he's looking for . . . what he's lost . . ."

Miranda longed to ask more questions, but brakes were squealing and Etienne was already out of the car. As the truck slammed to a stop behind them, Gage hit the ground running.

"Let's get him in the house!" Etienne shouted. "Gage, you go around to the other side and—"

"No . . . no . . . you're not listening." Even as Parker turned off the engine, the old man was struggling to sit up. "You have to help him! Why won't you believe me? Why won't anybody believe me . . . ?"

The only thing Miranda could do was stay put while the three boys pulled Jonas Hayes off her lap. Ashley retreated to one side of the driveway and nervously chewed her bottom lip.

"I can walk," the old man said weakly. He waved the boys away, then sagged against the passenger door, his dazed eyes scanning the house, the lawn, and the faces of his rescuers. Miranda wasn't sure he even knew where he was. When Gage and Etienne propped him up between them, he didn't resist. Slowly they turned him toward the veranda.

"It's okay, Jonas," Etienne assured him. "You just need to rest yourself, that's all." He took a few steps, then glanced back at Miranda. "You gonna help us here, or what?"

Startled, she saw the accusation in his gaze.

"You're the one who wanted to stay with him," Etienne reminded her. "It's not gonna do a whole lotta good if he's in there and you're out here."

The truth of it hit her then—all those things she should have considered first, before making her snap decision. She'd been forbidden to meet her grandfather. She had no idea where to put him or what to do with him once they got him inside. And her mother would be absolutely furious.

But before she could answer, Jonas Hayes broke away. He jerked free so suddenly that Gage and Etienne nearly went sprawling to the ground.

"You're the one, Miranda!"

The voice of her grandfather reached out to her. She could hear the desperation in it, and the sorrow. His eyes, so wild before, now fixed on her with the utmost gentleness, like a silent prayer.

"You'll have to do it, Miranda." The old man's tears spilled over. "You're the only one who can."

As everyone watched in amazement, Jonas Hayes stumbled off across the yard. He half climbed, half fell up the steps of the veranda. Then the front door closed, and he was gone.

8

"**Well! Okay, then!**" Parker smacked his palms together, sounding much too relieved. "Looks like we're through here, huh? So I guess we'll be going now!"

He jumped quickly into the front seat, motioning the others to hurry. Ashley didn't waste any time. Roo followed, but seemed doubtful. Gage and Etienne stood talking for a moment before finally climbing into Etienne's truck. As the BMW jumped the curb and fishtailed onto the street, Miranda saw Ashley waving good-bye.

"Don't forget!" Ashley called. "Tomorrow, ten o'clock! In front of the Battlefield Inn!"

With a sinking heart, Miranda watched them go. How could they abandon her like this? Leave her here with this crazy old man? She turned and gazed miserably at the house. She'd had the sincerest intentions earlier when she'd offered to stay with her grandfather. When he'd recognized her and said her name, all her emotions had taken over. She'd honestly believed he was going to be okay.

So what am I supposed to do now?

She had no idea when Aunt Teeta would be home. She couldn't just wait around and do nothing in the meantime. What if her grandfather got confused again, and sick, and terrified like he'd been at the Falls? She had to go inside; she had to check on him. *Why didn't I listen to Etienne?* Etienne had been right— her grandfather belonged in a clinic with doctors.

But he's not in a clinic. And it's my fault he's here, and there's only me now to take care of him.

Miranda drew a deep breath. Squaring her shoulders, she walked to the front door of Hayes House and gave a tentative knock. It didn't really surprise her when no one answered. Summoning all her courage, she let herself in.

She wasn't sure what she'd expected. In her daydreams, she'd always pictured Hayes House as a kind of small plantation, something straight out of *Gone with the Wind.* She knew from Aunt Teeta's letters that the house was very old, that it had survived the Civil War but had been updated and added onto throughout all the generations. That it was close to the Historic District, located on a shady side street about a block off the Brickway. And that it backed up against one quiet area of Rebel Park.

Now, as she moved slowly across the threshold, Miranda let her eyes wander over the hardwood floors, the wide staircase, the high ceilings. Through half-open pocket doors she could see what must be the living and dining rooms. The wallpaper looked old, the furniture was dusty, and there were brown stains on the ceiling where water had leaked in. It might have been a grand house once, but now it felt sad and tired. And it was hard to think of Mom growing up here—Mom, who loved open spaces and plenty of light.

Miranda gazed a moment longer. *Still . . . Mom would think this place has potential.* Before, when Mom ran her own interior design studio, Miranda had seen her work miracles out of the shabbiest impossibilities. She couldn't help wondering what Mom could do here.

The muffled sound of a voice brought her back to attention. It seemed to have come from above her, though she couldn't be sure. Approaching the staircase, Miranda peered up at the landing, then stopped and listened. Yes . . . it *was* a voice.

Grandpa?

Calling for me?

She knew she hadn't imagined it. For an endless moment she stood there, trying to decide what to do. He hadn't wanted anyone to help him earlier—it would probably be better if she just left. And those weird things he'd been mumbling? *What if he really* is *crazy, like Roo said?*

A cold wave of fear rippled through her.

Just go, Miranda. Leave now.

Yet she put her hand on the banister. And she started up the stairs.

The second floor was much darker than the first. As twilight slanted in through a stained-glass window, it bathed the landing with soft, multicolored pools of light. A long, empty hall stretched out before her, and she could see heavy doors on both sides, most of them shut. She didn't want to be alone here—she didn't want to be here at all—but she'd reached the first doorway now, and had found what she was looking for.

His eyes were closed. He was lying on a narrow, wrought-iron bed that took up one wall of a narrow, cluttered room. A room that might just as well have been a museum.

No, more than a museum. A shrine.

For it was exactly that—an overflowing, overstuffed memorial to the Civil War. Faded photographs of soldiers and battlefields. Hand-rendered portraits of officers dressed in gray. A mounted gun with bayonet, a small collection of knives. An old-fashioned doctor's bag complete with surgical instruments. Rebel caps and a shaving mug, papers and pens, a bent pair of spectacles without lenses, a tobacco pipe. And row upon row of dusty jars, rusty tins, and musty boxes containing God knew what. There was even a sword with a dull, stained blade and a moth-eaten sash around its handle.

Curiosity got the best of her. Quietly, careful not to wake him, she began lifting lids off the jars and boxes and tins. Eclectic assortments, she saw at once—yet everything was neatly organized. Bullets and various-style buttons. Scraps of rotted cloth. A locket . . . some rings. Gold chains of different lengths; a short strap of braided leather. Cutlery so tarnished, she doubted it would ever come clean. Crumbling pages of a Bible. Locks of hair tied up with brittle ribbons . . .

These are real things; they belonged to real people. Real people who had lives and who used these things before they died . . .

She picked up a small, round tin from the nightstand. As fine hairs prickled at the back of her neck, she glanced at the bed and saw her grandfather watching her.

Miranda dropped the tin. It clattered down onto the floor

and rolled noisily out of sight beneath a dresser, but she was powerless to retrieve it. She couldn't look away from her grandfather's face. That surprisingly powerful gaze that held her, that unsettling gaze of infinite calm and profound knowing. Another shiver went through her, though it was different this time. For a split second, it was almost as if that gaze had opened to her—allowing the briefest glimpse of immeasurable wisdom and immeasurable pain . . .

"Miranda," he whispered.

His eyes began to change. Pale, blue eyes growing kind, glowing warm, with a tenderness and clarity that pierced her heart.

This was the grandfather of her photograph.

The grandpa she'd hoped for, the grandpa she'd prayed for and imagined for so long.

And as his hand lifted and beckoned, she walked to his side and offered him a smile, half fearful, half shy.

"I've been waiting for you," he said softly. "All this time. So many years. I was beginning to think this day would never come."

She didn't know how to answer. His voice was still so weak, his face so chalky white. She felt his long, frail fingers close around her hand.

"It always skips a generation," he mumbled. "That's why your mama won't ever understand."

"Grandpa, I don't . . ." Miranda hesitated . . . shook her head. He was obviously still delusional; she didn't have a clue what he was talking about.

"They'll come to you because they know you can see them.

They'll speak to you because they know you'll hear." The old man gave a restless sigh. "It's a burden sometimes, all that listening and helping. But you can't turn them away."

I shouldn't have done this. I'm just making him worse.

Casually, she tried to free herself, but he only squeezed her hand tighter. "Promise me, Miranda. Promise me you'll never turn them away."

He was growing more agitated now, more insistent. Miranda feared what he might do if he worked himself into another frenzy. Not wanting to risk it, she gave him a solemn nod.

"Yes. I promise."

What have I done now?

But the change in him was remarkable. Relief shining from his eyes . . . peace drifting over his face.

"Good girl," he whispered. "I knew I could trust you."

Glancing away, she wrestled with her guilt. She'd promised, and he'd believed her. She'd promised him something, and she didn't even know what it was.

"Let him help." Her grandfather's voice was fading. As Miranda looked down at him once more, his body went limp with exhaustion, his ramblings lowered to murmurs. She wondered if he'd already slipped into his strange, private dreams.

"Ssh . . ." Freeing her hand, she placed it gently on his forehead. "Ssh . . . just rest now . . ."

"It's lonely, Miranda. He'll help you. Let him do that."

She stepped back from the bed, watching the rise and fall of her grandfather's chest—his deep, easy breathing of sleep. All around them, the shadows had grown darker. They'd lengthened and thickened and crept in from the musty hall, and now they slid along the walls and over the headboard, covering the old man's face like a death mask.

"Oh, Grandpa," Miranda whispered, "I wish I knew what you were talking about."

"I think," said a voice behind her, "he's talking about me."

9

ALL THE STRENGTH DRAINED OUT OF HER. As Miranda whirled around, a scream rose up and caught silently in her throat.

At first he seemed merely a shadow, one shapeless form among many. But when he shifted and started toward her, she recognized Etienne's tall silhouette etched sharply against the gloom.

"You're with him. That's good." Etienne's voice, like his arrival, was quiet and matter-of-fact. "I was hoping you would be, but I couldn't be sure."

Miranda didn't answer at first. Their earlier conversation— his knowing about the screams—flashed back to her, and she pressed against the dresser, trying to put distance between them.

"Sorry." Etienne moved closer. "I didn't mean to scare you. I thought you knew—"

"Knew what?" Though the intrusion hadn't disturbed her grandfather, Miranda felt wary and unnerved.

"Knew I was here," Etienne finished.

"All I know is that you seem to show up—*uninvited*—at very weird times."

"Okay, you're upset, I understand that. But I left to take Gage home. And you and Jonas needed a little time alone together."

"Why would *I* care whether you left or not? And who are *you* to say what I need?"

Etienne's gaze drifted to that elderly face upon the pillow. "It's what *he* needs."

"Oh, really? And I suppose he told you that?"

"He didn't have to tell me, *cher*. You're practically the only thing he cares about."

It was a revelation she certainly never expected. Swallowing a lump in her throat, she watched Etienne cross to the window, angle himself against the wall, and stare out at the gathering dusk.

"Gage didn't want to leave either," Etienne added offhandedly. "But I talked him into it."

Miranda scarcely heard the remark. "What did you mean just now? What you said about my grandpa and me?"

"Why? Is it so hard for you to believe?"

"To tell you the truth . . . yes."

"Your *grand-père*, he's saved every letter you've written to your aunt Teeta. Every picture you've ever sent. He talks about you like he's known you for your whole life. Like the two of you've been together forever." Etienne's tone went thoughtful. "Well . . . maybe you really have."

"Why would you say that? We've never met each other, never communicated. For ten years I never even knew he existed."

For a moment Etienne didn't respond. Then slowly he turned from the window, his black eyes narrowed hard upon her face.

"But Jonas, he always thought—always wondered—if that connection was there between you and him. And he knew if it was . . . then none of the other stuff mattered."

Miranda wished he would stop; she didn't want to hear any more. Yet at the same time, a fearful curiosity had sparked inside her, *wanting* to hear, *needing* to hear . . .

"He told me I'd know for sure when you heard their voices," Etienne went on. "And he said to ask you about the screams. He said only *you* would hear their screams at night."

Her curiosity vanished now, replaced by a growing panic. *This can't be happening to me.* It squeezed her heart and choked her words, though she fought to stay calm. Her hands clenched at her sides. She willed her voice not to tremble. "I don't even know what you're talking about."

"Look, Miranda—"

"I don't know about any voices."

"But you heard one in your apartment today, yeah? We *both* know that—"

"No. It was a mistake. I only thought I did . . ."

"I guess it'd be easier to believe that. *Safer* to believe that." Despite her angry glare, Etienne's voice softened. "Your *grandpère,* he cares about you. He knows what it's like. He wants your life to be happy."

"I'll be happy when you leave. Why'd you come here anyway? Why don't you just go?"

She was starting to shake uncontrollably. Deep, painful chills that ached all the way through. She couldn't get warm. She couldn't concentrate on what Etienne was saying. She hugged herself and tried to stop shivering, and that's when she realized Etienne's arms were around her.

"Your *grand-père*, he wants me to help you, *cher*," Etienne insisted. "So you won't be alone in all this."

The chills began instantly to melt. As Etienne pressed her firmly to his chest, she could feel his faint stir of breath through her hair, the length and shape of his body against hers. Her pulse quickened; her thoughts spun. She had to escape—from this room and this house, from Etienne and the way he was holding her, from these crazy things he was saying . . .

Miranda pushed him away.

"I told you, I don't know what you're talking about. My grandpa doesn't know anything about me, and neither do you. There's nothing to help me with. I don't *need* any help. And I'm not lonely."

"I didn't say you'd be lonely." Etienne seemed to be studying her, as if she were some unusual specimen under a microscope. "I said you'd be *alone*. But in this case, you might end up being both."

"I'm leaving. *You* can stay here with Jonas Hayes."

Shoving past Etienne, she headed for the door, but his calm voice followed her.

"You *have* heard the screams, haven't you? And he *told* you you'd hear things. He *told* you you'd see things. Things other people can't hear or see."

Miranda froze with one hand on the door frame. Etienne continued, unfazed.

"I've seen what this does—this gift of his. I see every day what it does to your *grand-père*."

"He's sick!" Even as the words left her mouth, she wished she could take them back. Feeling guilty and frightened and angry, she whirled to face Etienne. "He's just a sick, crazy old man. We should have taken him to a doctor like you said."

"Miranda—"

"You saw him at the cemetery. Is that your idea of a rational person? I mean, what was he doing running around in the woods like that anyway? He ought to be kept somewhere."

"So, what . . . you're saying he should be locked up?" Etienne's face went rigid. "For years he was caretaker at the Falls. And he still likes to go there—do some exploring, clean up the cemetery, fish a little."

"But that doesn't explain the way he was acting. Everyone says he's a lunatic. So why are you defending him? Why do you even care about him?"

Etienne held her in a long, cool stare. And yet there was something in his eyes that Miranda hadn't seen till this moment . . . something distant and almost sad.

"Because," Etienne said quietly, "he's my friend."

A heavy silence sank between them. For just an instant, Miranda felt as if she were seeing a different person standing before her—a stranger with Etienne's face. The briefest glimpse of loss and shame and vulnerability, the cold defiance of fierce pride.

And then it was gone. As quickly as it had come, it vanished again, leaving her to wonder at the mystery.

She heard the crunch of tires below in the driveway, the slamming of car doors. The familiar sound of voices—Aunt Teeta's and Mom's.

"You better get yourself outta here," Etienne told her. "Before your mama finds out."

"How do you know about—"

"Turn left at the bottom of the stairs and go two rooms down. There's a side door through the pantry; I'm just about the only one who ever uses it, and it's never locked. You can cut through the backyard—nobody'll see you with all those trees."

"But what about Grandpa?"

"Don't worry. I'll make sure Miss Teeta knows about him."

Miranda didn't waste any time. While Etienne went out the front door, she made a quick getaway, reaching the apartment well ahead of her mother. When Mom finally came in, Miranda was already sitting on the bed amid scattered piles of homework.

"Congratulate me!" Mom greeted her. "I got the job!"

Miranda couldn't have cared less about the job. In light of all that had happened today, a job hardly even seemed significant.

"Great." Miranda forced a smile. "Congratulations."

"I start tomorrow." For the first time in weeks, Mom sounded almost happy. "It's a renovation project—one of the oldest plantations on the bayou. Belle Chandelle? You remember Aunt Teeta telling us about it? The company was very impressed that I'd had my own design studio. They said my experience is just what they need!"

"That's good, Mom."

"Then afterward I picked up Teeta, and we stopped for a quick bite. We *did* come by here first, honey, to see if you wanted to eat with us."

When Miranda didn't respond, Mom did a quick appraisal of the books and papers on the bed.

"So how was your study group?"

"Fine."

"Think you'll make some new friends?"

"I guess."

"Well, it sure feels nice in here now, doesn't it?" Awkwardly, Mom groped for more small talk. "A lot better than it did before. So I'm assuming the air conditoner got fixed."

"It's a loaner."

A long pause followed. Then, "Miranda . . . about our discussion—"

"Not now, Mom, okay? I really need to get this done."

Mom's relief couldn't have been more obvious, though a slight frown creased her brow. "That's fine, honey. Maybe tomorrow, huh?"

"Maybe."

"Did you have dinner? Aunt Teeta and I are going to sit in the backyard and have ice cream if you—"

"No thanks."

She was glad when Mom left. There was too much to think about, too much to worry about, too much to figure out. The events of today swam crazily through her mind—the kids she'd met, the Ghost Walk they were planning, the eerie voice she'd heard, the Falls, her grandfather, Etienne . . .

Etienne.

Etienne, who seemed to know far more about her than she knew about herself . . .

"He told *you you'd hear things."* Etienne's words haunted her. *"He* told *you you'd see things. Things other people can't hear or see."*

"You're insane, Etienne Boucher. You and Grandpa and everyone else in this stupid town are all completely insane."

But what if it were true?

Because I did *hear a voice, and I* have *heard those screams . . .*

With one angry swipe, Miranda knocked all her books and papers to the floor.

What if everything Etienne said is true?

What does that make me?

10

THE SCREAMS CAME BACK THAT NIGHT.

Tossing and turning, Miranda tried to shut them out, to obliterate them once and for all. Only now they were *louder*—louder than they'd ever been—and the *voice* was there, too, drifting beneath them . . . muffled yet every bit as clear—

"*No . . . you're wrong . . .*"

That hollow male voice—*he's young . . . twenty at the most.*

"*I swear to you—for the love of God!*"

That raw, hopeless voice—*and his throat's dry, he can taste blood, his lips are cracked . . . he needs water.*

"*I'm the one you want . . . only me.*"

Like drowning waves, the voice and the screams flowed over her. Once again Miranda fought them, but they wrapped her in a cold embrace and drew her down into darkness.

She was lost in that darkness.

Lost and stumbling in that horrible darkness . . . yet not alone.

She couldn't see them, but they were there. Couldn't find them, couldn't touch them, but they were real. Real hands clawing and groping . . . real eyes vacant and staring, moving so close around her, just beyond her reach. Pain and shock and grief and rage—she could feel them all, the unbearable essence of them as they whispered the very words her grandfather had spoken . . .

"You're the one, Miranda . . . you're the only one who can—"

Bolting upright, she gasped for air. The apartment was sweltering hot, her flimsy nightgown completely soaked with sweat. As an unfamilar glow filtered through the darkness, it tinted the shadows red and thickened them into fog.

A deep, unnatural silence filled the room. Though she strained her eyes, she couldn't see anything—not the walls or the light from the bathroom, not the door, not even her mother's bed. As if, slowly and stealthily, that eerie red haze was shutting her off from the rest of the world . . . *no, no, not haze. Smoke!*

"Mom?" She wanted to throw back the covers, jump out of bed, and run to her mother, but suddenly she was so *scared*, too scared even to *move*. "Mom, are you there? Please answer me!"

Something's burning. We have to get out of here!

"Mom?" Miranda choked.

The smoke was swirling with nightmares, macabre silhouettes bursting into bright orange flames.

Fire!

Panicked, Miranda lunged at the darkness. Her fists pounded, and her legs kicked. The sheets felt tight, trapping her, and she struck out with flailing arms. As the smoke softly, gradually began to fade, her eyes opened to light.

For a second she didn't know where she was. Then the walls came into focus, and the air flowed around her, gentle and quiet and cool.

"Mom?"

Groggy and disoriented, Miranda sat up. The covers were tangled at the foot of the bed now; her head was throbbing, her stomach churned. She felt like she'd been run over by a truck.

"Mom, what time is it?"

Reaching for the clock, she let out a groan. *Nine forty-five?* Mom was probably at work already. *Why didn't I ask her to wake me?* She groaned again as a knock sounded at the door, and she stumbled over to answer it.

"Roo said you'd forget," Etienne greeted her.

"I didn't forget." Conscious of her thin nightgown, Miranda stepped behind the door.

"And Roo said even if you didn't forget, you still wouldn't be there on time."

His hair was damp, as though he'd just washed it. His black jeans fit casually over his narrow hips, and his black T-shirt had BOUCHER SWAMP TOURS stamped across the front in faded red letters.

"You should be feeling proud of yourself," he added offhandedly. "So far she hasn't told me one word about boiling you in oil. Not many people can pass the Roo test."

"Is that supposed to thrill me?"

"It thrills *me*. You sure don't want Roo putting a *gris-gris* on you. *Very* bad luck, *cher*."

"I have to get dressed," Miranda grumbled.

"I'll wait."

"I don't need you to wait for me."

"You might get lost."

"It's only a fifteen-minute walk to the inn, right? How lost could I get?"

She felt his eyes rake over her. She doubted if those eyes ever missed much.

"Bad night?" he asked her.

Miranda hesitated. Was he trying to be funny? Self-righteous? But the expression on his face wasn't joking or smug, and she didn't feel like answering any questions right now.

"I'll be out in a minute."

"Your *grand-père*? Miss Teeta says he's better," Etienne said. "Just in case you were wondering."

"Great. Maybe today he'll do something else for the whole town to talk about."

"The town, it won't talk if it doesn't know." Etienne's voice hardened. "I don't think you give your friends enough credit."

"What friends?" But she shut the door before he had a chance to respond.

She'd just assumed her classmates would tell everyone what had happened at the Falls—what a raving nutcase Jonas Hayes had been. It never occurred to her that they might keep it to themselves, and now she felt embarrassed and confused. Etienne had called the others her friends, yet she hardly knew them. Miranda realized she didn't quite know *what* to think—about *anything*.

Guiltily, she threw on her clothes, then smoothed her hair back behind her ears. She wished Etienne hadn't stopped by for her; she wished she'd thought up some brilliant excuse to stay home. She didn't feel like researching today, didn't feel like being with anyone or having to make conversation. She felt horrible, and she knew she looked horrible, too. *Well, how else would I look with no sleep?*

For the memory of her nightmare still clung to her. The smoke, the fire, the screaming. Despite its dreamlike aftermath, it hadn't *seemed* like a dream while it was happening—all those details, so frighteningly vivid.

She frowned at herself in the bathroom mirror.

Swearing under her breath, she brushed her teeth, then headed out the door.

Etienne was waiting for her at the end of the driveway. As Miranda approached, she could see Gage there, too, and the minute he smiled, she could feel her spirits lift. She walked between them, trying to match their long strides, then finally gave up and trailed behind. It was Gage who stopped and waited for her. Etienne slowed down but kept going.

Nearing the Battlefield Inn, they spotted Ashley and Parker sitting together on the front steps. Ashley immediately jumped up and started waving.

"There y'all are! We just got here, too! Isn't this fun!"

"Yeah," Parker grumbled, "I love spending Saturday morning out in the hot sun doing a crappy homework assignment."

"It's a beautiful day. Don't be such a whiner."

"If you say so. Can we please just get this over with? Look, I've got all this junk my mom gave me. So I don't see any reason to hang around here and waste time."

Reaching over, Ashley took the manila envelope he was holding. "I've already looked through it, and it's wonderful.

Brochures and little booklets and handouts—things like that. Plus, copies of actual newspaper articles, the history of the town. I mean, we've all heard *some* of the legends around here, but there's a lot of stuff I didn't know about."

"Fascinating. I'm overwhelmed with fascination."

"Mrs. Wilmington got us all this from the Historical Society. She's in charge of their museum, you know. Wasn't that sweet of her?"

"I'm overwhelmed with sweetness." Parker made a gagging sound in his throat. "In fact, let's nominate sweet Mrs. Wilmington for Mother of the Year."

"Parker, be nice."

"I'm always nice. You, of all people, should know how nice I am." Jumping to the sidewalk, he suddenly took Gage by the shoulders. He looked Gage up and down; he looked behind Gage's back. As the others started snickering, Parker stepped away again, his expression shocked. "That's *it*! I *knew* something was wrong. You're missing your worse half!"

Gage pointed to the old-fashioned bakery across the street. "She walked on ahead. She was hungry."

"Wow." Parker's eyes went wide. "I'm just not used to seeing the two of you separated. You look different. It's kind of scary."

Even Ashley couldn't help but join in. "What's *really* scary is when you see those people who spend so much time with each other? And they start to look alike?"

Etienne nodded at her, as if Gage weren't even present. "What do you think people like that *do* all the time they're together, anyway?"

"Ugh! Stop!" Parker gave an overly dramatic shudder.

As if on cue, Roo strolled out of the bakery, carrying a huge cinnamon roll in one hand and a giant cappuccino in the other. She wore a black taffeta miniskirt, black tights, black ballet slippers, and a black tank top over a purple T-shirt. Watching her a moment, Parker turned to the others and sighed.

"Look at her. Fashion Goddess of the Dark Realm."

"*She's creative,*" Ashley emphasized. "And her realm isn't always a bad place to be."

"Neither is hell. If you're the Antichrist."

This earned Parker a slug on the arm. Grinning, he pulled Ashley close and kissed her.

"Don't even ask," Roo announced as she joined them. "These are mine, and I'm not sharing."

Gage promptly tore off a fourth of the cinnamon roll and popped it in his mouth. Etienne took a third of what was left. Roo stood there looking down at her practically empty napkin.

"You didn't need that, anyway," Ashley insisted. "All those calories."

Parker gave Roo a serious once-over. "Since when has Roo cared about calories? No, wait. Since when has Roo cared about clothes? No, wait. Since when has Roo cared about how she looks?"

He stared at Gage. Gage stared at Etienne. Etienne stared at Parker.

"Since when has Roo cared about anything?" they all asked in unison.

Feeling a little envious, Miranda observed the good-natured

teasing. The kids back home hadn't shared this kind of camaraderie. Not that they hadn't been close—their own special group of girls and guys—but what Miranda saw here was different.

Stronger, somehow.

Like a real family.

Miranda refocused on the three boys. Roo didn't seem the least bit bothered by their comments. As Gage reached for the last bite of cinnamon roll, Roo stuffed it quickly into her mouth. Etienne just as quickly snatched the cappuccino from her other hand.

Giving Etienne a shove, Roo gestured knowingly in Miranda's direction. "I told you she'd forget."

"I didn't forget," Miranda defended herself for the second time.

"I told you she'd be late."

"Okay," Miranda grumbled. "I'll give you that one."

Roo looked smugly pleased. She took back her cappuccino.

"I think we should get started." Ashley, as usual, seized command of the situation. "Did y'all come up with any good ideas? I brought stuff for us to take notes with."

Parker grudgingly accepted the pad and pen she handed him. "Wow. Just what I always wanted."

"You'll thank me when you get an A on the project."

"I can think of other things I'd rather thank you for."

A memo pad came down on his head. Wincing, he rubbed his scalp and shot Ashley an injured look.

The six of them started walking, heading down the east side

of the Brickway, pausing often along the route. Other than the information Parker had gotten from his mom, Gage was the only one who'd bothered to do any actual research last night. Now he pulled a crumpled list from his pocket and read out interesting facts from time to time.

"Like the courthouse," Gage began, while Parker immediately dismissed the idea.

"Yeah, yeah, we all know about the courthouse. Every town in America has a haunted courthouse."

"We didn't." Miranda looked curiously at Gage. "What about the courthouse?"

"Supposedly, Judge Girard sentenced a lot of innocent people to death. Legend has it that he attended every single hanging, and that he'd actually laugh each time another body swung from the noose."

Roo's tone was matter-of-fact. "He liked to see them twitching."

"The thing is," Ashley picked up the story, "I guess a lot of prisoners really hated that judge."

Parker snorted. "You think?"

"When they spoke their final words, they cursed him." Gage's voice lowered. "One morning the judge was found dead in his own courtroom. Hanging from the rafters. Most people *didn't* believe it was suicide."

"Some people swear they've seen the judge's ghost," Roo finished.

Parker was obviously pleased with the outcome. "Yeah! The only good judge is a dead judge."

"Parker Wilmington the Sixth!" A slug from Ashley. "You stop that right now!"

"Parker's dad is a judge," Roo explained. She and Miranda had fallen behind the others, and out of earshot. "Parker really hates his dad."

Though Miranda had no desire to get involved, she couldn't help stating the obvious. "He doesn't sound like he's real fond of his mom either."

"He's not. His folks are into all the big social and political stuff around here. Parker hardly ever sees them; they're never home."

"But . . . I'm sure they love him, right?"

"Would *you* love Parker if he were *your* son?"

Miranda didn't know whether to laugh, be sad, or both. She decided on a more positive approach.

"He really likes Ashley."

Roo's shrug was noncommital.

"What I mean is," Miranda tried again, "he seems to really care about her."

"Sometimes I'm not sure what he cares about." Another shrug as Roo stared at the back of Parker's head. "He'll get thrown off the team permanently if they catch him drinking again. And his dad expects him to get a full football scholarship. Which Parker doesn't want to do."

So Parker's deliberately trying to get kicked off the team. Keeping the obvious conclusion to herself, Miranda asked, "What *does* Parker want to do?"

"Self-destruct would be my guess."

Suddenly aware that part of their crew was missing, the others stopped and waited. Roo and Miranda caught up to them, and the walk continued.

Despite her distracted state of mind, Miranda couldn't help being fascinated by the Brickway. Things about the old South that she'd watched on TV and in movies, things she'd read about in books—all that long-faded past was coming to life around her. Whether antebellum house or step-front shop, each held the promise of mystery and romance.

"Maybe we should start with commercial buildings," Gage suggested. "I think we'll have a better chance of getting inside than we would with most of the houses."

Ashley consulted the contents of her envelope. "What about the park?"

"Yeah! They're having the Rebel Rouser there today!" Parker's eyes shone with the possibility of escape.

At Miranda's questioning look, Ashley elaborated. "It's like a fair—all the money's used to maintain the park. The Ladies of the Southland sponsor it every year."

"They're this women's club," Gage said. Then, as an afterthought, "They do garden tours."

"And tea parties." Parker daintily crooked his little finger, as if holding a china teacup. "They wear hats. With fake flowers on them. And plastic fruit."

Chuckling, Gage shook his head. "Let's forget about the park. That could be a whole other tour by itself."

The others readily agreed. As they moved down the sidewalk, Ashley linked her arm through Miranda's and kept up a steady flow of information.

"Here's the museum—the one Parker's mom is in charge of. It belongs to the Historical Society. And that over there? It's all closed in now, but it was the original public market. You know, like a farmer's market? And that's Grace Church. And that's the library."

"Actually, I found out it used to be a funeral parlor." Gage smiled, glancing at Ashley.

Ashley shuddered. "I bet there's *tons* of creepy stories about *that*!"

"And a lotta other buildings maybe you wouldn't expect." Without breaking stride, Etienne pointed out a charming yellow house on the opposite side of the street. "Mama said a Dr. Fuller used to have his office in that place. Who knows who might've been sick or died there."

"Ewww!" Ashley stopped in her tracks. Gage promptly plowed into her from behind.

"We should do some research on voodoo, too," Roo reminded them. "Lots of people around here practiced secret voodoo rituals."

"How do you know that?"

"Why *wouldn't* she know that?" Parker returned. "She of the Deep Underworld who keeps decomposing mice and many other dead things in her locker."

Roo's stare was calm disdain. "*One* mouse."

"We still don't know how it got in Roo's locker," Ashley explained, looking distressed at the memory. "But she threw her books in and squashed it."

"It was hiding. How was *I* supposed to know it was there."

"Maybe if you cleaned out your locker once in a while?"

"Hey!" Snapping his fingers, Parker gave an exaggerated gasp of excitement. "I think we should put Roo's locker on our tour! The mummy of the murdered mouse!"

Gage held back a smile. "Why don't we just put *Roo* on our tour?"

"No, no, *mon Dieu,* way too scary." With one smooth motion, Etienne crooked his arm around Roo's neck and pulled her sideways against him. Roo tried to elbow him, but he expertly dodged the blow. "Okay, I think we got it, yeah? What information we have now, that's where we're gonna start. And once we get into all that research, we'll probably be finding even more ideas."

He seemed to be waiting for Miranda's confirmation. Realizing the others were staring at her, she quickly nodded. "Anything dark, mysterious, unsolved, or unexplained. As long as you don't make it up. The Ghost Walk's all about having fun and giving people a good scare. But it's also about factual events, the real history of the town."

"Well done," Gage murmured.

Doing her best to pay attention, Miranda wiped a hand across her brow. The morning had started out hot and humid, but she hadn't expected the temperature to rise so quickly. No one else looked uncomfortable, she noted. *Maybe I'm just tired from last night.*

"This fancy house?" Ashley still had Miranda firmly in tow. "Can you believe it started out as a one-room feed store? The family that built it had a little boy who died. I don't remember the exact details, but there's a newspaper article about it in this stuff from Parker's mom."

Miranda gave Ashley a puzzled frown. It suddenly occurred to her that she'd scarcely heard anything the girl was saying.

"What about that building over there?" Miranda asked.

"That one? Oh, that's the bank."

"Not the bank." Halting abruptly, Miranda spun Ashley halfway around. "That one."

Ashley caught her balance at the last possible second. Bewildered, she followed the point of Miranda's finger. "You mean Magnolia Gallery?"

"It's not a gallery," Miranda murmured.

Coming up beside them, Gage shot her a quizzical glance. "Yes, it is . . . an art gallery. Not just paintings though. We have a lot of local—"

"No." Her voice had gone stubborn. She realized the others had gathered close, watching her in quiet dismay. "Before that."

Gage glanced from Parker to Roo to Etienne. "Hasn't it always been a gallery?" Receiving only shrugs, he skimmed the list of research he'd done.

"*No, that's not it!*" Out of patience now, Miranda's tone sharpened.

God, it was so *hot* out here! Why were they all staring at her again? And why did she suddenly have such an overwhelming urge to go over and look at that building?

"Miranda?" Ashley asked worriedly, but Miranda didn't answer.

Pushing Ashley and Gage aside, she hurried across the street to the old building set back behind magnolia trees. Stately white facade; high, round columns; tall French shutters; upper-floor balconies—all the details rushed over her, familiar somehow, as if she'd seen them all before. She took the wide front steps two at a time and shoved open the massive doors. She paused expectantly on the threshold.

Music?

Her body grew even warmer, curiously detached. A strange but not unpleasant sensation of being removed to some different place—some close but hidden place where she could watch herself frozen there in the doorway. She could feel her mind opening, her heart searching, her senses reaching out . . .

Yes, definitely music. The tragic refrains of a finely tuned orchestra.

And a voice—such a voice!

An angel's voice!

Soaring to heaven and back again in sweetly pure soprano . . .

Again Miranda felt the pull. The pull to give in and go farther, the urge to completely let go.

The swishing of skirts and handheld fans, the clinking of crystal glasses, flow of fine wine, heady sweetness of roses . . .

The final fall of a curtain . . .

And one voice.

"Nathan . . . why?"

The angel's voice, sad and alone . . .

Sobbing . . .

Now silent.

Miranda whirled around. She was here, right here on the threshold of the gallery, and she could see the others gathered in behind her on the steps. Parker and Ashley, Roo and Gage and Etienne—all of them just standing there, watching her with half-stunned expressions. After what seemed an eternity, Etienne started toward her, but Gage got to her first.

"It was an opera house," she mumbled. Letting the doors swing shut, she peered up into Gage's startled eyes. "And something terrible happened here."

11

THE RUSH, THE HEAT, THE EERIE DETACHMENT WERE GONE.

No roses now, no ghostly sounds.

Instead, Miranda felt as though a raging fever had broken, leaving her weak and shaky, but remarkably clearheaded. She remembered every detail—every sight and scent and sound. She recalled her senses heightening to almost painful intensity before fading back again to normal.

And she was positive that time had come to a standstill, even while passing her by.

Oh my God . . . did I really say that out loud?

Etienne had stopped midstride. She could see the way he was looking at her—beyond curious, beyond surprise, almost as if he'd suddenly recognized who—or what—she truly was. The others, exchanging wary glances, hadn't moved.

It was Parker who finally broke the silence. Slapping both hands on his knees, he doubled over in forced laughter.

"Man! That was *great*! You really had me going there for a second!"

But Ashley's voice held a slight tremor as she snapped at him. "Parker, have you completely lost your mind? What is wrong with you?"

"Well, don't you get it? The way she set us up like that? It was brilliant!" Straightening, he grinned from ear to ear. "Hey, Miranda, did you take acting lessons at your old school? I think *you* should be the guide on this Ghost Walk thing—I mean, you were convincing as hell!"

"Um . . . excuse me?" Roo's stare was as condescending as her tone. "Reality check here. I don't think she was acting."

"Well, sure she was. She—" Parker broke off. Realizing he was the only one laughing, he glanced at Miranda's blank face, at Gage standing uncertainly beside her, at Etienne's fixed expression. Then he laughed again, though not as loud as before. "Y'all aren't buying this, are you? She's just screwing with us."

"*Were* you?" Ashley murmured, her wide-eyed gaze on Miranda. "Is that supposed to be part of the tour?"

Roo pulled a cigarette from one pocket, matches from another. She lit up, crossed her arms over her chest, and blew out a long curl of smoke.

Avoiding Etienne's stare, Miranda forced an amused smile. "Come on, you guys, how would I know anything about an opera house?" *Could I have read it somewhere?* "How would I know anything about *any* of these buildings?" *Could I have heard it from Aunt Teeta?*

Ashley immediately looked relieved. "So you *were* acting! Oh, Miranda, that was so good—you really have it down! I totally believed you!"

"She wasn't acting," Roo said again.

But Miranda couldn't listen to any more. Etienne was standing next to her now, and Gage was on her other side, and she was beginning to feel trapped. She had to get away from here.

"Sorry." Faking a look at Etienne's watch, she bolted down the steps and past the others. "I didn't realize how late it was—I promised Aunt Teeta I'd help her with something. See you later!"

She hurried along the route they'd taken, knowing full well how lame her excuse had been. She thought she heard someone call her name, but she didn't stop, and she didn't look over her shoulder. Had she managed to convince them that she'd been making everything up? For what else *could* she have done at the mercy of an event so totally unexpected and unforeseen? She could hardly believe it herself—how could she ever expect *them* to?

Yet she *did* believe it. Because this time was different.

This time she hadn't been afraid or alone or confused like she'd been before, when the voice had spoken, when the screams had come. This time she hadn't been lost in some nightmare. There had been a real opera house, a real tragedy within its walls, and though she wasn't sure how or why she could have known this, she was certain about it now. She just *knew*.

I have to go home. She had to escape before *it*—whatever *it* was—happened to her again. As she picked up speed, it dawned on her that there was one person who would understand.

I have to talk to Grandpa.

Miranda walked even faster. She prayed no one had followed, but there were footsteps behind her, gaining steadily.

"Miranda! Wait up!"

She pretended not to hear. When Etienne grabbed her arm,

she gasped as he swung her around to face him.

"Come on, *cher,* where you going?"

"It's a mistake!" Miranda insisted. "What I said at the gallery. I don't know anything about it—I made it up!"

"You know you didn't."

She tried to shake him off, but he only held her tighter. "Etienne, please—I need to talk to my grandfather. I need him to explain. I need to understand what this *is*—what's *happening* to me!"

"He already told you. You can communicate in ways the rest of us can't. With people the rest of us can't."

"Dead people." Miranda could barely choke out the words. "That's what you're saying, isn't it? That suddenly I've got this— this horrible power . . ."

"*Gift, cher.*"

As his eyes fixed on hers with calm intensity, she found it impossible to look away. She wondered if those eyes had ever shown the slightest trace of fear. She wondered why her own fears seemed to be calming inside her, leaving only a quiet resentment in their place.

"So I'm supposed to believe that. And accept that. Like it's perfectly normal."

"Yes. Your *grand-père,* he always helped them. When they had secrets they needed to share. When they were in pain. He was the only one they could turn to."

Miranda's heart was an icy knot. "Please don't tell me this."

"You need to hear the truth. And I promised him."

"This is crazy. You know that, right? Things like this don't happen to normal people." Biting her lip, she fought back sudden tears. "Why did that hurricane ever have to hit? Why did I ever have to come here in the first place?"

"Because," Etienne said gently, "maybe this is the place you're supposed to be."

His solemn words struck deep. With a puzzled frown, she gazed into his night-black stare.

"I heard what Jonas said to you yesterday," Etienne reminded her. "He asked you not to turn them away."

Thinking back to that strange conversation, Miranda gave a reluctant nod. "I *have* heard things. Voices. Sounds. And those screams Grandpa told you about. And something happened last night, too—I couldn't be sure what was real and what wasn't." She paused, her brow furrowing. "And now today. No warning, no time to think. What if it happens again?"

"It *will* happen again."

"I don't like being surprised. I don't want people staring and laughing at me."

Etienne sounded thoughtful. "There's only one person I know of who was laughing back there just now. And some people, they laugh just to hide how scared they are."

She knew he was referring to Parker, but it didn't ease the sting. "Parker can't be half as scared as I am."

"Listen to me, *cher*." Sliding his fingers beneath her chin, Etienne tilted her face toward his. "You got a lot on your shoulders right now—a lotta thoughts, a lotta questions, a whole lotta things to get used to. It doesn't seem real to you—and it probably won't for a while. But you better accept it. 'Cause, if you're anything like your *grand-père*, it won't be going away."

His honesty did little to reassure her. She noticed the rest of the group approaching now, and the urge to escape grew stronger.

"Aunt Teeta's waiting for me," she mumbled.

Twisting free, she took off once more, determined to put as much distance between herself and the others as she could. Thank God she didn't have far to go. She rounded the last corner and could finally see Hayes House ahead of her. She saw the neatly lettered sign on the curb stating PRIVATE HOME—NO TRESPASSING. And she saw a mass of people crowded along the driveway and across the lawn.

That's weird . . .

As Miranda started to run, neighbors continued to gather, all talking somberly to one another while they watched the house. For the first time she spotted several police cars and an ambulance. With rising dread, she forced her way through curious onlookers and up the front steps.

It was Mom who met her at the door. Mom with an expression much too serious, and a hint of tears glistening in her eyes.

"Mom?"

"It's your grandpa," Mom said quietly. "He's gone, honey. Teeta found him about half an hour ago . . . dead in his room."

12

THE AWFUL REALITY WAS SLOW TO SINK IN.

It seemed forever that Miranda stood there, regarding her mother in stunned disbelief.

She felt Mom take her arm and steer her gently inside the house, then close the door behind them. She heard Aunt Teeta crying. She could hear the hushed voices of police and paramedics, the creaking of footsteps on the second floor, the muffled maneuvers on the stairs as a stretcher was carried down.

Mom coaxed her into the nearest room—what Miranda had guessed to be the living room on her first visit here.

Yesterday. It was just yesterday.

How could that be? She'd finally found her grandfather. After all these years, all her dreams and imaginings, she'd met him at last. She'd talked with him, held his hand, touched his face. She'd been happy and disappointed; she'd been hopeful and had her hopes dashed. She'd been angry and yearning and horrified and confused, and she'd been given a shocking, secret revelation that she couldn't comprehend and certainly didn't want.

There would be no understanding now.

No answers, no explanations, nothing.

"It always skips a generation . . . that's why your mama will never understand . . ."

"Maybe this is the place you're supposed to be . . ."

Words pounded in her head. Grandpa's words, Etienne's words, useless words, meaningless words. She'd been afraid of her grandfather—she'd been embarrassed and ashamed. But now she was all mixed up. Now she didn't know *how* she felt.

I know I loved him. Tears filled her eyes at the realization. *And I really* wanted *to love him.* Had he known? Had he been able to see beneath her resentment and defenses? Had he been able to see that love in her heart?

Miranda looked down at the glass of water Mom was putting in her hand. The two of them were side by side on the couch, though she didn't remember sitting. She wondered about her mother; she searched Mom's face for telltale signs of emotion. But what she saw were features like stone, a dazed expression, and movements strangely mechanical.

Miranda waited till her grandfather had been taken away. Should she comfort Mom? Strong, stoic Mom who never asked or even liked to be comforted? Mom hadn't shed a tear when they'd left Florida, their friends, the empty rubble of their old life. Mom had been in total control, and she'd *taken* total control. *Does she feel guilt? Sadness? Pain? Regret?*

Miranda didn't know. And there were no clues to tell her.

"I need to check on Teeta," Mom said softly. "I guess you and I will be moving into the house now. I'm sure she's going to need us."

Miranda could only nod. Mom sounded so calm and practical, already making plans. *Just like when Dad died.* Setting her glass on the coffee table, Miranda stood on shaky legs.

"I think I'll go outside for a while."

"Not where people can stare, honey. They're like a pack of vultures out there, wanting to know every detail."

How could she be like that? Miranda wondered. Even now, in the midst of another tragedy, Mom was obsessed with what people thought. Fighting down a wave of anger, she slipped out the side door that Etienne had shown her. The trees hid her from view, and without hesitating, she hurried along the back wall and away from the house.

She hadn't intended on going to the park.

She just suddenly found herself at the entrance.

Swept inside by the crowd, Miranda was immediately assailed by a carnival-like atmosphere. *Oh, right. The Rebel Rouser today.* The air was filled with laughter; rich smells of barbecue, boiled shrimp, fried fish, and grilled burgers; the pounding, earsplitting rhythm of a zydeco band. From a petting zoo, goats and sheep bleated nervously as squealing kids chased them with handfuls of food. Bells clanged for lucky prizewinners at dozens of game booths. Flags flew, men in Civil War uniforms flirted with hoop-skirted ladies, and from somewhere in the distance came the boom of a cannon and the muffled discharge of guns . . .

Miranda stopped in her tracks. Yes . . . she was certain now that what she'd heard from her window yesterday hadn't been a car backfiring or kids playing with firecrackers . . .

"They *were* gunshots," she mumbled. *But not these gunshots.*

A chill clawed through her veins. How many other things

had she seen and heard since coming to St. Yvette? Things she hadn't paid attention to, things she should have noticed?

But how could I have realized? I didn't know! I didn't know till now—and now I don't want *to know!*

Forcing down panic, she moved on. She'd hoped to lose herself here—to blend in, be inconspicuous, retreat from the rest of the world. *How many clues have I missed? How many signs have I ignored?* She couldn't stop thinking about it. Why wouldn't it leave her alone?

She wandered farther into the park, along winding, tree-shaded pathways, looking for a place to sit down. The muggy heat had grown way past stifling. The sun blazed down without a cloud in the sky. In the wider, more open spaces, both Rebel and Yankee regiments impressed spectators with various marching and marksmanship skills, while in a small amphitheater, folksingers performed nostalgic Civil War ballads. Miranda paused briefly at each, then continued on to the cemetery.

Unlike the Falls, the Confederate Cemetery had been lovingly cared for. Located on a gentle rise, its grass was lush and green, its graves peaceful and undisturbed. Each tomb looked freshly whitewashed, banked with masses of flowers and foliage, decorated with vintage photographs, religious figurines, yellow ribbons, rosaries, and votive candles that flickered among the crosses. Markers and memorials stood proudly. Every name and message was distinct.

Spotting an empty bench, Miranda went over and sat down. It was a beautiful spot, facing the graveyard across a flower-bordered path, but the beauty did little to console her. As families strolled past, she thought of her grandfather—all the things left unsaid and undone, all the unexpressed feelings and unanswered questions.

A fine sheen of sweat glazed her brow. She was feeling warmer by the minute—warm from the inside out—getting so hot, she could hardly stand it. She wondered vaguely if someone had set up a grill nearby; she could see fine tendrils of pale, gray smoke curling through the air.

I just never expected Grandpa to die. I just never expected any of this.

Leaning forward, she propped both elbows on her knees . . . covered her face with her hands. She wanted to cry, but she felt so empty. When she finally lifted her head again, she was surprised to see even more smoke in the air, floating slowly in her direction, bringing with it a faint, familiar smell . . .

That smell! That smoke!

Only now the odor was stronger—more recognizable—and thoughts and images were tumbling wildly through her brain. Sweat and sulfur, dirt and blood and open sores, stagnant water, charred flesh, ashes, and hot, hot metal . . .

Miranda stiffened and looked around. There weren't any grills in sight, no cookouts, no food vendors. Not a single blade of grass stirring, not a single leaf rustling on a tree, though the smoke kept drifting toward her.

Alarmed, she jumped to her feet, waved her arms, tried to fan back the smoke. It was getting thicker, and with a slow, sick awareness, she watched it darken to red. *Like last night . . . oh, God, just like last night . . .*

"Please!" A dark haze was all around her now, she couldn't see the path anymore, not even six feet away. "Can someone help me?"

And, yes, thank God, someone *was* coming to help! She could see the vague silhouette materializing in front of her . . . the shadowy hand reaching out . . .

She realized then why he hadn't been completely visible at first. Why he'd blended so perfectly into the smoke. The tattered, gray uniform he was wearing . . . the dark smears of blood on his face and his clothes. *Was he from one of those reenactment regiments she'd been watching?* Yet his body seemed to hover there, suspended.

"For Miss Ellena," he whispered.

Miranda was totally paralyzed. All she could do was watch helplessly as he came forward to meet her.

"Take it . . . the rose . . ."

That sorrowful voice. That raw, empty, pleading voice, heartbreaking in its anguish.

That voice Miranda knew, for she had heard it before.

"Who are you?" From some distant place inside her head, Miranda knew she hadn't spoken aloud. Yet she heard the echo of her question, and she understood somehow that the young man heard it, too. "Who *are* you?"

The answer came like a death rattle.

"Nathan."

"What do you want?"

His face began to appear through the gloom. *Pale hair, bleached skin, eyes like bottomless, black holes. Sunken cheeks streaked with blood, parched lips caked with blood, but none of that as horrible as the blood soaking his uniform, as the wide, crimson stain blossoming over his shirt, directly over his heart . . .*

"Take it," he murmured. *And those lifeless eyes staring, staring, all the suffering there, the hopelessness, the aching regrets . . .* "Help me . . ."

As a faint, ragged breath stirred the air, Miranda felt something slide across her upturned hand. Not a rose, as he'd said, but something like twine . . . a short length of twine, knotted or twisted or woven . . .

Braided? She couldn't see it in her open palm. *Braided twine?*

"For Miss Ellena," he whispered. "The rose . . . the rose . . . the . . ."

And he was fading now, just as his voice was fading, just as the smoke was fading . . . fading to nothing but shadow . . .

She felt the sun.

She heard the people.

As the park came back into jarring focus, Miranda blinked against the light and looked down.

Her hand was empty.

And she was crying.

13

THAT NIGHT FOR THE VERY FIRST TIME, Miranda slept in Hayes House. Or rather, *tried* to sleep, in between tossing, turning, checking her windows, and keeping an eye on her door. Even the mirror made her nervous—not to mention the closet, the space under the bed, and every shadow in every single corner.

That poor soldier . . . that poor, tragic soldier.

Nathan, he'd called himself.

She couldn't stop seeing his face, hearing his voice. *"Take it . . . the rose . . . the rose . . ."* And his blood, his sorrow, his unbearable pain . . .

No matter how much Miranda longed to deny it, ignore it, and forget it—in her heart she couldn't.

She didn't remember coming home from the park. She'd suddenly found herself locked in a downstairs bathroom, crying into a towel and unable to stop. When she finally slipped out to the kitchen, no one seemed to have missed her, and she was relieved that Mom was too distracted with Aunt Teeta and pending funeral arrangements to focus on her.

But later, lying there in her mother's childhood room, Miranda almost wished she had someone to talk to. Not just about the soldier, but about so many other things. News of death traveled quickly in St. Yvette, and there'd been a constant procession of neighbors throughout the day, bringing casseroles, cakes, and condolences. She'd spent most of her time being introduced to people she didn't know and didn't care about knowing. She'd felt confused about her grandfather—how she should feel and how she should show it. She'd wondered what to say to her mother, who seemed rock solid, and what to say to Aunt Teeta, who was devastated.

Her only source of comfort had arrived later that evening, when she'd started down the hallway to go outside and found Gage at the front door.

"Are you okay?" was the first thing he'd asked. And then, before she'd been able to answer, his arms were around her in a gentle hug. Miranda had fought back unexpected tears and felt herself surrendering—just as unexpectedly—to his concern.

"We weren't really sure what to do," Gage explained as she led him into the deserted study at the back of the house. He'd waited till she sat down before taking the chair across from her. "We all wanted to come, but we didn't know how you'd feel about it. We didn't want to make you uncomfortable."

Miranda simply stared at him. "Nobody needed to come."

"We *wanted* to come."

She hadn't known what to say. Despite her best efforts, she'd felt embarrassed and strangely touched. "I've only known you guys for two days."

"Sometimes that's long enough."

When he smiled, she couldn't help smiling back at him. After a moment, he leaned toward her, his voice more solemn.

"Do they know what happened to your grandfather?"

"They're pretty sure it was a stroke. And that it was quick, so he didn't suffer."

Gage hesitated. "Did what happened at the Falls yesterday have anything to do with it?"

"I don't know. Maybe we should have taken him to the clinic."

"I think Etienne was right, Miranda—I think we did the best we could."

"Etienne hasn't been by this afternoon." She'd been startled when the words popped out—she hoped they hadn't sounded— what? Judgmental? Disappointed? The truth was, she'd honestly expected him to show up at the house, at least for Aunt Teeta's sake.

Gage's eyes were full of sympathy. "They were pretty tight, Etienne and your grandfather. I know Etienne's heard the news, but I haven't talked to him yet. He . . ." Again Gage paused, as though choosing just the right words. "I know he'll be really upset. And he never lets anybody see him that way."

"Macho thing?" Miranda couldn't help asking.

A dimple flashed in Gage's cheek. "Something like that, I guess."

They'd lapsed into a companionable silence. To Miranda, it felt so good just to sit there with him, not feeling the need to pretend or explain or keep up any sort of appearances. He'd seemed in no hurry to leave, and she'd been glad for him to stay. And when his attention focused on the comings and goings out in the hallway, she'd taken that chance really to study his face.

Yes, there were definitely resemblances between Gage and

Etienne—the same high cheekbones, lanky frames, and dark good looks. She guessed both their mothers were beautiful. But what was even more apparent up close was the stark contrast in the boys' eyes. One, soulful and sensitive . . . the other, suspicious and blatantly defiant.

"You're staring," Gage mumbled.

As Miranda realized she'd been caught, the two of them laughed self-consciously. Gage lowered his eyes and slid back in his chair.

"Do you know when the funeral is?" he'd asked her.

"I heard them talking about Tuesday."

"Let us know for sure."

"But—"

"So we can be there."

"But—"

"Because." His hands went up to ward off her question. "Because we want to, okay?"

"Okay."

"Oh, and um . . ." Frowning slightly, he traced one finger across his upper lip. "I'm not sure it's the right time to bring this up . . ."

"No, go ahead."

"That building you wondered about this morning? Magnolia Gallery?"

The change she'd felt had been immediate—that tightening in her stomach, that tensing of her nerves—though Gage didn't seem to notice. In fact, he'd seemed almost *too* casual as he continued talking.

"I've been trying to find some information on it. I haven't really come up with much yet, but what I've got so far is pretty interesting."

Miranda swallowed nervously, half expecting him to bring up her odd behavior of that morning. But Gage only cleared his throat and looked down at the floor.

"I thought . . . maybe later . . . when you feel better? Maybe we could talk about it."

"Yes. Later's good. I'd really like that."

"Great. Well . . . I better go." As the two of them stood, he'd fished in his shirt pocket and handed her a folded slip of paper. "Here's my cell phone number. And Etienne's. In case you . . . you know . . . need anything."

"Thanks."

Giving her another hug, he whispered, "I'm sorry, Miranda. Just remember I'm—we're—thinking about you."

His body was warm and strong, and there was nothing the least bit shy about the way he held her. Miranda had a sudden, silly urge just to stand there in his arms and never leave. But instead, she pulled free and walked him to the door, her mind in turmoil. *Should I tell him? About what happened in the park today? And how I knew about the opera house?* Because somehow she was sure Gage would listen . . . somehow she was sure he'd understand.

"Gage?"

Stopping on the walkway, he'd turned to look back at her. "Yeah?"

"Nothing. Just . . . thanks."

"I didn't do anything."

"Yes, you did. More than you know."

That dimple again, and a modest shrug. "See you."

Exhausted, Miranda had dragged herself through the rest of the evening. After the last visitor had gone, she and Mom and Aunt Teeta had sat together in the kitchen, picking at the vast assortment of food, but eating little. Aunt Teeta showed Miranda her new room—a cozy little hideaway tucked up on the third floor—then immediately went to bed. While Mom insisted on tidying up, Miranda made a quick run to their apartment to fetch nightgowns and toothbrushes.

And now she couldn't sleep.

It had been a long and grueling day, a bizarre and upsetting day. Even with her soft mattress and feather pillows and the privacy she'd been longing for, Miranda could only pitch restlessly back and forth and stare wide-eyed into the darkness.

This room had been Mom's, Aunt Teeta had told her—this room was where Mom had spent all her growing-up years. It sat right at the top of the narrow third-floor staircase, small and sparsely furnished and nestled snugly back under the eaves. Instead of air-conditioning, French doors stood open to a small sunporch where screened windows on three walls allowed for breezes, but could also be shut against bad weather. There'd been many a slumber party out there, Aunt Teeta recalled—girlfriends staying up till all hours, talking and giggling throughout those long, carefree summer nights. At one end of the porch a door led out to a flight of wooden steps. The banister was overgrown with ivy and honeysuckle vines, and the steps went all the way down to a thickly shrubberied back corner of the house.

Miranda wondered if her mother ever thought about this sunporch, about this room, about childhood. If her mother ever had any happy memories at all . . .

Memories . . .

But Miranda had her own memories to deal with tonight. Memories trudging heavy through her brain and flashing back at her like snapshots, making her heart race and her head pound. The walls seemed to be squeezing in. The stagnant air whispered with faraway screams. Unable to fight it any longer, she jumped up and made for the door, not even bothering with the bedside lamp.

Smart, Miranda. Real smart.

She'd forgotten how dark the staircase was. Groping along the wall, she couldn't find a light switch anywhere, but she *could* follow the sudden rumble of Aunt Teeta's snoring. With a relieved sigh, she reached the dimly lit second-floor landing, then continued on down toward the kitchen.

That's when she heard the crying.

Miranda froze at the foot of the stairs. *Oh, please God, not again.* Yet almost at once she realized *this* crying was different. Not the same ghostly sounds as before, but almost as heartbreaking. And very, very close by.

Still fearful, she peered through the kitchen doorway. The room was mostly in shadow, though a pale, silver moon shone in at the window above the sink. Then, as her eyes adjusted to the gloom, she finally recognized the figure at the table. Mom sitting there with her head lowered on folded arms, and her whole body shaking with sobs.

Miranda had never seen her mother cry like this before. In fact, she couldn't remember having seen her cry at all since Dad died. Mom—the strong one, the invincible one—always unflappable in the face of every situation, no matter how bad.

Startled, her mother gasped and looked up in alarm. "Oh, Miranda, it's you. What's wrong, honey, can't you sleep?"

Just like that, in total control again. While Miranda could only stand there and watch helplessly.

"Mom?" she whispered.

For an endless moment their eyes locked. Mom's hands fluttered uselessly toward her coffee cup, as if searching for some viable excuse.

"Mom . . . what's wrong?"

Her mother's shoulders sagged. Miranda moved slowly across the floor and took the empty chair across from her.

"What are you doing up?" Mom asked again.

"I was . . . thinking about stuff."

"Me, too." Mom made a feeble attempt at a laugh. "Well, your grandpa, mostly. But a lot of other stuff, too, I guess."

From her mother's red, puffy eyes, Miranda could tell she'd been crying for a long time. Now she asked cautiously, "What were you thinking about Grandpa?"

"About . . . oh, time, I suppose. How fast it goes. How much it can end up robbing you, if you let it."

Mom idly stirred her cold coffee, gazing down at her spoon.

"We were so different, Miranda—your grandpa and I. Teeta

was younger, and she was always closer to Daddy. I was the one closer to Mother, and after she died, I felt . . . I don't know . . . excluded, I guess. Teeta was always so good, and I was always the rebellious one."

"You!" Miranda couldn't hide her shock.

"Yes, me. And don't get any ideas." Mom frowned in mock sternness. "Daddy was . . . different. Teeta always seemed to understand that. Accept that."

"How do you mean?"

"He was . . . I don't know. Just *different*. Sort of quiet, never shared much. Strict with us and overly protective—at least that's how I saw things when I was growing up. He had his hobbies, his books . . . He kept to himself a lot. I never knew what he was thinking. But Mother—well, she was so animated, so happy all the time. You always knew where you stood with Mother, and people really loved her. But Daddy had these . . ." She shrugged. "Moods. That's what Mother called them. His moods."

Miranda said nothing. Simply waited for Mom to continue.

"I don't know how else to describe it, just that he'd get . . . *weird* about things. Like when Teeta and I would have our hearts set on going somewhere. And at the last minute Daddy would tell us we *couldn't* go, that something *bad* had happened there, and he'd forbid us to even step foot *near* the place."

"So . . . what'd you do?"

Mom gave a rueful smile. "We didn't go. No matter what Daddy said, no matter how irrational he sounded, and no matter how much Teeta and I argued—Mother would put her foot down, and we'd stay home."

"*Had* anything bad happened in those places?"

"Who knows? Daddy never explained how he knew about these so-called 'bad' things. Or where—or who—he got his inside information from." Mom's sarcasm was tempered with sadness. "Whatever the reasons, he completely believed them. And Mother completely believed *him*."

Chills raked at Miranda's spine. She didn't want to hear any more about Grandpa or his warnings, yet something held her tightly in her seat. Something that compelled her to keep listening.

"There was *one* time though." Mom's brow furrowed in thought. "I remember Teeta and I were going to a carnival in the next town. But sure enough, at the very last second, Daddy said we couldn't go. We were devastated. I wouldn't speak to him for days. Then about two weeks later, we found out five girls had been raped at that carnival."

The chills were growing steadily worse. Miranda could feel herself starting to tremble.

"Apparently every night this carnival worker would pick out a certain girl in the crowd to follow. He'd go up to her, looking very upset, and say he was worried about his wife—that she'd gone into one of the public restrooms but hadn't come out again. He'd say he'd been waiting for a long time, and he'd ask the girl to go in and check on her. Well, of course, all the girls wanted to help. He'd take each of them back to the very farthest shelter, back where nobody else was around. Then he'd pull a knife. And when it was over, he'd threaten them—tell them he knew where they lived, and if they ever said a word, he'd find them and kill them and kill their families, too."

"My God, those poor girls. They must have been so terrified."

"Thank goodness one of them finally found the courage to talk. She and her parents went to the police. But the carnival had left town by then . . . and the guy had left the carnival."

"Did they ever find him?"

"Yes. But . . ." Mom looked slightly incredulous at the memory. "After the news got out, Daddy walked over to the police station one morning and said he knew where the rapist was. Told them the guy was in River Camp—a town about five hundred miles from here. He gave them a physical description, down to the missing ring finger on the guy's left hand. The trailer park where he was staying, the color of the trailer, and the backcountry road where the park was located."

"Well, that was good, right?"

"Except that Daddy'd never been to River Camp. Never in his life."

"So..." *No. I can't ask. I won't ask.* "How did Grandpa know?"

"That's what the police wondered—along with everyone else in town. Daddy said he'd stopped at the gas station and overheard a man talking on the pay phone outside. And that when the man saw Daddy watching, he jumped in his car and took off before Daddy could get the license number."

Kind of lame. But kind of believable, too. Miranda's hands clenched together on the tabletop. She couldn't even look at her mother now. She could barely choke down the fear in her own throat.

Intent on the story, Mom didn't seem to notice. "But after Daddy went to the police, I heard him and Mother talking in their room that night. I didn't mean to listen—I was right outside their door, on my way downstairs. I think . . . Daddy was crying. I'd never known him to show that much emotion before, and it scared me. Mother was trying to comfort him, I guess, talking real quiet. I heard Daddy say something about another victim, and a hayfield, and that's how he'd known where the rapist was. That one of the *victims* told him."

Stop, Mom, please stop, don't say these things, don't make them true, don't make them real—

"I couldn't believe what I was hearing. I thought Daddy was very sick—*mentally* sick—that Mother had just been protecting him and not telling us the truth. And then . . ." Pausing, Mom drew a deep, shaky breath. "And then, a few days later, there it was in the newspaper. The police found a girl's body dumped in an old hayfield on an abandoned farm. Only a mile from where the carnival had been. They said she'd probably been there about three weeks."

Without realizing it, Miranda reached across and touched her mother's hand. "So you believed him *then*, right?"

It was a heartfelt plea. But one, Miranda knew at once, that her mother couldn't recognize.

"Of course I didn't believe him." Mom's tone bordered on

regret. "Because things like that are impossible. When Daddy was in one of his moods, we never knew *what* he might say— *what* he might make up."

"But . . . the rapist. Did they catch him in River Camp?"

Mom's lips pressed into a grim line. "They caught him, convicted him, and sent him to prison for life."

"And . . ." Miranda paused, her heart fluttering out of control. "And the girl in the hayfield. *Did* he kill her?"

A long silence fell between them. And even before her mother spoke, Miranda knew what the answer would be.

"Yes," Mom said at last. "He confessed to everything."

For an instant, Miranda felt the kitchen receding around her—she felt a thousand different emotions battering her from all sides. She was shivering violently now; she didn't know what to say. *Argue? Defend? Confess? Explain?* Clamping her arms tight around her chest, she fought to keep her voice level.

"Did your mother believe your dad?"

Mom wasn't looking at her now. Instead, she twirled her coffee cup slowly between her palms. "Oh, Mother always stood by him, no matter what. But things just got worse after that."

"How?"

"Well, maybe I should say, *Daddy* got worse after that. Or his *moods* got worse after that. Or maybe they'd been that bad all along, but till that night when I heard him and Mother talking, I just didn't realize *how* bad."

"Did you ever tell Aunt Teeta what you heard?"

"Of course. We started watching Daddy more, and he

started having more moods. We'd hear him talking to himself—sometimes for an hour, sometimes even longer—except it was like . . . like he was talking to another person. Of course, there wouldn't be anybody else *there*. And especially after Mother died—then we'd hear him having long conversations with *her*."

"So what'd you do?"

"Well, it was obvious he was having a breakdown. But you didn't talk about things like that in St. Yvette; families kept personal things to themselves. Even though all our neighbors knew about it. Something like that's pretty hard to hide."

"Small town?"

Miranda was getting used to the cliché. Mom gave a faint smile.

"Small town," she agreed. "And Daddy became the small-town eccentric. People pretended not to notice the glazed look in his eyes, or the way he'd walk down the street, discussing things with invisible friends. Everyone considered him fairly creepy, but harmless. And naturally, Teeta refused to put him away. And naturally, I couldn't stand knowing what other people thought of him—*and* of us. The stares, the gossip, the jokes. I was embarrassed. And ashamed."

Briefly her eyes met Miranda's. As a wistful look passed over her face, she cleared her throat and pushed away her half-empty cup.

"I wish I could have been like Teeta. Maybe if I'd tried to understand Daddy more . . . help him more . . ."

It must have been so hard for you, Mom . . . so hard being

Grandpa's daughter. A million questions rose up in Miranda's mind, but she recognized the fragile edge to her mother's voice. Biting hard on her bottom lip, she resisted the urge to keep nagging.

"But at the time," Mom continued tonelessly, "all I wanted to do was get away from him. Away from *here.* As far away as I possibly could. And then I met your dad . . ." She hesitated, drew a ragged breath. "And I *did* get away."

Her mother's eyes had gone distant now. Tears trickled down her face. "Honey, I loved your dad so much. And then you came along, and things were even more perfect. I never dreamed that anything bad could happen to us—to your dad. That someone so young could have a heart attack . . . could be here one minute, so full of life, then be taken from us the next."

"Oh, Mom . . ."

"No, honey, I'm okay. When your father died, your grandpa and Aunt Teeta begged me to come back here. They wanted to take care of us. To help us and watch you grow up. But I just couldn't. I just couldn't come back to all the gossip and staring and everything else I'd put behind me. All I could see were the same things happening all over again. I didn't want you to grow up the way I had."

"Why didn't you ever tell me this before?"

"I guess . . ." Mom ran a weary hand over her wet cheeks. "It was just easier not to. Not to involve you in things you couldn't possibly have understood. Children shouldn't have to carry their parents' burdens."

"But maybe I could have helped you."

A wan smile touched her mother's lips. "You help me just by being you. And by being happy. That's all I could think about after the hurricane—keeping you safe and happy. But we *had* to come here, Miranda; we didn't have a choice. And I was scared. And I'm *still* scared, but I'm ashamed of myself, too."

"Mom, *why*?"

"Because you didn't get to meet your grandpa, and all he ever really wanted was for us to be a family."

Miranda felt tears on her own face now. "And do you really believe that? That we can be a family again? A *happy* family?"

"Yes. I do." Mom's voice was firm. "And I want you to believe it, too, Miranda. I tell your dad every day how proud I am of you, and how brave you are, and what a great life you're going to have."

"Really?"

"Well, of course. Why do you sound so surprised?"

"I never . . . I guess I never realized you thought about him. I mean, you never talk about him. Not to me, anyway."

Now it was Mom's turn to be surprised. "Oh, honey, how can you say that? Your dad was my whole world—and I know he was yours, too. And I thought if I brought up memories, it would just make both of us too sad. I wish I could wave a magic wand and make everything like it used to be, when he was here and everything was good. But I can't. And someone *had* to be strong. Had to be strong then *and* now, to hold you and me together."

Miranda felt another wave of emotions surge through her. For the moment, every suspicion, every bad thought, was forgotten.

"I'm here," she insisted. "You have me."

"Thank you, honey." Bending forward across the table, Mom tenderly kissed her brow. "I know that. And I promise I'll try to be better."

"Me, too, Mom. Me, too."

14

AFTER HER MIDNIGHT TALK WITH MOM, Miranda slept peacefully the rest of the night, even waking up much later than usual. She spent most of Sunday at home, meeting and greeting more neighbors, making room in the refrigerator for more food, jotting down more names for thank-you notes. From time to time she caught her mother smiling at her, giving an appreciative nod. Since Aunt Teeta was too upset to be of much help, Miranda was glad to give Mom some much-needed support.

To her surprise, Ashley, Roo, and Parker dropped by together, bringing a perfectly arranged tray of gourmet hors d'oeuvres from Mrs. Wilmington's favorite deli, a fresh pot of jambalaya from the girls' mother—Miss Voncile—and a homemade pie from Roo.

"We don't know *what* kind of pie exactly," Parker said, his face perfectly composed. "But I've heard it's the thought that counts."

A slight frown settled between Roo's brows. She'd changed the streaks in her hair from dark purple to bright orange.

"It's something I haven't tried before," she said solemnly. "It's made with cottage cheese."

Ashley instantly looked alarmed. "You didn't use the cottage cheese in the fridge, did you?"

"What other cottage cheese would I use?"

"For God's sake, Roo, that's been in there for weeks. It's nasty by now."

"Well, I'm sure the cooking part must have killed the bacteria, if that's what you're worried about."

Despite Parker's vivid portrayal of death by poisoning, Miranda made a special point of exclaiming over the pie. Then she dumped it in the trash can as soon as they left.

By late afternoon, she was beginning to feel trapped. The steady stream of visitors had finally dwindled, so she went out onto the veranda and sat in the porch swing, swaying back and forth, lulling herself into a doze. When she heard her name being spoken, she jumped guiltily, only to find Gage seated beside her.

"Didn't mean to wake you," he said.

"You didn't."

"Uh-huh."

"I was just . . . thinking."

"Do you always snore when you think?"

"I was *not* snoring."

"I could hear you all the way down the street."

Despite his insistence, she saw the teasing in his eyes. She looked around for the rest of the group, but he appeared to be alone.

"Feel like getting away?" he asked her.

"That obvious, huh?"

"The Tavern has the best burgers in town, if you don't mind walking."

"Just let me grab my purse."

After a quick check-in with Mom, Miranda was ready to go. The Tavern was at the opposite end of the Brickway and mostly uphill, but in spite of the heat, she welcomed the fresh air and exercise. Gage seemed in no particular hurry to get there. Side by side, they settled into a leisurely stroll, discussing various points of interest along the way.

"You know, I never thought much about St. Yvette before this project," Gage confessed.

"I never thought about my own town either. I guess when you live in a place, you just take it for granted."

"Now that I've started doing some research, there really is this whole dark-history thing going on. Bad stuff behind closed doors. Buildings that look so normal from the outside . . . but terrible tragedies inside."

"You *have* been doing research." She waited for him to bring up the gallery, but he didn't.

"It's interesting. Sad sometimes . . . scary sometimes . . . but definitely interesting."

I can certainly agree with that. Once again she toyed with the idea of confiding in Gage. Once again, she kept quiet.

"You just never know about people, do you?" Gage went on seriously. "You think you know somebody so well. Then it turns out you don't know them like you thought you did. Maybe we never really know anybody at all. Even the people we're closest to."

"Or maybe, *especially* the people we're closest to."

His lips hinted at a smile. "Maybe that's because we're so used to seeing certain people a certain way. The way we *want* to see them. It sort of gives us tunnel vision."

Now it was Miranda's turn to grow thoughtful. "Have *you* ever been disappointed? By people you thought you knew?"

"Wow. There's a loaded question."

"Or . . . have you ever trusted your instincts, and then found out you were completely wrong?"

"I let Roo talk me into playing doctor once when we were little." Gage sighed. "Unfortunately, she *really* meant *play doctor*. She decided my mosquito bite needed surgery and cut my knee open with a pair of blunt scissors."

Miranda's expression flinched between pain and laughter.

"I still have the scar." Gage cast her a sidelong glance. "But that's not what you were asking, is it? I'm guessing this has something to do with your grandfather."

Reluctantly, she nodded. "I just wish . . . can you tell me anything about him?"

"I didn't really know him."

"But you must know something about him."

Was Gage deliberately hedging? She couldn't tell.

"Why don't you ask your mom?" he suggested. "Or your aunt?"

"I just couldn't, especially not now. Not with what they're both going through."

"Then talk to Etienne. He spent time with your grandfather."

And confided in him, too, Miranda thought uneasily. "How did they get to be friends?"

Gage's only answer was a shrug. Miranda decided to keep trying.

"How is Etienne, anyway? About my grandpa, I mean. Has he gotten in touch with you yet?"

"No. He'll come out when he's ready."

"Are you close to him?"

"You mean, where we live?"

"No, Roo told me that you and he are cousins. I just wondered if you're close to him."

"Nobody's close to him," Gage said matter-of-factly. "But if anybody *were* close to him, then I guess it'd be me."

"So where *does* he live?"

"He and his mom have a little place down on the bayou. About a mile or so from the Falls."

Should she admit that Roo had told her about Etienne's past? "What about his dad?"

"He died."

Gage was facing forward, yet Miranda still caught the subtle change in his expression. The slow, rigid set of his jawline. The carefully fixed stare. Almost as though he were watching something too distant for her to see.

"Sorry," she murmured. "That's too bad." Then, after a split-second pause, she took a chance. "How did it happen?"

Another shrug from Gage. His straight-ahead stare didn't waver. "He had an accident."

She wondered why Gage didn't elaborate. Was it one of those personal things he didn't like discussing? Had Etienne asked him not to mention it? Whatever the reason, Miranda took the hint and let the subject drop. She could see The Tavern coming into view on a small cul-de-sac. When they got there, Gage held the door for her, and they went inside.

They found an empty booth in a back corner away from the noise. Miranda couldn't help noticing how many girls perked up as Gage walked through—waitresses and customers alike, calling his name, delighted to get his attention. Miranda recognized serious flirting when she saw it. Gage, on the other hand, seemed not to realize the obvious.

After ordering hamburgers, the two of them settled back in their seats and talked generalities—the high school volunteer program, favorite and not-so-favorite teachers, the football team, movies they loved, books they hated, and, ultimately, hurricanes.

"It never happens to somebody you know," Gage said. He angled himself into the corner, one elbow resting on the table, a Coke in his other hand. "It always just happens on the six o'clock news."

"You're right. And that's why you still can't believe it, even when it *does* happen to you. You just want to change the channel and watch something else."

An awkward silence followed, as if Gage were working up the courage to ask something personal. When he finally did, Miranda was caught off guard.

"I . . . just keep thinking. I mean, about you and . . ." Gage avoided eye contact. "I guess you must really miss everybody. And the way everything used to be in your life."

Thank God he wasn't looking at her. It was all she could do to force back tears. "It's all gone. Nothing will ever be the same."

"I'm sorry." Gage's voice lowered.

And then, without warning, the need to talk about it became overwhelming. "We lost everything when the hurricane hit. Our house, our furniture, our car, our clothes. Everyday stuff you don't even think about. I probably won't see my friends again for a really long time. Maybe never. And there's just this huge hole in my heart."

Gage kept silent, but his eyes had gone sad.

"I know Mom's really worried about money, too. I mean, she just found a job yesterday, but I know Aunt Teeta's helping us a lot." Miranda paused, embarrassed. She didn't know why she'd told him that; she didn't know why she was telling him *any* of this. As the waitress set down their food, she was thankful for the interruption; another second and she'd have been bawling her head off. *No more moments of weakness, Miranda. Way too risky, feeling that much at one time.*

"I shouldn't have said anything—" she mumbled, but Gage immediately stopped her.

"It stays between us, okay? Maybe this just happened to be the right time, when you really needed to tell somebody. And . . . you know . . . I'm glad it was me."

An unexpected warmth spread through her. She twisted her napkin in her hands. "Maybe we should talk about something else."

He smiled that smile. Picking up the bottle of ketchup, he poured it liberally over his Ultra-Supreme-Everything-But-the-Kitchen-Sink Burger.

"That building you were interested in . . ." He agreeably

switched the subject. "Magnolia Gallery. I told you I found some information about it."

"And . . ." Miranda was all ears.

"And . . . you were right. It *was* an opera house."

"It . . . are you sure?"

"It was originally built in the early eighteen hundreds. But a long time after the war, it changed from being the opera house to being the gallery."

A shiver of excitement went through her. She could hardly sit still as Gage continued explaining.

"St. Yvette might have been small, but it was known for its culture back then. There were lots of rich planters around here, and I guess that original opera house was all about prestige. And I guess some pretty famous people performed there."

Music . . . applause . . . swishing of fans . . . roses . . . a curtain falling . . . a voice singing . . .

Miranda drew in a slow breath. "Really? Like who?"

"Nobody I ever heard of." Gage chuckled. "But I guess some of them came all the way from Europe."

While the waitress refilled their glasses, Miranda chewed thoughtfully on a French fry. "Where'd you find this out?"

"The Internet didn't have much at all. So I stopped by the library yesterday and started looking through their private collection on St. Yvette. We can't take any of it out, but we can always go back there and do more research. The Historical Society might have some information, too. I thought maybe we could go there tomorrow after school."

Miranda wasn't sure she could hold out till tomorrow. She

was amazed at Gage's findings, at how closely they matched the impressions she'd received. And now that this eerie reality began to dawn on her, she wanted to find out all she could.

"Gage, did it say that anything bad happened at the opera house?"

"You mean, besides opera? That's pretty bad."

She couldn't help smiling. "Are you sure something *else* bad didn't happen?"

"I'm not sure at all. But *you* seem pretty sure."

Miranda tried for casual surprise. "I do?"

"And you seemed to know an awful lot yesterday about a place you'd never seen or heard about before."

It wasn't said accusingly, not even suspiciously. More like a gentle reminder. And once again Miranda felt torn. Gage obviously knew something was going on. And though Etienne was the one her grandpa had advised her to trust, she'd trusted Gage enough to share other personal things with him. *So why can't I tell him about the voices, the screams, the soldier in the park—*

Startled, she felt a slight pressure on the tip of her chin. She hadn't noticed Gage leaning toward her, napkin in hand.

"You have mustard," Gage murmured, "right . . . there."

She held very still while he cleaned it off. She wanted to concentrate on the opposite wall, but it was impossible to look anywhere but at him. Those big, brown eyes with their long dark lashes . . . innocent and wise at the same time . . . incredibly sweet . . . amazingly sexy . . .

"*He was* amazing . . ." Roo had said.

As the memory of Roo's confession caught her off guard,

Miranda tried once more to look away from Gage. To focus on anything but his eyes. The fantasy potential there was both endless and irresistible.

"One of the books I found showed some old playbills." To Miranda's relief, Gage drew back to his own side of the table, intent again on research. "There were a few pretty bad photos of the building, too. It didn't say when they were taken though."

Miranda fidgeted with her napkin. "What about entertainers?"

"Their names and their acts were listed on the playbills. Singers. Actors. Dancers. Clowns." His frown was genuinely disturbed. "Why are clowns so creepy?"

"You're afraid of clowns?"

"I didn't say that. I just said they're creepy."

Miranda watched him, amused. The best defense was an even better offense.

"You're staring," Gage mumbled.

"I can't help it."

"Why? Do I have a messy face, too?"

"No." Miranda couldn't resist. "You have dimples."

He squirmed self-consciously. "I guess."

"I bet you get teased a lot."

"Is there some relevant point to this?"

Miranda did her best to keep a straight face. "Just that they're so cute."

"Stop it."

"Are you blushing?"

"Shut up."

Oh, Gage, you have no idea . . . if Marge and Joanie were here right now, they'd jump all over you.

Still flustered, Gage signaled the waitress. But it was someone else who walked over instead.

"Private conversation?" Etienne greeted them.

"No," Gage answered, a little too quickly.

"*Intimate* conversation?"

"I was just telling him about his . . ." Miranda began, but Gage looked so trapped, she didn't have the heart to bring Etienne into it. "Just telling him about—"

"We were talking about the gallery," Gage broke in. "That building she was wondering about."

Etienne glanced purposefully from Gage to Miranda and back again. "I don't know, from where I was standing over there, you were looking a little embarrassed."

"The opera house. I was telling her what I found out."

"Okay, if you say so."

"It's true!"

"And I said okay. I believe you. You gonna eat the rest of those fries?"

Gage slid his plate across the table as Etienne slid in beside Miranda. Etienne shot her a secret wink.

"It's not the thing with the dimples again, is it?" he asked innocently. "I don't know what it is with girls, the way y'all love his—"

"Why are you here?" Gage asked. Getting to his feet, he pointed toward the restrooms. "I'll be right back. *You* can leave the tip."

"I was going to anyway."

"No, I'm paying for my own." Miranda picked up the tab, but Etienne's hand came firmly down on hers.

"Gage and me, we are *nothing* if not true southern gentlemen. And a lady *never* pays on her first date."

Now Miranda was flustered. "It's *not* a date. We really *were* talking about that building."

"I know that." Shrugging, he yanked a napkin from the metal holder. "I also know Beth, your waitress. She's the one who heard you teasing Gage."

"You are so bad."

With a vague frown, Miranda settled back to watch him eat. Unlike Gage, it didn't seem to bother him, being the object of her scrutiny. She could only marvel at his focus.

"Magnolia Gallery," she said at last. "Etienne . . . it *was* an opera house."

"You sound surprised."

"I . . . I don't know what to think."

"How about the truth?"

For a long moment, she gazed down at her plate. It was the intensity of Etienne's stare that made her look up again.

"I'm sorry I didn't pass by your house." His voice, though lower now, had tightened. "I should have. I wanted to."

"Don't apologize. You were my grandpa's friend. This must be really hard for you."

Etienne didn't answer. Resting his elbows on the table, he wiped his mouth with the napkin, then crumpled the napkin in one fist. Miranda wondered what he was feeling. She understood that sense of loss, of being left behind. But with Etienne, it was almost impossible to know what emotions he was hiding.

"Maybe . . . maybe there's something of Grandpa's you'd like to have?" she suggested. "To remember him by? I could make sure you get it."

He seemed to mull this over. "Thanks. I'll think about it."

"I'd really like to."

The hard lines softened around his mouth. "I know," he said quietly.

Well . . . I guess this is as good a time as any. She hadn't been able to tell Gage, but Etienne . . . "Something happened to me in the park yesterday. And I know I didn't imagine it."

This time she'd definitely piqued his interest. He seemed about to question her when Gage suddenly leaned over the back of their booth.

"I just remembered," Gage said to Miranda.

Etienne shifted easily to one hip, fished into his pocket, tossed some money on the table. "What's that?"

"The *name* of the opera house."

Gage stood aside as the other two got out. He added his own money to Etienne's.

But Etienne was only half listening. "Come on, I'll give y'all a ride."

"So what is it?" Miranda asked. "What's the name?"

Gage squeezed in close to her as they pushed their way to the door. "The Rose."

"The *what*?"

"The Rose Opera House." Gage's expression turned curious. "Have you heard of it?"

Quickly Miranda shook her head. They were at the truck now, and she climbed in tensely between the two boys. Etienne started the engine, and her mind raced back, back to yesterday, to the old building and the sweet smell of roses . . . to the park and the ghostly plea: *"Take it . . . the rose . . ."*

Connections, somehow? Coincidences?

"Miranda? Here's your house."

"What?" Both Gage and Etienne were looking at her. She managed a sheepish smile. "Oh. Sorry. You guys want to come in?"

She was conscious now of Etienne's thigh against hers. And of Gage's arm along her shoulders, resting lightly on the back of the seat. The guys seemed to exchange a mutual glance.

"Better not." Etienne shrugged. "Night job."

"Homework." Helping her out, Gage walked Miranda to the door. "Don't forget about the Historical Society. Right after school tomorrow."

"I won't. And thanks for tonight, Gage. I had a really good time."

Smiling, he turned and headed back to the truck as Miranda let herself in.

Surprisingly, no one seemed to be around. Aunt Teeta's door was closed, and though the TV still blared from the den, Miranda found her mother sound asleep on the couch. Deciding not to wake her, she shut off the television, covered Mom with an afghan, then hurried upstairs.

The Rose Opera House!

Is that what the Gray Soldier—Nathan—was trying to tell me? Not a flower, but a place? That must be it—why else would I have known about the gallery once being an opera house?

Flopping down on her bed, she gazed numbly at the ceiling. More puzzle pieces fitting together . . . but still so unbelievable . . . still so impossible!

No . . . not impossible. The truth. Grandpa knew the truth. And you know it, too, Miranda.

Turning off the bedside lamp, she closed her eyes and drifted. The darkness was sultry and still, a deep hole to hide in. She wished she could turn off her mind as easily as she could turn off the light, but her thoughts refused to cooperate. *If only I could find answers . . . figure things out . . .*

The Rose Opera House.

"For Miss Ellena . . . take it . . . the rose . . ."

"Help me."

Miranda shuddered as Nathan's words echoed over and over in her head. Like a song, like a spell. Over and over and over again . . . exhausting her into sleep . . .

Miranda was floating . . . surrounded by darkness, suspended in time. And there was a faint, faraway voice . . . like an echo underwater . . . rippling softly . . . shimmering sadly . . .

Miranda strained to hear.

"Take it . . . for Miss Ellena . . ."

She was apart from everything—she was part of everything; he could see her—she was invisible; she suffered with him—she was at peace—*helpless and trapped in the smoke and the fog and the downpour of rain and the earth running dark, dark crimson with blood . . .*

"Help me," Nathan said to her. The soldier in gray, the young man with the helpless, haunted face. *"You're the only one."*

And his pale, outstretched hand . . . a short length of twine, woven, knotted . . . only *this* time her fingers brushed over it, *this* time her fingers closed around it.

Miranda touched his hand. His skin was ice cold; her fingers passed right through.

"Take it . . ."

Jerking upright, she saw the figure beside her bed.

The figure veiled in shadows, just beyond reach of the moonlight through her windows.

She tried to cry out, but couldn't; her heart leapt into her throat and stuck there as she gasped for breath.

"No!" Miranda choked.

She closed her eyes, willing him away. When she opened them again, he was gone.

Yet Miranda wasn't comforted. Tears ran down her cheeks; her covers were damp with sweat. She reached for the lamp on her nightstand, then suddenly froze.

She was holding something. Something clutched tightly in her hand.

Puzzled, she spread her fingers and looked closer. In the room's pale glow, she could see the small, familiar object nestled there against her palm.

"Oh my God . . ." she whispered.

It was a piece of braided twine.

15

PRAYING NO ONE WOULD HEAR HER, Miranda sped downstairs to use the kitchen phone. As she punched in Etienne's number, she was still shaking.

"Please, Etienne," she whispered. One ring. Two. "Please pick up."

She had to tell someone. There was nobody here she could talk to, and she had to tell someone what had just happened, what she'd just found.

Three rings. Four.

Her grandpa had told her to trust Etienne, and she wanted to—more than anything right now, she *wanted* to trust him. *And I need to trust him. Because he's the only one now who'll believe me.*

Five rings. "Come on, Etienne, where are you?"

"Yeah?" That deep, husky voice, slightly breathless. "Yeah, hello?"

"Etienne—"

"Miranda? What's wrong?"

"I'm sorry. I hope you weren't asleep."

"Me, no, I never sleep." His tone sharpened. "Something's wrong, I can tell. What is it?"

Hesitating, she cupped her hand around the phone and

glanced nervously over her shoulder. She took a deep, steadying breath, barely managing a whisper. "I need to talk to you. I need your help."

"Wait for me in your room."

"What! Now?"

Realizing he'd hung up, Miranda stood there, still clutching the receiver. She hadn't actually asked him to come by—she'd have been thankful for just a comforting conversation over the phone.

But now that he *was* coming, she felt better . . . *and* safer. She only hoped he'd get here fast.

Reluctantly she crept to her bedroom, pausing on the threshold to make sure she was alone. She switched on every lamp, put on her robe, and curled back against the headboard with her pillows around her. She figured Etienne would sneak in the side door downstairs, so when she heard footsteps out on the sunporch, her heart nearly stopped.

"Miranda, it's me," Etienne said softly. "You okay?"

Ducking his head, he slipped through the low doorway. As he stopped beside her bed and gazed down at her, Miranda went limp with relief.

"How'd you know where my room is?" she asked.

"Your *grand-père,* he had me fixing things in here the week before you came. He was always hoping you'd live in this house."

The reminder stabbed painfully through her. Trying not to cry, she gestured past Etienne toward the sunporch. "How'd you get in?"

"What, you think I don't know how to pick a lock?"

She couldn't tell if he was teasing or not, but his eyes were dead serious, sweeping the room with one keen glance. "What's going on, *cher*?"

But now that he was with her, she couldn't say it. All she could do was point to her nightstand and the piece of knotted twine she'd tossed there when she'd run for the phone.

Etienne's brow furrowed. "This?" And then, when Miranda finally nodded, he scooped it up to examine it more closely. "What the hell is it?"

"I don't know."

"So . . . what am I missing? Where'd you get it?"

"Nathan gave it to me," she whispered, but not loud enough for Etienne to hear. She watched him hold it near the lamp, turn it carefully over in his palm. It was about six inches long, narrower than a pencil, and shone dull in the lamplight, the color of rust.

"It's solid . . . really tight. But it's not twine . . . I don't think it's any kinda string. See here, how it's braided?" Etienne shot her a sidelong glance. "More like hair, yeah? Like a piece of braided hair?"

Miranda couldn't look at it anymore; it made her skin crawl. "You're not serious, are you?"

"It's been braided once . . . and then back over itself." Etienne's long fingers stroked the woven edges. "And look—there's something on each end . . . hard to see, they're so tarnished. Like some kinda clamps or clasps—what, to keep the hair from unraveling?"

"Etienne, *please* tell me you didn't just say—"

"Hair. I think this is human hair."

Clutching a pillow to her chest, Miranda fought off a fresh wave of horror. "Then what does it mean? And why did Nathan give it to *me*?"

"Nathan? Whoa, now. Just a minute. Who's Nathan?"

"The Gray Soldier." She was shaking again; she could hear her words tumbling out all wrong. "That's his name—the soldier in the park. Except he wasn't real. I mean, he was *real*—but a real *ghost*. And then tonight when he was here . . . tonight in my room when—"

Abruptly she broke off. The confusion in Etienne's eyes had faded to understanding; his face blurred through her tears.

"Start at the beginning." Slowly he sat beside her on the bed. "And don't leave anything out."

Somehow she was able to do it—to recall her experiences in detail; to answer his occasional questions; to explain as best she could. She knew Etienne believed her, yet she longed to know what he was thinking. She wished she could see inside that calm, black stare, into the carefully guarded places of his mind.

As Miranda finished, Etienne refocused his attention on the braid. "So where does this fit in with everything?"

"And all the stuff about roses?" Miranda added. "I smelled them at the gallery that morning . . . Nathan talked about a rose . . . and then tonight Gage tells me the name of that opera house was the Rose. Those can't be just coincidences."

"You got any idea who Miss Ellena is?"

"None."

"And I'm guessing this Nathan, he's in the Rebel army, him wearing that gray uniform and all."

Again, she nodded. "He was so sad, Etienne. I don't know how to describe it exactly, but . . ." Miranda made a futile gesture. "*More* than sad, even. *Worse* than sad. Just empty . . . completely lost."

The room fell silent. Only night sounds now, mingled faintly beyond the open windows. She was all too aware of Etienne's gaze, though she'd closed her eyes. And sensing he might reach for her, she picked up another pillow to hug, and leaned her head back against the wall.

"So I guess this is how my life's going to be from now on," she murmured. "Just like Mom said it was for Grandpa. All kinds of bad surprises coming out of nowhere."

"Not all bad," Etienne answered quietly.

Opening her eyes, Miranda fixed him with a bitter stare. "Being scared all the time? Having to see the very worst tragedies? And hear the very worst sufferings? How can I—how could *any* person—be expected to live that way?"

"'Cause you've got to." Etienne was firm, though not unkind. "'Cause like it or not—*want* it or not—it's who you are. Look, your *grand-père,* he loved you so *much.* Do you think for one second he'd have wanted you hurt or unhappy?"

"Then why didn't he just tell me how I could escape the family curse?"

"If he'd thought it was a curse—and if there'd been a way out—I'm sure he'd have told you. For your sake."

Despite her resentment, Miranda needed to believe that. She remembered the last time she'd seen her grandfather, and her smile began to fade. "So what happens now? What can I do about it?"

"Not turn them away."

Just what Grandpa said.

"Listen to them. And help them." As Etienne's voice softened, some deep, hidden emotion flickered briefly in his eyes. "Your *grand-père,* he made a whole lotta differences in their world. And when *they* found peace . . . then *he* found peace. Let them guide you."

"You mean, like Nathan? Is *he* trying to guide me?"

"Think about it. When you see him—when he talks to you—besides feeling sad for him, what do you know? Down here in your gut, what do you really *know*?"

"I know . . ." *Yes, Miranda, look inside . . . you do know.* "I know . . . he wants me to deliver a message. I know the message is really important. And I know it's for someone named Miss Ellena."

"So that's where you need to start, yeah? With what you know."

"But how will that help him if I can't figure out the rest?"

"You *can,*" Etienne assured her. "And I'm gonna help you. Whatever kind of research we need to do, we'll take each clue as it comes. And right now"—he held up the braid, dangling it between his fingers—"this is the best clue we've got."

Miranda's face went grim. "Well, the only clue we can actually see and touch, anyway. Even if we *don't* know what it is."

"But something might come to you, yeah? Maybe if you just look at for a little while . . . or hold it in your hand?"

"No. I can't." As more tears threatened, she fought to control the quiver in her voice. "I don't want to see him in my room again. I'm sorry . . . I just can't."

"Ssh . . . it's okay. I'll take it with me, how's that? You need to rest anyhow, and I need to go."

Almost fearfully, Miranda looked up again. She watched Etienne get to his feet and slip the braid into the front pocket of his work shirt. She watched him bend over to peer solemnly into her eyes.

"The next few days are gonna be hard, *cher*. The wake and the funeral and all. You gotta be strong, you gotta be good for your family . . ." His voice trailed off. His hand brushed lightly over her hair. "Jonas, he was always so proud of you," Etienne whispered. "Now I know why."

The words stayed with her long into the night. Long after Etienne had left her, long after her eyelids finally closed.

And *"Who'll watch out for them?"* she heard her grandfather whispering. *"For all of them? After I'm gone?"*

16

Somehow Miranda dragged herself through Monday. She didn't remember falling asleep the night before, or if any ghostly voices had sought her out in dreams.

Exhausted and depressed, she was already in a foul mood by the time she got to school—and the morning went steadily downhill from there. She'd translated the wrong chapter in her Spanish workbook; she'd completely forgotten about a math assignment. She flunked a pop quiz in English lit. Parker was in her first class, Ashley and Gage in her third, and she could swear they were acting differently toward her today. Evasive, she noted, and somewhat distant. She even caught Parker staring from time to time, but when she made eye contact, he quickly looked away.

She told herself that it was all in her mind, that she was being paranoid—yet she couldn't shake the feeling that something was wrong. When noon rolled around, she decided to hide out in the library. She didn't expect Ashley to show up at her locker before she could escape.

"Have lunch with us." Ashley smiled, as friendly as ever. Almost *too* friendly, Miranda couldn't help thinking. "We've got this great spot outside where we always eat."

Miranda had seen them and their great spot on her first day of school. The close-knit group eating at their special table, in their own private corner of the schoolyard. Now Ashley's invitation made her feel irritable and trapped. She had too much on her mind; she needed to find a quiet place, be alone, sort things out. She didn't *want* to be part of their group. They'd forced her into it, and now everything was a mess. They were getting too close to her, and now her life was worse than ever.

"I'm not hungry," she insisted, slamming her locker door.

Instantly sympathetic, Ashley laid a comforting hand on her arm. "Are you worried about that quiz? Don't be. There was a death in your family—Mr. Klein's really understanding about things like that. All the teachers are. Trust me, he won't even count that grade."

"I just can't eat right now, okay?"

"You don't have to eat. We need to talk about the project—get your opinion on some things before we turn in that outline."

Miranda cringed. She'd forgotten that their project outline was due today, but Ashley was quick to reassure her.

"We didn't want to bother you with it, Miranda. You had enough on your mind this weekend. Anyway, Gage and I put something together. Like we always do, when we're working with Roo and Parker." She paused for a long-suffering sigh. "But I think the outline's good. Very good and very thorough."

"Then you don't need my opinion," Miranda replied stubbornly. "I'm sure whatever you did is perfect."

"We really need you, Miranda. Please come. The group's not complete without you."

Don't you get it? I don't want to complete the group, I never wanted to complete the group. I want to be left alone.

Without giving Miranda another chance to refuse, Ashley practically dragged her down the hall. There were a lot of kids eating outside, some at wooden picnic tables, others at round umbrella tables, many on benches, steps, and blankets, or just grabbing quick snacks at the vending machines. Miranda saw the four familiar faces in their usual hangout—Etienne among them—but again she sensed that something had changed. As if they were all studying her. And trying not to. And hoping she wouldn't notice.

"Hey, there you are." Gage immediately slid over to make room. "We tried to catch you after class, but you disappeared."

Miranda settled beside him. Parker was gulping down a Coke, watching her over the rim of his cup. Ashley sat down next to Parker, her smile fixed firmly in place. Standing, Etienne leaned casually against the table. Roo was the only one who met Miranda's eyes.

"You met a ghost," Roo said. "How cool is that?"

Parker choked, spitting ice in all directions.

There followed a moment of stricken silence. Then, turning to Roo, Gage shook his head in disbelief. "Very nice. Hell of a lead-in."

"Subtle as always," Parker muttered, brushing ice chips and cola off the front of his shirt.

Even Ashley looked distressed. As Roo's words began to sink in, Miranda could only sit there in stunned silence, pinned by five pairs of eyes. Then she turned slowly to Etienne.

"You . . . told them?" Her voice hardened with the pain of betrayal. "You told them what happened?"

"Right, like we're not already involved." Roo gave a dismissive shrug. "Like we all didn't see you freaking out at the gallery."

Parker and Gage closed ranks. "Roo, shut up."

"What? What's the big deal?"

Throughout the exchange, Miranda kept watching Etienne, searching for some sign of remorse. But his stare—and his words—weren't the least bit apologetic.

"Look, with all of us, there's a whole lot better chance of figuring things out. I thought Gage might know what the braid was. Or Parker might've seen one sometime at the museum. You and me, we can't think of *everything*, yeah?"

"So you *told* them," Miranda repeated, still shocked.

"It was the right thing to do—the *smart* thing to do. And they needed to know."

"You had no right." Pain had turned to anger now. Miranda's throat squeezed tighter and tighter. "You wanted me to trust you."

"And I meant it."

"You were supposed to keep this secret. This is a secret thing."

"Get used to it," Parker snorted. "No secrets in *this* motley crew."

Taking her elbow, Gage turned her gently back toward the others. "It's okay, Miranda. We—"

"We'd just like to help." Ashley broke in.

It was all Miranda could do not to break down. Numbly she

stood up and started walking away, but what Etienne said next stopped her.

"Your *grand-père*, it's what he wanted, Miranda."

"No," she replied, fixing him with a bold, accusing stare. "He wanted *you* to help me, no one else."

"I *am* helping you."

"How? By sneaking around behind my back? By making fun of me?"

"Uh-oh," Parker mumbled. "Soap-opera time."

"Listen to me." Before Miranda could take another step, Etienne blocked her path and caught her firmly by the shoulders. "I already told you, I *saw* what it did to Jonas. And I'm *not* gonna let that happen to you."

There was cold, hard truth in his eyes. And a determination so strong, it nearly overpowered her.

"Miranda?" Ashley's concern broke the tension. "Please?"

Etienne released her. As Miranda reluctantly faced the group around the table, she could see every intent expression waiting for her response.

"We really can help you," Ashley said softly. "Please let us."

Miranda turned back to Etienne. His gaze was sure and steady.

"You need friends, *cher*. And we're your friends."

Seconds dragged by while she tried to think. She was hurt and confused; she was flattered and touched and even strangely relieved. The reality of her life was crowding in on her, much too close, much too quick.

"It wouldn't be so scary with us around." Roo said philosophically.

Tipping his cup, Parker shook more ice into his mouth and slanted Roo a look. "Not true. It's always scary with you around."

"Give us some credit." Gage winked at Miranda. "We might surprise you if you give us a chance."

"You don't have to be in this alone," Ashley insisted.

Yet despite the positive support, Miranda couldn't shake her bewilderment or her doubts. "Why are you doing this?" she asked them. *You're already friends, and people like you don't let strangers into your exclusive little group. Besides that, how could you possibly understand what you're getting into, when I don't even understand it myself?* "You don't even know me."

"Etienne threatened us." Yawning loudly, Parker gave a long stretch, then wheezed as Ashley punched him in the ribs. "I'm *kidding*! Hey, I'm *kidding*, okay? *Damn*, Ashley!"

"You might as well say yes, Miranda," Ashley persisted as if Parker weren't there. "Because we're going to help you find out about poor Nathan one way or another."

"How?" Miranda challenged. "*How* are you going to do that?"

"Well . . . we . . . don't know yet. We're still . . . still . . ."

"Trying to decide if I'm as crazy as my grandpa was?" To Miranda, the uneasy silence spoke volumes. It lasted only a second, but that was long enough for her heart to drop. "Look, you guys." Her tone came out harsher than she'd intended. *What was I thinking? I should have just kept on walking.* "This is private, okay? And I don't need any help, and it really doesn't matter if you believe me, so—"

"I believe you," Gage said quietly.

"You know *I* do," Roo echoed.

"And me." Ashley's head bobbed up and down.

Scowling, Parker glanced at each of them. Then he folded his arms across his chest, leaned back, and scowled harder. "Well, I don't believe her. I don't believe any of y'all, and I think you're *all* crazy. But . . . what the hell."

"Well, *cher*." Etienne faced Miranda. "The sooner we start, the better, yeah?"

The bell rang then. Grateful for the distraction, Miranda trailed the others back across campus. She was just starting into the building when Etienne suddenly took her arm and steered her into an alcove where they couldn't be seen.

Flustered, she peered up at him. He wasn't holding her now, but the alcove was small, and their bodies were practically touching. As his eyes fixed on hers, she realized he'd moved nearer, and there was nowhere she could go.

Her pulse began to race. He was standing so close—*too* close—and she wanted him closer, even as she wanted to push him away. She was afraid he might actually hear her heartbeat or her quick intake of breath.

"Miranda," Etienne murmured, "I promised to help you. To protect you."

His stare never wavered. His lips were only inches from her own.

"I keep my promises."

Before Miranda could react, Etienne was out of the alcove and backing slowly away, one corner of his mouth hinting at a smile.

17

WHEN MIRANDA MET GAGE AFTER SCHOOL, she found the whole group waiting there with him.

"Gage said y'all were going to the museum," Ashley announced. "So it only makes sense for *all* of us to go."

"Yeah, you two didn't want to be alone, did you?" Roo shot Gage a sly glance, hiding a smile as he looked away.

Ashley tugged excitedly on Miranda's arm. "Then we can research our Ghost Walk *and* Nathan's ghost at the same time!"

They headed toward the Brickway, while Ashley systematically checked off topics in her notebook.

"Okay, here's how we figured things out. Are y'all listening?"

Parker instantly looked suspicious. "Who figured what things out?"

"Parker, were you paying *any* attention in class when I handed in our outline? Research for the project, of course. And who *else* would do it? Gage and I *always* do all the work."

"Not true." Roo frowned. "I contributed."

"You criticized. And complained. A lot." Not bothering to hide her annoyance, Ashley continued down her list. "I'll take the courthouse."

"No, I want the courthouse," Parker insisted. "I'm all into that evil judge."

"This is *not* about your father. You take the museum."

Incredulous, Parker gaped at her. "My mom works there!"

"I know your mom works there. That's why we gave it to you. You won't even have to do anything—just ask your mom about stuff."

"No. No way I'm working with her."

"Oh, fine then, Parker. Just fine. You can take Grace Church."

"Hell, no!"

"Just give him the courthouse," Roo spoke up. "Maybe that curse'll rub off on him and he'll hang himself."

"Then *I'll* do the museum." Ashley's sigh was exasperated. "Roo wants the doctor's house. And the library–funeral parlor."

Glancing at Ashley, Parker feigned amazement. "Don't you ever find this disturbing? That your sister's so obsessed with dead things?"

"Why should it?" Roo threw back at him. "She goes out with *you*, doesn't she?"

Ashley doggedly kept on. "Gage said he'd do Grace Church."

"Way to go, Gage!" Parker clapped Gage hard on the shoulder. "Who's Grace Church?"

"Parker Wilmington, nobody here thinks you're funny."

"Come on, Ash, admit it. Everybody here thinks I'm *kind* of funny—"

"Etienne's going to find out stuff about voodoo. Oh, and Roo and I are going to research that little boy who died at the feed store. And Miranda gets Magnolia Gallery—but of course we'll all help her with that. And . . . and I guess that's about it."

"Damn." Parker did his best to sound disappointed. "I was hoping for a whole lot more."

Nodding sympathetically, Roo swept him with solemn eyes. "How sad. That's exactly what Ashley always says about you."

"Oh, except for this other idea I had." Ashley glanced hopefully around the group. "Instead of calling it Ghost Walk, why don't we call it something else?"

"*Great* idea." Parker was adamant. "Why don't we call it *off*?"

"How about"—Ashley paused dramatically, her eyes sparkling—"Walk of the Spirits?"

As everyone traded glances, Gage repeated it several times out loud. "Yeah. I like it."

"Me, too," Miranda spoke up. "I think it's good."

"I think it's romantic," Ashley sighed. "Walk of the Spirits . . . don't you think it's wonderfully romantic?"

"I think it's wonderfully . . . you." Etienne patted Ashley's shoulder. "But could we move a little faster here? I got me a lotta work to do this evening."

"That's okay, this is just our first outline. We still have to refine it. And we still have a lot more research to do."

Gage nodded. "Then we have to write up a script for the tour. And everything has to be timed. And—"

"Enough torture." Parker glowered at each of them. "I get the idea."

"But hey, y'all." Ashley fairly glowed with pride. "The important thing is that Miss Dupree loves our project even more now. Did you see the look on her face when she was reading our outline? I've never seen her that excited about any assignment before, have you?"

"I've never seen her excited about anything." Parker exchanged guy looks with Etienne. "She needs to get laid."

"You know, at some point, we really need to do a trial run of this thing," Gage advised, ignoring Parker. "Seeing it in daylight is totally different than seeing it at night. If we're gonna get the full effect, we need to walk it after dark."

"He's right," Ashley agreed. "Just . . . not tonight."

"How come not—" Parker began, then winced as Ashley squeezed his arm. Noting her glance toward Miranda, he was instantly contrite. "Oh. Sorry. I forgot about the wake."

Miranda was quick to reassure him. "If I didn't have to be there, I wouldn't go either."

They'd reached the Historical Society. Before anyone could go inside, Parker started backing away.

"Oh, for heaven's sake," Ashley scolded him. "It won't kill you to see your mother."

"But I haven't seen her in weeks, so the shock really *could* kill me." He paused on the curb, grin widening. "Besides, I wouldn't even know what she looks like. And besides that, somebody still needs to find out if we can take tours inside some of these businesses. So I volunteer."

"Right," Gage answered. "Like you're suddenly so interested."

"Hey, never let it be said that I'm not a team player!"

"A *cowardly* team player!" Ashley shot back.

As Parker sauntered away, Roo nudged Miranda. "See what I mean?"

They'd barely walked through the door when a tall, willowy blond woman glided toward them. Her hair was swept back into a diamond clip, she had Parker's eyes, and her tailored suit was unmistakably designer label. She was lovely and elegant and smelled faintly of expensive perfume.

"Why, hello, Ashley darlin'!" Mrs. Wilmington caught Ashley in a carefully distanced hug. "I see the whole group is here."

Whole group? Miranda felt a twinge of defensiveness. *Parker's not here.* She studied the woman more closely. Mrs. Wilmington was staring at Roo, and not quite managing to hide her distaste. Roo looked smugly victorious.

"And you must be Miranda." Parker's mother offered a welcoming handshake. "Well, aren't you just the sweetest thing."

Embarrassed, Miranda was all too aware of Roo and Ashley hiding smiles, while Gage and Etienne seemed to find the whole thing silently hilarious. Mrs. Wilmington's handshake was limp.

"My, my, you look so much like your granddaddy," the woman observed.

"Dead?" Roo mumbled, while Gage elbowed her in the side.

Mrs. Wilmington didn't notice. "He was a very special person, your granddaddy. He and I were close friends for a long, long time."

"Run for your life," Roo hissed in Miranda's ear. "She's after something."

"Parker told me about the project y'all are working on, and that you'd probably be stopping by." Mrs. Wilmington made an all-inclusive gesture of the room. "And I think it's just wonderful. Whatever it takes to get our young people interested in their community—I fully support it!"

She paused, fingering the strand of pearls around her neck. Her frown was brief, but compassionate.

"I'm so sorry to hear about your granddaddy, Miranda," she said. "Really, it's such a shame."

Miranda managed an awkward nod. "Thank you for the food and flowers, Mrs. Wilmington."

"You are most welcome. *Most* welcome. Now. How might I help you ladies and gentlemen today?"

To Miranda's relief, Gage stepped forward. "We were wondering if you knew anything about an old opera house. We think it used to be where the Magnolia Gallery is."

"Opera house . . . opera house." The woman's face sank into deep thought. "You must mean the Rose Opera House."

As Gage nodded, Mrs. Wilmington's voice grew nostalgic and sad.

"The Rose was almost completely destroyed by fire around . . . 1863? Well, very near the middle of the war. A small portion of the remaining building *was* salvaged, however. And many years later that became part of a brand-new gallery."

Catching Miranda's eye, Gage smiled encouragement. Parker's mother gestured them all toward a doorway.

"Come along in here," she instructed. "Let me just see what we've got on that subject."

They followed her into an adjoining room—part library, part office—where she quickly scanned several tall bookcases, then consulted the computer on her immaculate desk. After studying the screen for several moments, she turned to them again, adjusting small, dainty reading glasses on the bridge of her perfect nose job.

"Built in 1830 . . . let's see now . . . and my, yes, just as I suspected. Quite the hub of cultured society."

"Oh," Ashley sighed. "How romantic."

"There are several photos in these files. I can print them out for you, if you like."

Gage glanced at the others. "Thanks. That'd be great."

While the information was being processed, Parker's mother spoke the rest from memory. "Only the rich and titled could afford such luxuries, you understand. The operas—and plays—usually came here from New Orleans. In fact, any traveling shows passing near or through St. Yvette were always welcome. But there were local events, too, and local talent. Theater troupes and ballet, special events and extravaganzas."

Strolling behind Mrs. Wilmington, Roo made a face. "*Extravaganzas?*" she mouthed silently.

"You said aristocrats were the main audience." Arms folded over his chest, Etienne angled himself back against the wall. "Who exactly would that've been?"

"Well, the upper class, obviously. The ones who held all the power. Plantation owners . . . doctors . . . lawyers . . . wealthy merchants, just to name a select few. And, during the Civil War, high-ranking Confederate officers, of course. Until the Union army laid siege to the town."

Mrs. Wilmington removed her glasses and toyed with one pearl earring. Ashley stared longingly at the jewelry.

"Normally, there would be quite lavish parties at the opera house after the performances. Some of the performers were regarded as royalty—they were the famous celebrities of their day."

Roo was not impressed. "How famous? Like rock stars?"

Ashley gave her a lethal frown.

"They were honored and esteemed wherever they went." Mrs. Wilmington sounded deeply insulted. "They came here to St. Yvette not only from New Orleans, but from every major city in the United States. And some actually traveled from Vienna and Paris and London."

As the printer churned out copies, Etienne picked one up and began studying it. He motioned Miranda over so the two of them could examine it more closely. The photograph didn't seem particularly exceptional, Miranda decided—just like any other public building of that era, except on a much grander scale. Wide, tall columns; wide, shallow steps rising to the entrance; wide, massive doors; a wide, curved drive.

"Notice the architecture," Mrs. Wilmington said proudly, peering over their shoulders. "The driveway was specifically designed for horse-drawn carriages. So ladies and gentlemen could alight close to the building, without mussing their clothes."

"*Alight?*" Roo mouthed again to Miranda. "*Mussing their clothes?*"

Ashley's face took on a dreamy expression. "All those hoop skirts and fans . . . I just love hoop skirts and fans."

Trying to view the photo, Roo crowded in next to Mrs. Wilmington. The woman discreetly cringed and moved away.

"Can I see one of those?" Gage asked, coming over to join them. He retrieved another printout, then leaned in close to Miranda, comparing both photographs side by side. The photo he held had been taken on the night of a performance— the building crowded with people, the driveway lined with carriages.

The entrance overflowed with flowers.

Miranda made a small, choked sound in her throat. Curious, Ashley and Mrs. Wilmington walked up behind her while the others exchanged lowered glances.

"Ah, yes," Mrs. Wilmington said, apparently recognizing the picture. "All the roses. Aren't they lovely?"

With a gentle tug, Gage coaxed the paper from Miranda's hand. She didn't even realize she'd grabbed it away from him.

"What about the roses?" Gage's tone was casual, but Miranda could hear an underlying hint of excitement. "There're so many of them."

"And hundreds more you can't even see here," Parker's mother informed him. "Red roses had a special significance at the opera house."

Miranda had begun to shiver. From some distant place, she was vaguely aware of Gage's hand on her back.

"And," the woman added, "when red roses lined the driveway and spilled from every door and window of the opera house, it always meant that Mademoiselle DuVrey was performing that night."

"And why was that?" Roo stared pensively into Mrs. Wilmington's enraptured face. "Did she have body odor or offensive personal habits?"

Gage choked down a laugh. Ashley looked horrified. Etienne shifted from one foot to the other and mumbled under his breath. Mrs. Wilmington maintained her dignity.

"Through all these years, we've found precious little information about Mademoiselle DuVrey. We do know that she was originally from New Orleans, and that she was considered somewhat of a heroine by the Confederate soldiers. Apparently, she was so passionate about the southern cause, she frequently insisted on crossing enemy lines just to visit our camps and rally our troops. One can only assume she had *no* trouble acquiring escorts." Parker's mother gave a suggestive little smile. "But as for details of her personal life? Only that she was stunningly beautiful and had the voice of an angel."

"I bet men admired and adored her." Ashley's sigh was a little more yearning this time. Mrs. Wilmington seemed equally smitten.

"Yes, I'm sure of it. Whenever she performed at the Rose, it was to sellout crowds, standing room only. And *she* was the one who always insisted the opera house be filled with red roses."

Miranda realized the others had surrounded her now, all of

them curious and expectant, waiting for Mrs. Wilmington to continue. The woman's expression went thoughtful.

"It was her signature, really. You know, many people thought the opera house was named simply for all the flowers. But, actually, the Rose was rather like a nickname of the utmost respect. From Mademoiselle DuVrey's stage name. Ellena Rose."

18

SOMEONE WAS SQUEEZING HER HAND. No, *both* hands, Miranda realized—Gage on one side, Etienne on the other. Roo was staring at Ashley. Ashley was staring at Gage. Gage was staring at Etienne over Miranda's shoulder.

It was Etienne who finally broke the startled silence. "You wouldn't have any pictures of her, would you?"

"Of Mademoiselle DuVrey?" Mrs. Wilmington shook her head. "None here in the museum—well, at least no actual photographs. Apparently, they're quite hard to find, if any even exist. Some written accounts say that she was quite phobic about having her picture taken or even her portrait done. But there are several newspaper articles that mention her—and I do seem to recall an old playbill. In fact, there might even be a small caricature of her face on that. You'll find everything in our display featuring the arts."

Etienne jerked his chin toward the door. Without a word, they all walked back into the main room.

"Miranda, dear, I guess you know that your granddaddy is—was—an avid collector of Confederate memorabilia."

"Yes, he was." Images of all her grandpa's things came back to her. *The Civil War shrine.* "I think he really liked collecting things." *Profound statement, Miranda. Well, at least that's* one *thing about him you know for sure.*

Mrs. Wilmington seemed intrigued by the subject. "Oh yes, he was quite obsessed with it. It's not that difficult to find artifacts in this area—folks are always discovering buttons and bullets and old coins. But your granddaddy found some real treasures. In fact, a lot of what you see here in the museum is actually on loan from him."

"Told you. Here it comes." Muttering under her breath, Roo nudged Miranda. The warning escaped Mrs. Wilmington's notice.

"I can't help but wonder what his estate will decide to do with all these lovely things. It would be such a shame for them to end up in somebody's attic, where they can't be fully appreciated." The woman paused, her brow furrowing. "I don't suppose you know what *other* interesting things he might have kept at home?"

Roo seemed dangerously on the verge of responding when Gage quickly steered her away. As Miranda followed them, she could hear their muffled conversation.

"Don't even think about it." *Gage.*

"What?" *Roo.*

"Don't 'what' me. I know that look."

"Did you hear what she said to Miranda?"

"I heard."

"She's such a—"

"Dammit, Roo, shut up."

Mrs. Wilmington was still talking, but Miranda had tuned her out. *"Take it . . . the rose . . ."* The Rose Opera House . . . roses *spilling everywhere . . . Ellena Rose. So Nathan was talking about a place and a person. He wanted to get a message to Miss Ellena—Mademoiselle DuVrey—at the opera house.*

Thoughts and questions tumbled wildly through Miranda's brain. *But what's the message? And how am I supposed to deliver it to someone who lived a century ago?*

"Now, where did we move that display?" Mrs. Wilmington's voice drifted back to her. "We rotate the exhibits in here every six months, you know—there are *so* many things of interest, and we simply don't have the space."

Miranda tried to catch Etienne's attention. He was standing uncomfortably with Roo and Gage, while Mrs. Wilmington went on and on about charitable donations. Gage had Roo's shoulder firmly in his grasp—each time she tried to ease away, he held on tighter. Miranda felt as if the walls were closing in. She needed to get some air. She needed—

"Miranda, you were right!" With a conspiratorial whisper, Ashley tugged at her arm. "It's amazing! You were right about all of it!"

"Of course she was," Etienne mumbled, giving Ashley a wink. He'd finally managed to slip away from Mrs. Wilmington's lecture. Now, as a telephone rang and the woman hurried to answer it, Roo and Gage quickly followed him.

"Miranda was right, y'all!" Ashley said again, but Miranda didn't share the excitement.

"Okay, so we have a name. But how will I figure out the rest?"

"With time," Etienne reminded her. "It was the same way

for Jonas, yeah? He told me how frustrated he'd be, thinking he had something figured out, then having to do it all over again. But with time—and practice—he got more feelings about it, stronger feelings about it. With time, he just started trusting that he *knew*."

Before the discussion could go further, Mrs. Wilmington returned from her office. She directed them over to some framed documents on the wall, where they all proceeded to crowd in.

"Here are the articles—reviews mostly, nothing really personal—and here's the playbill. Ah yes, with this very tiny sketch of Mademoiselle DuVrey, which I'm sure is *quite* unflattering and does her absolutely *no* justice whatsoever. Plus, there are a few more photographs of the opera house. No interior shots, unfortunately."

"What about the fire?" Etienne asked. "You said the opera house burned during the war?"

"Yes, but not from any battle. I don't think anybody ever knew for certain what started that fire. Oh, there were speculations, of course—jealous actors, spurned lovers, disgruntled employees, drunken soldiers—all the way to a carelessly discarded cigar or an accidentally overturned lamp. Luckily, there wasn't a performance that night, so no audience was present. But there *were* some rehearsals going on."

Miranda was only half listening. Intent on the playbill, she gazed at the crude sketch of Ellena Rose that appeared alongside the diva's name. *Fair skin. You had very fair skin . . .*

Puzzled, she tried to pull back but couldn't. She realized the air had grown stuffy, and the conversation around her had become a low, indistinguishable hum. She couldn't take her eyes off Ellena Rose's face. *Fair skin . . . red hair . . . green eyes—no. One blue and one green . . . entrancing and irresistible . . .*

"No performance?" Miranda snapped back to the present. Her own voice was speaking out loud, and she was completely coherent, fully aware that no time had passed at all. "So then no one was hurt?"

For a brief second, Mrs. Wilmington seemed flustered. Then, with an apologetic laugh, she said, "My goodness, I'm getting ahead of myself. Yes, the opera house was closed to the public that night—but Mademoiselle DuVrey was in her dressing room." As if on cue, the woman's face went grief-stricken. "Poor thing. So young. Such a tragedy."

"She *died*?" Though the others glanced at one another in surprise, Ashley was close to tears.

"Heartbreaking, isn't it? A young woman like that, with everything to live for . . . the whole world at her feet . . . her whole life ahead—"

"Her whole story dragged out," Roo mumbled, before Gage could stop her.

Mrs. Wilmington gravely proceeded. "Apparently, the fire spread very quickly; there was total confusion and panic. By the time someone went searching for Mademoiselle DuVrey, it was already too late. She was trapped in her dressing room that terrible night. She perished in the flames."

"Burned?" Roo's dark-ringed stare was genuinely curious. "Or smoke inhalation?"

Mrs. Wilmington shuddered. "Her body was recovered the next day."

"And everybody was sure it was just an accident?" Gage asked.

"That's what history tells us."

"But history's not always right," Etienne spoke up. "A lotta history gets changed just through telling about it, yeah?"

After a brief hesitation, the woman's voice grew hard. "Times change very little. Tragedies occur—in many ways. Some people are simply self-destructive. Some people have everything they could ever want, and everything to live for, and they still throw it all away."

An uncomfortable silence filled the room. Miranda suspected that Mrs. Wilmington was referring to Parker, and from the others' strained expressions, they apparently thought so, too.

"So how come people around here don't know about the opera house?" Etienne smoothly changed the subject. "Me, I've lived here my whole life, and I never heard anybody talking about it."

"It's not marked either," Gage added, "like a lot of our other historic places are."

Mrs. Wilmington's nod was understanding. "I think it's mainly because the original building—or should I say, *most* of the original building—isn't there anymore. Once it burned, it stayed in ruins till long after the war. We have no way of knowing how much of it was left, or what parts of it were recovered and reconstructed into the gallery. I suppose it's unrealistic to hope that anything should last forever. But I fear one of these days, the Rose won't even be a memory."

"That's so sad." Again Ashley fought back tears. "Poor Ellena Rose. Nobody should ever be forgotten like that."

"But she hasn't been forgotten," Miranda whispered.

She realized Etienne was watching her, standing close, hearing every word. She looked up at him, her face solemn.

"Nathan *never* forgot Ellena Rose. That's why he's still here."

"I'm sorry, Miranda." Mrs. Wilmington smiled politely. "Were you asking a question?"

"We should probably be going," Etienne said.

Ashley, however, couldn't resist one last look at the photographs on the wall. "The opera house was such a beautiful building. Wouldn't you just love to hear all the stories it could tell?"

Parker's mother seemed amused. "Not all of them respectable, I imagine."

"Why is that?"

"Ashley?" Gage prompted, but Mrs. Wilmington was again in her element.

"Leading ladies often entertained suitors in their dressing rooms. People were expected to be discreet and look the other way."

"I bet she entertained lots of men," Ashley decided. "I bet she had lots of lovers."

Roo clenched her teeth. "Ash. *Come on!*"

"No, wait a minute, this is so interesting. I want to hear it."

"Yes, no doubt many lovers," Mrs. Wilmington picked right up.

"Women like her would have been constantly—and ardently—pursued."

While their discussion continued, Miranda began edging toward the door. A strange restlessness had settled over her, as though the room were suddenly too small, as though some sense of urgency were trying to get her attention. Her thoughts spun, connected by the most fragile of threads—she needed to untangle them. Now. Now, before they faded and disappeared, like the Rose Opera House.

Outside, the blazing heat was merciless. She leaned into the brick wall of the building and closed her eyes against the sun, too distracted to realize Etienne had followed her.

"Hey, *cher*, you okay?"

Startled, she took a second to hone in on his face. "It's there, Etienne. Answers . . . reasons . . . everything's there. Nathan, Miss Ellena, the message—all I have to do is put the pieces together and make them fit. I just don't know how."

She could see her frustration reflected in his eyes. *Or is that his own frustration?* She couldn't be sure, and when she looked again, it was gone.

"I don't know how," she repeated irritably.

"You don't *have* to know that now. You don't have to *do* that now." Etienne's gaze was steady, his voice calm. "You have the wake tonight and the funeral tomorrow. That's enough to handle."

"I had another vision. In the museum. When I looked at that playbill."

"So that's why you came out here." His features softened.

He lifted one hand toward her face, then drew back again as the front door burst open. Almost guiltily, Miranda stepped away to make room for the others on the sidewalk.

"Well, I am just *so* happy y'all stopped by today," Mrs. Wilmington gushed, though Ashley seemed to be the only one listening. "And be sure to let me know if there's *anything* else I can help with. Anything at all."

Gage and Etienne were having their own conversation at the curb. Roo was yawning. Impatient to get home, Miranda started pacing back and forth, past the front window of the museum.

"Oh my God."

It was only a glance, but it was enough to stop her. To freeze her there with both hands on the windowpane while the others curiously squeezed around.

"What is it?" Gage was there first, trying to follow the direction of her shocked eyes. "What are you looking at?"

"Him," Miranda whispered.

Her finger shook as she pointed to the photograph. An old, yellowed photograph of Rebel soldiers.

He was standing in the very back row, crowded in among many others, but proudly holding the reins of two magnificent horses. His gray uniform hung too loose on his thin frame; his face was just visible beneath the lowered brim of his cap. And though the quality of the photograph was poor—much of it faded to near obscurity—Miranda would have recognized him anywhere.

The Gray Soldier. Nathan.

He was strikingly handsome—nothing like the grim, haunted

specter of her visions. And yet the eyes were the same—she could see that now—and the pale hair was the same, and the lips, relaxed in an easy smile, were definitely the same lips that had spoken to her.

"Him," she murmured again.

Her pointed finger was still trembling. Gage's fingers closed around it and coaxed it down.

So young, so determined, all those soldiers. So strong and full of life. No thoughts of fear there, no hesitation; no thoughts of dying or losing the war. So certain of a quick return to homes and loved ones and the world they'd always known.

Eyes misting, Miranda focused on that one familiar face. *He looks happy.* Then, easing her hand from Gage, she touched the windowpane once more.

"Mrs. Wilmington, who is this?"

Readjusting her glasses, the woman peered over Miranda's shoulder. "Who? This man here?"

"Yes, him."

"Goodness, I have no idea. Some poor Rebel soldier, obviously."

"Do you know where this was taken?"

"Hmmm . . . well . . . it *might* have been one of these old houses on the Brickway. Or close to here, at any rate. So many of them look alike, you know. And unfortunately, some were torn down before we could save them."

But Miranda was scarcely listening. She caught her breath and struggled to choke out the words.

"That's our house. Hayes House."

"You're kidding." Gage glanced from her to the photograph. "Are you sure?"

"I'm sure. I mean . . . I'm pretty sure—"

"I don't think so, Miranda." Ashley sounded sorry for disagreeing. "That doesn't even *look* like your house."

Noting Etienne's pensive stare, Roo gave him a shrug.

"That's Hayes House," Miranda said firmly.

True, it wasn't the *exact* Hayes House of today. A different color, different windows, a slightly different shape. It looked smaller, and stood at the end of a dirt road, the roofs of several outbuildings barely visible in back. There was no wall behind it bordering a park, not as many trees, no landscaped gardens. But she knew it was Hayes House just the same.

"How can you tell?" Gage asked her.

I feel it. I know.

"This picture is from your grandfather's collection," Mrs. Wilmington offered helpfully. "He kept excellent records—he documented everything. The photograph should be fairly easy to trace."

Though Roo arched a look at Miranda, none of them spoke. Only Mrs. Wilmington, who commented again on the picture.

"I especially love the officers' uniforms, don't you? So sophisticated, so noble. And this one officer here . . ."

Miranda hadn't paid any attention to the man in front. Tall and distinguished, but with his hat tilted rakishly, he had dark hair, a dark goatee, and a long dark mustache, impeccably trimmed.

"This was Travis Raleigh Fontaine," Mrs. Wilmington finished.

"He was a very well-known, high-ranking Confederate officer. Quite the ladies' man of his day. But you can tell *that* just by looking at him."

Trying to be inconspicuous, Miranda gestured to Etienne. Her restlessness was getting worse, tiny pins and needles all over her body, but there was something about this photograph— *something important!*—something else she couldn't quite figure out . . .

"Notice his sash." Mrs. Wilmington was clearly enamored. "The cut of his clothes, the shine on his boots. And, of course, a true southern gentleman was never fully dressed without his pocket watch."

Rolling her eyes, Roo tugged on the back of Gage's shirt. "Save me," she muttered. "I can't take any more."

Gage batted her hand away. Roo tugged more determinedly on his back pocket.

"You can actually see the chain here." Parker's mother tapped the window, demanding their attention. "Even in black and white, that chain seems to glitter. Solid gold, you know."

Leaning forward, Ashley strained to see. "It really *does* glitter! Oh, I think men with pocket watches were so handsome."

"Distinguished, without a doubt. A pocket watch and chain were as unique as the man who owned them. Take watch chains, for example. There were various lengths depending on where the watch was to be worn. In a vest pocket, perhaps. Or in the pocket of one's trousers. There were even shorter chains, which attached the watch to a small ornament called a fob—and which in turn anchored the watch to a side pocket. But no matter its length, a chain assured that the watch was easy to handle and didn't get lost."

Something . . . Miranda rubbed at her temples. *Something . . . what is it? It's there . . . answers . . . if only—*

"Were all chains fancy like this one?" Ashley asked.

Mrs. Wilmington was delighted to elaborate. "Oh no, they could be made of many different materials."

Etienne's body tensed. Miranda felt the quick catch of his muscles . . . the slide of his hands up her back . . . as he slowly gripped her shoulders. And she knew the realization had struck both of them at the exact same time.

"They could be gold-filled or platinum," Mrs. Wilmington rattled on. "Or expensive leather, or studded with precious stones. But some were much plainer—a ribbon, or a common strap. Even string. Oh, and some women even wove them out of their hair."

The silence was sudden and stifling. Five bodies held together by an undercurrent of shock.

Mrs. Wilmington was clueless about the response she'd just caused. She tapped again on the window glass.

"Yes, indeed," she said, "that was the truest devotion. To have a watch chain woven from your sweetheart's hair."

19

"LET'S SEE THAT THING AGAIN," Gage said, reaching toward Etienne. Obligingly, Etienne handed him the braid.

The six of them were on the veranda of Hayes House, drinking lemonade. Ashley had called Parker on his cell phone, and he'd met them there within minutes. Now he and Ashley shared the porch swing, while Gage and Etienne slouched in wicker chairs. Roo sat cross-legged on the floor, pressing a frosty glass to one cheek. And Miranda sat beside Roo, leaning back against the wall, with her eyes wearily shut.

"People are still bringing food," Ashley whispered while more visitors came up the walk. "I feel like we shouldn't be here."

"I want you here," Miranda assured her. "Just let them step around us."

They all grew quiet as more people walked past, as solemn looks and sympathetic smiles and comforting words were offered. Without bothering to open her eyes, Miranda nodded and mumbled politely in response to each comment. She'd probably hear about it later from Mom. About how rude people thought that niece of Aunt Teeta's was. Right now she couldn't care less.

"It sure looks like human hair." Gage marveled, turning it over in his palm. "It sure *feels* like human hair. Sort of."

"It's old. And who the hell knows where it's been all these years." Etienne took a long swallow of his drink. The front of his T-shirt was damp with sweat, and he'd carelessly shoved his hair back from his forehead.

"I can't believe I didn't make the connection." Seriously put out with herself, Miranda groaned. "I saw some watch chains in my grandpa's room. I just didn't know what they were."

Gage handed the braid back to Etienne. "Well, whoever's hair this was must have been a redhead."

"Ellena Rose," Miranda said. "She was a redhead."

There was a brief pause as everyone traded glances. Then Ashley scooted to the edge of the swing.

"Miranda, how do you know that?"

"I just . . . the playbill."

Parker gave a derisive snort.

"Wow. It wasn't even a photo of Ellena Rose." Roo set down her lemonade and lit up a cigarette. "So you got her hair color from just a black-and-white sketch?"

"Yes. She had red hair and different colored eyes—one green and one blue."

"Maybe she was wearing contacts," Ashley suggested. Five stares aimed in her direction. Her smile began to fade. "She was a celebrity. Celebrities wear contacts to match their clothes."

"You know, Ash," Roo stated, "even after all these years, your keen powers of perception continue to amaze me."

Etienne gamely switched the subject. "That picture of the soldiers? Miranda's right. I'm sure that's Hayes House in the background."

Without a word, everyone looked warily toward the front door, as if half expecting the house to come alive.

"Why didn't you say something before?" Miranda glared at him.

"'Cause I needed to think about it. And"—he hesitated, almost sheepish—"I didn't want you freaking out any more than you were already."

"I'm more freaked out that you didn't say anything."

"Sorry. But it *is* the same house—the way it was originally."

Now it was Parker who groaned. "Oh, don't tell me. The house contacted you. You talk to dead houses."

"The thing is," Etienne continued, unfazed, "I've worked plenty construction, and I've done plenty work on *this* house—I know good renovation when I see it."

Roo cast Miranda a bland look. "Construction sites are popular in this town. A chance to see Etienne Boucher without his shirt on. Very hot."

The others could hardly keep from laughing. As one more sad-faced visitor approached the house, they all tried to compose themselves.

What's wrong with me? I shouldn't be joking at a time like this. Miranda felt both guilt and defiance. *What did Etienne say? About people laughing the hardest when they're scared and don't want to show it?*

"Your *grand-père's* things." Focusing on Miranda, Etienne steered the conversation back again. "You're gonna have to go through them, yeah? See what else you can find out?"

"I can't do that."

"Why not?"

"I can't just tell Aunt Teeta I want to go through his things."

"You're his granddaughter. Just say you want to know more about him. It's true."

"Just say it's for our project," Ashley said helpfully. "Which is also true."

"If he documented anything about that photograph, it could really help us."

"I didn't see any files in his room," Miranda added. "And I didn't see any papers in there either."

Etienne gave a distracted nod. "He didn't keep things like that in his room. He kept them in the attic."

"Well, if you know so much about them, why don't *you* go through his things?"

"Look," Gage broke in, "we can *all* go through his things. We can *all* help."

"Oooo, I love attics." Ashley gave a little squirm of anticipation. "Maybe your grandpa has some old trunks up there, do you think? Like attics in the movies? With clothes and old hats and those dressmaker dummies?"

Roo drew on her cigarette. "You're looking for dummies? Don't tempt me, Ash."

"Well, as tempting as it is to continue this fascinating and stimulating discussion"—Parker grimaced—"I've got to get home." Standing, he pulled Ashley up with him. "I guess we'll see y'all later?"

As the others got to their feet, Ashley gave Miranda a tight hug. "We're coming tonight. You know, to the wake."

Miranda, once more, was touched. "Look, you guys, I appreciate it—really. But you don't have to. It's going to be so depressing."

"We're coming," Roo said.

"Yeah, Roo likes depressing," Parker insisted. "She'll feel right at home."

"Parker, that's so rude," Ashley scolded him. "This isn't anything to joke about."

"Right. Sorry."

The last to leave, Gage paused on the top step to look back at her. "We'll be there."

An evening had never felt so endless.

As a steady stream of people—all friends of Aunt Teeta; the whole town, it seemed—came and went from the funeral home, Miranda was forced to stand and shake hands, endure countless introductions, and say "thank you" till she wanted to scream. She couldn't concentrate on the wake or anything else around her. Clues kept flitting through her mind—unknown connections between a soldier and an opera singer, a watch chain, a fire, and Hayes House.

"Oh, Miranda, are you doing okay?"

Deep in thought, Miranda was startled by Ashley's hug. She hadn't noticed the group coming in, but now she saw them talking quietly to Aunt Teeta in one corner of the room. They all looked as strained as she felt. Especially Etienne.

Despite her own misery, Miranda's heart went out to him. She still didn't understand the closeness he and her grandfather had shared, but it was obvious Etienne was hurting. She watched his gaze shift slowly, reluctantly, toward the casket. His jaw was rigid, his features like stone.

"Is Etienne—" she began, but Ashley was already shaking her head.

"He's taking it really hard, I think. But he doesn't want anybody to know it."

Before Miranda could respond, the others were there, all offering sympathetic hugs. When it was Etienne's turn, his hug was tense and brief.

Feeling dangerously emotional, Miranda tried to lighten the mood. She scanned Parker, Gage, and Etienne with a critical eye.

"Look at you guys," she said at last. "I didn't even recognize you. Y'all clean up real good, as Aunt Teeta would say."

Parker grinned. Gage and Etienne seemed vaguely embarrassed. Amused, Roo and Ashley deliberately looked the boys up and down.

Leaving Miranda to her family duties, the rest of them began drifting away, recognizing friends and neighbors in the crowd, making rounds to say hello. Miranda was relieved when Mom told her to get some air. The place was close and stuffy and reeked of lilies, and as she made her way through the many visitors, it suddenly dawned on her how haggard her mother looked.

She couldn't help feeling a twinge of guilt. Mom, as usual, had had to take care of all the burdensome details—wake, funeral, burial, eulogy—and had already made lists of even more things that would need attention afterward. Papers and various legal documents, bank boxes, the will, and Grandpa's possessions—the sheer thought of what Mom would have to deal with was staggering. Miranda made a firm mental note to help her out more and complain less.

Noting that everyone was engaged in conversation, she slipped out the front door. A few strangers lingered on the walkway, chatting quietly, but, to her surprise, she spotted Parker at the far end of the porch. He was alone, bent forward with his arms crossed on the railing, staring up at the sky.

"Parker, what are you doing out here all by yourself?"

He didn't seem particularly surprised by the interruption— just turned his head to look at her. No cocky grin now, no smart-ass jokes. Just a pensive face and a nice smile.

"Hey," he said.

Had he been drinking? Miranda thought she could smell a faint trace of liquor on his breath, but she didn't see any evidence. Maybe he was hiding it—in his car or in a suit pocket.

Keeping a friendly tone, she tried again. "What happened? Did Ashley kick you out?"

"Actually"—his smile tightened—"I'm not very good at these things."

"Me neither. You want to know something?"

"Sure."

"I keep wondering if all these people are just here out of curiosity. Like this is a sideshow—step right up, come see crazy old Jonas Hayes."

Parker shrugged. "Some of them, I guess. He *is* kind of a legend in this town."

"I'm glad it's a closed casket. I don't want everyone staring at him."

"People have always stared at him."

Though it wasn't said unkindly, Miranda frowned. "But maybe if people had really gotten to know him, they wouldn't have thought he was crazy."

"Maybe. But you're talking about St. Yvette. Most people his age who lived here are dead now. A lot of people your mom's age have either moved *away* from here or moved *to* here from someplace else. And with our generation, we hardly ever saw him at all. So most of what people know about Jonas Hayes is probably from stories they've heard."

"But stories get changed through the years. So who knows what's even true?"

"I guess it depends on the story," Parker said quietly. "Don't tell me you've never heard any of them."

"Not really." Sure, Mom had shared that one episode with her, but ever since then Miranda had longed to know so much more. "I mean, it's not like I've never asked my mom about it. But somehow it just never seems to be the right time."

"You get that, too, huh? Always something better to do than

sit down and talk with your kid. Oh, unless it's to criticize, of course."

Miranda heard the bitterness in his tone. She thought of all the arguments she'd had with her own mother, and she sympathized.

"I feel that way sometimes," she admitted.

But Parker had returned to their former topic. "I can tell you something about your grandfather. Well, something my mom remembers. I've heard her talk about it."

"And it's really true?"

"She says it is." Sighing, he wheeled around and propped back on his elbows, stretching his legs out in front of him. "A little girl disappeared, and your grandfather told them where to find her."

"That's all? That's not much of a story."

"Okay. Did I mention that the little girl *told* him where to find her? And that she happened to be *dead* at the time?"

Miranda felt the hairs lift at the back of her neck. "Go on."

"They searched for this kid for weeks. She was like, five or six years old. The whole town was out looking for her. And then Jonas Hayes walks into the police station one night and says he knows where she is."

Just like the other time Mom told me about. Swallowing hard, Miranda leaned against the railing beside Parker. "And *did* he know?"

"He led them straight to her. They found her body stuffed inside an old tomb near the Falls."

"So . . . she really was—"

"Dead. Strangled. Just . . . you know . . . a little kid." Parker's voice lowered harshly. "The killer ended up being some relative—some cousin or something. The guy was so freaked out that they found the body, he confessed in a note and then shot himself."

Miranda hesitated, yet she had to ask. "But before they found the note, did the police ever think my grandpa did it?"

"Hmmm . . . let's see." Parker began counting on his fingers. "First, he'd been caretaker at the Falls for years. Second, the tomb where they found the girl's body was way back in those woods, really hard to get to. Third, the Falls had already been searched, but nobody found anything. And fourth, he told the cops that the girl—the *dead* girl—had asked him to come and get her." Turning slightly, Parker seemed amused. "Hell, no. No suspicions there."

For a split second the night seemed to recede around her, stars spinning out in all directions. Miranda met Parker's stare full on.

"Parker, he wasn't crazy."

"Excuse me? Did you happen to notice him scaring the crap out of us the other day?"

"He *wasn't*," she insisted. "And he really *could* communicate with spirits."

"Hey, I don't know, okay?" Distractedly, Parker ran one hand down the front of his jacket. For the first time Miranda noticed the slight bulge from an inside pocket. A flask? She stared at the jacket. Then she stared at Parker. Noting her scrutiny, he gave a wan smile.

"Yes. To answer your question, yes, I have. But just a little."

"Parker—"

"Don't start. I get enough of that from Ashley."

"Only because she cares about you. She doesn't want to see you hurt yourself."

The bitterness reached out from his voice . . . spread across his face. The smile disappeared. "Maybe I *want* to hurt myself."

"But *why*? You have . . . you have so much—"

"What? Potential? All that wonderful, perfect potential I'm expected to fulfill?"

Miranda softened. "I wasn't going to say that. I was going to say you have *so much*. That's just it. You have everything."

"Maybe I don't *want* everything. Maybe I want something else *besides* everything."

"Then what is it, Parker? What is it you really want?"

Silence fell between them. As Parker gazed out into the night, Miranda noticed the tension in his shoulders, the tightening of his jaw.

"Etienne told me how your grandfather loved you," Parker murmured. "Jonas Hayes, the lunatic—how he loved you so much and felt like he knew you, even though he'd never met you before now."

Miranda couldn't speak. She watched Parker's expression go darker.

"Weird, huh. Everybody thinks *my* mom and dad are perfect. But you know what? They don't even know me. I've lived with them my whole life, and they've *never* known me."

He looked at her then, and for one brief second there was such sadness in his eyes. A glimpse of truth that was raw and aching and vulnerable. "You're a nice girl, Miranda. I'm glad your grandfather loved you so much."

As though suddenly self-conscious, he drew back from her. The bare emotions vanished; the old carefree facade took their place. When Ashley walked out on the porch, Parker gave a loud, shrill whistle that echoed clear across the parking lot.

"Parker Wilmington!" Ashley hissed. Trying to ignore the offended stares of onlookers, she marched over and planted her feet angrily in front of him. "What on earth has gotten into you? I am *so* sorry, Miranda."

Parker grinned. He lunged for Ashley, grabbed her around the waist, and pulled her close. "I'm leaving. You staying or going?"

"Go," Miranda insisted. "This thing's almost over. There's no reason for you guys to hang around."

Ashley didn't seem convinced. "Are you sure? The others are leaving, too, but I can stay. I can always walk home—"

"No walking home," Parker ordered.

"I can always get a ride later with Etienne—"

"No riding with Etienne!" Parker's hands went up in despair. "Dammit, I'll be competing with that guy for the rest of my life!"

"*And* Gage, don't forget," Ashley teased.

"*And* Gage." Wrapping her in a hug, Parker steered Ashley toward the steps. "I'll be competing with Etienne *and* Gage for the rest of my life!"

Ashley gave Miranda a see-what-I-put-up-with sigh. Hiding her concern, Miranda watched the two of them get into Parker's car and drive away.

By nine-thirty, the dreaded ordeal was over. As Miranda watched the final visitors leave, her mother and Aunt Teeta went off with the funeral director to discuss last-minute details for tomorrow's service. A welcome silence descended around her, along with a crushing wave of exhaustion. She felt numb and totally drained. And standing there in that sudden quiet of the viewing room, she realized that she and her grandfather were alone together for the last time.

It wasn't supposed to be like this, Grandpa. We were supposed to get to know each other and be happy. You and Mom were supposed to make up. And you were supposed to live for years and years and years, and always be there when we needed you . . .

Bitter tears blinded her. Grief and regrets tore at her heart, the ache almost unbearable. She hadn't expected to feel so much— not this depth of emotion, certainly not this depth of pain— but even more than that, not this fierce and burning anger. *You weren't supposed to do this, Grandpa—you weren't supposed to leave me.*

With no distractions now, she let herself focus on the casket. It rested there at the front of the room, covered by a spray of roses, flanked by plants and flower arrangements, serene and dignified beneath carefully dimmed lights. Nothing had really changed in here, Miranda reminded herself, nothing except the subdued chatter and crowds of people, yet the room was different somehow. Definitely and somberly different. This was death. This silence was death . . . these shadows were death. And this aloneness—this coffin abandoned when everyone else went home tonight—this terrible aloneness was also death.

Miranda thought of her father.

And she thought of the Gray Soldier.

That haunted, hopeless face of his; that desperate, endless wandering.

Because he's searching for something, for someone . . .

Because he's alone.

All at once the awareness was too much for her. All at once she wanted to go to her grandfather, to see him, hold his hand, hear his voice. *Tell me what to do, Grandpa. If this had to happen to me, why couldn't you have stayed here to tell me what to do!*

She started toward the casket when something stopped her. Some slight noise just outside the door, a footfall so soft, she wasn't certain if she'd actually heard it or only sensed it. Panic stabbed through her—fears of restless phantoms—and, though she told herself she was being irrational, she ducked down behind a chair and held her breath.

The footsteps entered . . . paused . . . and passed her by. Summoning all her courage, she forced herself to look out around the chair.

Etienne.

He was standing alone beside the casket. Just standing there with his arms at his sides and his head bowed. The tension that had gripped him earlier was gone; now his shoulders sagged, and his whole body seemed tired. As Miranda watched from her hidden place, her heart cried.

"Jonas," he whispered. Again, a sound so soft, Miranda wondered if he'd even spoken aloud. "I had to come one more time, yeah? Say good-bye . . . say thank you . . ."

Etienne's voice broke. Stepping slowly forward, he slid his

hands across the top of the casket and rested his face against the polished wood. The words he murmured were hushed and foreign and filled with pain. His body shook with silent tears.

"Our secret," he choked then, drawing a deep, unsteady breath. "You saved me, Jonas. I'll keep our pact, I swear. I'll never tell . . . I'll never forget."

A muffled sob escaped him. And then, everything went completely still, as though the aftermath of his sorrow had spread a gentle calm throughout the room. Overcome by what she'd just witnessed, Miranda could scarcely keep her own emotions under control. She sank lower out of sight, and when she looked again, Etienne was gone.

Oh, Etienne . . . I'm so sorry . . .

More determinedly this time, she walked to the casket. She straightened the roses on top, and ran her fingertips lightly over the lid. She could feel wet streaks there from Etienne's tears, but after a brief hesitation, she left them where they were.

What is it, Grandpa? The pact you and Etienne made? The secret you two kept? And what did you save him from? For it was clear to her now that whatever connection her grandfather and Etienne shared went far deeper and was far more important than she'd imagined.

Closing her eyes, Miranda conjured up her grandfather's face, the kindly face from her cherished photograph. *I need you, Grandpa. I've always needed you. Only now I need you more than ever, and it's too late.*

She realized then that she was waiting for him to answer—

expecting him to answer as she strained her ears so desperately through the silence, as her thoughts groped so pleadingly in every direction. *Wanting* him to speak to her, but terrified as well; craving something that only he could give her—peace, closure, a gentle word of confirmation—yet, at the same time, *willing* him to prove her wrong.

"Miranda? Honey, let's go home."

Whirling around, Miranda saw her mother and Aunt Teeta in the doorway. As Teeta began to cry, Mom automatically braced her in a hug.

"I'm being silly." Aunt Teeta tried to smile through the tears. "I just hate leaving Daddy behind like this. I hate to think of him being here, all alone in the dark."

"But he's not really here." Though Mom's voice was strong, Miranda heard a tremor below the surface. "You and I both know he's finally at peace. He's gone on to a better place. Where it's never dark, and there's Mother and lots of other people who love him."

Aunt Teeta listened and seemed comforted. With one arm pressed firmly against Teeta's back, Mom steered her toward the front door. "Miranda, are you coming?"

"Another minute, Mom."

"Sure, honey, take your time. We'll be in the car."

Miranda waited till they'd walked away, till they'd spoken quietly with the funeral director, who glanced back at her with an understanding nod, showed the two women out, and politely disappeared. Once more she turned to the casket. Her breath was coming faster, and her heart gave a curious flutter in her chest.

"This is what you meant, isn't it, Grandpa?" she whispered. "What Mom just said—*this* is what it's all about . . ."

Images rushed back at her—vivid scenes and conversations, words and pictures overlapping and blocking out everything else.

She shut her eyes tightly to ward them off, but they grew only more insistent. *Grandpa at the Falls . . . Grandpa so sick in his room . . . the Gray Soldier standing by my bed—"Listen . . . help them . . . don't turn them away."*

"Oh, Grandpa . . ."

"Listen, Miranda . . . watch . . ."

"Grandpa?"

She knew it was him. Here in this empty viewing room, in this deserted funeral parlor, in this vast and eternal silence of death, she knew his voice, and she felt the gentleness of his smile.

"Listen, Miranda . . . watch . . ."

"I hear you," she whispered. "And you *are* in a better place, aren't you? You're *not* alone, just like Mom said. But all those others—" She broke off tearfully, then drew a deep breath. "All those others who can't find what you've found—peace, and someone to love them, and a place to go home to, and how to get there . . ."

How to get there . . .

The air stirred softly behind her. For a split second, Miranda could almost swear that a hand had touched her shoulder, coaxing the next solemn words from her mouth.

"It's *me*, Grandpa. *I'm* how they'll get there."

20

"HONEY, you don't have to be at the funeral tomorrow, you know."

Back at the house again, Miranda and her mother had taken refuge in the kitchen. While her mom sorted listlessly through all the food, Miranda sat at the table, cradling her head on folded arms.

"I know. But I want to be there for you and Aunt Teeta. And Grandpa."

Mom smiled at that. "Your aunt Teeta's better, she really is. She just needed to get her grief out of the way."

Get her grief out of the way. Is that even possible? Can you ever really get it out of the way, or does it just hide someplace deep inside you, ready to crawl out again when you least expect it?

"Mom, do you think Aunt Teeta would mind if I went through some of Grandpa's things in the attic?"

Mom looked surprised. "Goodness, why in the world would you want to go through that old stuff?"

"Mrs. Wilmington at the museum said he kept really good records of everything he collected. We thought we might find something to help with our project."

"Of course I don't mind!" Aunt Teeta appeared in the doorway, wrapped in her chenille bathrobe, with kitty slippers on her feet. She seemed almost her jolly self again, though her face still looked tired. "You just help yourself to whatever you need up there. I'll probably end up donating all that stuff to the museum. I don't want anything old or depressing in this house anymore."

Mom looked amused. "You wouldn't be talking about Daddy, would you?"

"Well . . ." Reaching for the teakettle, Aunt Teeta couldn't help chuckling. "He *was* pretty old and depressing, bless his heart. But I'm going to miss him all the same."

Mom didn't respond to that. Miranda reached out and touched her mother's hand.

"All your friends are welcome here, darlin'," Aunt Teeta asssured her niece. "It'll be good to have young people in the house. It needs some laughter and enthusiasm and fresh ideas."

"You'll love Ashley, then," Miranda told her. "I wish I had her enthusiasm."

"I wish you had Etienne Boucher. But that Gage is awful cute, too." Winking, Aunt Teeta picked up her mug of mint tea and started for the stairs. "I'm off to bed, dear ones. Sleep tight."

Mom gave Miranda a teasing look. "What's all this about Etienne Boucher? Teeta seems awfully determined to get you two together."

"He's just a guy at school. In my study group. It's nothing." Then, as Mom lifted an eyebrow, Miranda added, "He's the guy who fixed our air conditioner."

"I like him already. Who's Gage?"

"His cousin. And I'm not getting together with anyone."

"You don't have to convince *me*, honey." She pointed to the counter covered with leftovers. "Potato casserole?"

In spite of herself, Miranda couldn't help but laugh. "No potato casserole."

"Ham? Jell-O salad?"

"No, I just want—" *I just want to talk to you about what's going on in my life. About Grandpa. About the things he needs me to do, now that he's gone.*

But of course she couldn't. Not now . . . probably not ever. Not after all the baggage left over from Mom's childhood, not with all the burdens on Mom's shoulders. For the first time it was beginning to dawn on Miranda what her grandfather had meant, how alone she would be with this gift she'd never asked for or expected.

"Baked beans?" Mom was staring at her. "Buttermilk pie?"

Again Miranda laughed. "No food. Just sleep. See you in the morning."

Wearily she made her way to the third floor, changed into pajamas, and climbed into bed—but she couldn't shut off her mind. Along with all the questions, there was now a new and very real sense of responsibility that she found both disturbing and comforting. *What do I do? How will I know? And how should I do it?* Oddly enough, when the screams came that night, they seemed more sad to her than frightening. And when she finally dozed off, it wasn't a cry that woke her, but the soft sound of a footstep.

"Psst. You awake, *cher*?"

Miranda fought her way up from sleep. "I am now." Annoyance gave way to relief. She wondered why she wasn't more startled; it was almost as if she'd expected Etienne to show up. "What do you think you're doing?"

"Well, you musta been wishing for me, yeah?" he teased. "'Cause here I am."

Switching on the lamp, Miranda solemnly patted the edge of the bed. "Sit down. We need to talk."

"Awww, don't be mad now. I just—"

"I know. You wanted to check on me. And I'm glad—I'm glad you came."

"Good. 'Cause I also wanted to leave you this." Holding out his hand, he showed her the braided watch chain. "Look, I know how you feel about it, but I really think you should be keeping it with you. Just in case you pick up on something, yeah?"

Miranda instantly recoiled. *But this is part of it. This is part of what I have to do.* Taking a deep breath, she pointed reluctantly to the dresser.

"Put it in the drawer. I don't want to look at it." As Etienne did so, her voice tightened. "Something happened tonight, Etienne. And I need to tell you."

Pausing a moment, he scanned her face with narrowed eyes. Then he lowered himself beside her.

"Something's changed, hasn't it, *cher*?" he murmured.

"Yes."

"And you've changed with it."

And then she told him. About her feelings at the funeral

home, her sadness and sense of loss, her sudden and over-whelming revelation of purpose, and hearing her grandfather's voice. Everything but having hidden and watched and eaves-dropped on his own personal sorrow. When she'd gotten it all out, neither of them spoke. He'd moved closer to her, and, for the moment, it made her feel safe.

"You know what I keep wondering?" Miranda's tone went even more serious. "I keep wondering if all those spirits think *I'm* the one who's lost."

That not-quite-smile brushed his lips. "We're all a little lost. We're all trying to find something."

Miranda considered this. "I know you and Grandpa tried to tell me before. About my gift . . . and how I can do so much good with it. But tonight—for the first time—it was *real* to me. Like I finally *got* it. Like it finally all made sense."

"Sometimes we can be hearing the same stuff over and over again, yeah? And we know it's true, we know it *there*"—Etienne lightly tapped her forehead—"but what matters is when we finally know it *here*." As he touched his heart, she couldn't help giving a wan smile.

"The weird thing is . . . I'm okay with it. I mean, I'm still sort of scared . . . but I'm okay."

"You've always been okay, *cher*. Way more than okay."

As her cheeks flushed, she hoped he hadn't noticed. "How am I ever going to know all the stuff I need to know? I mean, I need to learn *everything*."

"Tonight?" Etienne kept a perfectly straight face. "I'm not sure I'm up to it."

Miranda's stare was deliberately reproachful. "This is about Nathan. He needs me. *Now.*"

Groaning softly, Etienne lay back, pillowing his arms beneath his head. "I can see I'm gonna have to be humoring you. So what do you wanna talk about?"

"Why spirits stay earthbound."

"For a lotta reasons. Attachments. To certain people. Or places. Or things they can't let go of."

"Because they're sad. Or angry."

"Maybe they want revenge."

"Or they have unfinished business. Or they're afraid to leave, because it's familiar and they were happy."

"Or maybe 'cause they don't know they're dead."

"It makes sense, doesn't it?" Tucking her hair behind her ears, Miranda stared into the shadows. "Like in war. All those soldiers who never expected to die. All of them caught up in such intense emotions."

"Fear. Grief."

"Most of them probably died so fast, there wasn't time to think. There wasn't time to realize what happened to them." Her face grew pensive. She recalled what Mom had said about Dad. "What would that be like: Here one second, and gone the next? Would you feel surprise? Shock? How long would it take you to know you'd actually died?"

"Your *grand-père*, he said their concept of time's not the same as ours. Maybe to them, a century's the same as a day. Maybe to them, time doesn't exist at all. And they have to keep doing the same things over and over again. And nothing ever changes, nothing ever gets fixed."

Miranda thought back. In her mind she could see Nathan's ravaged face; she could see the hopelessness in his eyes.

"I don't know how any of these spirits—or the people they once were—can survive the pain they're in."

"You'd be surprised what people can survive," Etienne murmured. "When they have to."

Something about the way he said it caught at her heart. She lowered her pillow and started to reach for him, but he was already off the bed, moving swiftly and silently toward the dark, open doorway to the sunporch.

"Etienne, what—"

"Ssh," he hissed at her. "Something's out there."

21

MIRANDA FROZE WHERE SHE SAT. As Etienne slid into the shadows beside the door, she caught the quick movement of his left hand—the glint of something sharp.

"Well." Parker grinned, creeping slowly across the threshold. "This is cozy!"

A stream of undecipherable words burst from Etienne's mouth. Parker immediately looked offended.

"Hey, I don't have a clue what you just said to me, but it wasn't very polite."

"Good way to get yourself killed," Etienne muttered.

Parker stared at him, incredulous. "Is that your *knife*? You were actually going to *stab* me?"

"Knife?" Miranda echoed. Startled, she craned her neck for a better view, but as suddenly as it had appeared, Etienne's knife had vanished.

"I told you not to sneak up on him. You know he always has that hunting knife when he's not in school." Behind Parker, Roo poked her head in. "Hey, mind if we join you?"

As Parker, Roo, Ashley, and Gage crowded into the room, Etienne threw up his hands, turned his back, and continued his muttering. Miranda could only stare in disbelief. Roo was barefoot, wearing baggy pajama bottoms and a St. Yvette High jersey; Ashley had on a long robe and tennis shoes. Both girls were carrying food, and Parker and Gage held flashlights, which they'd switched off.

"Sleepover!" Ashley giggled while Parker pressed a finger to her lips.

"Ssh! This is a covert operation! You want to wake everybody up?"

Miranda didn't know whether to laugh or be upset. For the time being, her discussion with Etienne was on hold. "*What* is going on?"

"Etienne told Gage he might stop by here tonight." Parker's grin widened. "We're not interrupting anything, are we?"

Etienne frowned at his cousin. Gage returned it with an innocent shrug.

"That's right," Ashley picked up. "So we figured, why should y'all have all the fun?"

"Ashley brought chips," Roo added, then brandished a greasy paper bag. "I made popcorn."

Leaning toward Gage, Parker mumbled, "She can't ruin popcorn, can she?"

"I wouldn't bet on it," Gage mumbled back.

Miranda was still trying to process the intrusion. "Just tell me one thing—how do you guys get away with sneaking out at night? My mom would have a fit!"

"Right." Parker's grin turned scornful. "Like *my* mom and dad ever know if I'm there or not."

Ashley was totally unconcerned. "Oh, we just tell them we're going to the tree house. They never check on us there."

"What's the tree house?" Miranda wanted to know.

"Well, when we were little, Gage's daddy built a tree house for the three of us in his backyard. We used to have a secret club. And we'd play over there, and hide from people, and pretend we were knights in a castle."

"Gage and I were knights," Roo corrected her. "*You* always had to be rescued."

"Well, I liked the way Gage threw me over his shoulder and carried me down from the tower."

"Gage did that?" Clasping his hands over his heart, Parker sighed. "My hero."

Gage ignored him.

"We used to camp out in that tree house at night." Ashley nibbled a potato chip. "In fact, we *still* like sleeping together over there."

Parker wiggled his eyebrows and gave Miranda a stage whisper. "Very kinky."

"Oh, for heaven's sake, Parker—not *that* kind of sleeping together." Ashley paused for a second. "It *is* just Gage, after all."

Gage stared at her. "What's *that* supposed to mean?"

"Oh, nothing." Ashley plopped down on the bed next to Miranda. "Just that we love and respect you so much, we wouldn't *dream* of taking advantage of you."

"Sometimes *I* dream of you two taking advantage of him," Parker said seriously. "It's one of my favorite fantasies."

Gage tried unsuccessfully not to look embarrassed. "You need a life."

"So what's on the agenda for tonight?" Ashley asked.

Miranda couldn't keep from laughing. Although she and Marge and Joanie had done lots of spur-of-the-moment things together back in Florida, nothing could compare to the surprises from this crazy bunch. She realized she was starting to get used to—and even enjoy—these unexpected adventures.

"Popcorn, anybody?" Roo opened the paper bag and held it out. Parker immediately backed away. "Uh . . . I pass."

"Y'all keep it quiet," Etienne warned.

He'd positioned himself near the door of the sunporch, while Parker sat beside Ashley, and Gage claimed the rocking chair. Roo sank cross-legged to the floor near Etienne's feet, her back propped on a pillow that Miranda tossed down to her. They could all hear the TV blaring and Aunt Teeta snoring from the rooms below.

"Well, as long as we're all here," Miranda began, while Parker let out a prolonged groan.

"Uh-oh, I sense drama."

"Impossible," Roo said offhandedly. "You *have* no sense."

"This might be a good time to talk about our project?" Miranda continued. "How's the research going?"

"Oh! Me first!" Waving her arm, Ashley gave an excited little squirm. "You know how the museum and those shops on both sides of it are all attached to each other? Well, Parker's mom said they all used to be just one big building!"

The others waited. When Ashley merely sat there beaming at them, Parker drew back in exaggerated surprise.

"Wow! That's really fascinating, Ash!"

"No, that's not the fascinating part." Ashley looked slightly offended. "I haven't gotten to that yet."

"Then hurry and *get* to that part. The suspense is killing us."

"The building used to be a club. Like a private gentlemen's club. Except upstairs, that's where they'd meet their mistresses."

Parker smacked a hand to his forehead. "Hookers! Damn! And I took the courthouse!"

"*Not* prostitutes." Another offended look from Ashley. "*Mistresses*. It's not just about sex, you know. There's a very big difference."

"Is that the sad part?" Parker asked.

Ashley continued, undaunted. "I found out there was a murder in one of those upstairs rooms. That when a very rich plantation owner wanted to end the relationship with his mistress, she stabbed him to death. In bed."

Calmly munching her popcorn, Roo gave a supportive thumbs-up.

"And the drugstore next door to the museum? People who work there say they've heard *moaning* at night in one of those storage rooms on the second floor."

The boys traded glances.

"And this moaning," Parker said, straight-faced, "did it come *before* or *after* the guy was stabbed?"

"*Any*way," Ashley concluded," that's what I've got so far."

Noting her sister's outstretched hand, Roo obligingly relinquished the popcorn. "Did y'all know that furniture makers ran some of the first funeral homes? Because they were the ones who built the coffins?"

"Fascinating." Parker was all dignified solemnity. "And such a grave undertaking." He ducked as Ashley's popcorn sailed at his head.

"I know embalming really got its start during the Civil War," Gage spoke up. "With all those dead soldiers sent home to their families, the bodies had to be preserved."

Nodding, Roo stretched out her legs, frowned at her toes, then sat cross-legged again. "So my two buildings are the funeral parlor and the doctor's house. But when I started finding stuff on Dr. Fuller, I started finding stuff about an epidemic, too. I mean, they *called* it an epidemic, but nobody knew what was causing it."

"And when was this?"

"Around nineteen hundred. The statistics were unbelievable, so many people died. And lots of them were children."

Parker automatically grabbed a tissue off the nightstand and gave it to Ashley.

"Did they ever figure it out?" Gage asked.

"Not really. The research kept saying how Dr. Fuller was so dedicated, he had all those patients to take care of, he was trying to identify the epidemic, he was trying to find a cure. But so many patients kept dying, the funeral parlor could hardly keep up. There were funerals going on practically all the time."

"So did the doctor end up dying?" With a sad sigh, Ashley rested her head on Parker's shoulder. "And did the undertaker end up dying? Whatever that disease was, it must have been really contagious."

"That's what I thought, too. But Dr. Fuller and Mr. McGrail

lived to be very old men. Which leads me to a theory." Roo paused, one eyebrow raised. "What if my buildings had this really sinister connection? Dr. Fuller poisoned his patients, Mr. McGrail did the funerals, then the two of them split the profits?"

"I bet you're right." Ashley's sadness gave way to indignation. "That totally creeps me out."

Roo looked mildly gratified. "So what about your voodoo, Boucher?"

Arms folded over his chest, Etienne leaned lazily against the wall. "Mama, she had me go talk to my *tante* Bernadette—she's my *grand-mère's* sister. And she's about a hundred years old."

"She's great." Gage laughed softly. "She tells the best stories."

"Yeah, well, she remembers some of that voodoo around here. In fact, she *saw* some of those wild parties going on back in the bayou. And that house on the west side of the Brickway, where the antique shop is now? There was a cook who worked there way back then—an old lady named Dominique, all heavy into voodoo. She had herself a secret place in the attic, and some pretty high-class clients sneaking over there to see her. My *tante* Bernadette, she says you never wanted to eat any of Dominique's cooking—you never knew what kinda spell she might be putting on you."

"Oooh." Ashley gave a delicious shiver. "This is going to be the *best* tour! Gage, you go next."

"No problems researching the church," Gage replied. "They keep records of just about everything. There's almost *too* much information—it's hard to narrow it all down. But I'm sort of leaning toward these old manuscripts Father Paul told me about. They were handwritten by French monks and brought over here by some of the earliest missionaries. Could be some good stuff in those."

Roo took the potato chip bag from Miranda and passed it on. "Okay, Parker. Enrapture us once again with your dullness."

"You mean, my evil courthouse." Giving a mock shudder, Parker lounged comfortably back on the bed. "Evil judge. Unfair convictions. Botched hangings. Judge swings from rafters and dies a slow, painful death. Judge gets exactly what he deserves. Nothing we don't already know."

Ashley was clearly annoyed. "That's it?"

"What else do you want?"

"Some historical facts would be nice."

"Like what?"

"Well, tell us something about the prisoners. What kinds of crimes did they commit?"

"I don't know anything about the prisoners. Why would I need to know that?"

"Parker!"

"Come on, crime is crime. You got murder. Stealing. Murder. Treason. Murder. Oh, and did I mention murder?"

"That's incredibly historical." Roo's stare was bland. "And incredibly descriptive. Wow. I feel like I was there."

Parker grimaced. "Okay, fine. Let me run through the prisoners for you. Murderers. Thieves. Murderers. Spies. Murderers. Oh, and did I happen to mention killers, too?"

Frowning, Ashley shook her finger at him. "I will say this one more time. If you mess up our project—"

"Miranda!" Parker broke in quickly. "Update us on your dashing, see-through soldier!"

"Parker Wilmington, shame on you. Don't call him that. And Miranda has enough on her shoulders right now without you being so insensitive."

"I'm not being insensitive. All I said was—"

"Actually," Miranda interrupted, "I *have* been thinking about Nathan. And I've had some ideas."

She was the sole focus of attention now. As the room grew expectantly quiet, she tried to organize all the thoughts scrambling in her brain.

"I keep thinking about what he said." Miranda addressed the five rapt faces. "'No, you're wrong' and 'I swear to you, for the love of God' and 'I'm the one you want, only me.' Like he was really trying to convince someone. Like he really wanted someone to believe him."

"You!" Ashley exclaimed. "He wanted *you* to believe him!"

"No, I don't think so. It wasn't like in the park—I *knew* he was talking to me then. But those other times, he was definitely talking to someone else—and I was only hearing *his* side of the conversation."

"So what does that have to do with what happened in the park?"

"That's my point. I think it has *everything* to do with what happened in the park."

In possession of her popcorn once more, Roo dug absentmindedly through the bag. "Sounds to me like he's confessing."

"Or defending someone?" A frown settled between Miranda's brows.

"More than that," Etienne offered. "Protecting somebody."

"And maybe taking the blame for something he didn't really do."

Shrugging, Gage slowly swept his hair back from his forehead. "Sacrificing himself?"

Roo nodded. "Yeah. To defend and protect and save somebody else."

"He was suffering," Miranda recalled, while Parker promptly rolled his eyes.

"Not such a stretch, O Psychic One. The guy *did* have a bullet hole in him."

Miranda disregarded the comment. "No . . . before that, I mean. Some kind of punishment. His throat was raw, and his lips were all cracked. He could taste his own blood. And he really needed water."

"Bar fight and hangover. Mystery solved."

"I think he was being tortured."

"By who?" As Ashley gasped in horror, Etienne began pacing the length of the room.

"Prisoner of war?" he mumbled. "Makes sense."

"It does," Miranda agreed. "Maybe he had important information the Yankees wanted. And he wouldn't talk—he wouldn't betray the Confederacy."

"The Union army *did take* St. Yvette," Gage reasoned. "And there's documented accounts of how bad some prisoners were treated."

For a brief moment, Miranda looked down and clenched her pillow tighter. *Yes . . . yes . . . I've heard how they were treated . . . I've heard their cries, their screams . . .*

"Oh, poor Nathan." Ashley's voice caught. "I can't stand to think of people being mean to him."

Parker clutched his head with both hands. "For Christ's sake, Ashley. You're doing it again. You're talking about that imaginary guy like he's real."

"Of course he's real. Miranda saw him. And we all saw the braid he gave her."

"So he was tortured and then killed?" Still pacing, Etienne glanced at Miranda. She'd sunk deep into thought, unaware the room had grown quiet. "Miranda?"

Something . . . something . . . not quite right . . . As Miranda slowly raised her eyes to Etienne's, he came to a stop. "I don't know. I'm not sure."

"What about?"

"The way we're putting it together."

"Well, Miss Ellena has to come in there somewhere." Gage tried to be helpful. "We know she and Nathan had some kind of connection. And he did want you to get a message to her—"

"But I still feel like we're missing something."

Parker's scowl swept the faces around him. "Yeah, your minds. Your sanity. Should I go on?"

"Yes, go on," Roo said dryly. "Go right on out that door."

"Actually, we should *all* be going out that door." Checking his watch, Gage immediately stood up. "It's getting late. And tomorrow . . ."

None of them mentioned the funeral. Even after everyone had left, Miranda tried not to think about what the next day might bring.

Something more ... something I'm not quite getting ...

But it was there. She knew it was there, so close, just beyond her grasp.

Something important ...

Something unexpected ...

A tragic secret only she could discover.

22

THE NEXT MORNING COULDN'T HAVE BEEN MORE DREARY.
The sky was overcast, the air thick with the promise of rain.
A hot, restless wind scattered broken leaves and crushed petals
around the casket. Thunder growled low in the distance, and the
mourners looked as wilted as the flowers.

Perfect, Miranda thought glumly as she and Mom and
Aunt Teeta sat beneath the canopy beside the gravesite. *Perfect
weather for a funeral.*

But her new friends had come, just as they'd promised. She
spotted them standing respectfully toward the back of the huge
crowd, and she wondered why she suddenly felt sentimental,
watching them. She'd known them only a few days, yet it seemed
a lifetime. Already—for so many reasons—she felt closer to
them than she ever had to Marge and Joanie.

With the service ending and people drifting away, she
longed to escape—with Parker and Ashley, Roo and Gage and
Etienne—back to school, back to noise and laughter and chaos.
As the group approached, she was overcome with emotions.
When Etienne laid a flower on her grandfather's casket, she
nearly broke down.

"Hey," Gage whispered, wrapping her in a hug. His eyes were

so gentle, so compassionate. He slid his fingers beneath her chin and tilted her face toward his. "It'll all be okay. You'll see."

She knew the others were watching. Embarrassed, she lowered her head, but Gage's arm was still around her, keeping her close. Even Etienne's face had a certain tenderness about it; he seemed glad that Gage was consoling her.

It struck her, then, the irony of her grandfather's passing. The end of one chapter, the start of another. Jonas Hayes had fulfilled his legacy; now he'd passed the torch on to her. And Miranda's new life was not merely with the living now . . . but with the dead, as well.

"We'll see you later," Gage whispered. Releasing her, he stepped away and smiled, showing a dimple in one cheek.

Miranda smiled back. "Thanks so much, you guys. Thanks for helping me get through this."

"Always," Ashley replied, and waved to her while they headed for Parker's car.

Miranda was exhausted by afternoon.

She'd hoped that after the funeral, the constant flow of visitors might stop—but it seemed to get only worse. More food kept arriving, and more people filled the house, spilling out onto the veranda, the front and back lawns. But Miranda had had her fill of death. All she wanted now was to get away from everyone and everything, and with so many distractions, she figured no one would miss her.

Slipping up to her room, she closed the door, changed her

clothes, and stretched out across the bed. She hadn't planned on falling asleep, but when she lifted her head from the pillows, it was almost six o'clock.

Their company had gone. When Miranda went to the living room, she found Aunt Teeta snoring in the recliner and Mom asleep on the couch, the TV shut off. *Why don't you sleep in a bed anymore, Mom? Do these walls and closed doors scare you? Old, dark memories of this house? But the past is over; you and Aunt Teeta and I are together. Things will be better for you now.*

Starting upstairs again, she suddenly remembered the attic. This was a perfect time to look through some more of her grandpa's things, to see if she could find any information on St. Yvette or that old photograph of the Gray Soldier. After a brief search, she located the attic door and made her way up a narrow flight of steps to a landing.

It opened onto a large, low-ceilinged space—the very kind Ashley would love. Stale and musty and swelteringly hot. Mysterious beneath deep shadows and heavy layers of dust. Bathed in a jaundiced glow from the old, yellowed shades at the windows. There was even a dressmaker's dummy.

Miranda picked her way cautiously through a maze of boxes, bags, trunks, and suitcases; piles of outdated magazines and newspapers; rusty file cabinets; wooden crates; claw-legged furniture draped with dirty sheets; paintings and portraits shoved back into corners. But Mrs. Wilmington had been right about one thing—nearly every item was labeled with a concise, hand-written description. Intrigued, Miranda raised a window shade, pulled one of the cartons into a shaft of dim light, and sat down to explore its contents.

Here was photo after photo of southerners posed in their best finery; plantations and gardens; quaint shops and markets and modest antebellum homes; an eclectic assortment of buildings. But there were many other pictures, as well—the grim realities of war. Maimed and mangled soldiers, ravaged by disease, wrapped in dirty bandages. Row after row of corpses—unknown, unidentified, unclaimed. Amputations, grim surgeons at work, field hospitals, embalmings. Stockades and armed guards; weary prisoners, sunken-eyed, emaciated skeletons in filthy, ragged clothes . . .

Miranda frowned. It was getting hard to breathe with all this dust. Distractedly, she ran a hand back through her hair; cobwebs clung to her fingers, and she choked back a sneeze. *Something . . . something . . .* Shadows were beginning to lengthen through the uncovered window and around the grimy edges of the window shades. *Damn—what is it? What's missing?* She didn't want to be up here anymore, yet she couldn't shake the feeling that whatever she was looking for was beckoning again, practically within reach. Here somewhere, hidden among all these old things. *Why can't I figure it out?*

Frustrated, she gathered up the photographs and crammed them back in the box. No pictures of Nathan. No pictures of Ellena Rose. No pictures of Hayes House the way it used to be. Just that nagging sense of being so close, *so close,* to some sort of answer . . .

Without warning, her whole body went rigid. She could swear she'd seen a movement just then, from the corner of her eye. An ever-so-subtle movement near one of the windows, where dust motes hovered in the air like waves of heat over a summer road. For a second she could even swear those ripples of dust had taken on human form . . .

"It *is* you, isn't it?" she murmured. "What do you want?"

But he didn't speak aloud this time. His mouth hung open in a silent plea, his stare was without hope. And as one empty hand reached out to her, she heard the anguished crying from his heart. "*Take it . . . the rose . . . help me . . .*"

Miranda shut her eyes. Slowly, cautiously, she focused on his presence, his nearness, his tenuous reality. Pain flowed out from him in waves. She was aware of her own senses sharpening, just as they had at the gallery that day—curious, open, accepting. *You know, don't you? You know I'm trying to help you.*

A current passed between them.

An understanding so powerful, it took her breath away.

She opened her eyes to look at him again, but he was gone.

You came to me in the park because that was your battle-field . . .

Trembling, she set down the box of photographs. She leaned heavily against the wall and gazed at the spot where Nathan's ghost had just disappeared, her thoughts still trying to follow him.

But the first time I heard your voice, I was in the apartment over the garage. And then you came to me in my bedroom. And now here to the attic . . .

Why here?

Miranda got quickly to her feet. Images and emotions swept through her, and she welcomed them, invited them. In her mind she could see the photograph—the one from the museum—Nathan and his comrades posed in front of a much older and much different Hayes House.

Hayes House . . .

It was more than just having your picture taken, wasn't it? There was something else that tied you to this house—a connection so much stronger than a photograph.

Scarcely able to contain her excitement, she headed for the stairs.

You spent time here. There were things you had to do: important things . . . hidden things . . . secret things . . .

Deep, dark, dangerous secrets . . .

And because of those secrets, you died.

23

BACK IN HER ROOM AGAIN, Miranda waited impatiently for Mom and Aunt Teeta to wake from their naps. When she finally heard signs of life downstairs, she found both of them busy in the kitchen—Mom washing dishes, Aunt Teeta fussing over several potted plants that had been delivered earlier. Miranda decided not to mention Hayes House in front of her mother. Instead, she waited till Aunt Teeta went out to the veranda, then sat down with her in the porch swing.

"Aunt Teeta, I was going through one of those boxes in the attic—"

"Oh, that's just fine, darlin'." Fanning herself with a magazine, Aunt Teeta scooted sideways to give Miranda more room. "Did you find anything y'all could use for your project?"

"There's so much up there. Did Grandpa really collect all that stuff?"

"Every bit of it. Treasure hunting—that's what he always called it—treasure hunting always made him so happy."

A smile lit Aunt Teeta's face, then began to fade. "Well . . . till near the end, anyway. He seemed different . . . not as enthused about it. Not as satisfied. And he was so tired."

Miranda thought of that day at the Falls . . . her grandfather's erratic behavior . . . the confessions he'd made. "Do you know why? I mean, did he ever give you any reasons?"

"He never talked about himself much. He suffered from these . . . dark moods from time to time. But this wasn't the same."

Dark moods. Miranda remembered that midnight discussion with Mom, those stories about Grandpa's moods. She decided to play innocent and let the remark pass.

"Maybe I should have paid more attention," her aunt reflected. "Made him rest more . . . forced him to take better care of himself . . ."

"From what I've heard about Grandpa, nobody could force him to do anything."

"Well, you're certainly right about that. And your mama's just like him, but don't you ever tell her I said that, 'cause I'll deny it till the day I die." Giving a conspiratorial wink, Aunt Teeta began to laugh—that deep, merry laugh that everyone loved. After a few seconds of uncontrolled hilarity, she caught her breath and dabbed at her eyes.

"Oh mercy, that felt good. And you know what, darlin'? *You* remind me of your grandpa, too. Funny—I can't quite put my finger on it, but it's there, all right. In a really *good* way."

As Aunt Teeta wrapped both arms around her, Miranda nestled into her hug. *I wish I could tell you, Aunt Teeta. I think you'd understand . . .*

But now was not the time. And when Aunt Teeta finally pulled away, her face had gone thoughtful once more.

"You know, honey, maybe after all these years, your grandpa's hobby just got to be too much for him. More work than fun. Maybe he should have given it up a long time ago."

But he couldn't, Aunt Teeta. And it did get to be too much for him, but he still couldn't. Not till he found me.

He was waiting for me. He'd always been waiting for me.

It was another realization that struck to the core of her being. Miranda fumbled to change the subject.

"Aunt Teeta, do you know if Hayes House was ever anything else?"

"What do you mean, darlin'?"

"Since it was first built, has it ever been anything else besides a house?"

Leaning her head back, Aunt Teeta wrinkled her brow in deep thought. "No, it was always just a house, as far as I know. But way back when, one of your grandmas *did* take in boarders here for a while. Especially during the Civil War, with so many people coming in and out of town and not enough places to put them up. It worked out good for everybody—she loved to cook, and I'm sure the extra money came in handy. And folks could board their horses, too, out in her barn."

"There was a barn?" Miranda's pulse quickened. *Nathan with those two beautiful horses . . .*

"Well, not since *I've* lived here, but I know I've seen a picture or two somewhere. A barn . . . or maybe stables. I can't imagine what happened to those old pictures, though. Your grandpa kept track of all that."

"But the barn—stables—were here?"

"Out back behind the house. Of course, the property was much bigger then. Hayes land has been sold off little by little through the years."

"Did any famous people ever stay at the boardinghouse?"

"Hmmm. *That* I couldn't tell you."

"Maybe there was a guest book? Or a ledger? Old receipts, things like that?"

"Oh, honey, if there were, then they'd be somewhere in all your grandpa's stuff. Either here or at the museum. I wouldn't have the slightest idea where to look."

Miranda couldn't recall seeing any of those items at the museum. But she hadn't really been looking for them—and hadn't Mrs. Wilmington said the exhibits were changed on a regular basis?

"Back then, it was common for travelers to stay over at plantations." Frowning, Aunt Teeta rolled up her magazine to swat at a mosquito. "Of course, the hotel was more convenient for business in town, but there were only so many rooms, and not everybody could afford the prices. Lots of times, local families handled the overflow. Good ole southern hospitality— I don't imagine they'd have turned anybody away."

Just what Mrs. Wilmington said. Miranda's thoughts were jumping again, bouncing from one possibility to another. "So someone famous *could* have stayed here."

Her persistence seemed to amuse Aunt Teeta. "Anybody *could* have stayed here. Or *eaten* here. Or *slept* here. Or kept their horses and *carriages* here. Goodness, is this all part of your research?"

"We need all the information we can get." Deliberately evasive, Miranda looked up to see her mother smiling at them from the doorway.

"I've got bacon and eggs," Mom announced. "For whoever's hungry."

The porch swing stopped. Aunt Teeta lifted her arms, a comical hallelujah.

"That's the best news I've heard all day! I'm so tired of funeral food, I could scream." Then, a little guiltily, she added, "Though the intentions *were* kind and generous."

As Aunt Teeta stood up, Miranda headed quickly for the front steps. "Go on and eat without me, you guys. I won't be long."

"Miranda?" Mom was surprised. "You didn't tell me you were meeting your friends tonight."

"I'm not meeting them. I just want to take a walk."

"Now? Alone? Honey, it's nearly dark—"

"Oh, let her go," Aunt Teeta scolded, motioning Miranda to make a run for it. "She'll be fine. It's perfectly safe around here."

"Yeah, Mom." Miranda couldn't resist. "It's a small town, remember?"

Mom knew when she'd lost the battle. "Two against one— that hardly seems fair."

Relieved, Miranda watched her mother and aunt close the screen door behind them. She was halfway down the steps when she heard the door creak open again, and Aunt Teeta's voice unexpectedly stopped her.

"I'm sorry, darlin'—but something just came to me."

Miranda turned around. Aunt Teeta was standing at the edge of the veranda, her expression vaguely distressed. While an uncomfortable silence stretched out between them, Miranda felt a stab of alarm.

"Aunt Teeta, what's wrong?"

Her aunt roused. She fixed Miranda with troubled eyes and spoke hesitantly. "I was thinking about our talk. When you asked me about your grandpa—why he was so different near the end. I said I didn't know, and that's true. Only . . ."

Miranda's heart gave a sudden lurch. "Only what?"

"He brought something home a few weeks back. Something he'd found on one of his treasure hunts. And after that . . . well, it might be my imagination, or it might be nothing at all. But that *really* affected him. Like he got restless and depressed at the same time. Researching for hours and hours, exploring till way past dark."

"What was it?" Miranda could hardly keep her voice level. "What did he bring home?"

"I have no idea. But he was truly obsessed with it."

"Do you know where it is? Did he store it somewhere?"

Her aunt gave a helpless shrug. "All I can say for sure is that he *wouldn't* have thrown it away. He never threw *anything* away."

"Then do you at least remember where he found it?"

"I'm pretty sure it was at the Falls. He went back there a lot after that." Aunt Teeta's expression grew sad. "And you know, when I think about it now, it was almost like he knew he was running out of time."

24

IT'S CLOSER.

Whatever this is I'm supposed to find, whatever I'm meant to do, it's so much closer, I can feel *it.*

Moving along the Brickway, Miranda could still hear Aunt Teeta's words echoing through her head. She felt both stunned and excited; her thoughts and emotions were in complete turmoil. Pausing to catch her breath, she realized she'd been running.

Concentrate, Miranda. You have to concentrate.

But focusing right now was too much to demand of herself. And getting more answers seemed only to raise more questions.

What was it you found, Grandpa? Because that's when it started, wasn't it? That's when Nathan's spirit started contacting you.

It all made perfect sense—her grandfather's desperation, his frantic mumblings at the Falls that day. *That's where you found something important, some treasure the Gray Soldier was connected to. That's why you kept going back to the Falls. You were looking for clues. You were looking for a way to help him. Because you* did *know you weren't going to be here much longer.*

I won't let you down, Grandpa. Not you or *Nathan . . .*

It had started to rain. Not very heavily yet, more a warm,

clinging drizzle that thickened the air like fog and distorted everything around her. There weren't many people out this evening. Hazy light glowed from lampposts and houses and a few shop windows, but the sidewalks were mostly deserted. And yet . . .

There are things in this fog.

Many presences in this fog.

Miranda couldn't see them, but she knew they were there. All around her, very real and very close.

"Help us . . ."

"We're lost . . ."

"We want to go home . . ."

A clammy breeze trailed over her, as if ghostly fingers were plucking at her clothes, urging her to reach through the mist and into the past.

"You're the way, Miranda. You're the way between the living and the dead . . ."

Miranda stopped walking. Her hair and clothes were wet, and she didn't know where she was. She hadn't meant to stay out here this long, or to walk this far. But as she squinted through the rain, she saw the Magnolia Gallery looming high above her.

She was standing on the steps of the entrance. Her hands were pressed against one of the tall, round columns, and she could feel a warm rush starting through her, stirring her deepest instincts.

Take your time. Trust yourself.

She slipped into it so naturally, it was like breathing.

Suddenly she was there amid the muffled applause and conversation . . . the clinking of glasses . . . the flow of champagne.

She was drowning in the sweet scent of roses. She heard the sobbing—*"Nathan . . . oh, Nathan, why?"*—the swish and fall of the curtain onstage, and the silence, the terrible silence . . .

And footsteps. No . . . *heavier* than footsteps . . .

Boots. Strong and solid, a bold walk, a man's boots . . .

Something brushed past her in the fog.

A tall figure—a stranger—imposing and silent, his gray uniform woven from swirling mist . . . bringing bad news . . . bringing terrible news . . .

Miranda's senses kicked into high alert. She could feel danger emanating from that stealthy, solitary figure, washing over her like waves of a drowning tide. She could hear him muttering, words low and fierce, intense but hard to make out. An official tone, a tone of authority. And all the while, like sorrowful background music, came that constant, heartbroken sobbing, *"Nathan . . . why?"*

Miranda was trembling and invisible. She was a ghost in this specter's world, and his world was a cold, black night. He didn't see her, didn't know she was there, even though they were close enough to touch. She could smell his sweat, and the sweat of his horse, the duties and atrocities of war clinging to his body, the sad and angry tears dried upon his cheeks . . .

She watched him pause . . . examine a small glass bottle in his hand. And she could smell *that*, too, as faint as it was—bitter and swift and final—a smell of certain death.

Without warning, he turned around. Miranda could see him clearly now, and as she silently whispered his name, Travis Raleigh Fontaine slipped the vial of poison back into his pocket.

"A fair exchange, Ellena." His voice trembled . . . a voice of eternal torment, a voice from beyond the grave. "My mercy . . . for your betrayal."

There was one sharp hiss as he struck the match. One brief spark between his fingertips, before he flung it to the ground, before it burst into flames.

The tread of his boots faded. The glory of the opera house flickered once more, brightly, then disappeared. As Miranda sank to the gallery steps, the evening turned dark, and the drizzle became a downpour.

Oh, God . . . what really happened that awful night?

The spirit had gone, yet she still had an eerie feeling she wasn't alone. When she glanced over her shoulder and saw the dim glow of light floating toward her through the rain, she wondered hopefully if it might be her mother or Aunt Teeta, carrying a flashlight, coming to find her.

"Mom?"

But it wasn't Mom who stood before her, holding a lantern in one pale hand. With a hooded cloak of fog . . . long red hair tumbling down . . . bone-white face . . . eyes unearthly, shining tragic with tears.

"You were my life, Nathan," Ellena Rose whispered. *"And now you are my death."*

25

MIRANDA WAS BACK IN HER OWN WORLD.

The only thing she could hear now was the pouring rain and her pounding heart. Ellena Rose had vanished, yet the lantern light remained, moving steadily closer.

"Hey, Miranda, is that you?"

"Roo?"

Surprised, Miranda saw that it really *was* a flashlight this time—no, *two* flashlights—and that Roo and Gage were hurrying up the steps to join her beneath the covered entrance of the gallery. Both of them were soaked. As they pinned her with the beams of their flashlights, she squinted and ducked her head.

"What are you guys doing here?"

Roo's reply was matter-of-fact. "Looking for you."

"You're kidding."

"We called your house." Gage smiled, shoving wet hair back from his eyes. "Just to see if you felt like getting out for a while. Your mom was really worried—she was about ready to search the town."

"When she told us how long you'd been gone, we thought maybe you'd walked over here," Roo added. "And we were wet anyway."

Gage passed Miranda his cell phone. "Hit redial. And tell your mom we'll bring you home after we get something to eat."

"Are you sure Etienne's picking us up?" Roo frowned at him. "I'm starving."

"You're always starving. And yes, I'm sure. I already called him."

"I don't see any extra umbrellas," Miranda teased, seeing no umbrellas at all.

Gage gave a long-suffering sigh. "Roo likes the rain. She likes walking in it. Playing in it. Sitting in it. Thinking in it—"

"It's a spiritual thing." Roo shrugged. "It makes me feel clean."

"So would taking a shower. Or me spraying you with a hose."

With a dismissive wave, Roo plopped down next to Miranda. She set aside the flashlight and started digging through the pockets of her overalls. "Damn. Most of my cigarettes got wet."

"Then this is a perfect time to quit." Sitting across from her, Gage grabbed for one of her pockets, but she twisted away.

"Leave those alone. They keep me calm."

"Right. Like you're so nervous all the time."

"See? They work."

"Call your mom, Miranda."

Miranda did so. After squaring things with her mother, she handed the phone back to Gage.

"So," Roo began nonchalantly. She struck a match, lit her cigarette, then flicked the match out into the rain. "Do we have to guess, or are you going to tell us what happened?"

Staring at Roo's match, Miranda couldn't help but shudder. "How'd you know something happened?"

"You have that look."

"Of wisdom?" Miranda tried to joke.

"Of wiped out."

"I am wiped out. And you're not going to believe what I just saw."

"Do we look like Parker? Hey, we believe in everything."

"I know how Ellena Rose really died."

Impressed, Roo took a drag on her cigarette. Gage offered an encouraging nod. And by the time Miranda related the details, both Roo and Gage were as enthralled as she was.

"So Travis did it," Gage murmured. "He poisoned her, then set the building on fire to hide the murder."

"A clandestine meeting." With a vague frown, Roo tapped off her ashes. "They make love, he pours the wine, and no more Ellena Rose."

But Miranda met Roo's frown with one of her own. "I don't think there was any romance that night. And I'm not so sure he hid the poison in wine . . . or in anything."

"Explain."

"From what Travis said . . . and the feeling I got when he said it . . . What if he wanted her to *know* he was poisoning her?"

"Double cruel."

Gage paused to mull this over. "If there were rehearsals going on that night, there must have been people around. Wouldn't she have called for help or fought back when he tried to poison her? She must have figured *somebody* would hear her and come to help."

"You're right," Miranda murmured. "I think she took the poison deliberately. And willingly."

Tossing her cigarette, Roo fixed Miranda with a level stare. "He definitely had something on her. Otherwise, she *would* have fought back. And whatever he threatened her with must have been pretty bad if she thought dying was better."

"Blackmail," Gage insisted. "Any ideas why?"

Frustrated, Miranda shook her head, but before she could answer, a horn honked from the curb.

"Hey!" Parker leaned out the passenger side of Etienne's truck. "Don't y'all have enough sense to come in out of the rain?"

Peering over his shoulder, Ashley waved at them. "Come on! Let's go to The Tavern!"

"We'll ride in the back!" Roo yelled.

Grumbling, Gage ushered the girls ahead of him. While Parker helped Miranda into the front seat, Gage boosted Roo onto the truck bed and climbed in after her. There weren't any close parking spaces when they got to the restaurant. By the time they made a mad dash for the door, the rest of them were as wet and bedraggled as Roo and Gage. They found a large table in the back—and their waitress, who spoke Cajun to Etienne, took their orders, then brought a roll of paper towels so they could all clean themselves up.

"Did Miranda tell you?" Flipping her bangs from her eyes, Roo stared at Etienne. He immediately looked suspicious.

"Tell me what?"

"I can't believe she didn't tell you, riding over here."

"Tell me *what*?"

"I thought girls told you everything. You must be losing some of that charm."

Before Etienne could manage a comeback, Miranda held up her hands for quiet. "I was waiting for all of us to be together."

Seeing she had everyone's undivided attention, she recounted her whole experience again, as well as her discussion with Roo and Gage. It didn't take long for a ripple of expectation to travel around the table—to everyone but Parker. He shook his head in disgust but stayed quiet.

"So Ellena's life for his mercy," Etienne mused. "That was Travis's exchange?"

"He said 'my mercy for your betrayal.'" Miranda knew the words by heart.

"Yeah, well, it musta been a pretty big betrayal if he thought poisoning her was merciful."

Thoughtfully, Gage leaned forward. "We know Travis was an officer—both from Miranda's vision and from the picture in the museum. And we also know from the picture that he and Nathan probably knew each other."

"Nathan was holding those horses," Ashley recalled. "Only . . . soldiers didn't ride horses, did they? Soldiers walked."

"But officers rode horses. So maybe—"

"He could have been in charge of them, right? Like a . . . some kind of vet? Or . . . or maybe he was like their horse trainer? Or a horse assistant?"

"Aide-de-camp?" Roo shrugged. "What if he was Travis's aide-de-camp?"

"Aid the what?"

"Aide-de-camp. It's like a personal assistant."

"Isn't that what I just said?" Confusion wrinkled Ashley's brow.

"If Nathan *was* Travis's aide-de-camp, he must have had special privileges," Gage pointed out. "A position like that meant lots of comforts a regular soldier wouldn't have. And he probably wouldn't have been sent to the front lines."

"Which makes it less likely he was killed in battle." Glancing at Parker, Roo couldn't help sounding smug. "And which also supports Miranda's theory about his being tortured and shot."

Though Parker rolled his eyes, Etienne nodded agreement. "Look, he'd probably have known a lot about Travis, yeah? Seen a lotta things going on . . . heard a lotta things being talked about—by Travis and the other officers."

"Official correspondence." Solemnly, Gage ran through the possibilities. "Battle plans. War strategies. All kinds of classified information."

As the food arrived, there was an impatient time-out. After mustard, ketchup, and hot sauce were hurriedly passed around, drinks refilled, and the first few satisfied bites taken, the group's discussion resumed in earnest.

"If Travis had access to classified information, maybe that's how he found out something about Ellena." Miranda's voice tightened with excitement. "And it was something so awful, something she felt so threatened by, she was willing to kill herself over it."

Parker shot each of the girls a mock scowl. "Women. What can I say? They can't be trusted. They end up breaking your heart. All of them are traitors."

"Oh my God," Miranda mumbled. "Parker . . . oh my God . . ."

Traitor.

It was only a word . . . but suddenly she knew.

"Parker, you are *brilliant*!"

Parker lifted clasped hands toward heaven. "It's a miracle! Somebody who finally recognizes my *genius*!"

"She was a spy!" Straightening in her seat, Miranda gripped the edge of the table, her eyes going wide. "Don't you see? That's why she drank the poison—she knew that if she didn't, she'd be hanged. Ellena Rose—Miss Ellena—she was a *Yankee spy.*"

26

IT WAS AS IF ALL THE PUZZLE PIECES WERE NEARLY IN place. As though the whole picture were finally coming into focus, with details vivid and intact. As the noise of The Tavern continued around her, Miranda felt a swift and sudden detachment. In the space of a heartbeat, time stopped and slammed her into the past, where scenes and people and conversations raged like a hurricane through her senses. *Nathan . . . Ellena Rose . . . Travis Fontaine*—lives intertwined and shattered and forgotten . . .

Until here . . . until now . . .

Until Grandpa and me.

"That's got to be right," she heard Roo mumble. "Once they discovered she was a spy, she'd have been executed."

"And think of her career." Ashley sighed. "The scandal."

Etienne's tone was humorless. "Hell, in *this* town, the *locals* mighta strung her up. Me, I'd have taken that poison, too."

The mood around the table had gone somber, as though none of them really wanted to admit Miss Ellena's guilt. Even Parker seemed to be considering Miranda's theory.

Leaning back in his chair, Etienne stroked his fingers along his chin. "She coulda gotten secrets from anybody. Or passed secrets to anybody. Especially if she was somebody's mistress."

"Or *many* somebodys' mistress." Parker chuckled.

"It would have been so easy for her—men would have told her anything. They'd have given up secret information just like *that*." Snapping her fingers, Ashley coolly confronted Parker's indignation.

"Come on, give us guys a little credit. Why would any high-ranking officer share classified information with his little groupie, huh?"

"Because those high-ranking officers were men." Roo's stare was as condescending as her tone. "And men only think with their—"

"Downstairs brain," Ashley finished.

While the guys conceded with slight embarrassment, Roo and Miranda laughed. "Good one, Ash."

"Everything we know—or think we know—about Ellena Rose fits the spy profile." Etienne tried to steer the conversation back again. "Remember the part about her crossing enemy lines—how she never had any problems? And how she loved traveling through the South?"

"She probably had contacts all over the place," Gage reasoned. "Nobody would ever have suspected her."

"And even if they did, nobody else woulda believed it."

"Till Travis Fontaine." Reaching across Gage, Roo traded her empty glass for his half-full one. Gage stared into the empty glass and frowned.

"So Travis must have been one of her informants, except he didn't know it." Miranda picked up the probable scenario. "And when he found out, he felt betrayed for himself *and* the Confederate army."

"And he wouldn't have had a choice, really." Gage's expression was troubled. "He knew he'd have to turn her in. He knew she'd have to be executed . . ."

Nodding at Gage, Ashley lowered her voice. "So he gave *Ellena* the choice."

"Some choice." Parker grinned. "Either *I* kill you, or *you* kill you."

Despite Parker's twisted attempt at humor, a heavy silence settled over the group.

At last Etienne cleared his throat. "So Travis, I guess he musta loved her, yeah? To give her a way out like that?"

"I can't even imagine." Ashley fixed Etienne with a sorrowful gaze. "The fear she would have felt . . . the shame and humiliation—"

"But he let her die with some dignity. You gotta give him that."

"And then he burned down the opera house," Miranda whispered. "He burned down the Rose."

Ashley's eyes misted over. "Both Roses. He destroyed both Roses."

For a long moment, they all seemed lost in their own thoughts. Then Parker spoke up.

"Yeah." Tilting his chair back, he winked at Gage and Etienne. "That's the way to a girl's heart, all right. Give her poison, then burn down her house."

Roo's stare was openly curious. "Tell us the truth, Parker. Are you really just a changeling in human form?"

"Look, *if* I believed all this poison-betrayal crap—which I *don't*—but if I *did*? I'd be looking at your Gray Soldier guy."

"Nathan," Ashley corrected him.

"Whoever. I mean, y'all said yourselves, it all has to be connected, right? So Miss Ellena might have been a spy, but how does that tie in with Nathan's message and him being tortured and shot?"

As a new thought hit, Miranda put down her fork and tapped Parker lightly on the arm. "Parker, what you just said—"

"*Another* brilliant revelation, no doubt." Parker smirked.

"Actually, it was. If Nathan was trying to get a message to Ellena, maybe it was information about the Confederate army. What if *he* was a spy, too?"

"Ellena's accomplice?" Roo arched a quizzical brow.

"If he and Ellena were in this together, then it makes sense. He would have been sending her *lots* of secret messages."

Leaning toward Miranda, Etienne folded his arms on the tabletop. "Travis, he musta been plenty mad, yeah? When he found out Nathan was a spy? And I'm guessing that's when he found out about Ellena, too—when he was torturing Nathan."

"Do you think that's when Nathan got shot?" Ashley groaned and covered her face with her hands. "Do you think Travis killed him after Nathan told him about Ellena?"

Roo's shrug could have been either yes or no. "Talk about betrayal—your assistant *and* your mistress."

"And I bet they were the two people he trusted most in the whole world." Pushing back her plate, Ashley gazed morosely at her burger. "I can't eat any more. This whole thing just gets sadder and sadder."

Miranda's glance was sympathetic. "But I still don't know what Nathan's message is. Or why he's still trying to get it to Ellena."

She'd felt so hopeful while they'd all been talking—so close to solving the mystery, so close to helping Nathan's restless spirit. *But with each step forward, I fall back three.*

By the time they were ready to leave, the rain had tapered off to a saunalike drizzle. The group headed for the truck, Parker and Ashley walking ahead, while the other four took their time.

"You know," Miranda ventured, not sure if it would help or make things more confusing, "I think I've figured out where this whole thing with Nathan started."

She could tell they were intrigued. Repeating the information Aunt Teeta had given her, she told them about her grandfather, the unknown treasure he'd found, and his obsession with it.

"And I think," she said gently to Etienne, "that might have been what Grandpa was talking about that day . . . when he said he should have told you about it but never did."

A muscle clenched in Etienne's jaw. Gage threw him a look, but said nothing.

Pulling another cigarette from her pocket, Roo lit up, turned sideways, and fanned away the smoke. As Etienne reached toward her, she automatically passed the cigarette over to him.

"I believe Grandpa really wanted to help Nathan," Miranda concluded. "And I believe he tried really hard, as hard as he possibly could."

"So we'll keep trying, too," Gage assured her. "We'll figure it out."

Etienne took several long drags on Roo's cigarette. When he handed it back, his expression was more serious than ever.

"Whatever it was Jonas found, he'd have kept it close. Probably in his room somewhere."

"And how does that help me?" Miranda made a futile gesture. "There must be a *million* things in his room."

"But only *one* that belongs to Nathan. And only one person who can find it." Etienne gave her a sidelong glance. "And that's you, *cher.*"

27

"CAN YOU COME UP THE BACK WAY?" MIRANDA ASKED.

Etienne had dropped the others off. Now he and Miranda sat in his truck, parked in the driveway of Hayes House. The stress of the evening had eased since they'd left The Tavern, and she leaned back with her eyes closed while Etienne stared silently out the fogged-up windshield.

"Can you?" she asked again. She still hadn't told him about the attic, about Nathan's unexpected appearance, or about the connection she'd sensed between Nathan and Hayes House. Several times during dinner, she'd wanted to bring it up, but with so many other things to talk over, she'd decided to put it on hold till a later time. *And now's that time.*

"Etienne?"

"We gotta stop meeting like this," he said, poker-faced. "The neighbors, they're starting to talk."

"*You're* the one who started it."

"What, you don't want me to meet your mama?"

"It's not that—"

"I promise she'll like me. Your aunt Teeta, *she* likes me."

"My aunt Teeta *loves* you. She thinks you're wonderful."

"See. What'd I tell you?"

"She also thinks Gage is adorable."

"What can I say? Gage *is* adorable."

Miranda had to laugh. "Look, if we go in the front, they'll both want to fuss over you, and we won't have any privacy, and I can't mention ghosts and weird things in front of them."

"You know, *cher*, I've had a lotta girls talk me into their bedrooms, but this is the first time I've heard *that* excuse."

"This is *not* that kind of invitation. Understand?"

Etienne gave her a solemn stare. He let out a long-suffering sigh. "Okay. Since you twisted my arm—I'll come up the back."

Miranda thought maybe this time he might actually smile. But like all the times before, only a fleeting hint of amusement touched his lips.

"Fifteen minutes," she said, climbing out.

"At least. I gotta park my truck somewhere else. And walk all the way back. And sneak all the way in. Secret rendezvous, you know . . . they take time."

Laughing again, Miranda left him and went inside. To her relief, only Aunt Teeta was up, and she was on her way to bed.

"Your mama was exhausted," Aunt Teeta explained. "Bless her heart, I don't know how she's lasted this long. I told her I'd wait up for you. And I did, and here you are, and now I'm going to tuck myself in. I'll see you in the morning!"

"Aunt Teeta?"

"What, darlin'?"

"Did Mom sleep in her bedroom tonight?"

Aunt Teeta gave a wink. "She sure did. And that's a *real* good sign!"

Gratefully, Miranda hurried up to her room, shocked to find Etienne already waiting for her.

"Hey," he greeted her. "What took you so long?"

"You're impossible." While he stretched out on his side across the end of the bed, she grabbed her favorite pillow and scooted back in her corner against the wall.

"So what's the big mystery?" Etienne focused on her face. "And don't tell me we're gonna be looking through your *grandpère's* room tonight for that little treasure."

"I think Nathan has some special connection to this house. To the treasure, yes, but also to this house."

Etienne's dark eyes narrowed. "What kinda connection?"

While he listened attentively, she told him about the boardinghouse and barn; she reminded him of the old photograph of Hayes House, of Nathan with the horses, of local families taking in visitors.

"Suppose Nathan took care of Travis's horse and boarded it here. And suppose Ellena stayed here on some of her visits. Maybe this is where the two of them first met. Maybe this was even where they traded information. Probably no one would have suspected them."

Leaning back, Etienne propped himself on his elbows. "So now you gonna be exploring all through the house and all over the yard, trying to come up with clues?"

Miranda couldn't help but smile. "Maybe. I still can't figure out what that stupid watch chain has to do with everything."

"Don't be trying so hard."

Giving a long, languid stretch, he folded his arms beneath his head. His T-shirt had slipped higher, exposing part of his stomach. His jeans had slipped lower, his skin smooth and tan. Miranda looked quickly away.

"Now see?" Etienne scolded. "You're getting yourself all tense, all worked up. And you're never gonna find answers that way. So what'd I tell you?"

"You said . . ." She tried to concentrate. She watched him sit up, move closer.

"You said . . . just surrender to it."

"That's right," he murmured. "That's all you gotta do."

Very slowly, he leaned toward her. He took her face between his hands. His lips were gentle, but his kiss was firm—she melted beneath it as he pressed her tight against his chest. His lips traced a shivery path to her neck and lingered at the base of her throat. His hands slid to her shoulders and down her body, an embrace both relentless and tender—burning where it touched, but never forcing, never intrusive. He whispered to her in his secret language . . . their lips locked in a kiss . . .

"Miranda?" Aunt Teeta called softly.

Miranda's cry was instantly muffled beneath Etienne's lips. Shocked, she stared at him, even as he pulled away from her, snapped off the light, and slipped out of sight beneath the covers. After a second's hesitation, Miranda slid in beside him and yanked the bedspread up to her chin.

"What?" she called back, with what she hoped was convincing grogginess.

Aunt Teeta opened the door, her bathrobe askew, her hair disheveled, and several oversize curlers bobbing on top of her head.

"Oh, darlin', I'm so sorry. I didn't think you'd be asleep yet. You know, I was just thinking—since you and Etienne have been spending so much time together, why don't you invite him over sometime? So your mama can meet him? And ask Gage over, too—he's such a cutie."

Miranda yawned loudly. "That's a great idea, Aunt Teeta. Thanks a lot."

"All right now, hon, you go on back to sleep. Love you."

"Love you, too."

Miranda waited till the door closed. Till Aunt Teeta's footsteps faded down the stairs, till the house was silent once more. She waited a long time.

At last the covers moved, and Etienne, after a thorough look around, threw them back and sat up. He seemed immensely amused.

"Damn, that was close. Your aunt, she woulda skinned me alive if she'd caught me here."

Miranda sank back on the pillows. Her heart was still racing at top speed. She felt excited and happy and breathless, confused and strangely frustrated.

"I think you better leave now," she mumbled.

"Yeah, I think I better."

The kiss he gave her this time was on the cheek and almost brotherly. He jumped from the bed, but paused when he got to the sunporch. As Miranda saw him turn to look back at her, her whole body felt warm.

"What is it?" she asked him, embarrassed now.

But Etienne didn't look embarrassed at all.

"It's good, *cher.*" He winked. "And next time, it'll be even better."

28

"WELL, GOOD MORNING, SLEEPYHEAD!" As Miranda shuffled drowsily into the kitchen, Aunt Teeta met her with a big hug. "Your mama already left for work, but look who's decided to grace us with their presence!"

Startled, Miranda saw Gage and Etienne sitting at the table, both with heaping plates of food in front of them. Gage wiped his mouth quickly on a napkin; Etienne watched her over the rim of his coffee cup.

Her mind spun back to last night, cheeks flaming at the memory. *What was I thinking? I should know better! When everything about Etienne Boucher screams GUARANTEED HEARTBREAK and even though nothing really serious happened—I should definitely know better!*

Halfway standing, Gage pulled out a chair for her. "We thought maybe you'd like a ride to school."

Oh yes . . . and now here was Gage. With that face and that smile and those big brown eyes that just melted her heart whenever she looked at him. And especially since Roo's candid confession— *"He was* amazing*"*—how could a girl *not* imagine other secrets behind the shyness?

Still flustered, Miranda turned and bumped into her aunt, upsetting the coffeepot, splashing the floor, nearly burning her arm in the process. As Gage and Etienne exchanged glances, she had a second of panic. What if Etienne had said something about last night? What if Gage suspected? Did she look guilty?

"Oh, mercy, did you burn yourself?" Aunt Teeta fussed, trying to mop the floor, trying to tend to Miranda.

"I'm sorry, Aunt Teeta. No, I'm okay."

"Here, let me get your breakfast."

"I'm really not hungry."

Ignoring her, Aunt Teeta bustled to the stove. "Gage, honey, I'm *so* glad you came this morning."

"Thanks. It's been a while."

"I used to see you all the time at the office," Aunt Teeta went on. Then, in an aside to Miranda, "His mama and I worked together for years. But she decided to leave and spend more time with her family."

Though Etienne and Gage exchanged glances, neither of them said anything. Miranda wondered if Gage's mom might have quit her job when Etienne's mother got sick.

"So I've had the pleasure of watching these two little rascals grow up." As Aunt Teeta passed the table, she gave Gage's shoulder an affectionate squeeze. "Isn't this Gage just the cutest thing?"

Shaking his head, Gage flushed slightly and tried to concentrate on his scrambled eggs.

"And those dimples," Aunt Teeta teased. "Aren't they just precious?"

Before Gage could ward him off, Etienne leaned over and pinched his cheek. "Just precious. Cute and precious."

"Cut it out," Gage mumbled, lowering his head.

"Miranda, honey, sit down. I wish you'd eat something." Peering out the window, Aunt Teeta gave a shudder. "Y'all be sure and take umbrellas. There's supposed to be a doozy of a storm coming in."

"How much of a doozy?" Etienne asked. "Medium doozy or big doozy?"

Aunt Teeta flapped her dishtowel at him. "*Monster* doozy. Big bad winds, flash-flood rain, and maybe even tornadoes kind of doozy. Miranda, don't you feel well?"

"Just"—Miranda brushed it off—"kind of sick to my stomach, I guess."

"What, darlin', something keep you awake last night?"

Etienne stared at her. Gage stared at her. Aunt Teeta stared at her. Thank God for Gage, who finally seemed to sense her growing distress. Cramming the last bite of sausage into his mouth, he scraped back his chair from the table.

"I'll make sure she eats something later," he promised Aunt Teeta. "Come on, we better go. We're gonna be late."

Miranda threw him a grateful look as the three of them trooped out the door. Still, once they reached Etienne's truck, she couldn't resist.

"You really are cute and precious," she said, touching a fingertip to one of his dimples.

Gage's face went redder. He grabbed her hand and boosted her into the front seat. "See if I come to *your* rescue anymore."

"And I have to agree with Roo and Ashley. You're *especially* cute when you're embarrassed."

"Yeah?" Gage's lips moved against her ear. "Don't tempt me.

I bet you're especially cute when you're embarrassed, too."

Miranda stared at him in surprise. Gage gave her an innocent smile, then climbed in beside her. Etienne seemed completely unaware of their little exchange.

While the boys argued sports scores and statistics, Miranda gazed nervously out at the pewter sky. Thunder rumbled in the distance, and the windshield glistened with the first few sprinklings of rain. As Etienne reached to turn on the wipers, she felt a deep and unexpected chill.

"Listen, Miranda . . . watch . . ."

Surprised, she straightened in her seat. She glanced quickly from Gage to Etienne, but the two of them didn't seem to notice and kept right on talking.

"Watch . . ."

A shiver, even colder now, gnawed at her spine. *Grandpa?* But of course it was him, she recognized his voice—the same tone, the same words she'd heard at the funeral home the night of the visitation. *But why here? Why now?*

"Listen, Miranda . . . watch . . ."

"You okay?" This time Gage looked down at her, half amused, half concerned.

"Somebody walk over your grave?" Etienne teased.

Miranda had heard that old expression many times before— only now it seemed more scary than funny, and she edged slightly nearer to Gage.

Muttering to himself, Etienne bent forward, eyes narrowed on the school ahead and the ominous clouds behind it. There were even more of them now, gray darkening to black, and all of them churning like restless waves.

Gage pointed out a parking space in the student lot. "Did Ashley call you about revising that outline?" he asked Etienne. "She wants to meet at lunch and brainstorm."

"Did you say rainstorm?" Etienne grumbled. "'Cause this one looks like it's gonna be a killer."

"There's tornado warnings," Ashley fretted, pulling a chair up to their table.

The school cafeteria was packed, much noisier and more chaotic than usual. No one was eating outside today because of the rain.

Balancing his tray on one hand, Parker slid into the empty chair next to her. "Hey, don't worry so much. We never have tornadoes around here."

"Well, we *could* have tornadoes around here."

"Ash, when was the last time you heard of a tornado touching down in St. Yvette?"

"What if our house blew away? That would be a really horrible thing!"

"What if your *boyfriend* blew away?" Roo asked mildly. "That would be a really *good* thing."

And then, as everyone suddenly realized the impact of what they were saying, all eyes turned guiltily to Miranda.

"Oh, God, Miranda," Ashley was horrified. "I'm so sorry. I didn't mean . . . I would never—"

"Come on, it was a joke." Forcing a smile, Miranda did her best to brush it off. "Please, don't worry about it."

Neither Gage nor Etienne looked convinced. Miranda stared back at each of them and forced her smile a little more firmly.

"Maybe they'll let us out of school early." Parker sounded hopeful. "Hey, my folks are out of town for a few days—we could all party at my place."

Roo leaned over and lifted the top piece of bread from Gage's sandwich. As Gage watched her, she took out a slice of cheese and a tomato, then put the sandwich back together.

Gage shook his head and resumed eating.

"Full fridge." Parker tried again. "Home theater, swimming pool, and well-stocked bar. Any takers?"

"Yes, the *police* when they come to take you *away*," Roo said.

A clap of thunder violently shook the building. Though the storm had held off so far, Miranda's uneasiness had grown. That feeling of dread in the air—that feeling of grim expectancy. It was like her worst nightmare all over again.

She realized now that Ashley was talking, something about their ghost tour. The others were casually listening, a comment or question or insult tossed out here and there. Laughter and conversation were at full pitch around them. Life at St. Yvette High was going on as usual, and nobody else seemed paticularly bothered by the weather. All Miranda wanted to do was get home to Aunt Teeta's, where she'd be safe. *Well . . . safe from the storm, anyway . . .*

The real downpour began just as Etienne dropped her off after school. Bolting for the door, Miranda got inside and dried off, changed clothes, and fixed herself something to eat. With Mom and Aunt Teeta both at work, the house loomed large and silent around her. Her footsteps echoed over the parquet floors. Thunder shivered the walls and trembled the old foundations.

But she couldn't stop thinking of Ellena Rose.

She'd finally worked up enough courage to take the watch chain from her room, and now, sitting at the kitchen table, Miranda went back over everything she knew—or thought she knew. There was still so much missing. Clues and answers and truths . . .

"Listen, Miranda . . . watch . . ."

Her grandfather's words made her even more restless. *I have been listening, I have been watching. What am I missing? How do I find it?*

She thought of his treasure. Some small and seemingly insignificant artifact that Jonas Hayes had picked up one day at the Falls and become completely obsessed with. He wouldn't have thrown it away, Aunt Teeta had assured her. And what had Etienne said? *"He'd have kept it close . . ."*

Some connection . . . something important . . . something that Nathan's spirit is connected to . . .

Leaning forward onto the table, Miranda rested her head on folded arms and let her eyes drift shut. She could see Hayes House the way it used to be—the way she imagined it would be—warm and solid and welcoming, with the aroma of home-cooked meals, and a big, roomy barn out back. And he'd be there—*Nathan*—brushing down the horses, when Ellena Rose strolled by. She'd be inquiring about a carriage maybe, but

Nathan would be her *real* reason for stopping. *To exchange a whisper. To exchange information.*

Miranda's thoughts flowed. Back through years and seasons and moonlit nights . . . the opera house and the battlefield . . .

"No . . . you're wrong . . ."

"I swear to you . . . for the love of God . . ."

"I'm the one you want. Only me . . . only me."

"Take it . . . the Rose . . . Miss Ellena . . . "

Miranda's head was spinning. Too many images . . . too many scenes . . . all of them painful and heartbreaking. Nathan—rope burns around his wrists . . . cuts from horse-whip lashes; Ellena Rose—a lingering taste of poison on her tongue, and in her throat, her last words choked, her sweet song silenced forever.

"You were my life, Nathan . . . and now you are my death . . ."

"No. Please stop." But Miranda's senses reached out; her mind searched. *You thought Nathan betrayed you . . .*

"I'm the one you want . . . only me . . ."

"Only me."

Tears ran down Miranda's cheeks, and they were Ellena's tears and Nathan's tears. She clutched the braid tightly to her heart.

Why did Nathan betray you, Ellena? How could he have been that selfish? That unfeeling?

Frustrated, Miranda pressed both hands to her forehead. She was here in Aunt Teeta's kitchen, yet it was *another* kitchen, a long-ago farmhouse kitchen. In a house where a beautiful red-haired diva and a handsome stable boy traded secrets and . . .

And kisses . . .

For Miranda could see them now—Nathan and Ellena—alone in the barn at midnight, while Hayes House slept. The way they held each other, clung to each other, in the soft glow of lantern light, as though they were the only two people in the world.

Accomplices . . . and sweethearts.

Slowly, reluctantly, they drew apart. Nathan, handing Ellena his pocket watch . . . Ellena, giving Nathan a watch chain braided from her beautiful red hair . . .

"*Someday,*" Nathan whispered, wiping tears from Ellena's cheeks. "*Someday when this terrible war is over, we won't have to hide like this. We won't have to hide our feelings for each other . . . we'll finally be together.*"

"*But I'm afraid, Nathan. I'm so afraid! Something bad is going to happen—I can* feel *it!*"

"*Hush now. Nothing's going to happen, my love. We've been careful; we'll be safe.*"

"*Promise you'll come back to me . . .*"

"*Yes. Always. I promise.*"

Very gently Ellena touched the braid in his hand. "*And promise me you'll keep this close to your heart.*"

"*I swear it. And someday, I'll wear my watch and your chain together.* Together, *Ellena. Just like you and me . . .*"

Miranda began to come back to herself.

She could feel the watch chain pressing into her skin—she wanted to hold it close, she wanted to fling it away.

"*A fair exchange,*" Travis Fontaine had said that tragic, deadly night. "*My mercy . . . for your betrayal.*"

Through a slow, lingering haze, Miranda stared down at the braid. This beautiful red hair over a hundred years old, yet she could still feel the love, the devotion, the tears in every strand . . .

Ellena's tears . . . Nathan's tears . . . the tears of Travis Fontaine.

Because he's the one, isn't he, Ellena? When Nathan was caught, Travis Fontaine—the other man who loved you so much—saw that watch chain and recognized that watch chain . . .

Because he recognized your hair.

Miranda was quivering. Shaking with fear, with grief, with regret. Shaking with over a century of emotions, the emotions of three people trapped in a pitiless fate.

Oh, Ellena Rose . . . he knew your hair.

Nathan didn't betray you. Even though he was captured, even when he was tortured, he never *betrayed you.*

Miranda's eyelids finally opened. She was sitting at the kitchen table; the hands on the clock had scarcely moved. And instead of the questions that had haunted her, there was only a deep, sad wisdom.

For she knew the rights and the wrongs . . .

The truths and the lies . . .

The betrayed and the betrayer.

"Listen, Miranda . . . watch."

And she knew now what her grandfather had found at the Falls.

29

A HUGE CRASH OF THUNDER BROUGHT HER UP OUT OF her chair. As the lights flickered ominously, Miranda ran for flashlights, laying them out on the table within easy reach. Rain gushed at the windowpanes and pounded on the roof; trees flailed helplessly in the wind. When the front door suddenly burst open, she let out a yell and went running into the hall, convinced the whole front of the house was blowing away.

What she found instead was Etienne, alone in the entryway, shaking off water like a wet dog.

"You!" She let out a sigh of relief while Etienne glanced around the corridor.

"Yeah. Last time I checked, anyhow."

"What are you doing, coming here in this weather? It looks *horrible* out there."

"It *is* horrible out there. But Miss Teeta, she just called me and she was worried, so I figured you might like the company."

"You figured right."

One corner of his mouth twitched. "Yeah, I usually do."

He followed her into the kitchen, then stood dripping in front of the sink. Miranda brought him towels, made a pot of strong coffee, and pulled out Aunt Teeta's latest homemade confection—bread pudding with rum sauce—which she popped into the microwave.

"Great. My favorite." Nodding approval, Etienne continued towel drying his hair.

"Aunt Teeta told me you say that about every single thing she makes."

"And it's true. They're *all* my favorites." Pausing, he shoved his wet hair back from his face and stared at her, eyes narrowed. "Hey, you okay, *cher*?"

"Well"—Miranda drew a deep breath—"I wasn't okay just a few minutes ago. But I think I am now."

"Ah. Is that your way of telling me I'm your hero?"

Miranda couldn't resist. "No. It's my way of telling you that I had a nightmare, but I woke up."

"That's cruel, *cher*. You just stabbed me straight in my heart."

"You'll live."

She watched his lips quirk at the edges, his dark eyes shining with amusement. But then, the amusement began to fade.

"So what *really* happened?" he asked quietly.

She felt silly as her eyes brimmed with sudden tears. She started to turn away from him, but his arms went around her.

"Miranda?"

"Can we just . . . sit down first?"

While Etienne chose a spot at the table, she busied herself with his food, brought him another towel. Anything to distract herself, to keep all the new revelations from crowding in and overwhelming her too fast. Finally Etienne stopped her, took the bread pudding, then gently—but firmly—pushed her down in a chair.

"Whatever it is, you're not gonna get rid of it by running. And I'm always gonna believe you, no matter what."

"I know what really happened now. To Nathan. And Ellena. And Travis Fontaine."

With a look of mild surprise, Etienne pushed his bowl away and leaned toward her. "I'm listening."

"They're all connected, just like we thought. Only the betrayal wasn't just about Travis and Ellena. Ellena thought Nathan betrayed her to Travis. But Nathan didn't. It was the chain and her hair. And the two of them were in love, which made it even worse. And Nathan made a promise to her, but they both died, and they couldn't be together—"

"Whoa, whoa . . ." Etienne's concern had turned to confusion. "Time out. Back up." While Miranda took a deep breath and started over, he retrieved his bowl and ate the bread pudding. He chewed slowly, deep in thought. Then he leaned back in his chair.

"Maybe I should put this another way," he said. "Is there something you *didn't* figure out before I got here?"

"Where the watch is."

"The . . ."

"Watch. That's what Grandpa found at the Falls that day. And what he's been trying to tell me." Miranda's voice tightened. "I think Nathan wants me to take the watch chain to Ellena. And connect it to the watch like they promised."

"A watch. Nathan's watch."

"And I think if I do that, Nathan will be at peace. See, all this time I thought Grandpa was telling me to listen *and* to watch. But he was telling me to listen, because it *was* the watch. So now we have to find it."

"Your *grand-père*," Etienne murmured. "He talked to you?"

"Yes. I heard him. I'm certain of it."

For just the briefest moment, something shimmered in the black depths of Etienne's eyes and softened the chiseled features of his face. "That's good, *cher*," he whispered. "Good for you."

As the two of them continued to talk, the weather continued to worsen. Mom and Aunt Teeta both called to check in—and though neither of them could come home yet, they were grateful Etienne was there. While he went in search of candles, Miranda made another pot of coffee. Refilling his cup, she suddenly had the feeling of being watched, and when she turned around, Etienne was in the doorway, observing her every move.

"I wish you wouldn't look at me like that." Miranda frowned.

"Like what?"

"Like . . . you can see things I don't want you to see."

"Too late."

"Stop." She did her best to sound stern. "Now I know how Gage feels."

"Except for the dimples."

"Right. Except for those."

"Not to worry, *cher*. You got a whole lotta other redeeming qualities."

Picking up a napkin, Miranda tossed it at him. "Drink your coffee."

"Yes, ma'am."

But she could still feel him watching. And when she passed his chair, he caught her and pulled her close.

She stood silently, facing him. She set the coffeepot on the table. Gently she ran her fingers through his thick, dark hair . . . along the angles of his face. She heard his slight intake of breath, felt the sudden tensing of his muscles.

His hands encircled her waist. She gazed down at him, and bent slowly to kiss him . . .

The phone shrilled loudly, jarring them apart. As Miranda hurried to answer it, she could hardly breathe.

"Hello?"

But she couldn't make out the voice on the other end. The voice crying and babbling so fast, words spilling out, making no sense. When she finally heard the name "Etienne," she quickly handed him the receiver.

It was as though he already knew something was wrong. Even before he saw the fear on Miranda's face, even before he took the phone. And then there were only those few short words, those few foreign words he spoke, before jumping up and heading for the door.

Miranda stood frozen with dread. "What is it?"

"Roo's gone. Ashley says she never came home after school."

"What—"

"She's afraid Roo might be at the Falls."

"Now? *Why*?"

"Some argument they got into, something about Parker. And Roo was plenty mad and wouldn't ride with them and said she was gonna walk home so she could think."

"Ashley told me Roo always goes to the Falls when she's upset. But it floods there, doesn't it?"

"That's why I gotta go. *Now.* I'm gonna stop and get Parker."

"What about Gage?"

"Aunt Jules—Gage's mom—just called Ashley's house, looking for him. Ashley told her they were all there studying—she didn't want Aunt Jules to worry." Etienne's expression darkened. "I guess Aunt Jules's van is gone."

"What about Ashley's parents?" Yet as Etienne sighed, Miranda knew what the answer would be. "Let me guess. Ashley told them Roo and Gage are at Gage's house."

"You got it."

"Look, you know Gage must have driven Roo to the Falls. And you know he'll take good care of her."

"Stay here. I'll call as soon as I can."

But Miranda was already grabbing a rain jacket from the front hall closet. "Absolutely not. I'm coming with you."

Before he could say no, she ran after him, out into the storm.

30

"IT'S ALL MY FAULT," ASHLEY SOBBED. "What if she's dead?"

The four of them were squeezed tightly into Etienne's truck. With every shift of the clutch and each turn of the wheel, Etienne's right arm jabbed sharply into Miranda's side, and Ashley bounced back and forth between Miranda's lap and Parker's. The old Chevy truck, way past its prime, rattled and clanked and groaned at every pothole and puddle, but it hugged the roads like glue.

"It's not your fault," Parker reassured Ashley for the dozenth time. "You didn't know what she was planning to do. How could it be your fault?"

"The water always gets so deep at the Falls. The bayou always floods. If she's dead—"

"She's not *dead.*" He paused, then mumbled, "I couldn't be that lucky."

"Parker Wilmington, I can't even believe you said—"

"I was *kidding*, Ash. Okay, sorry, bad timing, but I was *kidding*, okay? Roo's fine. And none of this is your fault."

Gulping down a hiccup, Ashley glared at him. "You're right. It's *your* fault."

"*My* fault?"

"You know she caught you drinking in the parking lot!"

"Just a little! I swear, I only had one sip—"

"You're heartless and insensitive, and you hate my sister."

"Christ, Ashley, I *don't* hate your sister—"

"You told her I care more about you than I do about her, and that's not true!"

"I know it's not—and *Roo* knows it's not. It was a joke! I wasn't serious!"

"I'm always defending you, and Roo's always been smarter than me. Roo would *never* get involved with somebody like you."

Parker shot Etienne another helpless glance. "Is that good or bad?"

"I wouldn't be doing any more talking right now, if I were you," Etienne advised him.

"Roo looks out for me. Roo has better sense than I do," Ashley went on miserably. "It's always been that way, ever since we were little. She's always had the brains. And I've always had . . . not the brains."

Etienne's eyes and Parker's eyes met behind Ashley's back.

"Not going there," Etienne mumbled. Then to Ashley, "Don't be worrying about Roo, *cher*. Parker's right—she's gonna be fine."

"Yeah." Parker's tone was equally reassuring. "Gage is with her right this minute."

Miranda could tell Ashley wanted to believe them. But the girl's eyes were still bleary with tears, and her lips were quivering.

"If something happens to Roo, I'll never forgive myself." Sniffling, Ashley stared dejectedly out Parker's window. It was impossible to see anything but gusting rain.

"Nothing's gonna happen to her, *cher*."

"You promise?"

Etienne didn't miss a beat. "Sure, I promise."

As Miranda glanced at his silhouette, she saw that telltale muscle clench in his cheek. His body was rigid. He was clutching the steering wheel so fiercely, his knuckles were white. For the first time, she realized just how worried he actually was—far more worried than he wanted anyone to suspect.

A fresh wave of fear washed over her.

Hunching down inside her jacket, Miranda tried to concentrate on a happy ending. Tried to believe how someday they'd all look back on this and laugh, just another crazy adventure. Outside, the storm shrieked and roared; in here, it was stuffy and hot and damp. She could smell fear and sweat, mud and wet hair and wet clothes, the faint sweetness of Ashley's perfume.

"The road's already flooding." Ashley sounded alarmed. "How long do you think till the bayou—"

"Hours yet," Etienne replied, a little too quickly.

But Miranda's imagination filled in the rest. She braced against Parker as Etienne began swerving more often, more sharply, around broken limbs and downed trees. The wipers were no match for the storm now; the headlights barely penetrated the rain. She couldn't even see the hood of the truck.

"Can't you go faster?" Ashley pleaded.

"Any faster, and *we'll* be the ones needing a rescue." Etienne gripped the wheel even tighter. He hunched his shoulders and took another angry swipe at the windshield.

Miranda leaned in close to his ear. "Don't worry. Gage will be fine, too."

For just a brief instant, Etienne's defenses seemed to crumble. For just a brief instant, she caught a glimpse of emotions—both panic and hope. And then, just as fast, his jaw set in a determined line, and he cast her a smooth, sidelong glance.

"Is that you, smelling like an old cheeseburger?"

Startled, she couldn't help laughing. "That is *not* me—that is something, *somewhere*, in this disgustingly dirty truck of yours."

"No, I don't think so. No, I definitely think it's—Hey, that's Aunt Jules's van over there."

"Where?" Leaning across Miranda, Parker squinted out Etienne's window. "Are you sure?"

"As sure as I am that it's stuck in the mud," Etienne grumbled. "And as sure as I am that Gage is gonna be grounded for the rest of his life."

"At least we know they're here." A tiny bit of relief crept into Ashley's voice. "Do you see them anywhere?"

"It doesn't look like they're in the van, but—*Merde!*"

As the brakes slammed and held, the truck skidded deep into water. Parker managed to catch Ashley right before she hit the dashboard.

"Now what?" Parker demanded.

Etienne's tone was as grim as his face. "Well, I guess we know why they got stuck, yeah? No way we can get any farther on this road. The water's too high."

"Is there another way in? Maybe from another direction?"

"Only the bayou."

"What about your boat?"

"That'll take too long, and we can't risk the time." Gunning the engine, Etienne tried backing the truck onto a stretch of higher ground. But when the tires spun uselessly, he shut off the ignition, twisted around, and grabbed two flashlights from behind the seat.

"Take this." Handing one to Parker, Etienne kept the other for himself. "You girls stay here where it's safe."

"Safe!" Ashley wailed. "It's flooded, and we'll float away!"

"You won't float away, Ashley. I swear."

"Hey, we'll take our chances with you," Miranda shot back, scrambling out with Ashley before Etienne could shut his door.

Holding on to one another, the four of them made slow, painstaking progress. What rain gear they wore did little to protect them; within seconds they were all completely soaked. Clutching both Etienne's hand and Ashley's, Miranda stayed alert for alligators and water moccasins and other creepy things that might be escaping to higher ground. She couldn't see into the murky water, couldn't see where to step. She had no sense of direction, no clue where they were headed. *Maybe Ashley and I should have stayed in the truck.*

CUSICK

But Etienne seemed entirely sure of himself. He led them steadily through the downpour, all of them shouting as loud as they could.

"Roo! Gage!"

"Why aren't they answering?" Ashley looked so pathetic, shivering like a drowned rat. When Miranda stopped to hug her, Parker wrapped both girls in a tight hug of his own.

"Roo!" Etienne kept calling. "Gage!"

A blinding flash of lightning ripped the sky. Miranda caught a split-second glance of what she thought might be the Falls, just ahead of them. She tried to go faster, pulling Ashley along with her.

"Roo! Gage!" Mockingly, the storm flung all their shouts back at them. "Roo! Where are you? It's us! Gage! Come on, y'all—*answer*!"

The four trudged on. As Ashley slipped and jerked Miranda down with her into the water, Parker immediately hauled them both up again.

"They're not here!" Ashley wept. "I know something terrible's happened. I *know* it!"

"No, Ashley, they're okay," Miranda insisted. "I'm sure they've taken shelter somewhere—they just can't hear us, that's all."

But Miranda was just as terrified—totally panicked and trying not to show it. It was like being forced back into the hurricane— the awful tragedy happening all over again—*howling wind . . . drowning rain . . . the house falling in . . . the world falling apart and nobody to help . . .*

Once more she stumbled, then realized that Parker still had

a firm grip on her, that he was tucking her inside his jacket, the same way he was tucking Ashley against his other side, shielding them both, steering them both to safety.

"*Roo!*" Parker was hoarse from yelling. "Dammit, are you out here? *Gage!*"

And then . . . miraculously . . . came the faint sound of a voice—thin and weak and frightened, and not so far away . . .

"Here!" it called back. "We're over here!"

"*Roo!*" Ashley screamed. "Oh God, that's *Roo!*"

New strength surged through them as they tried to run, sloshing through mud and muck and water and debris, flashlights slicing the dark.

"I see her!" Etienne called. "Roo! You okay?"

"Yes! But Gage—"

"*Gage!*"

It was the fear in Etienne's voice that pierced Miranda's heart. The stark, raw fear as Etienne shouted his cousin's name and struggled on ahead of them, then suddenly dropped to his knees.

At first Miranda didn't notice anything but the tree. The gigantic tree uprooted and split open on the ground, its massive branches splayed in all directions. But as she got closer, there was movement among the layers and layers of drenched leaves—just a slight movement—and the small, huddled figure of a girl, and the sobs of her desperate pleading.

"Help him! You've got to help him! *Hurry*!"

Scrambling easily over the twisted limbs and foliage, Parker was the next to reach Roo, with Ashley and Miranda right behind him..In shocked silence, the three of them stared at the cuts and bruises on Roo's face and arms, the blood on Roo's clothes . . . but nothing could have prepared them for what they saw next.

"Gage," Roo choked. "He pushed me out of the way. I think . . . I think he's . . ."

Miranda's heart stopped. Gage was sprawled on his back, pinned under one section of the tree. A huge, gnarled branch sloped down across his chest, another had caught his left leg, twisting it behind him at a grotesque angle. Blood had pooled in the wet grass around his head and beneath his shoulders. His eyes were closed. His face was white and still. He looked like some macabre rag doll, tossed carelessly out in the rain.

But almost as wrenching was the sight of Etienne. Etienne kneeling there beside Gage, feeling for a pulse, listening for a heartbeat, his features cold, hard stone.

Miranda didn't realize she'd been holding her breath. Not till Etienne finally glanced up at them, his voice thick with emotion.

"He's breathing. Let's get him outta here."

31

EVEN THEN, it took a moment for the terrible reality to sink in. While Roo and Ashley clutched each other, crying. While Parker, grave and stunned, slid his hand along Roo's shoulder, then squatted down on his heels beside Etienne. And while Miranda bent low over Gage, to smooth the hair back from his forehead.

The storm was growing worse. As the five of them struggled frantically to free Gage, the wind blew wilder, the rain fell harder, and the limbs became heavier to move. Several times Gage roused and cried out, temporarily halting the rescue. Miranda doubted he really comprehended much, but she also knew that if his pain had managed to cross the boundaries of unconsciousness, even for a second, then it had to be excruciating.

"Shit!" Parker exploded. "This is taking too damn long!"

Roo glanced at Gage, then at Miranda. Her dark makeup was runny and smeared, her expression shocked and bewildered. "I just wanted to get away, that's all. But he said he was coming with me, that I always think better with him around. I never thought the rain would get this bad. And he's lost so much blood . . . and I couldn't call 911 . . ."

"Right," Parker remembered. "No phone signal out here." Planting his feet wide apart, he balanced himself on the tree's enormous trunk. He ripped off a limb, flung it angrily, then wiped a muddy hand across his brow. "And Etienne's truck is stranded. Which means we can't go for help."

Ashley's fearful eyes swept over Gage. "It's just . . . like Roo said . . . he's lost so much blood."

It was bad enough not knowing the extent of Gage's injuries; it was even worse not being able to reach the ones they could see. The helplessness was unbearable. Miranda felt as if she were watching all the life drain slowly and steadily out of him.

"I've got some tools in the truck." Shrugging out of his jacket, Etienne passed it to Miranda. "Here—try and keep him warm. I'll be right back."

He was off before anyone could stop him. Holding the jacket at arm's length, Miranda wondered what good it could possibly do—like all the rest of their clothes, it was soaked. With Roo and Ashley's help, she managed to work it in beneath the branches, to tuck it around Gage's chest. Gage moaned, his eyelids struggling open. Most of his right arm had escaped serious injury, so Miranda reached down and gently squeezed his fingers. They were slick with blood.

"Look at his eyes." Crouched there with the others, Ashley began rocking slowly back and forth. "He's hurting so much . . . I can't stand it."

Miranda knew exactly what Ashley meant. Gage's big brown eyes, always so soft, so expressive, were now dull with pain, hazy and unfocused. As a muscle flinched in his jaw, the girls crowded even closer, determined to protect him however they could.

"I think he's coming to," Roo mumbled. Stroking his cheek, she leaned in close to listen.

"Cold," Gage whispered.

Up till now, Miranda hadn't really noticed the bluish tinge to his lips. Alarm bells immediately sounded in her brain, but before she could get up, Parker's hand came down on her shoulder.

"Here," he said, "give him this."

With Roo and Ashley looking on in surprise, Miranda accepted the small flask Parker slid from his pocket. She nodded him a grateful smile.

"What happened?" Gage whispered again. "Roo . . . is Roo okay?"

"He doesn't see me," Roo choked, while Ashley and Miranda forced a few sips of whiskey down Gage's throat. Roo took a deep breath, tried to collect herself. "Hey, I'm fine," she told Gage. "And you're fine, too. And everybody's here, and . . . dammit, Gage, why'd you come with me? I told you not to. I *told* you I wanted to be by myself. Why don't you ever listen to anything I say?"

"So . . . cold," he murmured. "Can't . . . feel . . . legs."

"Gage, no. Oh, God."

Miranda glanced over her shoulder. Etienne had waded back from the truck, bringing tools with him. The boys were standing about twenty feet away, locked in grim conversation. Etienne was pointing to the last cumbersome branch that trapped Gage. Parker was nodding, making air measurements with his hands.

This can't be good. As new prickles of fear crept up Miranda's spine, she refocused on Gage.

"He's still saying he's cold," Ashley said.

For the first time Miranda stared at Ashley's pink headband. The girl had pulled it from her hair and was running it tenderly over Gage's face, trying to clean off dirt and blood. How long had Ashley been doing that, Miranda wondered—how long had they all been out here? She didn't even recall *seeing* that headband before—but seeing it now, with Gage's blood all over it, was almost too much for her. She closed her eyes, swallowed hard, tried to concentrate on what Ashley was saying.

"I don't think it's just his legs he can't feel. I'm not sure he can feel *anything*."

Miranda opened her eyes. All this time she'd been holding Gage's hand, squeezing his fingers, getting no response. "It's temporary," she answered, determined to be hopeful. "He's fading in and out right now, and that's good. If he could feel everything—everywhere he's hurt—I'm not sure he could take it."

"Miranda"—Ashley's eyes were wide with fear—"what are we going to do?"

Miranda could only shrug in frustration. As Ashley pressed the headband to Gage's forehead, and Roo continued to stroke Gage's cheek, Etienne and Parker walked over.

"This should do it," Etienne announced. "Now y'all need to hold him down. *Tight*, you understand? 'Cause when we cut this last branch, and it shifts around, he's probably gonna feel it. And it'll hurt like hell."

Roo's stare went slowly from Etienne to Parker. "He's going to die, isn't he."

"And leave you?" Parker snorted. "Not a chance."

And then everything happened so fast. Surreal, like a dream—age-old instincts of love and survival, guiding them, giving them strength. The girls trying to restrain Gage—Parker and Etienne shouting—the crushing branch turning and scraping and tilting, suspended there for mere seconds—just long enough for Gage to be dragged out from under it.

Miranda was distinctly aware of two things.

Gage screaming in agony.

And the world turning red with his blood.

"Quick!"

"Got him!"

"Move!"

As the tree came down again, it hit with an earth-shuddering crash. But Gage was clear of it, and—at least for now—he was still alive.

"Come on—take him to the shelter!"

"The picnic shelter? Are you sure it's safe?"

"It's concrete, and it's raised. What, you got any better ideas?"

Sharp tableaux swept through Miranda's head, imprinting themselves on her brain—bright, piercing snapshots she knew she'd never forget.

The raging storm and the raging emotions. Gage's face twisted in anguish, his broken body, shards of white bone, torn muscles, raw flesh. Gage trying so hard to be brave, trying so hard not to feel, not to cry, even as tears streamed helplessly down his cheeks. And the blessed relief of unconsciousness that followed;

the limp, easy weight of him in their arms; their rushing him to the picnic shelter, laying him down, standing guard—close and watchful and protective—around him.

"Anybody here ever set a broken bone?" As the others regarded him with blank expressions, Etienne pointed to Gage's leg. "Great. Anybody here wanna help me?"

And once again it was as if somehow, instinctively, they all knew what to do. Parker and Etienne tearing off their shirts to stanch the bleeding. Every jacket, every extra bit of clothing commandeered for makeshift blankets and bandages. Caring for Gage, crying for Gage, praying for Gage. When all had been done that *could* be done, only then did everyone finally give in to exhaustion, resolved to wait out the storm.

"Listen," Etienne said. For the last half hour he'd been leaning up against the wall, arms folded across his bare chest, narrowed eyes gauging the flooded woods around them. "I'm gonna try to make it home."

"Now?" Parker gaped at him as though he'd lost his mind. "In *this*?"

"Etienne, that's crazy!" Curled along Gage's side, Ashley raised up in alarm. "There's no way you could get home. Don't even think about it."

Etienne's sigh was tolerant. "Look, it's not that far—"

"I know how far it is," Parker broke in. "But going by truck is one thing. And going by boat is another thing. But trying to swim—"

"It's not that bad yet. I can still make it through if I leave now. And it won't be this deep, the closer I get to the road."

"Roo, say something." Half turning, Ashley appealed to her sister. "He'll listen to you. Tell him not to go."

Roo calmly considered. She'd been sitting cross-legged beside Ashley, with Gage's head cradled in her lap. Her glance flicked from Etienne to Gage, but when she didn't answer, Parker resumed the argument.

"Have you noticed it's very dark out there? Does the word *night* mean anything to you?"

"Nobody knows we're here." Etienne's reply was matter-of-fact. "It's not like they're gonna be sending search parties for us anytime soon."

"At least wait till the rain lets up a little."

"This rain, it could go on for hours." Etienne's mouth settled into a hard line. "And if the water keeps rising . . . I mean . . . Gage needs help."

Throughout the exchange, Miranda kept her thoughts to herself. She didn't want to admit how terrified she was, watching Gage with an increasing sense of dread. His breathing was more ragged now, catching tight in his chest, stabbing deep through his muscles. And even though he was covered with sweat, he'd begun shivering uncontrollably.

At last she stood up. She walked solemnly over to Parker and Etienne. "I think . . . someone needs to go."

As the three of them stared at one another, Etienne pushed away from the wall.

"No." Parker grabbed Etienne's arm. "I'll go."

Surprise crept slowly over Etienne's face. Instinctively, Miranda glanced at Ashley, who seemed oddly frozen.

"Parker—" Ashley began, but Etienne interrupted.

"I know the way better than you do," he said firmly.

"Like I haven't been to your house a million times?" Grinning, Parker shrugged and jerked his chin in Gage's direction. "You got one too sick to go, two too tired to go, and her"—he winked at Miranda—"too damn cute to go. And besides, who's the athlete around here anyway?"

"No, Parker. I—"

"Look." The grin faded from Parker's lips. He moved closer to Etienne, putting his back to Roo and Ashley so they couldn't hear. His voice was soft now, and serious. "You and Gage, you're each other's family. If something happened to you—" He broke off, glanced away, then pulled his eyes back to Etienne. "What would Gage do if something happened to you? Hell, what would *any* of us do if something happened to you?"

Their gazes held steady. Parker swallowed . . . gave a slight nod.

"Let me do this, Etienne. I want to."

Silence fell between them.

A silence louder, wider, deeper than any storm.

It was Ashley who broke it. "Parker, what's happening?"

Almost guiltily, Miranda jumped. She'd been so engrossed in the boys' conversation, she hadn't noticed Ashley approaching. At once Parker and Etienne turned toward Ashley, their expressions somber.

"Parker?" Ashley asked again. But then, as she stared long and hard at the boys, a slow dawn of awareness crept over her. "No, Parker. Please don't be stupid."

Miranda waited for Roo's usual insults. Roo kept silent.

"Hey, I'm up for this." Grin firmly back in place, Parker struck a heroic pose. "Parker Wilmington—explorer, adventurer, and super-swimmer!"

"Parker, you can't go out there—"

"Battling the elements! Wrestling man-eating alligators! Laughing in the face of danger!"

"Parker, I'm serious!" Ashley was close to tears. "It's too far to Etienne's house!"

"Hey, I need the exercise. And the fresh air. And the good news is: I won't even have to worry about dehydration."

But the tears came now, rolling down Ashley's cheeks, while Etienne tactfully moved away and Miranda joined him.

"Please." Slipping her arms around Parker's waist, Ashley leaned into him, peered up at him. "It's too horrible out there. I'm scared."

Parker raised his arms, flexed his muscles. "Fear? Fear is foreign to me!"

"Don't joke about this! I'm really scared something bad will happen. I just *feel* it."

"Ash, nothing bad is going to happen. I'll be careful, okay? I'll be safe."

Miranda suddenly realized she'd been eavesdropping. She hadn't meant to intrude on their private conversation, yet she'd been watching their faces and hearing every word. An eerie chill had settled at the base of her spine. She felt anxious and restless and afraid.

She glanced at Roo. Roo hadn't said anything in such a long

time, just sitting there holding Gage, her head bent over his face. Miranda's heart reached out to Roo, but her own uneasiness persisted. *Something dangerous, something tragic . . .*

Something familiar . . .

Reluctantly she turned her attention to Ashley and Parker. Though Ashley's features were pale and drawn, she seemed composed now, even quietly resigned. Parker was squeezing her in a tight hug.

"You better hurry, Parker Wilmington." Ashley's voice was muffled against his chest. "Promise you'll come back to me."

Parker rolled his eyes. "Yeah, yeah, sure. I promise."

"*Tonight.*"

"Tonight," Parker echoed dutifully.

"Cross your heart."

"Oh, for Christ's sake, Ashley, I said I'd be back, didn't I? Don't I *always* come back? Even when you *don't* want me to?"

Miranda's breath caught in her throat. Fear squeezed in her chest.

It can't be . . . it's impossible . . .

For she knew now why she'd listened so intently to Ashley and Parker, why their conversation had seemed so familiar . . .

Oh, God, no . . .

"Parker," she whispered.

Starting forward, she saw Ashley and Etienne standing at the edge of the shelter. Ashley was shivering, and Etienne's arm was around her shoulders. Miranda tried to call out, to shout a warning, to stop Parker from going, but he'd already dashed into the rain; she could already see the beam of his flashlight growing smaller and dimmer, swallowed by the storm.

Yet his words were still here. They lingered in this dark, frightening, abandoned place—the words he'd spoken to Ashley, and the words Ashley had spoken to him.

Prophetic words and fatal words. Words that tore at Miranda's heart and echoed over and over again in her mind.

The words Nathan and Ellena had spoken . . .

Right before the end.

32

"**Where is he, Miranda?**" **Ashley whispered.** "What's taking him so long?"

Hours had passed since Parker vanished into the storm. Hours of waiting and worrying and watching hopefully for his return. And though Miranda had kept up a steady show of confidence for Ashley's sake, secretly she was scared to death.

Nathan promised Ellena he'd come back to her . . .

And Ellena never saw him again.

Miranda noticed Ashley's grave expression. She remembered Ashley's fears that something bad would happen . . . and Parker's attempts to reassure her.

Ellena never saw him again.

"Something must have happened." Glancing from Roo to Miranda, Ashley ran her hand lightly over Gage's cheek. "I just have this horrible feeling—"

"Listen to me, *cher*," Etienne broke in. "He's fine. It's just gonna take him some time, that's all. But he'll come rescue us. You'll see."

Miranda could tell how much Ashley wanted to believe him. But as the girl's face began to crumple, Etienne stretched out his arms. "Aw, now, don't cry. Come here to me."

Ashley got up and started toward him, just as Etienne started toward her. He drew her gently against him. And then, while she sobbed quietly, he held her in a strong, solid embrace.

"You're tired, *cher*," Etienne mumbled. "We're all tired; we're all a little scared. It's okay to cry. Just get it all out. We're all gonna be fine. You'll see . . . you'll see . . ."

Miranda also wanted to believe that, though the words of Nathan and Ellena continued to haunt her. She couldn't even share her fears with Etienne, not when he had so much to deal with already.

She couldn't help marveling at him. His calm in the midst of chaos. His detachment holding them together. The way he rested his chin on top of Ashley's head. Patting her back, swaying her ever so gently . . . murmuring comfort and hope. Even though he looked far more strained and exhausted than the rest of them. Even though Gage still lay battered and unconscious, and there was nothing more any of them could do. And even though the storm blew savagely around them, and the black water was creeping over the foundation of the shelter, and inching slowly toward Etienne's feet.

"But Parker *should* be back by now," Roo suddenly murmured to Miranda. "Maybe something really *did* happen."

Miranda threw her an anxious glance. Nodding, Roo fixed a worried gaze on Ashley.

Time crawled endlessly. Minutes stretched to hours, and those hours grew more fearful. The girls kept their vigil around Gage. Etienne continued to stand, his keen eyes watchful for some sign of Parker's return. Miranda could only pray that Gage wouldn't rouse from unconsciousness.

As the night drew on, Parker's absence became almost unbearable. Etienne had started pacing. Roo had scooted closer to her sister, occasionally leaning her head on Ashley's shoulder. Watching Ashley stare so sadly out into the night, Miranda could only imagine what the girl must be thinking. Once again she tried to make positive conversation.

"It's so brave, what Parker's doing." Miranda offered Ashley an encouraging smile.

But Ashley's own smile seemed emotionless. "He should have been there by now. We all know it. People should be rescuing us."

"They'll come, Ash," Roo mumbled.

"He must not have gotten there."

"He did. I'm sure he did."

Ashley took a deep breath. She touched her head against Roo's, then gazed at Miranda.

"I'm not as nice to Parker as I should be."

"How can you even say that?" Miranda was startled. "Parker's crazy about you."

"But I'm mean to him sometimes."

Again Miranda expected Roo to chime in with her usual sarcasm. But again, Roo was uncharacteristically quiet.

"I am," Ashley admitted, almost shamefully. "I *am* mean to him."

"You're *true* to him," Miranda corrected. "And *truthful* to him. I can't think of a better way to love someone."

Just like Nathan and Ellena. Oh please, God, let Parker be okay.

Ashley seemed to find solace in Miranda's words. Lowering her head, she spoke softly to Roo.

"I don't care about Parker more than I care about you."

"I know," Roo said, without looking up. "I just don't want you riding in Parker's car when he's been drinking."

"I know."

"Hey!" Etienne called sharply. "They're here—they're coming!"

Even then, Miranda could hardly believe it. Even then, as she and Roo and Ashley jumped to their feet and saw Etienne signal with the flashlight. To her amazement, other lights were signaling back to them—flashing lights from police cars and ambulances, spinning lights from fire trucks—and there were sirens, and shouts, men running, confusion and chaos—

"*Parker!*" Ashley cried.

He grabbed her into his arms and held her, burying his face in her hair. His sides were heaving, his voice was hoarse. He looked completely drained. "I told you I'd come back."

"Yes—yes—you did. And don't you ever leave me again!"

"How's Gage? Is he—"

"He's alive, but it's bad, Parker; it's much worse. He hasn't woken up, and he's hardly breathing and—"

"It's okay, Ash, they'll take care of him now."

Releasing Ashley, Parker turned to Etienne. A look passed between them . . . a nod . . . a thousand silent words. As emergency teams swarmed around them, Parker spotted Miranda and caught her in a hug.

"God, Parker." Miranda's voice broke. "Are we glad to see you."

"Likewise. And you don't have to call me God. *Saint* Parker's good enough. Where's Roo?"

"Back there with—"

"Gage. Yeah, I see her."

The relief was overwhelming. Miranda had been so terrified, so determined not to cry, so intent on holding it together—at least till she could get home. Now suddenly there were paramedics wrapping her in blankets, examining her cuts and scrapes and bruises, asking her questions, passing her hot chocolate, and she felt so grateful and so relieved and just so glad to be alive . . .

"Oh, Roo," she whispered.

Because all at once she had a straight, clear view of Roo, and the view was heartbreaking. Roo, who was being quickly and efficiently forced out of the way as rescuers honed in on Gage's critical injuries. Roo, who was standing there alone, looking lost and scared and pathetically childlike . . .

"Roo!" Miranda called and started toward her.

But she realized then that the others had noticed, too. Ashley and Parker and Etienne, all of them hurrying in Roo's direction, though it was Parker who reached her first.

"So what'd you do?" he teased gently. "Take bets I wouldn't make it back?"

Despite her best attempt at annoyance, Roo's voice was shaking. "A girl can hope, can't she?"

"Hey, I came back to save you."

"Hey, you came back to spite me."

Parker ruffled her hair. Roo punched him in the abs. While the five of them watched Gage being carried away on a stretcher,

Parker slid his arm around Roo's shoulders. And Roo didn't pull away.

Dangerously close to tears again, Miranda sagged back against the wall and tried to collect herself. In all the commotion, she hadn't even noticed the woman running over to Etienne, but it was quickly apparent that the rest of the group knew her. They crowded in close, everyone talking at once, while the woman listened attentively, scrutinizing each bedraggled appearance, feeling every forehead, stroking every cheek.

"Miranda." Ashley motioned her over. "Come meet Etienne's mom."

She was small and delicate—almost frail in her oversize jacket, floppy wide-brimmed hat, and wading boots that reached up to her knees. She had Etienne's nose and Etienne's hair, and a knowing half-smile that was currently being leveled at her son. Catching his face between her hands, she held Etienne's gaze with her own. Her wide dark eyes caressed and scolded him. His eyes teased back and adored her.

"—want all y'all to get checked out, just in case," Etienne's mom was saying. "Your aunt Jules and uncle Frank will meet us at the hospital. Gage . . . our baby . . ."

Etienne whispered something that seemed to reassure her. She stepped back from him as Ashley touched her arm.

"Miss Nell," Ashley said, pulling Miranda over. "This is Miranda."

Miranda felt the instant appraisal of those coal-black eyes. When Nell Boucher took her hand, Miranda sensed strength, survival, and a heart of immense kindness.

"It's nice to meet you, Mrs. Boucher," she answered shyly.

"Nell," the woman corrected, a dimple showing at each corner of her mouth. She cocked an eyebrow at Etienne. "Okay, I guess you win the bet. She's just as cute as you said she was."

Blushing, Miranda was all too conscious of the others' amused stares. As she had with the rest of them, Miss Nell put one hand to Miranda's cheek and leaned in close.

"I'm glad we're finally meeting," she murmured. "Because I've certainly heard a lot of wonderful things about you."

Miranda was at a loss for words, but Miss Nell didn't seem to mind. Instead, the woman calmly herded the five of them together, then led them out through the storm to safety.

33

"OKAY, Y'ALL," ASHLEY ANNOUNCED. "This is our dress rehearsal. Our last chance to get everything perfect before the big night tomorrow. Any questions? Ideas? Opinions?"

"Yeah, I have an idea." Slumped on the front steps of the Battlefield Inn, Parker choked down a mouthful of cough syrup and tried not to speak above a whisper. "Let's call it off. That would *really* make it perfect. No more ghost tour."

"Walk of the Spirits," Ashley corrected him, irritated. "*Walk of the Spirits.* And we're *not* calling it off. After all this time? All this work?"

"All this suffering?" Roo added. She was perched one step below Parker, and was digging through her pockets for a cigarette. Her face still bore some major bruises from the storm, and a wide gash zigzagged across her forehead, not quite healed. She'd taken great pains to highlight this zigzag with dark, red lipstick.

"You *like* suffering," Parker reminded her. "And, excuse me, but *you're* not the one with pneumonia."

"You don't have pneumonia. You're just jealous because Gage was in worse shape than you, and he got more attention."

"Well, it's *almost* pneumonia. It's turning *into* pneumonia." Tensing, Parker let out a gigantic sneeze. "Shit, I hate this. I feel like my brain's ten times its normal size."

Roo gave him a bland stare. "You know, when people lose a leg or an arm, they think they still feel it, even though it's not really there."

"Will you two behave?" Ashley scolded. "And, Parker, where's that newspaper article your mom was going to give us?"

"Somewhere." Parker thought a moment, then shrugged. "In my car, I think."

"Well, will you please go get it? The sooner we start, the sooner we can all go home."

"She's right." Though unable to hold back a laugh, Miranda came loyally to Ashley's rescue. "Let's just walk it through, and read the script, and make sure we've covered all the basic information. Ashley, what about your costume?"

"I've got the final fitting after I leave here." Ashley's eyes shone with excitement. "Can you believe Mrs. Wilmington went to all that trouble to make it for me?"

"She didn't." Parker scowled. "She got her *dressmaker,* or *designer*, or *whoever* the hell she calls him, to make it for you."

"Parker, that doesn't matter—it was still really nice of your mother to do that."

"You're a southern belle—how could she resist that?"

Ashley shot Miranda a grateful smile. "That was Miranda's idea."

"It made sense," Miranda explained. "A costume sets the mood. It's all about southern history and heritage, so our tour guide should be a southern hostess—hoopskirt and all."

"And I'm the only one who gets to dress up! And I can't wait to wear it! It's like cotton candy!"

Roo arched an eyebrow. "Sticky?"

"No! All pink and fluffy and . . . sweet. I love the way I feel in it."

"I agree," Parker said hoarsely. "I love the way you feel in it, too. And I love the way you feel *out* of it even better."

Roo stared at him. "Wow. You should write greeting cards."

But before he could manage a comeback, Ashley stood on her tiptoes and started waving frantically toward the curb.

"There's Gage and Etienne! Hey, y'all! We weren't sure you were coming tonight! Gage, you are *just* looking better and better!"

Miranda watched the two guys climb from Etienne's truck and start up the sidewalk. Nearly three weeks had passed since that awful night of the storm, and though Gage wasn't fully recovered yet—his left leg was still in a cast—he could hobble unsteadily on crutches. And, Miranda noted, despite his lingering cuts, scrapes, and bruises, his eyes and his smile were just as irresistible as before.

"So we haven't missed anything?" Etienne greeted them. Leaving Gage at the bottom of the steps, he couldn't resist sprinting up and tapping Roo on her forehead. "Hey, love the scar. *Very* Bride of Frankenstein."

Roo looked pleased. Ashley was still focused intently on Gage.

"You're still kind of pale though," she worried, gazing at his face, running her finger along one of his cheekbones. "And your face is still pretty thin."

Gage glanced sideways, trying to avoid the attention. "I'm fine. My leg looks worse than it feels."

"No, it doesn't," Etienne teased him. "You're just being brave."

"No, I'm not. It really doesn't feel that bad."

"Well, at least you can feel *something* now," Parker remarked offhandedly. "The night you got hurt, you couldn't feel much of anything."

"I couldn't?"

"You mean, the girls didn't tell you?" Feigning concern, Parker shook his head. "Well, they had to . . . you know . . . *test* a lot of places on you. Just to see if you *could* still feel."

The flush had already started up Gage's cheeks.

"That's true," Roo agreed. "Of course . . . some places were a lot more fun to test than others."

"A *whole* lot more fun to test than others," Ashley insisted.

Gage's embarrassment reached full blush. Hiding a smile, Ashley pressed her palm to his forehead.

"But you're sure you feel fine now? Because you look a little hot."

"He *is* hot," Roo answered. "Oh. Oh, you meant his temperature."

"Stop," poor Gage mumbled. "I'm fine."

Etienne motioned to Ashley, his expression perfectly serious. "Come on. Y'all know how Gage is—he's suffering in silence 'cause he doesn't want to look weak in front of you women."

"Cut it out," Gage said.

"No, really. We all know you're just being modest."

"Shut up."

Roo fixed Gage with an owlish stare. "You cried when you broke your leg."

"I did not."

"Yes, you did. You cried. You're a crybaby."

The best Parker could offer was a sympathetic shrug. "Sorry, little soldier. You cried."

Gage looked longingly at the truck. Taking pity on him at last, the others stopped teasing and turned their attention back to their project.

In the days since the storm, they'd held many discussions about Nathan and Ellena Rose. Miranda had finally been able to offer them the insights she'd shared with Etienne that day—about the boardinghouse and the secret meetings, Nathan's and Ellena's work as spies and their passionate love, their promise made with the watch and chain, and finally—most important—the tragic truth of the betrayal. Everyone except Parker had been captivated by her story. Everyone except Parker had insisted Hayes House be added to their tour. All of them had speculated as to where Jonas might have put the watch, but none of their guesses had panned out. And though the whereabouts of Nathan's watch remained a mystery, Miranda was still determined to find it and reunite it with the braid of Ellena's hair.

Now, preparing to rehearse their ghostly tour, Miranda was still thinking about her grandpa and the long-ago tragedy he'd passed on to her. She'd hoped to have all the questions answered by now . . . the puzzle pieces together . . . the spirits at peace. *So close . . . but not there yet . . .*

"I wish we could put Nathan and Ellena and Travis on our walk." Ashley sighed. "It just doesn't seem complete without them."

"They're on our walk." Taking Ashley's notebook, Roo calmly pointed to the neatly lettered, neatly organized tour script. "See? Right here. Magnolia Gallery. Opera house fire."

"That's not what I meant. Each of them really, really loved somebody very much. That's what I want people to remember." Ashley put a hand over her heart. "The loves that never die."

"The loves that *made* people die." Parker downed another swig of cough medicine, capped the bottle, then slid it into the back pocket of his jeans. "Sorry, Ash, but that's not the way of the world. If you tell their real stories, people will only remember all the dumb mistakes they made. Like . . . oh, you know . . . torture and murder and arson and treason and—"

"Ah, yes," Roo acknowledged coolly. "Parker Wilmington, the last of the true romantics."

Retrieving her notebook, Ashley hugged it to her chest. Her sigh was more wistful this time. "I know you're right. I mean, we can't ever give away their real secrets. Not on the Walk of the Spirits . . . not to anybody . . . not ever. I mean, Nathan and Ellena and Travis lived and sacrificed and died, protecting those secrets about themselves. If *we* told their secrets, it would be like betraying them all over again."

"Or we could call the tabloids and paparazzi," Parker deadpanned. "They pay big money for secrets and betrayals."

"Parker Wilmington, if I told even *half* your secrets and betrayals, I'd be a very rich woman!"

Even Parker looked amused as the group broke into raucous applause. Looking entirely pleased with herself, Ashley curtsied, then motioned them all toward the Brickway.

"I'm going to be so nervous tomorrow," Ashley confessed, linking her arm through Miranda's. "What if our whole class hates it?"

"Then I'll say I told you so," Parker replied. Roo, Gage, and Etienne had moved several feet ahead to argue something about the script. Hanging back, Parker tried to swallow, but winced at the effort. "Anybody got anything stronger than cough syrup?"

When no one responded, he pointed to his BMW parked along the opposite curb. "You know what? As sad as I know this will make you, ladies, I'm going home and to bed. Alone."

"Parker—"

"Oh, yeah, right—I've got that stupid article in my car. Go on ahead. I'll give it to Miranda."

"Parker, do you really feel that terrible?"

"Christ, Ashley, my throat's like raw hamburger. Is that terrible enough for you to believe me?"

The suspicion on Ashley's face turned to guilt, and Miranda felt just as bad. They both knew Parker had gotten sick trying to save them. Maybe he wasn't faking so much after all.

As Ashley caught up to the others, Miranda followed Parker across the street.

Dusk had fallen, and shadows lay deep. While Parker grabbed an envelope from the glove box, Miranda watched Ashley and the others talking beneath a lamppost on the corner . . . heard their muffled laughter and conversation.

"Miranda?" Parker said suddenly.

Startled, Miranda saw him turn around. In the dim light, something in his face caught her attention. Something like bewilderment . . . or even fear . . .

"Parker, what is it?"

He handed her the envelope. After a brief hesitation, he leaned slowly against the side of his car. "Miranda, I just wanted . . . needed to tell you."

"Tell me what"

"Damn. This is . . . really hard."

A spark of worry flared inside her. "Parker, *tell* me. What's wrong?"

"Something happened that night, Miranda." Another short pause before he spoke again. "In the storm."

"What do you mean?"

"When I left y'all there at the shelter, and I tried to get to Etienne's house."

"But you *did* get there. You brought back help, and you saved us."

"I didn't." His voice dropped to a whisper. "I didn't."

"Parker—"

"I mean, I *did*. But not like everybody thinks."

She realized she was shaking. She realized Parker was shaking, too, and there was something unnerving about his stare.

"I got lost," he mumbled. "I got so lost, I didn't have a clue where I was or what direction I was headed. And it was shit-awful scary out there."

As though the memory were too much for him, he sank to the curb and squatted back on his heels.

"The flashlight was like nothing. *Nothing.* And suddenly I just stepped off—tripped—I don't know, the ground just disappeared, and I went down. And I thought, This is it: I'm drowning; I'm going to die."

She gazed at him sympathetically, but he avoided her eyes. His words were tight with emotion. "And then . . . something happened. I . . ."

"Parker?"

"I swear to God, Miranda, there was this light. Like a flashlight, only . . . only *not* a flashlight. More like a lantern, I guess . . . and this . . . I don't know . . . *something* just sort of floated out of the rain, floated right out of the storm toward me. I could feel it on the back of my neck, and on my shoulders—and it grabbed me under my arms and pulled me out."

Parker's hands clenched into fists. He pressed them hard against his temples. "I heard this voice . . . this voice sort of talking, sort of singing. And it sounded . . . like a woman's voice."

"Was the voice familiar? Did you recognize her?"

"No." Adamantly, Parker shook his head. "But she called me Nathan."

34

MIRANDA WENT ICE COLD. As she and Parker locked eyes, time seemed to halt around them.

"And then . . ." Parker drew a ragged breath. "I was totally free. And the lantern sort of . . . *moved* . . . like somebody was swinging it, you know? Waving it in one direction?"

"What happened next?"

"Hell, I ran, swam—both. I was so damn scared, and so damn glad to be alive."

He'd turned his head away. His voice was hollow now, and she had to strain to hear.

"And then it was like I kicked into autopilot or something—I didn't even think about where I was going, I just went straight to Etienne's house. It was like I'd been dreaming, and then I woke up, and I was just *there*. And I found his mom, and she got help—"

Parker's words choked off. For an endless moment neither he nor Miranda spoke.

Then, at last, he looked at her again. Gave a sheepish smile, gave a strained, self-conscious laugh. "So what, am I crazy?"

"No." Reaching out, Miranda firmly took his hand. "No, Parker, you're not. Not at all."

Another laugh, more hoarse this time. He tried to clear

his throat. His nose was running, and his eyes shone with embarrassed tears; he wiped one sleeve angrily across his cheeks. On a sudden impulse, Miranda threw her arms around him.

"What's that for?" Parker asked, both flustered and surprised.

"Just . . ." Miranda pulled back again. She gazed anxiously into his eyes. "Parker . . . you saw it. You saw it was real."

He wanted to forget about it, she could tell. He'd opened himself and shown her his fears, and now he wanted to forget it ever happened. *But you won't forget, Parker. You'll never forget. I've been there. I know.*

"You believe me," she whispered.

"Okay, fine, I believe you."

His stare, always so bold, faltered a little. He tilted his head back and made a frustrated sound in his throat.

"We're not going to be like best girlfriends now, are we?" he accused her. "I mean, you're not going to be squealing at me every time somebody says the word *ghost*, are you?"

"Of course not."

"Because . . . I swear to God, Miranda, if you *ever* tell anybody—"

Miranda hugged him tighter. "I won't tell a soul."

"A *soul*? Is that supposed to be funny?"

"I won't tell anyone. I'm just hugging you because you're you."

"Yeah, I get that a lot. Girls want to *love* me, and guys want to *be* me."

Another coughing spasm racked through him. Catching his breath, he shifted away from her, reached wearily for his back pocket, and pulled out the bottle of medicine. Miranda saw him fumble it between his fingers—she heard the sharp clink as it fell and struck the curb.

"Oh shit," Parker muttered. "There goes my fix."

But the bottle hadn't broken. Instead it began to roll slowly into the street, turning over and over . . . over and over—a rhythmic, monotonous sound.

That sound . . .

And Miranda realized she *knew* that sound—or something very like it—it was *familiar*, she'd heard it before . . . *but when? Where?*

"Parker?"

"Yeah?" He'd gotten up now, gone after his bottle of cough syrup. With one smooth motion he scooped it up, unscrewed the top, and took a satisfied gulp.

"Parker, I . . ." *Something . . . I know it's there . . . I want to remember . . .* "I want you to take me home."

Parker froze, the bottle at his lips, poised for another swallow. He shot her a sidelong glance.

"This is so sudden, Miranda. I mean, we hardly know each other, and I *do* have a girlfriend. And there *is*, of course, the issue of my extremely high moral standards. But . . . okay. What the hell. I'll take you home with me."

"Not *your* home. *My* home. Hayes House."

"What? Hayes House? Oh! Sure! Hayes House! Did you think I meant—that I wanted to—hey, I was just kidding!"

The irreverence was there again, the cocky grin back in place. As Miranda climbed into the passenger seat, Parker slid behind the wheel, then gunned the engine to breakneck speed. In less than five minutes they were squealing into the driveway of Hayes House. But even when Parker reached across and shoved open her door, Miranda made no move to get out.

"Let me guess." Parker watched her expectantly. "You really *do* want to go home with me. You were just playing hard to get."

Slowly Miranda shook her head. She gazed down at the envelope in her lap. "I forgot to give this to Ashley."

"Forget it. Why the big rush to get here?"

The sound . . . the rolling sound . . . it's close . . . it's important. "I'm not sure, Parker. There's . . . something—"

"No. Don't tell me. Whatever it is, I don't want to see it, hear it, or go through it ever again."

Getting out of the car, Miranda walked a few steps before turning back to face him. "But aren't you even curious about what happened to you out in the storm? Don't you even want to explore all the—"

"Stop right there. There's lots of things I *want* to explore, and things I most definitely *will* explore. But ghosts aren't one of them. See you later."

She watched him back down the driveway. Within seconds, the BMW had faded from sight, yet the sound—*that sound!*—stayed with her. Parker's bottle of cough syrup rolling out into the street . . . *that rhythmic, monotonous sound . . .*

Why did it seem so familiar? Nagging her and bringing back memories—*except I don't know what the memories are! They're right here, close enough to touch, and deep inside, but I can't reach them!*

Frustrated, she went into the house. Mom and Aunt Teeta had gone out to eat; she was glad to have the whole place to herself. Within seconds she found herself upstairs in her grandpa's room, surrounded by so many things, so many connections to so many worlds . . .

Help me, Grandpa. Nathan . . . Ellena Rose . . . help me.

The room was silent, yet full of echoes. Ghostly whispers from forgotten voices . . . desperate pleas from her grandfather . . . comforting words from Etienne . . .

"Help me, Etienne," she murmured.

"*Whatever it was that Jonas found, he'd have kept it close to him,*" Etienne had insisted.

Especially if it was your last treasure, your last quest, your last responsibility—right, Grandpa?

She walked to the nightstand. Not much had been moved in this room since the death of Jonas Hayes. As her eyes did a sweep of her surroundings, as her hands slid over the nightstand, her mind spun back to that day she'd been in here—*that day I first met Grandpa. He was asleep; I was curious, looking through all his stuff. I touched something, some kind of container, and Grandpa looked at me, and something fell on the floor . . .*

A tin. I remember now.

It rolled under the dresser, and Grandpa spoke to me, and when Etienne came, I forgot about the tin, and I never picked it up again . . .

Her heart raced out of control. She reached under the antique dresser, groped along the hardwood floor. Her fingers closed around a small, round canister.

It rolled when she touched it.

Rocking back on her heels, she pried the round lid from the tin. Her hands were trembling so violently, she could barely lift the old pocket watch from its wrapping of yellowed cloth.

Oh my God . . .

It was as though she held something alive. Something that swelled through her heart and coursed through her veins and burst into a thousand different emotions. Tears flowed down her cheeks, and she touched a fingertip carefully to the tiny spring latch.

The top clicked open. The rusted hinge gave way.

Through shimmering tears, she saw the tiny scrap of paper that fell out into her palm. Very slowly, she began to unfold it, piece by painstaking piece, all too aware of the delicate memories she was holding.

Even after all this time . . .

The delicate memories, and fragile lives, and long-ago brittle promises, all of them crumbling into dust between her fingertips.

Yet the message itself remained.

Six simple words, binding two hearts forever:

Nathan, I love you,
your Ellena.

35

"**WHAT IF NOBODY COMES?**" Ashley wrung her hands.

"They'll show up," Roo assured her.

"If nobody shows up, it'll be my absolute worst nightmare."

Blowing his nose into a tissue, Parker looked up with bleary eyes. "And if you don't stop talking about it, it'll be *my* absolute worst nightmare."

"Parker Wilmington, how can you say that? For the millionth time, this counts for half our grade. And we can't very well have a Walk of the Spirits if there's nobody to walk with."

Miranda opted for practicality. "Well, we know Miss Dupree and our class will be here. And I know my mom and Aunt Teeta are coming."

"My folks, too," Gage added. "And some of the other kids at school—they said they were interested."

"Yeah. In laughing at us." Flopping into a chair, Parker slid low on his spine. His voice was even hoarser than yesterday, and he winced each time he tried to talk. "Shit, I'll be glad when this is over."

Etienne struggled to keep a straight face. "How come? You scared you might see a real ghost?"

Miranda caught the fierce, accusing glare Parker shot her. But when Parker read the honest bewilderment on her face, he forced a painful laugh. "Right. Good one, Boucher. Real ghosts. Very funny."

The six of them were in the lobby of the Battlefield Inn. While the others scanned last-minute notes and details of the tour script, Ashley was practically wearing out a path in the carpet.

"I'm just so nervous!" Taking the old-fashioned lantern Miranda handed her, she held it high above her head. "Oh, Miranda, carrying this was another wonderful idea of yours! And just look at my dress! Do I look okay?"

Roo gave her sister a bland appraisal. The southern belle gown was an airy, pastel confection of satin and lace and taffeta. "You look . . . pink. Pink and . . . pink. And—"

"Beautiful," Gage broke in. "You look beautiful, Ash."

"So sit yourself down," Etienne ordered. "Before I *hold* you down."

Sticking her tongue out at him, Ashley kept right on pacing, oblivious to her wide hoopskirt sweeping everything in its path—including Gage. Catching himself just in time, Gage backed out of her way and tried to realign his crutches. As Roo slyly tapped his left crutch with the toe of her combat boot, he shot her a warning glance.

"Don't make me teach you a lesson." He sighed.

"As if you could. In the shape you're in."

"Well, in case you've forgotten—you're the reason I'm *in* this shape."

Roo lounged slowly back in her seat. She fixed Gage with a long, unwavering stare. "I told Miranda you and I had sex."

The room went silent.

Everyone froze. And turned. And looked at Gage.

"I—you—what—" A slow, hot blush crept over Gage's cheeks. His eyes widened in disbelief. "Roo—I—you—"

"Gross!" Parker shuddered. "*Way* too much information!"

"*Valuable* information, *cher*." Etienne winked at Roo. "Girls at school, they'll pay a whole lotta money to find out if Gage has any *other* dimples."

While Ashley collapsed in giggles, Miranda tried her best not to laugh. Groaning softly, Gage ducked his head.

"Oh, look!" Ashley let out a sudden squeal. "Look, y'all! I see some people outside! I think they're coming over!"

It was true. After weeks and weeks of painstaking study and planning and rehearsing, opening night was finally here. St. Yvette's first Walk of the Spirits.

"They *are* coming!" Ashley exclaimed. "See, Roo, I knew they'd show up."

Dusk was settling over the Brickway. The air was warm, with a balmy breeze and the skies downy gray. No threat of rain, just a pale sprinkling of stars. Even the Historic District seemed different tonight, Miranda couldn't help thinking. Soft with shadows . . . hushed with secrets . . . sweetly sentimental with memories.

And tonight we'll remember Nathan and Ellena.

Tonight they'll be together again.

She hadn't told the others about finding the watch . . . she hadn't even told Etienne.

She wanted to surprise them.

And she wanted the moment to be just right.

"There's Miss Dupree!" As Parker joined Ashley at the window, the girl bounced eagerly on her tiptoes, using his arm for leverage. "Oh my God—it looks like our whole class is really here."

Parker scowled. "She probably bribed them. She probably told them she'd give them A's on all their projects if they came and walked through ours."

"And there's the principal—and assistant principal—Oh, there's lots of teachers here, too!"

Mildly curious, Roo squeezed in between Ashley and Parker. "Hey, Boucher, there's your mama. And Miss Jules and Mr. Frank. Oh, and Miranda, there's your mom and your aunt Teeta . . . and our folks."

Though no one said it, the absence of the Wilmingtons was painfully obvious. Parker shrugged and turned back from the window. Disappointment settled on the other five faces around him.

"Well," Parker managed a croak. "Better light up your lantern, Miss Ashley. It's showtime."

Ashley stared. Her eyes went saucer-wide, and she clutched her stomach. "I don't think I can go out there, y'all. There's too many people!"

As the others stared back at her, Etienne made a strangling motion with his hands. "Shall I do the honors? Or does *everybody* want a turn?"

He and Parker promptly escorted Ashley out the door. Roo fell into step beside Miranda, with Gage bringing up the rear.

"Just watch her." Roo's tone held mild but sincere admiration. "She's a pro."

Roo was right. As Ashley swept onto the steps, an audible sigh went through the crowd. Ashley dipped and swayed, both sweet and seductive, her voice flowing honey-warm.

"Why, welcome, y'all. Welcome to our Walk of the Spirits."

And so it went. Step by entertaining step along the Brickway, Ashley enticed and enthralled and utterly charmed the tour group. The history and heritage of St. Yvette came magically alive.

"Well," Etienne mumbled to Miranda as they trailed a watchful distance behind the crowd, "they're looking scared at all the right times. And they're laughing at all the right jokes. That's a good sign, yeah?"

"It's better than good," Miranda agreed with him. "It's great. It's unbelievable."

"She threatened them," Parker muttered, jerking his chin toward Miss Dupree. "I knew it! Damn! She bribed them *and* she threatened them."

"No, I don't think so," Miranda said truthfully. "I think it's really the subject matter. It's all so fascinating. And Ashley, of course. She's also fascinating."

"Look at her," Roo pointed out. "Didn't I tell you? She's got every single one of them in the palm of her hand."

Etienne couldn't resist. "You mean right where she's got Parker?"

"Well," Roo shot Parker a look. "Of course, some conquests are much easier than others. Especially with species of primitive brain."

"Is she just talking about Parker?" Etienne raised an eyebrow at Gage. "Or you and me, too?"

The Walk of the Spirits moved on. Through the velvety nightfall, by the eerie glow of lantern light, came haunting and heartbreaking tales. An evil judge and his tortured victims. A kindly doctor, a grave-robbing undertaker, and a mysterious, deadly epidemic. The eternal screams of a child plunging from a nursery window. Curses, spells, and grisly sacrifices; secret voodoo rites. The silent processions and eerie chantings of spectral monks. And finally . . . sorrowfully . . . a ghostly song, the ghostly sobs, from a long-ago opera house.

"As y'all know, this is Magnolia Gallery," Ashley explained. "But what y'all probably *don't* know is that during the war, an opera house stood in this very spot. An opera house with a sad and tragic history. It was called the Rose—for the beautiful red-haired diva who sang there. Her name was Ellena Rose, and whenever she performed, red roses lined the carriageway and spilled from every door and window. Though many men pursued her, Ellena loved only Nathan—a stable boy. But their happiness was not meant to be. One foggy southern morning—and unknown to Ellena—Nathan was mortally wounded. And when the opera house went up in flames that night, Ellena perished in the fire, calling for her sweetheart, who never came."

The tour group was mesmerized. There were gasps, sorrowful murmurs, and muffled tears.

"And sometimes . . ." Pausing dramatically, Ashley raised her lantern. "Sometimes you can hear the soft, sad singing from the opera house. Or see the pale glow of a lantern in the fog. As Ellena Rose searches eternally for her one true love."

Tenderly, Miranda's thoughts reached out. *We'll keep your secrets, Ellena. Your secrets and Nathan's secrets. Forever.*

"Excuse me! Wasn't there something about a watch?" Miranda asked loudly.

Startled, Ashley turned to look at her. Miranda saw the confusion on Ashley's face, her quick, anxious glance at the script. *No, Ashley, it's not written in there—nothing about the watch or the chain.* Etienne was studying Miranda with a shrewd gaze. Gage and Parker exchanged bewildered glances. Roo seemed to be assessing the reactions of everyone else in the crowd.

"Watch?" Ashley echoed, expression totally blank. "You mean . . . like . . . a pocket watch?"

Eagerly, Miranda nodded. "And wasn't there something about a watch chain?"

She had everyone's attention now. All around her, people's faces were tightening with curiosity. Ashley made a helpless gesture to Gage, who was still intent on Miranda. And then, very slowly, Gage began to smile.

"Yes," Miranda said seriously. "I heard this legend once. About Nathan and Ellena exchanging tokens of their love. That Nathan gave her a watch—like this one. And Ellena Rose gave him a chain—a braided chain—like this."

Calmly she pulled both objects from the pockets of her jeans. The tour group seemed intrigued, but her friends gasped out loud.

"Miranda!"

"Oh my God—"

"Where the hell—"

"I don't believe it!"

"You did it, *cher*. I knew you would."

"Just like Nathan and Ellena, the watch and chain are meant to go together," Miranda went on, holding both treasures up so the crowd could see. "One attaches to the other. So they don't get lost."

With her five friends gathered close, Miranda carefully, gently, connected Nathan's watch to the chain of Ellena's hair. Her fingers shook; her heart shed silent tears. And the onlookers, respectfully observing, could only wonder at this fragile, timeless moment they'd just been allowed to share.

May you have happiness, Nathan and Ellena . . .

May you have understanding . . .

May you have peace.

Somehow, Miranda knew they would.

Wiping away tears, Ashley recovered herself and motioned to the crowd. Once more she led them by lantern light through the magical darkness and into the quiet past.

They were nearing Hayes House now. As the group turned off the Brickway and onto the side street, Miranda purposefully lagged behind. Soft lights glowed from the Hayes House veranda and out across the lawn, and it dawned on her that she was smiling again.

I thought I'd never be happy here.

She stopped to gaze up at the windows. And back toward the stone wall that bordered the long-ago battlefield.

"Help us . . . we're lost . . . we want to go home . . ."

"Yes," she whispered. "I'll help you. And I'll listen. And I won't turn you away."

Because, after all, there was time. All the time in the world.

All the time in both our worlds.

Miranda lifted her head into the sweet, southern breeze . . .

And smelled roses.

SPIRIT WALK

SHADOW MIRROR

SPEAK
Published by the Penguin Group
Penguin Group (USA) Inc., 345 Hudson Street, New York, New York 10014, U.S.A.
Penguin Group (Canada), 90 Eglinton Avenue East, Suite 700, Toronto, Ontario, Canada M4P 2Y3
(a division of Pearson Penguin Canada Inc.)
Penguin Books Ltd, 80 Strand, London WC2R 0RL, England
Penguin Ireland, 25 St Stephen's Green, Dublin 2, Ireland (a division of Penguin Books Ltd)
Penguin Group (Australia), 250 Camberwell Road, Camberwell, Victoria 3124, Australia
(a division of Pearson Australia Group Pty Ltd)
Penguin Books India Pvt Ltd, 11 Community Centre, Panchsheel Park, New Delhi – 110 017, India
Penguin Group (NZ), 67 Apollo Drive, Rosedale, Auckland 0632, New Zealand
(a division of Pearson New Zealand Ltd.)
Penguin Books (South Africa) (Pty) Ltd, 24 Sturdee Avenue, Rosebank, Johannesburg 2196, South Africa

Penguin Books Ltd, Registered Offices: 80 Strand, London WC2R 0RL, England

First published in the United States of America by Speak, an imprint of Penguin Group (USA) Inc., 2010
This omnibus edition published by Speak, an imprint of Penguin Group (USA) Inc., 2012

1 3 5 7 9 10 8 6 4 2

LIBRARY OF CONGRESS CATALOGING-IN-PUBLICATION DATA:
Cusick, Richie Tankersley.
Shadow mirror / by Richie Tankersley Cusick.
p. cm.
Summary: Seventeen-year-old Miranda Barnes' ability to communicate with spirits gets her in trouble
when she crosses over to the "Other Side," and only love will bring her back.
ISBN: 978-0-14-241227-5 (pbk.)
[1. Ghosts—Fiction. 2. Space and time—Fiction. 3. Afterlife—Fiction. 4. Dating (Social customs)—Fic-
tion. 5. Louisiana—Fiction. 6. Mystery and detective stories.]
I. Title.
PZ7.C9646Sh 2010
[Fic]—dc22   2009027240

Speak ISBN 978-0-14-242791-0

Printed in the United States of America

For Alex & Cathy . . .
my guardian angels . . .
for always being there with love and prayers,
friendship and faith,
and comfort from Cathy's Cupboard.

I love you,

Richie

1

SHE WANTED TO BELIEVE THAT IT WAS JUST AN ACCIDENT.
That the broken mirror lying in pieces at her feet was simply
the result of carelessness, of trying to get ready too fast and not
keeping her mind on what she was doing.

*An accident, that's all. Don't be dumb, Miranda—everyone
breaks mirrors. No big deal.*

And yet . . . it didn't *feel* like an accident.

Standing there alone in the bathroom, Miranda was suddenly
aware of her heart pounding, of sweat breaking out on her
forehead. The air went sharply, unnaturally cold, and she could
feel the walls closing in around her. *Not* the mirror, she told
herself again firmly—*it's just me, some leftover symptoms from
that stupid flu.*

Thinking about it now made her queasy all over again. Only
two days after Walk of the Spirits—the ghost tour that she and
her friends had created for their class project—she'd woken up
with a raging fever, and then a week had passed without her. She
couldn't recall much of that time—only the haziest memories of
lying there aching and miserable in bed, while Mom and Aunt
Teeta took turns off from work to give pills, take temperatures,
force fluids, and coax down spoonfuls of Aunt Teeta's homemade

chicken soup. In a faraway blur, Miranda had tossed, drifted, and slept the sleep of the dead.

But her mind had never rested. Hour after hour, images had scattered and flowed back and forth between her present and her past, her new life and her old. St. Yvette and the Falls, the phantoms of Nathan and Ellena Rose. Scenes of Florida and the hurricane, of Marge and Joanie and the best-friend things they'd done together. The vacant spot on the white sandy beach where her house had once stood, where she and Mom had been so happy. Hayes House and Aunt Teeta. The Walk of the Spirits and Grandpa. Parker and Ashley . . . Gage and Roo . . . Etienne . . .

And wouldn't it be weird, she'd sometimes wondered, floating through that senseless fog, *if I woke up in my old bed, in my old house, and no hurricane had ever come, and Mom and I had never moved here to St. Yvette, and all of this*—my life now—*was just a dream?*

But of course it wasn't a dream. Eventually she *did* wake up only to realize that she was still here in Hayes House, tucked safely beneath the eaves of her cozy third-floor bedroom, with its French doors open to the sun porch, and the scent of Aunt Teeta's chrysanthemums and late-blooming roses drifting up from the backyard. And eventually she'd felt well enough to go back to school—was even looking forward to it . . .

Until just a few minutes ago.

Until the mirror.

"Stupid," Miranda whispered. "Think you could be any clumsier?"

But it was Monday morning, already seven thirty, and she was in a rush.

She'd heard Parker's car pulling into the driveway and hadn't wanted to keep him and Ashley waiting. He'd blasted his horn. Twice. Three more times. Yelling her name while she'd scrambled to pull on clothes and find her shoes and run a comb through her hair.

"Hey, Miranda, move it!"

"I'm not deaf, Parker," she'd grumbled. "And neither are the neighbors." But she was all thumbs and trying to hurry, giving herself a quick frown in the bathroom mirror, disappointed with what she saw. Her slight, not-very-tall self; those natural-curl ends of short brown hair shoved carelessly behind her ears. The dark, sleepless smudges lingering beneath her hazel eyes; her heart-shaped face, still a little too pale, with a light sprinkling of freckles across her nose. She'd stuck out her tongue at the sorry image, then yanked Aunt Teeta's hand mirror from the vanity drawer while fumbling the cap off a tube of lip gloss.

She'd never expected that mirror to drop.

She'd watched as it slipped through her fingers and shattered across the floor, her fractured reflection staring up at her, Miranda-shards-and-slivers glittering in the harsh bathroom light.

Since then she hadn't even moved. Her gaze stayed fixed on those shiny splinters of glass, and she realized that her hands were trembling, that the sweat on her forehead was trickling down her cheeks. For one split second, she drowned in a wave of irrational sorrow. A surge of irrational fear.

And that's when the *other* feelings started.

The warning feelings, the caution feelings, the unwanted feelings she was beginning to recognize all too well. Those nagging, unnerving suspicions that she wasn't quite alone, that some invisible—but all too real—connection had been made. A connection meant only for her.

Stop it, Miranda. It's just a mirror, it doesn't mean anything.

Yet her heart was racing, and she didn't take time to be careful. She scooped up the glass with her bare hands, gasping in pain as one large fragment lodged in her palm, clenching her teeth as she pulled it out. Then she wrapped *all* the fragments in bloody, wadded-up tissues, ran to the kitchen, and buried them in the garbage can, beneath coffee grounds, rotten banana peels, and soggy paper towels. She didn't want Aunt Teeta finding any leftover traces of broken mirror anywhere. She didn't want to hear what Aunt Teeta was sure to say. *Seven years' bad luck.*

One thing Miranda had learned since moving here to St. Yvette was that most Southerners were just as superstitious as they were hospitable. And the last thing she needed in her life right now was more bad luck.

"Miranda!" The horn was blaring again from outside, Parker's voice even louder. "Don't make me come up there! Even though I know you want me to!"

Gathering her things, Miranda dashed for the front door. She grabbed another tissue for the cut on her hand. She took a deep breath and swallowed down a wave of nausea.

Just a mirror . . . a plain, old, ordinary, silly broken mirror . . .

Except that it *wasn't* silly. And it *did* mean something—though she couldn't possibly guess what that was right now, or even explain how she knew.

The answer's waiting for me.

At some unknown time . . . but soon.

In some unknown place . . . but close.

2

"**MIRANDA!**" Ashley squealed. "Oh my God, I'm so glad you're feeling better!"

Tightly squeezing her tissue, Miranda hurried toward the shiny red convertible idling alongside the curb. While Ashley jumped out to give her a hug, Parker lounged back, rested his left elbow on the door of his BMW, and pounded his right fist on the horn.

"Parker, for heaven's sake!" Whirling around, Ashley glared at him. "Stop that! It's so rude!"

"We're late!" he said, but eased off the steering wheel. "And you're the one who wanted to be there early for your fun . . . fun whatever the hell it is."

"*Fund*-raiser." Ashley's glare faded to mild annoyance. She was wearing one of her black-and-white cheerleader uniforms—one of the more *modest* ones, Miranda noted—which usually meant some in-school activity going on. Modest or not, the dress still managed to look sexy on Ashley's petite figure. Today her long blond hair was swept into a loose ponytail and tied back with black-and-white ribbons, a few stray curls falling softly around her face. Sometimes Miranda couldn't help wondering how it would feel, being that beautiful. Being one of those special, picture-perfect girls who would always be drooled over, sought after, and passionately admired.

"Fund-raiser," Ashley repeated, her attention back on Miranda. Like most everyone else in town, both Ashley and Parker had distinct Southern accents—but Ashley's was extra rich and ultra thick, like warm, melted honey. "We're sponsoring our Win-A-Date contest again this year. And we don't have to hurry *that* much; it's not like the cheerleading squad can't sell tickets without me. Oh, Miranda, we *all* missed you! I called to see how you were—but Parker wouldn't let me bring your homework by."

"You owe me for that." Parker smirked at Miranda. "Big-time."

As Ashley's arms went around her once more, Miranda realized that she was returning the hug just as tightly. "Aunt Teeta gave me your message," she whispered, and for just an instant there was a catch in her voice. "I missed you too, Ashley."

She hadn't expected this sudden depth of emotion. Not just for Ashley, and even Parker—but for the whole group that would be waiting at school. . . .

My friends.

"Where's Roo?" she asked quickly, not wanting to cry.

"Gage's mom gave them a ride. He still needs help, you know, with his cast and all."

"So Roo's still helping him?"

"Still making his life miserable, is more like it. But his cast comes off in a couple days, so that'll be great." Drawing back,

Ashley studied Miranda closely, put a cool hand to her forehead. "Maybe you're coming back too soon. Maybe you should give it another week. You have been *awfully* sick."

Miranda forced a laugh. "Forget it. If I have to spend even one more second in bed, I will *kill* myself."

"You're obviously not spending your seconds in bed with the right person," Parker advised her. "Trust me. That can make *all* the difference. In fact, I'd be more than happy to volun—"

"Parker, shush. Now listen to me, Miranda." Hands on hips, Ashley leveled her friend a no-nonsense stare. "You need to be really careful. You need to take things *really* slow, and take *really* good care of yourself. Or else you could get a relapse! And then I'd be missing you all over again! We'd *all* be missing you *all over again*!"

"No more hugging," Parker groaned. "Get in the car—no, wait! Have you been de-germed, Miranda? Absolutely no riding in my car unless you've been de-germed."

"*And* I missed you, too, Parker," Miranda teased as Ashley leaned in to swat Parker's shoulder.

"Ignore him, Miranda. He won't admit it, but he missed you terribly."

"Okay, I admit it." Parker sighed, "I missed you, Miranda. Terribly. I fantasized the whole time about you in your pajamas. With your runny nose and greasy hair, lying there in bed, all sweaty and breathing hard. Man, what a turn-on."

Though Ashley wasn't amused, Miranda found it impossible to resist that grin. Hard to resist almost *anything* about Parker, she had to admit. Parker Wilmington—most popular boy at St.

Yvette High School. Tall and blond, incredible sea-green eyes. Those gorgeous, unruly strands of hair framing his handsome face, no matter how many times he shook them back. Star quarterback, not a single game lost last season. Self-confident swagger and cocky smile. More money than he could spend in ten lifetimes. And—much to the disappointment of every female student—most definitely taken by Ashley.

"Oh, Parker, honestly," Ashley scolded, climbing in beside him. "Just be quiet and drive."

True to form, Parker managed to break all speed limits without getting caught. He skidded into the student lot, screeched to a halt in the last empty space, then the three of them hurried across campus. Even before they reached the main building, they could see a big crowd gathered outside. Several long tables had been set up; ribbons, streamers, and pom-poms seemed to be everywhere—all black and white, official colors of the St. Yvette Pirates. Banners and signs had been decorated in huge black-and-white letters: WIN A DATE WITH A CHEERLEADER! TICKETS ONLY $1.00! And while a few of St. Yvette High's cheerleaders handled sales and information, the rest were jumping, leaping, dancing, clapping, waving, cartwheeling, and rallying student onlookers with rousing chants.

Parker stopped in his tracks. He looked at Ashley. He let out another groan. "Tell me you're kidding."

"You know we do this date thing every year," Ashley said, half defensive, half apologetic. "I can't get out of it."

"Right. And the guy who wins a date with you—what does *he* get out of it?"

"Honestly, Parker, it's—oh, look, there's Roo and Gage!"

As Ashley rushed ahead and Parker followed, Miranda was content to trail behind. She could see Gage and Roo now, standing a safe distance from all the commotion—Gage's left leg in a cast, his lanky form balanced on crutches; and Roo beside him, munching solemnly on a limp wedge of pizza dripping with ketchup.

Looking at Gage, Miranda felt her heart warm. *God, I swear he's gotten cuter. . . .*

Tall like Parker, though a little more slender, his shoulders not as broad. Big brown eyes; long dark lashes; sensitive features. Soft brown hair, always a little long and shaggy over his ears and forehead. And those lips—perfect lips—though she'd never actually kissed them. As Miranda continued to watch, Roo gulped down some pizza, slid her hand beneath Gage's shirttail, and wiped her fingers on the seat of his jeans. Gage shot her an over-the-shoulder frown.

Next to Gage, Roo seemed even shorter than her barely-over-five-feet height. Her solid little body, more curvy than plump, was swathed in its usual blackness from head to toe— heavy black eye makeup; long black old-fashioned dress; high black combat boots. Dark purple beads dangled from her multi-pierced ears; thick bangs practically obscured her brows. And today she'd threaded more purple beads—the same shade of purple as her lip gloss—through at least a dozen strands of her overdyed black hair. Hard to believe that she and Ashley were stepsisters since the age of three—Miranda had been totally shocked when Roo told her.

Before she could call out, Gage spotted her in the crowd and began to smile. Casually he nudged Roo, who turned and waved her over.

"Miranda. Back among the living."

"And"—Parker looked Roo up and down—"the living dead."

"Did somebody speak?" Roo pointedly ignored him. "No? I didn't think so. By the way, Miranda, do us all a favor and never be gone this long again. Gage was inconsolable."

Gage smoothly deflected their teasing. "Just a *little* inconsolable."

"Come on, y'all *have* to buy some tickets," Ashley pleaded.

Glancing at Miranda, Gage winked. Parker let out his usual groan. Ashley kept right on talking.

"They only cost a dollar. And you could win a date with *any* of the cheerleaders. All you have to do is buy a ticket for the cheerleader you want, and it goes in a jar with her name on it. And then our coach draws a winner for each girl. Parker?"

"Huh?"

"You of *all* people can afford some tickets—how many do you want?"

"None."

"None?" Roo echoed, around another mouthful of pizza. Chewing, swallowing, she fixed Parker with a stare. "No tickets. No tickets at all to maybe win a date with your own girlfriend."

Parker grinned. "Hey. Why pay for something I get free?" Then, at the expression on Ashley's face, he added, "*Dates*, Ash. Come on, I was talking about *dates*."

"I'll buy some tickets," Gage offered swiftly. "I know Etienne will too."

At the mention of the name, Miranda's eyes did a quick sweep of the crowd. She hadn't seen Etienne since they'd gotten to school—she realized that she'd been looking for him all along.

"Thank you, Gage!" Ashley threw her arms around his neck, nearly knocking him over. "Look, y'all, I know we've got one more fund-raiser this year, but our squad needs money really, really bad. Like, for road trips. And competitions. And cheerleader camp. And we need new uniforms. And we need new pom-poms!"

Parker nodded at the front of her shirt. "Trust me, Ash. Your old pom-poms are just fine."

Though Gage choked back a laugh, he and Parker obviously found this hilarious. Now both of them received a withering glare from Ashley.

"Funny, guys, very funny. And I wouldn't say *anything* if I were you," she added, poking Gage in the ribs. "*I* know Babette LeBlanc wrote her measurements down on your cast."

"What!" Parker looked incredulous. "*Where?*"

"Right there." Ashley pointed while Parker crowded in to see. "Right next to her phone number."

"Damn! Yeah, with pom-poms that big, it's *got* to be Babette LeBlanc."

Rolling her eyes, Ashley began dragging Parker away. "Come on. You can help me sell tickets."

"I don't want to help you sell tickets."

"Parker, you're the star of the football team. You need to set a good example."

"I'm already a good example. In fact, I'm a *great* example."

"Yes, you are," Roo agreed. "But I don't think she was talking about stupidity." Hoisting her gargoyle backpack, Roo trudged for the entrance, leaving Gage and Miranda to follow.

It took Gage a few minutes to speak up.

"I'm glad you're better," he said at last. That soft-spoken voice . . . a half-shy smile. "It wasn't . . . the group wasn't the same without you."

Miranda turned to look at him, but his eyes were downward, intent on steering his crutches. "Yeah?"

"Cross my heart."

"That makes me feel really nice."

"It's the truth." His smile widened, showing a dimple in each cheek. Lifting his head, he regarded her with gentle curiosity. "So how are you?"

"Good."

"I mean, really."

"What do you mean, 'really'?" Playfully she bumped against him. "Don't I *look* good?"

"You look great. I just figured you might feel . . ."

"What?"

"You've been out of school awhile. Maybe you're feeling a little nervous about being back."

They'd reached the front steps. Without hesitation Gage started up—a slow but easy rhythm.

"Wow," Miranda said, holding the door, following him into the building. "You've gotten really talented at this."

"I should be; I've had six weeks to practice. And don't change the subject."

"Was I?"

"It'll be okay, Miranda."

Miranda didn't answer. All morning she'd been determined to hide her nervousness from everyone; she thought she'd managed to pull it off. *Leave it to Gage . . .*

Since their lockers were on different floors, Gage said good-bye at the next corner while Miranda watched him maneuver up the stairs. It always amused her, seeing the female attention he attracted—Gage, on the other hand, seemed oblivious that the flirting was meant exclusively for him. When he finally reached the landing, he paused, swiveled around on his crutches, and gave Miranda an encouraging thumbs-up. Laughing, she returned it.

Okay, Miranda. Keep telling yourself you belong here . . . keep telling yourself it feels good to be here. . . .

The weird thing was—it really *did* feel good to be here. Good to be out of bed and out of the house, good to be here at St. Yvette High. It was as though, for the very first time, she was allowing herself to feel a part of it all.

To *be* a part of it all.

The morning flew by. Parker was in her first class, complaining and cracking jokes, as usual; Ashley and Gage shared third period with her, teasing each other about some test question they'd both gotten wrong. To Miranda's relief, she hadn't missed as much work as she thought she had. A weekend maybe, with Ashley's help, and she'd be caught up again—but in the meantime there were new assignments to focus on, plus a whole range of upcoming activities to learn about. The Win a Date with a Cheerleader raffle. A Halloween dance. Assemblies, pep rallies, and football games. Something called the Harvest Festival. Volunteer projects, Homecoming events, and holiday bake sales. When it was announced that classes were canceled Friday because of teachers' meetings, a wild cheer resounded through the entire school.

But by the time noon rolled around, Miranda was dragging. She knew the others were expecting her to eat lunch with them, but she wasn't the least bit hungry—she wasn't sure she could even last the rest of the day. *Maybe I'm still sick. Maybe I came back too soon.*

Promising to meet them outside, she waved the group on without her. She couldn't remember the combination to her locker, and as she struggled to get it open, she kept glancing into the corridor. Still no sign of Etienne, though not so unusual, she kept reminding herself. With him working part-time and coming to school part-time, no one was ever quite sure of his schedule. *And not like I expect anything from him. Or that I should have heard from him by now. Or that I'm particularly important in his life, or that there's any sort of arrangement between us, or that we're anything more than friends—*

She bit hard on her bottom lip. What was she thinking? Etienne Boucher—elusive, alluring, and unattainable. *Get real, Miranda. The truth is, he promised Grandpa he'd look after you, that's all. Just friends.*

And yet . . . they *had* shared some close moments, she *couldn't* have imagined those—could she? Some really special moments, some private, more-than-friend moments? In spite of Etienne's busy life. In spite of the long hours he spent at all his different jobs. In spite of his silences, his solitude, his fiercely guarded secrets. *And in spite of the fact that he can have any girl in this whole town.*

God, Miranda, you are so pathetic.

Finally recalling the combination, she opened her locker, tossed in her books, and stared at the messy jumble. Not a bad locker, despite her own disorganized habits; in fact, Ashley had helped her with lots of personal touches. Some very cool magnets and stickers, hooks for hanging things, a message board, an extra shelf, and two mirrors—one at the rear, and one on the inside of the door. Miranda gave everything a good hard shove, then stepped back, taking a second to check herself in the mirror on the door.

My God . . . no wonder I'm dragging. Startled, she stared back at her shocking reflection—eyes too wide; shadows underneath, darker than ever; cheeks pinched tight; skin more pale. And that fine sheen of sweat was breaking out on her forehead again, just like this morning, dampening her hairline, even though she could feel another chill beginning to ache inside her.

What's going on?

It came to her then that something was horribly wrong, that her image in the glass wasn't natural—even for being sick. That everything about it seemed disjointed and frightening—her cheeks more sallow than white; eyes too hollow, too bruised, too vacant; the sweat too feverish; the chill too deep. *Something's not right . . . something . . .*

Trembling, Miranda lowered her head, took short, shallow breaths. *Don't freak out, there's a perfectly logical explanation, I just have to calm down and think . . .*

But instinct told her that it was happening again, just like it had happened weeks before. When she'd first become aware of her "gift." When she and the others had first become friends, first begun planning their Walk of the Spirits, when she'd first met the ghosts of Nathan and Ellena Rose. It had happened then, just like it had happened in the bathroom this morning when she'd dropped the mirror. Some message . . . some purpose . . . some connection . . . *except it's not the same—signs, signals, senses all twisted, all different—why isn't it the same—*

She fought down a wave of panic. She had to get out of here, go to the nurse, call Mom or Aunt Teeta to come pick her up. For a brief instant she wished Grandpa were still alive, wished Etienne would show up, wished Gage would find her—she was feeling worse and worse by the second. She'd just spent a whole week being miserable in bed, but none of that could even *begin* to compare with what she was feeling now. . . .

Sick . . . so frighteningly sick . . .

Lifting her head, Miranda stared once more into the mirror. And felt a slow, icy fist squeeze around her heart.

She saw her own face and the empty corridor behind her. No crowds, no activity, not a single student in any direction . . .

But *someone* was there.

Someone.

Watching her with a wide, fixed gaze—eyes so intense, so powerful, *so close*, that they missed nothing. Watching her from a place outside the mirror, but from *inside* the mirror, as well—looking back at her from within her own reflection . . .

Oh God . . .

The hairs prickled at the back of her neck. Miranda couldn't move or escape, could scarcely even breathe.

"Who are you?" she murmured. "*Where* are you? What do you want?"

Finally, fearfully, she was able to lift her hand.

She pressed it to the mirror and felt a scream catch instantly in her throat.

Another hand pressed back.

She could feel it, every detail, as though it were real—the firm pressure of it through the glass, distinct shape molded to hers, fingers lengthened against her fingers, alive but deathly cold.

And then a silent whisper. A plea she couldn't hear. Scared . . . sad . . . a noiseless sob.

"Who are you?" Miranda begged again. "What are you trying to tell me?"

But the hand, the voice, were gone now.

And the eyes that had watched her were closed.

3

"**MIRANDA!** Here you are!"

Numbly, Miranda turned to see Ashley hurrying up behind her. She took one last look at the mirror in her locker, then firmly shut the door.

"I thought you were coming to lunch and—"

Stopping abruptly, Ashley took in Miranda's condition at a glance—and obviously didn't like what she saw. "Are you okay? You're so pale."

"Am I?" Miranda opted for innocence.

"Extremely. Are you sick again? Do you need to go home?"

"I . . . maybe. Maybe I came back too soon."

"Oh, I knew it! Didn't I say that just this morning when we picked you up?" Ashley's arms went around her, hugging gently. "*Please* come eat something—I bet that's why you don't feel well. How do you expect to get better if you don't keep up your strength?"

"Maybe some crackers, then," Miranda agreed distractedly, knowing that Ashley wouldn't give up.

"Well . . . it's not great, but it's better than nothing." Taking Miranda's elbow, Ashley steered her firmly into the corridor. "The others are outside, our usual table. I have to go sell tickets now, though. And . . . you know . . . cheer. Oh, and I just saw your aunt Teeta on my way in."

"Here? You mean, at school?"

"By the principal's office. She said something about an appointment with Mr. Clark—I guess he's a client of hers?"

Not surprising, Miranda thought. Aunt Teeta's real estate agency was the most popular and dependable in St. Yvette; practically every family and business in town had been a client of hers at one time or another.

"I bet she's still there." Ashley's tone grew more anxious. "You could just leave with her. Come on, I'll walk with you."

It only took them a few minutes. And even before Miranda spotted her aunt, she could already hear that familiar laugh echoing down the corridor.

Giggling, Ashley shook her head. "I just love your aunt Teeta."

"Who doesn't? She's the best."

It was always that way with Aunt Teeta. The biggest heart in the world; an endless supply of comfort and hugs; and a warm, contagious laugh that made everyone within earshot laugh right along with her.

"Well, hey girls!" Waving some tickets in one plump hand, Aunt Teeta bustled toward them. "Now, isn't this a treat, I get to see both y'all in one visit!"

Miranda went straight into her aunt's open arms. It was one of the few places where she felt truly safe these days; now she wondered why that particular feeling of security seemed so important to her at this precise moment. She could tell at once that Aunt Teeta wasn't fooled. As the hug tightened around her, she heard genuine concern in her aunt's voice.

"What's up, darlin'? Miranda, are you—"

"Glad to see you," Miranda said quickly, pulling away, trying to tease. "Are those cheerleader tickets?"

For a second Aunt Teeta hesitated . . . then smoothly redirected her attention. "They most certainly are."

"So what cheerleader are you trying to win a date with?"

"Why, Ashley, of course! And if I win, I'm going to pay for her and that handsome boyfriend of hers to go out to some fine, fancy place for dinner."

This time Miranda had to smile. "Aunt Teeta, Parker could *buy* any of the fine, fancy dinner places in this town."

"Well then, I'll just have to cook them a special homemade dinner. My famous chicken pot pie and red velvet cake. Served by candlelight!" Laughing merrily, she glanced down at her watch. "Mercy, I didn't plan on being here this long. I've got me a whole afternoon free for a change, and I promised your poor mama I'd help her—she's gonna be wondering what on earth happened to me."

"Why?" Miranda frowned. "Where is she?"

"Out at the plantation. Buried under about ten million wallpaper samples, I imagine."

Ashley's face immediately lit up. "At Belle Chandelle? Oh, I can hardly stand it, I'm so jealous! That's like, my total dream house!"

"Well, honey, I'm afraid right now it's more like a total nightmare house. Although I shouldn't complain—I'm just thankful somebody finally bought it and decided to renovate. These new owners are rolling in money. They seem to know what they're in for, and they're committed for the long haul. So someday . . . God willing . . . the place will be beautiful again."

"I've *always* thought it was beautiful." Ashley's sigh was wistful. "I mean . . . it probably wasn't. But when I was little . . . and growing up . . . in my mind, it always was."

Aunt Teeta fixed Ashley with a long, thoughtful stare. "Would you like to see it?"

A moment of shocked, total silence. Ashley glanced at Miranda, then back to Aunt Teeta. Her eyes went saucer-wide.

"Really? *Oh, Miss Teeta, do you mean it?*"

"Well, of course I do—bring the whole group, if they want to come. In fact, why don't y'all drive on out this afternoon?"

"But you have practice, don't you, Ashley?" Miranda heard the urgency in her own voice, almost a plea. She hadn't meant to come up with excuses; the words just popped out. "And Parker . . . he has football practice, right?"

Before Ashley could respond, Aunt Teeta responded for her. "Don't worry if y'all are a little late. Miranda's mama has a meeting to go to later, but I've got lots to do out there. I won't be finishing up till at least six thirty or seven."

"Parker probably won't want to go anyway," Miranda tried again, still surprising herself. "And I don't have a car. And Gage, with his broken leg and all—"

"It's okay, Miranda." Ashley's face was growing more puzzled by the second. "Gage's mom is picking him and Roo up after school—if you don't want to wait around for Parker and me, you can catch a ride home with them. I'm pretty sure I can borrow Mom's car and come and get you after cheerleading. The guys are totally on their own, though. Oh, Miss Teeta, thank you so much!"

"You're entirely welcome, darlin'. I'll see y'all later."

Miranda waved as Ashley hurried off. All around her the hall was growing busy and more crowded, but the only thing she really noticed was the way Aunt Teeta was staring at her.

"*What?*" She didn't mean to sound so defensive. But Aunt Teeta only smiled and linked one arm through hers.

"Come walk with me, darlin'."

They went out the entrance, strolled slowly across the fenced grounds toward the visitors' parking lot. It was hot and humid, no trace of a breeze. Aunt Teeta smiled again . . . drew Miranda closer to her side.

"So how's your first day back?"

"Good."

"Glad to see your friends again? Think you can get caught up with homework pretty easy?"

Miranda nodded.

"Have you seen Gage?"

"You know I have, and stop making it more than it is."

"More than what is? It's a simple question. How about Etienne?"

"How *about* Etienne?"

"Uh-oh. I surely don't like the sound of *that* tone."

"I haven't seen him."

"No? Well, that's too bad."

"I've told you, Aunt Teeta, we're not . . ."

"What?"

"Anything." Miranda felt a quick stab of irritation. She wondered where it had come from. Then she felt even more irritated for wondering. "And stop playing matchmaker."

"Mercy, that would be like taking away the very air I breathe."

She wished Aunt Teeta would quit joking around—the last thing she felt like doing right now was laughing. School had started out so positive this morning, but things had gone steadily downhill. She was grumpy and exhausted, her hand was hurting again from the cut, and all she wanted to do was to go home and sleep. *And* not *go to Belle Chandelle.*

"You know," Aunt Teeta was talking again, "you still look a little under the weather."

"I'm fine. Just tired, is all."

"And I get the feeling you're not too happy about going out to the plantation today. Or maybe *any* day."

Miranda kept quiet. She concentrated on her sandals scuffing through the damp grass.

"The thing is, honey . . . your mama's been kind of wondering why you haven't shown more interest in her new job. She told me she's even offered to take you out there to Belle Chandelle a couple times."

Miranda nodded, half guilty, half resentful. Because deep

down she *knew* what was bothering her—and what could she say, really? To Aunt Teeta *or* to Mom? Neither of them was aware of what she'd been through these last few months, inheriting Grandpa's legacy, coming to terms with her newly discovered powers; neither of them had the slightest clue about the ways her life had changed, or the deep secrets she was forced to keep, or the fateful responsibilities that she carried on her shoulders, now that Grandpa was dead. *Souls and suffering . . . not of this world.* So how could she expect Mom and Aunt Teeta to understand how physically and emotionally vulnerable she was . . . how cautious she needed to be?

Old houses—especially an old, historic plantation like Belle Chandelle—meant lifetimes of memories. All those people who'd ever lived there—births and deaths and everything in between. Spirits who would ask her to open to their tragedies, open herself to places where the past could reach out and pull her in . . .

"Etienne's mama." Aunt Teeta's words startled Miranda back again.

"What about Miss Nell?"

"Darlin', have you been listenin' to a single thing I've said?" Laughing, Aunt Teeta gave her a quick, tight squeeze. "Those new owners of Belle Chandelle—they want to turn it into a bed and breakfast. Now, isn't that exciting? And they asked if I knew anybody to head up the kitchen. Well, I didn't even have to think. Nell Boucher's always been the best cook in this whole parish. And she and Etienne's daddy *did* have that restaurant in town once upon a time—why, people came from miles around just to eat there, it was so popular. And the food? Honey, I'm telling you, it was to die for."

"Really? What happened to it?"

"What always happened whenever Lazare Boucher got his mean, sneaky self involved with anything. Oh, there were plenty rumors—but the hard fact was, the restaurant shut down, and he blamed Nell for it. Not a soul believed him, of course. And Nell was heartbroken."

Miranda shot her aunt a sympathetic glance. "But don't she and Etienne have a tourist business now? Swamp boats or something?"

"Yes, but Etienne talked her into letting *him* do the tours from now on; he *wants* his mama to take the job at Belle Chandelle." Aunt Teeta's voice lowered, went thoughtful. "I know that boy worries about her all the time. Even though he never shows what he's feeling."

"But . . . her cancer's in remission, right?"

"Last I heard. And Nell never complains. Even when I've seen her right there on death's doorstep, I've never once heard her complain." Aunt Teeta clucked her tongue . . . rummaged deep in her purse . . . pulled out a set of keys. "Enough of this sad talk! I'll see you later at the plantation. Oh, and by the way—there *are* some pretty amazing sights out there. One in particular I think you'll enjoy."

"What is it?"

"You'll see." Giving her one last hug, Aunt Teeta pulled free. "Well, here's my car. Love you, baby girl."

"Love you too."

But long after Aunt Teeta left, Miranda stood there staring off across campus . . . the morning's strange events still clinging to her like a gloomy fog.

From some distant place, she felt something trickle down her fingertips, and she realized that her palm had started to bleed.

A pain much worse this time . . .

Aching from her hand . . . deep into her heart.

4

"SHOULDN'T WE BE GETTING CLOSE?" Chewing her bottom lip, Ashley strained forward to peer out the windshield. "You'd think there'd be signs or something, wouldn't you? It feels like we've been driving forever."

"We *have* been driving forever," Roo complained. "*Whenever* you drive, we end up driving forever."

"I'm ignoring that. I'm not even listening." Ashley settled back in her seat again. She shot Miranda a troubled glance. "Miranda, you haven't said a word since we picked you up. Maybe this wasn't such a good idea, you coming out here and—"

"No, I'm fine," Miranda answered, though she didn't feel fine at all.

She'd been glad to go home to an empty house after school; she'd gone straight to her room and crawled into bed and stayed there. She'd tried to nap, but couldn't. She'd tried not to think about the creepy experience at her locker, but wasn't able to think of anything else. Most of all, she'd tried to psych herself up for this little outing to Belle Chandelle—and hadn't done a very good job of it.

Now she leaned against the passenger door, determined to sound convincing. "I *wanted* to come. I'm just sort of . . . edgy, I guess."

"Global warming," Roo said solemnly.

"What?"

"Global warming. Halloween's in a couple days, Thanksgiving's only three weeks after that, and it's still almost a hundred degrees outside. I don't remember October ever being this hot before. It doesn't feel like the holidays, and it throws everything off."

Right, Miranda thought glumly. *If only it were that simple.*

"Oh, y'all, I'm just so *excited!*" Ashley burst out, inching the car around a pothole. "I've been in love with this plantation my whole *life*! Ever since I was a little girl, I used to dream I'd live there someday and fix it all up! And now—to actually see it! Inside! And in person!"

Roo was less than enthused. "We'll never see it at all if you don't go faster."

"I can't go faster—it's muddy. And deer and little animals might run out in front of the car."

"Ash, the only thing you could hit at this speed is road kill."

In spite of her mood, Miranda couldn't help smiling. She sat straighter, did her best to focus—on Ashley pouting beside her, on Roo lounging into one corner of the backseat, earbuds firmly in place, expression totally bored. Turning halfway around, she tapped Roo on the knee.

"Hey, what are you listening to?"

"My soul."

At some point since leaving school today, Roo had obviously attempted one of her spur-of-the-moment makeovers—with the usual startling results. The purple beads had vanished from her hair, replaced now with bright magenta streaks and several newly chopped, very uneven layers.

"And what's your soul telling you?" Miranda went along.

"That it will be fully evolved by the time this trip is over."

"Roo, you are *impossible*!" Indignant, Ashley frowned into the rearview mirror. "If Parker were driving, you'd be nagging him to slow down."

"That's because *Parker* drives like a maniac. *You* drive like Great-Grandma Fern."

"But . . . Great-Grandma Fern can't drive."

"I know."

"Well, it's not my fault—I *hate* using Mom's car, it always makes me so nervous! I mean . . . the radio's broken, I can't concentrate."

As Roo rolled her eyes, Miranda guided the conversation to safer ground.

"So you guys grew up here all these years, this close to Belle Chandelle, but you've never been inside?"

"No, it was always so spooky!" Ashley's blue eyes widened. "And dangerous, too. The place had been empty forever—the roof was caved in, and the galleries had fallen down, and most of the outbuildings were all rotted away. Our folks wouldn't let us go near it."

"And it's not that close to town." Rousing slightly, Roo took a long drag on her cigarette, flicked ashes out her half-open window. "Sometimes we'd ride our bikes out here, though. And sometimes when we'd be at Etienne's house, we'd all sneak over."

"On your bikes?" Miranda asked.

"We walked. When we got older, sometimes we took his boat—but mostly we walked. It didn't really seem that far then . . . even though it was."

"Etienne lives pretty close to Belle Chandelle," Ashley explained to Miranda. "How close, Roo? About a mile . . . mile and a half . . . down the bayou? Sort of between Belle Chandelle and the Falls?"

Roo's shrug seemed affirmative.

"So you'd be at Etienne's," Miranda prompted Ashley. "And then you'd come over here and sneak through the buildings?"

"The rest of us sneaked," Roo corrected. "Ashley was always too scared."

Ashley's voice raised in quick protest. "I was . . . careful."

"You cried and ran away."

"Well, Gage and Etienne always hid and jumped out at me!"

"You cried all the way back to Etienne's house. And you told on us."

"I did not!"

"Yes, you did. You were a little tattletale."

"I was not! I never told on y'all."

"You were the only one crying. Same thing."

Picturing the scene, Miranda chuckled. "So then what happened?" she asked Roo.

"Etienne got in trouble."

"Just Etienne? No one else?"

"He was always the instigator. He was always the one who

brought us over here, but then of course, we always *wanted* him to. Nobody would have known, if it hadn't been for Ashley."

"I don't remember him getting in any *real* trouble," Ashley defended herself. "Well . . . okay . . . I *sort* of remember him getting fussed at a couple times."

"Yeah, Miss Nell didn't usually do much more than fuss. Not that Etienne cared. And she *never* told Etienne's dad." Roo paused, her expression darkening. "She'd never have done that."

For a moment there was only silence. Miranda had seen the faded scars along Etienne's arms; she remembered Roo telling her about the regular beatings Etienne had received from his father. Now it was Ashley who changed topics.

"Miranda, your mom's so lucky—getting to work at the plantation every day! She must be really happy."

"At least she's in a good mood most of the time," Miranda admitted. "She's smiling a lot more. And we're not fighting like we used to. It's . . . you know . . . nice to see her smiling like that again."

"Okay, I know your mom's an interior designer, but explain it again, about her job." Clutching the steering wheel, Ashley slowed the car to a near crawl, slammed viciously on the brake, then lurched headlong into a wide, shallow puddle.

There was an awkward moment of silence. Roo took a long drag on her cigarette before she finally spoke.

"Now what?"

"I'm trying to miss all this water."

"It's a puddle, Ash. Not the Mississippi River."

Struggling not to laugh, Miranda resumed their discussion.

"Mom's in charge of all the decorating. And not just for the main house—for all the outbuildings, too. I think it's a pretty big deal."

"The whole plantation? That *is* a big deal. Can you imagine getting to pick out all that furniture? The rugs . . . the wallpaper . . . the curtains . . . the candlesticks . . ."

"The mosquito nets," Roo added blandly.

"Your mother must *love* going to work every day, Miranda." Ashley sounded wistful. "Who wouldn't want a perfect job like that! And I bet everybody's so excited to have her there."

"They seem to be." Miranda considered a moment. "Even Parker's mom thinks it's a good idea."

"Mrs. Wilmington? Really?"

"Mom and Aunt Teeta and Mrs. Wilmington are all on some renovation committee together. And Mrs. Wilmington actually told the members that putting Mom in charge of the decorating was the smartest decision they'd ever made."

"She's after something," Roo concluded.

"Get this. One day Mrs. Wilmington brought in a whole bunch of fabric samples she wanted Mom to use in the plantation house. And Mom turned them all down."

Ashley's voice was half shock, half awe. "Are you serious? She stood up to Mrs. Wilmington? And told her *no*? And didn't get *fired*?"

"Way to go, Miranda's mom," Roo murmured, impressed.

"Hazel," Miranda said. "Mom wants all my friends to start calling her Hazel, not Mrs. Barnes. Like how you call each other's moms. Not so formal."

"Then way to go, Miss Hazel." Roo blew out a slow, sinuous stream of smoke. "Parker must be ecstatic over *that* little confrontation. Anything that pisses off his mom *always* makes Parker ecstatic. Not that I blame him."

"Roo, don't," Ashley scolded. "Mrs. Wilmington can be really nice."

"Yeah—when she's *after* something. Listen, Miranda, you know she's just sucking up because she still wants your grandfather's War collection. She'd *love* to get her hands on all those artifacts."

Miranda looked thoughtful. "Hmmm . . . maybe. I know Mom's been after Aunt Teeta lately to get all that stuff appraised."

"That proves it. Your mom must suspect something too. I swear, just because Mrs. Wilmington runs the Historical Society, she thinks she can run the whole town."

"With all their money, they pretty much *do* run the whole town," Ashley confirmed. "And . . . pretty much *own* the whole town."

"It's weird, though." Once more, Miranda reflected. "For some reason, Mom really seems to like Mrs. Wilmington."

Roo made a sound of disgust. "That's because your mom doesn't really know her."

"Well, she knows Mrs. Wilmington's the authority on local history. She said—and I quote—'It only makes sense to include her expertise.'"

"Well, I'm glad *we're* being included," Ashley piped up. "This is so great of your aunt Teeta—letting us see the house before it's even finished!"

"Aunt Teeta's even more nuts about the place than my mom is—she's out there helping every chance she gets. Did you know she had the listing for Belle Chandelle ever since she's been a real estate agent? She said she never gave up on it—she knew somewhere, someday, there just had to be the right people willing to save it."

"Well, I can't believe you haven't been out there yet. If it were me, I'd be there every single day—I'd be *living* there if I could! Maybe you'll get to help decorate, Miranda. You're so lucky."

Right. Broken-mirror-seven-years'-bad-lucky.

Abruptly Miranda changed the subject. "So, are the guys coming, do you think?"

"They said they were. Well, Parker said he absolutely wouldn't come, but I sort of . . . bribed him."

"Do *not* elaborate," Roo ordered.

"Oh, honestly, Roo. I just promised I'd write his English essay for him."

"You write *all* his essays for him."

"I *help* write them. I don't *totally* write them. We'd get expelled if I *totally* wrote them."

Roo shook her head at Miranda. "She *totally* writes them. But she puts in a bunch of really ignorant parts, so the teacher will think it's Parker."

"So are they coming?" Miranda asked again, managing a straight face.

Ashley slowed down for a fallen branch. "Yes. Parker said he'd pick up Gage after football practice."

"Poor Gage. He's going to be so happy to finally get that cast off."

"In a few days, right?" Roo mulled this over. "Hmmm . . . I bet he'll still be really wobbly for a while."

Ashley shot her sister a frown. "Roo, shame on you. The whole time he's been in that awful thing, you've tormented him. And now it's finally coming off, and you've got a million *new* ways to torment him. Even before his leg can get strong again!"

"Not quite a million. I'm still deep in my creative process."

"You know he'll get you back," Ashley warned.

"No, he won't."

"He will eventually. He always does."

"Never. I have too many advantages."

"Such as?" Miranda asked her, amused.

"First, I've always got my guard up. Second, Gage is way too easy to embarrass."

"And so *cute* when he's embarrassed," Ashley insisted. "Don't forget that."

"Three major strikes against him."

"But then . . . Gage is cute when he's *not* embarrassed too."

"*No*. I'm going for embarrassment. Complete and total embarrassment, every chance I get."

As Miranda and Ashley laughed, Roo gave a satisfied smile and draped herself between the seats. Miranda shifted her eyes to the heavily wooded landscape.

"And what about Etienne?" she mentioned casually. "I didn't

see him at school today. Did anyone ask him if he wanted to meet us?"

"Didn't have to," Roo said.

"What do you mean?"

"He's on the construction crew out here."

"You're kidding." *Pretty amazing sights, huh? One I'd especially be interested in? Good one, Aunt Teeta.*

"You mean he never told you?"

Ashley sounded exasperated. "How could he tell her, Roo? She's been sick. And besides that, Etienne never tells anybody anything, you know that."

"Actually, it's sort of an on-again-off-again thing," Roo explained. "Whenever somebody decides to renovate Belle Chandelle, then Etienne gets hired."

"He worked there all last summer," Ashley added. "At least till the owner ran out of money and shut the place down. After that happened, he said Belle Chandelle was probably lost forever."

The information surprised Miranda. "I didn't realize anyone owned it before."

"Well, nobody ever kept it very long. They'd start to fix it up, they'd sell it. They'd start to fix it up again, they'd sell it again. Last Christmas, some people in New Orleans finally bought it. Etienne says they never come here, but they seem to know all the best experts to hire."

"Aunt Teeta said they're making it into a bed and breakfast."

"Seriously?" Bouncing in her seat, Ashley let out a squeal.

"That's so perfect! I *love* these new owners, whoever they are! And I'm so glad they want to protect Belle Chandelle."

Roo gave a vague nod. "They've made it a private road now—and fenced in a lot of the property. And they *really* don't want trespassers around."

"So do people ever sneak in?" Miranda wondered. "Or try to—"

As a cold shudder crept up her spine, she went rigid, her glance darting to the slowly passing scenery.

"Maybe we should turn around," she whispered. "Maybe we should go back."

Startled, Ashley let up on the gas pedal. "You mean, go home? But I thought—"

"I think maybe it *is* out here somewhere." For a split second, Miranda's thoughts scrambled, her mind went hazy, her words echoed hollowly through her brain. *Did I just say that out loud?*

She hadn't meant to, hadn't expected to—but the dark mood that had plagued her most of the day was suddenly unbearable. As though the very atmosphere were shifting and closing in . . . intrusive . . . oppressive . . . the way a room could feel when it held too many people. . . .

"*What's* out here somewhere?" Ashley asked, confused.

"I feel dizzy," Miranda mumbled. "I need some air."

Rolling down the window, she breathed deeply, felt her senses opening wide. Outside it smelled of swamp water and last night's rain; of creeping animals and the twisted underbrush that hid them. The earth here was rich and dark. A soggy breeze snaked its way through the weeds and tangled trees, bringing with it a heady confusion of moss and mold and remembrances. . . .

She felt Ashley squeezing her shoulder. With enormous effort, she pulled back inside, took another deep breath, and turned to face Roo's bold stare.

"The plantation's still two miles away." Without breaking eye contact, Roo tossed her cigarette butt out onto the muddy road. "And you're already picking up spirit vibes."

Ashley was instantly alarmed. "Are you really? Oh, Miranda, I wish you wouldn't. I don't think I want to go there if you're already picking up spirit vibes."

"It's nothing," *No worse than staring eyes and a disembodied hand in my locker.* Swallowing hard, Miranda tried to sound reassuring. "Look, even though I've been through it once, I'm still getting used to all this, you know? Weird stuff coming out of nowhere, hitting me when I'm not expecting it? It catches me off guard, it's like . . . like . . ." Her voice trailed off. She saw the guilt on Ashley's face, felt a second gentle squeeze on her shoulder.

"Don't worry, Ashley." Miranda forced an overly confident smile. "Honest. I'm okay."

Yet even though Ashley seemed relieved, Miranda sensed that she hadn't fooled Roo for a second.

"Uh-huh." One of Roo's eyebrows arched beneath her bangs. "Keep telling yourself that."

But they were driving closer every second, and Miranda's

head was filling with echoes and whispers and secrets and cries, all jumbled, all muffled, like wind rushing softly, like time spinning out of control . . .

I shouldn't have come. I should have stayed away, I knew *better* . . .

"Dammit," she murmured, so the others couldn't hear. "Why today?"

For she was certain now that this was all meant to be, all happening for a reason. A reason of grave importance that she'd become part of, but still couldn't figure out. Like the eerie connection she'd felt in the bathroom this morning when she'd broken Aunt Teeta's mirror . . . and the frightening events that she'd experienced at her locker . . . *and here I am, getting ready to walk right into that plantation, right into God knows what* . . .

She realized that Roo was watching her. There was both concern and understanding in that steady, black-ringed stare.

"Think you're ready?" Roo asked.

Hesitantly, Miranda nodded. Events were already in play; she had no choice but to see them through. And yet deep down she *wasn't* ready, not ready at all.

Not for memories . . .

Not for mysteries . . .

Not for what's waiting for me at Belle Chandelle.

5

"**THERE'S A CAR BEHIND US,**" Ashley said. "Well, not *close* behind us. But it will be in a minute—it's coming really fast."

Grateful for the interruption, Miranda checked the side mirror, then once again craned her head out the window. The car was still at a distance, blocked from sight by drooping tree branches and long, gray strings of moss overhanging the road. But its engine was revving loud, bursts of rocks and shells and mud slinging wildly from beneath its tires. Annoyed, Miranda turned back to Ashley.

"I thought this road wasn't open to the public. Maybe it's some of the workers."

"Sure it's not Parker?" Roo asked, settling into her corner. "Whoever it is sure *drives* like Parker."

"That's not nice." Ashley frowned.

"It wasn't meant to be nice. It was meant to be true."

Miranda did another quick take in the mirror. "It's not a BMW. It's . . . I don't know. A station wagon? And it looks like maybe two people inside?"

"Ignore them, Ash." Digging through the pockets of her dress, Roo pulled out a matchbook and a crumpled pack of cigarettes. "Just keep driving."

"I can't keep driving," Ashley told her. "They're going to run me off the road."

"Pull over, then."

"There's no place to pull over."

"Sure there is. Just go between those trees."

"It's squishy over there. We might get stuck."

"We won't get stuck. Just do it."

"No. I'm stopping."

"You're what?"

"I'm going to stop here. They'll just have to go around me."

"Maybe Roo's right," Miranda echoed nervously. "Maybe you should pull over."

As Roo peered out the back windshield, Miranda heard the approaching car kick into high gear, accelerating rapidly, barreling down on them. The road was barely wide enough for two cars to pass, and Ashley had stopped in the middle. Thick stands of trees flanked each side, and both narrow shoulders were mucky with a week's buildup of rain.

"They'll stop." Ashley's eyes were glued to the rearview mirror. "When they see we're not moving, I'm pretty sure they'll stop."

"They're not stopping," Roo said.

The car burst into clear view. For a split second, it hurtled toward them at breakneck speed, then suddenly slammed on its brakes, fishtailing wildly, sliding to a stop beside them, angled half on, half off the road. Miranda didn't realize she'd been holding her breath. Not till the car's window rolled down and she saw the familiar face grinning out at them.

"What's this, Ash? A roadblock? Damsels in distress?"

Roo's stare was bland. "Roadblock. There's an idiot on the loose, but—oh. Never mind. I see we just caught him."

"Parker Wilmington!" Ashley exploded. "You scared me half to death! What on earth do you think you're doing?"

Despite their near collision, Parker obviously found the whole thing hilarious. And as Ashley continued to berate him, he only looked more and more amused.

"And why are you in that car?" Ashley demanded. "That's not your car!"

"No, it's Leo's."

"Leo's? You're driving your *gardener's car*?"

Parker started to answer, then stopped. His gaze redirected to Roo. "Hey. Your Gloominess. What the *hell* did you do to your hair?"

"Cut it."

"With what? A saw? A very dull meat cleaver?"

"I needed a change."

"Try a mask next time."

"You're driving your *gardener's car*?" Ashley asked again.

"Look, I got a flat tire; Leo told me I could use this. What's the big deal?"

"The big deal is, your family has a ton of brand-new cars, and you're driving this poor old car of Leo's, and you're totally trashing it in the process!"

"Hey, not to worry. I told him I'd fill the tank and wash it before I brought it back." Inclining his head, Parker's grin widened. "Hey, Miranda."

"Hi, Parker. And in case you didn't notice the speed limit back there—"

"I've got Gage," Parker interrupted quickly.

"Sounds contagious," Roo said. "Is it fatal?"

"Depends on where you touch it."

As Parker chuckled and glanced to his right, Miranda spotted Gage sitting next to him. The passenger seat had been pushed back to accommodate his cast, but he was leaning slightly toward Parker's window, staring out.

"Forget it," Gage informed Roo. "You're not touching me. I don't care where it is."

Parker made a dramatic show of checking the dashboard clock. "Ash, you left at *least* half an hour before I did. And then I *still* had to pick up Gage. I mean, even *I* figured you'd go over five miles an hour."

"She didn't go over *one* mile an hour," Roo grumbled. "I'm walking back."

"What's wrong with your broomstick?"

"You can ride with us," Gage offered, easing back into place.

"Excuse me?" Parker shot at Gage. "You can't invite her. It's not your car."

"It's not yours, either."

"Come on, y'all," Ashley scolded. "I just want to hurry so we can get there."

"Whoa, she's a speed demon!" Parker obligingly gunned the motor. "Christ, Ashley, the whole damn plantation will be rebuilt by the time you show up."

He left them behind within seconds. When Ashley finally

reached the turnoff to Belle Chandelle, the station wagon was nowhere to be seen.

"It shouldn't be too far now." Scooting to the edge of her seat, Miranda kept a sharp eye on their surroundings. "Aunt Tecta said there's a big gate and a barbwire fence. Maybe around this next curve?"

"I'm getting so excited again!" Ashley caught a quick breath. "Aren't you even the least bit excited, Roo?"

"Don't I look excited?"

"I can't wait to see—*oh my God!*"

"Now what?"

"Look, y'all! There it is!"

Magical. That's the first word that came to mind as Miranda stared at the scene ahead of them. Magical and make-believe, like something straight out of a movie. A perfect photograph, centuries old, caught in the fading glow of late afternoon, framed by those wild, tangled woods and the hazy aftermath of early rain.

Belle Chandelle.

"It's beautiful," Ashley murmured. "More beautiful than I even imagined."

"Except for the color." Miranda couldn't help making a face. "Why would anyone paint it such a horrible color?"

Set back among live oaks, cypress trees, and towering magnolias, the three-story plantation house rose majestically within deep, restful shadows and soft draperies of moss, where the full rays of the sun couldn't quite reach. Eight round columns adorned the front, rising all the way to the gabled roof. A row of tall, shuttered French doors lined the verandah and the wide, balustered gallery above it; a series of dormer windows marked the third floor. Higher still were the brick chimneys, while a railing-enclosed belvedere stood in silhouette against the sky, cresting the roof like a giant finial.

And all of it yellow. A dark, dull, nauseous yellow, with an ugly reddish tinge. Miranda's stomach instantly went queasy.

"It's not a horrible color!" Ashley objected. "It's *perfect*! Absolutely perfect. In fact, I can't imagine it being any better color than white."

"White? What are you talking about? It's—"

The words died in Miranda's throat. As she turned back toward the house, she could see all the creamy white walls, the tall white columns, the wide white galleries . . .

Not yellow—nothing *is yellow. It's all*—

"White," Roo finished. "What are *you* talking about?"

Flustered, Miranda tried to think, tried to concentrate, but the voices were whispering again, floating through her head telling secrets, and scenes were flowing, running together so fast, they were like one big blur that made no sense. . . .

"You're right," she mumbled, staring down at her hands, forcing herself to talk out loud. "I guess . . . the way the light was shining down, it just looked yellow to me." *Good . . . good . . . my head is clearing . . . the shadows are going.* "It must have been a reflection on something."

Yet deep down, though she *wanted* to believe that, she still wasn't sure. *It was too clear, too vivid, that hideous yellow.* And a cold, nagging dread had settled deeper in the pit of her stomach.

"Miranda, are you sure this is where we're supposed to be? It's all empty. I think we're the only ones here."

As Ashley's voice snapped her back to attention, Miranda realized they were still driving, that they'd come to an open gate at the end of the road. Beyond the high fence was a makeshift parking lot—a large, muddy tract of crushed oyster shells, potholes, and carelessly arranged lengths of plywood. *Pull yourself together, Miranda. Don't think about what just happened.*

"It's after five," she told Ashley now. "I don't imagine the work crews hang around."

Roo nodded toward the far corner of the lot, where two big pecan trees offered the only shade. "There's the station wagon. And Etienne's truck."

"I see Aunt Teeta's car."

"Do you want me to park next to them?" Brow furrowing, Ashley hesitated. "Because I need to warn you, I'm not very good at parking so—"

"No," Miranda said quickly, hoping she hadn't sounded too eager. "No, just stop the car right here. I think that's the path to the main house—over by the fence. This way we won't have so far to walk. Right, Roo?"

But Roo didn't take time to answer. She was already out of the car and onto the path, leaving Miranda and Ashley to trail behind.

It was obvious that this end of the property had been reserved strictly for construction—on all sides there were building materials, work vehicles, and heavy machinery. Deep tire tracks rutted the ground and seeped with water; any grass had been killed off long ago. The day was still warm and chokingly humid. Roo was right—even for south Louisiana, October had been unseasonably hot.

But as the girls walked farther, Miranda noticed the scenery begin to change. Despite more than a century of neglect, there were isolated spots of beauty here and there; colors peeking through the choked weeds and rambling vines; an overall park-like setting, tranquil beneath heavy layers of overgrown vegetation, dignified beneath the scars of blistering Southern weather.

"Miranda . . . do you know Kurt Fuller?" Ashley asked quietly.

Miranda threw her a glance. Ashley was frowning, eyes cast down, as if something important weighed heavily on her mind— but though Miranda was trying to listen, there were so many *other* things around her, tugging at her senses, demanding her attention. Wide-spreading trees dripping moss, some standing alone, some in thick groves, *cruelty happened here, beatings, hangings*—the promise of lush grass beneath heavy carpets of weeds, *duels were fought here, blood was spilled*—wildflowers springing up amidst piles of rotting boards, crumbling rocks and stones, *babies were buried here, mothers wept*—

"I . . ." Again Miranda tried to concentrate on Ashley. "He sits across from me in Spanish. He's on the football team, right?"

"He's our wide receiver."

"Don't they call him Sneak or something?"

"*Streak*, Miranda. Because he's so fast."

"Sorry."

Ashley's voice lowered even more. "He just broke up with his girlfriend Delphine. And after cheerleading practice today? He asked me to go out with him."

"Really?" Miranda glanced from Ashley's face . . . scanned the desolate surroundings. There were no buildings out here, only the trees and the empty sweep of land, *but the slave quarters were back there, two rows of cabins facing each other, raised up off the ground—and the cemetery, they had their own cemetery— almost like their own separate little neighborhood—the overseer's house—and sugarcane tall and ripe, growing for miles and miles in the scorching sun—*

"You can't tell Parker," Ashley said. With a start, Miranda realized that they'd stopped walking, that Ashley was waiting for her to talk. "And you can't tell Roo. She'd probably *want* me to go out with Kurt. Just to upset Parker."

"So . . ." *Focus, Miranda. Focus.* "What are you going to do?"

"I'm *not* going out with him," Ashley replied firmly. "Even though he *is* . . . you know. Handsome and godlike in every way. And he *knows* Parker and I are together. Why would he even ask me out? *Everybody* knows Parker and I are together."

"Maybe he just really likes you, Ashley."

"Or maybe he wants to make Delphine jealous."

"Or maybe he's liked you for a while, and he's been trying to get *out* of his other relationship, and now he's . . . you know . . . testing the waters."

"Or maybe he's trying to make Parker mad."

"Does he have something against Parker?"

"Well . . . they've always been really competitive on the field, but Coach won't put up with stuff like that."

"Hmmm. Sounds like they might be really competitive *off* the field too—especially now that Kurt's girlfriend's out of the picture. Did you tell him you wouldn't go out with him?"

"Of course!"

"And what happened?"

The girl's response was somewhat embarrassed. "He said he thinks I'm hot."

"What'd *you* say?"

"I told him it was because of the weather—you know, because I just finished practice, and I'm *always* hot when I finish practice. Oh Miranda, I don't *want* him to think I'm hot. Even though it *is* a really nice compliment. And he *is* a really nice guy. And charming. And he does things like send flowers and cards and candy, and he never forgets a special occasion, and—"

"How do you know all that?"

"All the girls know that—Delphine brags to everybody. In fact . . . Kurt's kind of obsessive about being wonderful."

"So . . . isn't that good?"

"I don't think he's going to leave me alone. I think he's going to keep asking me out, and I don't know what to do about it."

"Keep saying no?"

"I told you . . . the guy's obsessive."

"Then maybe you *should* tell Parker. If it bothers you that much, he might . . ."

Miranda's thoughts trailed away. As a soft warmth crept through her, her mind began to open . . . open . . . and for an instant she wasn't sure if she was actually turning around or only imagining it— peering off between long curtains of moss, far over the sweeping plantation grounds, back toward wild, overgrown fields. . . .

Magnolia blossoms, waxy cool fragrant trees—blazing sunshine, tall graceful green seas of sugarcane—low voices singing, work-weary chorus—meat curing billowing, thick black ribbons of smoke—sweet ripe orchards heavy with fruit—flies buzzing swarming, stinking outhouses on sweltering days—fresh herbs hot spices gumbo simmering in the fireplace, wafting from the open kitchen door—black rancid bayou water—sweat-soaked cotton shirts, dark oily grimy hands, bloody hands, hands thick with calluses, hands torn with scars—hammering chiseling sawdust underfoot, white hot sparks metal horseshoes—harvest wagons groaning, slow steady plodding of mules, whips cracking the air . . .

No. No . . . not the air . . . something else . . . whips cracking, snapping, striking, like a snake striking—cutting skin bone raw tender flesh . . . wrists bound bodies trapped and tortured—

"Parker would *not* handle it well." Ashley's reply jolted Miranda back again. "Sometimes he can get really jealous. And I don't want there to be any trouble between him and Kurt. I'd be so embarrassed, especially over something so stupid."

Miranda drew a deep breath. For a split second she felt shaky and light-headed—her usual transition between this world and another. Fortunately, Ashley didn't seem to notice. "Are you sure? It's not stupid if you're worried about it."

"Yes, I'm sure. I just . . . I guess I just needed to talk about it."

"You can always talk to me, Ashley."

"Look, Roo's waiting for us. Please don't say anything."

"I won't. And she still has her earbuds in anyway."

"Actually . . . I'm pretty sure they're not connected to anything. Sometimes she just sticks them in and walks around with the other end loose in her pocket. She thinks it's funny when people say rude things about her because they think she can't hear them."

"It doesn't hurt her feelings?"

"She says rude things back at them, just to see the looks on their faces."

Laughing, the girls continued walking. The sensations had stilled in Miranda's head; the sweeping images had faded. She felt stronger now and calmer, yet a tiny spark of wariness still flickered in the farthest corner of her mind. Instinctively she glanced in all directions. This place, this entire plantation property, was massive and overwhelming—over a century of human drama had played out within its boundaries. *And I'm only one person; it's too much, too much to take in. . . .*

She rubbed at her forehead, squinted down at the muddy edges of the path. *Stay focused, Miranda. Stay here, right in this moment. Don't look to the left or the right, don't let yourself think forward or backward, just stay focused and you'll be fine.* As she and Ashley caught up with Roo, she managed a smile and made an all-encompassing gesture with her arms.

"So what do you think, Roo? Anything familiar? Anything you remember from when you were little?"

Roo considered the question. Turning slowly, she scanned

the landscape, then brought her gaze back again, full circle. "There were some buildings off that way, behind the house. Or at least what was *left* of some buildings. That's where we used to play. But they were already in such bad shape then, I didn't really expect anything to be left."

"Mom said they'll have to reconstruct most of the outbuildings. Hardly any of the originals survived."

"It's so tragic," Ashley sighed. "I bet this whole place was really happy and romantic once upon a time. Can't you imagine— just like in the movies? Full of hopes and dreams and love and charm and—"

"They had slaves here," Roo said flatly. "I don't imagine *they* thought it was very happy and romantic."

"Roo, don't spoil it! That's not what I meant."

"I'm just saying."

Still deep in conversation, the three started off again. Miranda hadn't realized how far they'd come, and as they passed through the last dense stand of trees, the plantation house rose suddenly before them—silent, imposing . . . and sad.

She was instantly disappointed. And though Ashley gasped in delight, Miranda felt only pity.

From this vantage point, they could see the entire west side of the house and most of the front. Her eyes swept the stately facade, the enormous round columns, the shaded galleries— and for one second, she actually wondered if this might be a *different* place from that magical, faraway image they'd admired earlier from the road. Because here, viewed up close and despite the evidence of work in progress, Belle Chandelle's flaws were all too evident, all too glaring. The countless years of abandonment, vandalism, and neglect; the ruthless encroachment of animals, water, weather, and time . . .

And sorrow, Miranda realized. *Terrible, terrible sorrow.*

Apparently, Ashley didn't notice. "Oh, it just goes deep inside me!" With a wistful sigh, she clasped her hands to her heart. "How perfectly *gorgeous* it is!"

Roo arched an eyebrow. "Are you talking about the house or *Etienne*?"

Etienne? Feeling her pulse quicken, Miranda was instantly annoyed with herself.

"*Where's* Etienne?" she heard Ashley ask, and Roo motioned vaguely upward.

"There. On top of the house."

Miranda followed the point of Roo's finger. And saw Etienne standing at the edge of the roof.

His shirt was off. His jeans fit low on his narrow hips, and his feet were planted wide apart, straddling a stack of shingles. Sweat glistened on his bare chest and across his shoulders, down the sinewy cords of muscles along his arms. His body was lean, easily six feet tall; his tan was natural, not dictated by any season. Though he'd dropped his tool belt to one side, he was still clutching a hammer in his left hand. A few stray waves of black hair clung damply to his cheeks and forehead; the rest had been tied carelessly back at the nape of his neck. Watching him now, Miranda remembered the very first time she'd ever seen him, how he'd reminded her of some wild gypsy.

Today—more than ever—he still did.

"Well." Roo nodded toward Etienne. "That's *one* good thing about global warming."

"Etienne!" Cupping her hands around her mouth, Ashley shouted, then began to wave. "Etienne! Hey! It's us!"

He saw them at once . . . lifted one arm in recognition . . . wiped it slowly over his dripping face. Even from that distance, Miranda felt the force of those swamp-black eyes.

"Hey, Boucher," Roo greeted him. "What are you doing up there? Showing off?"

Etienne propped a work boot on some shingles. Leaning forward, he draped an arm across his knee, while the faintest hint of a smile played at one corner of his mouth. "*Mais*, yeah. I been waiting up here all day just to impress you."

That unforgettable voice, deep and slightly husky. That thick Cajun accent mixed in with Southern charm. Before Etienne, Miranda had never heard a language like his before— that distinct strain of Acadian French combined so effortlessly with English. It was both musical and mysterious . . . and incredibly sexy.

"I'm impressed." Roo arched an eyebrow. "Especially with your big hammer."

"Will y'all two stop?" Ashley groaned at their usual banter, though Miranda couldn't help but laugh. "After listening to that for all these years, I can*not* understand why y'all still think you're funny."

"We're not funny." Roo sounded mildly indignant. "We're passionate about each other."

Expressionless, she winked at Etienne. Slyly, Etienne winked back.

"So where y'all goin' at?" he asked, but his gaze was on Miranda. She told herself that the rush of heat she felt was merely from the sultry air.

Answer him—you're being totally silly. The truth was, she'd thought about him all day long and had watched for him to show up. Now here he finally was, looking as only Etienne could look, staring as only Etienne could stare, and her heart was skipping a beat, and she couldn't come up with a single, coherent word to say. *Get a grip, Miranda.*

"Miss Teeta invited us!" Ashley waved again. "Do you know where she is?"

"All over the place, usually."

"Did you see Gage and Parker? They got here way before we did."

"Then you musta been driving, yeah?"

"Don't make fun of me."

"What? I could never make fun of you," Etienne assured her, though his expression suggested otherwise. "They're probably all inside. Just go around front, door's in the middle."

He bent to retrieve his tool belt. As Roo and Ashley walked on, Miranda started to follow, then suddenly stopped and turned.

Etienne was poised on a ledge, just below the third-story dormer, his back to an open window. Most of the glass had broken long ago, leaving nothing but a few jagged edges at the corners. No curtains hanging, no shades . . . only darkness.

But Miranda saw what was there.

She saw it, dimly, and she told herself that it was only the fading sunlight flickering through moss and leafy branches. Even though her skin went suddenly cold.

Because for one instant, she could swear she'd seen a hand.

A small, shadowy hand; fingers pressed flat against the air, as though pressed flat against a windowpane.

As if something—someone—were trying to get out.

6

"**Miranda?**"

Startled, Miranda's gaze shifted from the window to Etienne. He'd straightened up again, frowning, eyes narrowed down at her

"Miranda? What's wrong, *cher*?"

"I—I—"

But it was gone now. The window was empty and black; whatever she'd seen there had disappeared. If, in fact, she'd really seen anything at all.

"I—just—nothing." She was backing away, trying to smile, trying to act as if nothing had happened. And knowing she wasn't fooling Etienne for a second. "See you inside!"

Damn. She felt his eyes upon her till she rounded the corner of the house. Those black, black eyes that always seemed to see inside places she didn't want them to look and stir up emotions she wasn't sure she wanted to feel. Which didn't change the fact that she hadn't heard from him for a week, ever since she'd gotten sick. Even though she was *still* telling herself that it didn't matter . . .

Flustered, she hurried along the low brick verandah and caught up with Roo and Ashley just as they were entering the house.

"Hey, cancel that APB!" Parker called to Gage. Standing just inside the French doors, he grabbed Ashley around the waist and pulled her against him. "I guess they didn't die after all."

"I'm not *that* bad of a driver," Ashley said indignantly.

Roo shot her a look. "Yes. You are."

"It's not like I would have gotten us in a wreck."

"We weren't worried about you dying from a wreck," Gage assured her. "Just from old age."

As Ashley stuck her tongue out at him, he smiled and angled himself back into the corner beside Parker. Roo, walking several paces ahead, stopped to fuss with her earbuds while Miranda paused on the threshold and did a split-second appraisal of the room.

Emptiness, was her first impression—but so much *more* than emptiness, more than just no furniture or people, more somehow, than just a deserted house. A vast, *overwhelming* emptiness that distorted her friends' conversation around her, and swallowed the sound of their laughter, and stirred the air with echoes she didn't recognize.

Like being in some lost cavern, she thought. Dingy and bare, filled with nothing but shadows. Stale and musty and damp. Surprisingly cool, despite the lingering late-day heat.

The floors had been partially laid, their rich, cypress beauty scarcely recognizable beneath layers of ground-in dirt and plaster dust. The ceilings, at least thirteen feet high, showed various stages of carvings, moldings, and friezes. On the other three walls of the room, carved pocket doors stood halfway open, revealing another connecting room beyond each.

Exterior rooms, Miranda guessed, from their rows of French doors, all tightly shuttered. Glancing off to her left, she noted a huge desk—Mom's, she was sure—surrounded by file cabinets and cardboard boxes, crates of dishes and glassware, and small items of antique furniture in various stages of disrepair.

"This is so amazing." There was no mistaking the awe in Ashley's voice. "I can't believe I'm actually inside this house."

Stay here, Miranda. Concentrate. Once again Miranda steeled herself, tried her best to pay attention to what was going on in the moment. Ashley, of course, was completely enamored, but what Miranda kept seeing was that empty third-story window; that small, shadowy hand pressed flat against the dark. . . .

"What'd you do to your hand?" a voice asked her.

Startled, she glanced up into concerned brown eyes. She hadn't noticed Gage moving close to her, but now he was lifting her injured palm and studying it.

"Just a cut," she stammered. "Some broken glass. No big deal."

"It's bleeding a little, though."

"Is it?" Parker, who'd been watching, reached out for Roo's back and grabbed the end of her long shawl. Before Miranda could protest, he swiped it over her hand, then dropped it again.

Roo instantly whirled to face them.

Parker pointed at Miranda. Miranda looked chidingly at Parker, who looked at Ashley, who looked at Gage, who gave Miranda a shrug.

"What?" they all chorused.

Roo frowned. Returned to her earbuds.

Ashley, however, had switched her focus to the room again— still taking it all in, still sounding slightly incredulous. "This house is so perfect. So *perfect*."

"It's a dump," Parker said, pulling her tighter. "It smells like mold."

"Let go—I want to explore. It was perfect once, and it'll be perfect again. You'll see."

"Yeah, perfect if you're *dead*." As Ashley pushed him away, Parker gave a mock shudder. "Am I the only one who sees the resemblance here? Or hasn't anybody else noticed how much this place looks like a tomb—inside *and* out?"

"Parker Wilmington, you are *not* going to scare me. So just stop it."

Though Miranda hadn't really thought of it, she realized that Parker was right. The house really *did* look like a tomb. *Inside and out . . .*

She'd heard Mom and Aunt Teeta explaining many times about how slow and tedious the work was, how early the stages of renovation—yet she'd certainly expected a whole lot more than what she was viewing now. Curious, she walked straight ahead, into the adjoining room. Ladders here, and scaffolding; sawdust and paint cans; drop cloths, tiles and grout; stacks of lumber. Enlarged blueprints on the wall, plumbing and electrical plans, landscape designs. Paint streaks, hundreds of different colors; wallpaper patterns, jig sawed and push-pinned with fabric swatches. And tables, straining beneath the weight of magazines, catalogs, bolts of material, binders, and sample books.

See, Miranda? Signs of progress and hope, signs that this house is trying to come alive again . . .

Then why did she still feel so sad?

Why did the *house* still feel so sad?

This area showed more damage, she noticed—holes pocking the walls and ceiling, glimpses of exposed bricks and lath strips, various stages of patchwork and plastering . . . *water seepage . . . rodents . . . rot . . .* Dust and debris had been carelessly swept aside, heaped against the French doors, pushed into corners and crevices, even stuffed inside the deep, massive cavity that had once been a glorious fireplace. Though obviously unused for years, the interior was still blackened—thick layers of smoke and soot—while from high up the chimney came the faint, far patter of bat wings.

"Great." Stepping back, Miranda kept wary eyes on the opening. Just her luck for some rabid bat to come swooping out and land right in her hair. The firebox was crammed with all kinds of garbage—no doubt the workmen threw their leftover lunches in here too; it was probably infested with mice and rats and roaches and God only knew what else. Not to mention all the centuries' worth of historical odds and ends that had most likely been swept up, then carelessly hauled off to landfills . . .

"Look," Roo said. She'd been pacing again, back and forth along the walls, but stopped now in front of the boys. As Miranda came back to join them, Roo lifted her arms wide. She held them up for a second, midair. She let them drop down again at her sides. "Look at this. This is weird."

Parker and Gage exchanged glances.

"I am looking," Parker agreed. "I am looking at you, and yes, you are weird."

Reaching out, Gage calmly pulled the plugs from Roo's ears and slipped them into his shirt pocket. "Stop talking to your soul. It's not polite when the rest of us aren't in on the conversation."

But Roo paid no attention. "I don't mean *me*. I mean being *here*. In this place. Who'd have thought?"

"Thought what?"

"We're connected."

"Who's connected?" Parker scowled. "Definitely not you and me in any way, shape, or form. *Ever*." Another glance at Gage. "Give those ear-things back. Maybe her soul can translate."

Amused, Miranda watched from the threshold. A wet, sluggish breeze crept in through the French doors, bringing long shadows of early twilight and the promise of more rain. There was muffled thunder in the distance . . . leaves rustling . . . bayou sounds . . .

Laughter . . .

Immediately she turned, eyes scanning left to right. Verandah . . . outbuildings . . . overgrown lawn . . . mossy oaks . . . discarded piles of rubble. A rusty, wrought-iron bench. A headless marble statue. A wooden swing hanging by ropes from a tree branch, jerking restlessly in the wind . . .

Deserted. No one there.

Yet she was sure she'd heard it. Faint . . . fleeting . . . nothing more than that, nothing she could really describe, but laughter all the same.

Without warning, a flock of crows burst from the nearest

oak, making her jump. For several long moments there were only hoarse, mocking cries and wings beating furiously at the air—then just as suddenly, everything grew still.

"—I know what she means," Ashley was insisting.

Turning back again, Miranda did her best not to shiver. *Must have been those crows . . . that must have been what I heard—*

"I *do* know what Roo means!" Ashley went on loyally, hugging her sister, oblivious to the frown Roo gave her. "And it *is* weird! *We* had a past, and the *house* had a past. And *we* played here, and the *house* was here. And *we* grew up, and the *house* grew up—"

"And do I care?" Parker cut in. "And is there a bathroom around this place?"

Without a word, Gage pointed outside. Ashley, suddenly noting the four pairs of eyes on her, stopped talking. She lifted her nose at Gage and Parker. She turned loose of Roo.

"We all share a common bond with Belle Chandelle," Ashley finished indignantly. "We're connected."

Tilting his head back, Parker snorted a laugh. "Yeah. You and all the other gazillion people who've ever walked across this property since the beginning of time."

"It's more than that," Ashley argued. "More than just us. More than just the history and the land and the soil . . . and . . . It's our *heritage.*"

"Uh-oh." Parker exchanged winces with Gage. "Is this where we get the Strong Southern Women lecture?"

"Yes!" Ashley declared. "Strong, brave, Southern women. And the strong, brave Southern . . . spirit . . . in . . . our blood!"

"Yep, there it is. I hear the background music playing. What is it with you girls, anyhow? All your stupid *Gone With the Wind* fantasies?"

Roo leveled Parker a look. She held out her palms, one at a time, weighing options. "Gosh, I don't know. Rhett Butler . . . Parker Wilmington. It's a total mystery."

"And it's the *romance*," Ashley scolded. "All that beautiful, old-fashioned romance. Girls love that."

Startled, Miranda felt a movement at her back. Before she could turn around, Etienne's hands settled firmly on her hips, easing her to one side of the doorway so he could slip through. Leaning close, his lips brushed lightly over her ear.

"You okay?" he murmured.

"Sure." Another shiver, only hot this time and not one bit controllable. Etienne must have felt it, though he gave no sign. Miranda was instantly annoyed with herself.

"Yeah?" he persisted.

"Yes. Why wouldn't I be?"

Reading the doubt in his eyes, she felt helplessly transparent. But Etienne simply focused on the others and asked, "So what y'all think?"

He'd put on a T-shirt—still wet with sweat, it clung to him like a second skin. And his hair was untied, so the damp, reckless waves tousled nearly to his shoulders. Roo offered a quick assessment.

"Of this place? Or you?"

That hint of a smile. "I already know what you think of me, *cher*."

"It's the most wonderful place I've ever seen." Ashley sighed. "When can we look around?"

Before Etienne could answer, there was rapid shuffling along the verandah, and the next second Aunt Teeta burst in, laughing, waving, and apologizing with every step.

"I am *so* sorry I'm late, y'all! The electricity just went out, and I don't have a clue what's going on! Why, Gage—you're lookin' better every time I see you, hon! And hey there, little Miss Ashley! And Roo—my goodness, just look how creative you've gone and done your hair! And Parker, I hear your shoulder's all healed up now—we're all countin' on you whuppin' that football team of yours into shape!"

Watching her aunt, Miranda couldn't help but marvel once again—the way moods always lifted whenever Aunt Teeta was around. Ashley, Roo, and Gage were laughing along with her; Etienne, as usual, looked amused. Even Parker couldn't hold back a grin.

"Etienne, darlin', is there anything you can do—" the woman began, but he was already walking toward her, brow creased in thought.

"It's been working fine, yeah? So what, it just quit, no reason?"

"Well, that's the darnedest thing! We've had power all day—then bam! Nothing! I'd say it was about . . . maybe twenty minutes ago? And everything died all at once."

Miranda caught Roo's stare, mildly accusing.

"When *you* got here?" Roo mouthed at her.

"No way," Miranda mouthed back.

Yet Etienne was staring at her now too, and so was Gage—till Etienne smoothly redirected everyone's attention.

"I'll go check it out," he promised Aunt Teeta.

Bestowing him a grateful smile, she turned back to the group. "Now, I know it's my fault we're runnin' behind—but Etienne, please tell me there's still time for a little tour?"

Etienne shrugged, ran one hand distractedly across his chest. "As long as we're outta here before it's too dark."

"Well, not all the house has power, anyway." Aunt Teeta reconciled herself. "So I think we can manage—it's not like there's a whole lot to see in those empty rooms. But I'm just wondering— if I give y'all a little bit of background first, would that help?"

There was a general chorus of assent. Motioning them to follow, Aunt Teeta moved toward the center of the room and began her speech.

"As y'all probably noticed from outside, the verandah and the galleries wrap completely around the building. We believe the *original* layout of the house was a typical Louisiana style—three rooms wide and two rooms deep, on both the first and second floors. Each room would have had at least one opening onto the galleries; some had more. And a few of the rooms connected to each other through interior doors—like these pocket doors y'all see here. There weren't any halls, and no central corridor, but there *was*—and still is—one sneak stairway at the back."

"Is that where the master sneaked in all his girlfriends?" Parker grinned wider, ignoring Ashley's jab in his side.

Aunt Teeta found this hilarious. It took several seconds till she caught her breath.

"Now Parker, I'm not saying it never served that particular purpose. But it got the name because it was hidden in the wall and used only by the servants. The rest of the family used the covered staircases at each end of the galleries."

"What about the third story?" Miranda asked quickly.

"That's the attic," Aunt Teeta replied. "And the access to the belvedere is from there."

Parker frowned. "The what?"

"Belvedere," Ashley repeated. "Honestly, Parker, will you please pay attention?"

"I am paying attention. What the hell's a belvedere?"

"It's a thing on top of the house."

"So are roofs and chimneys. And birds. Thanks, Ash. I feel completely enlightened."

"That little dome on the roof," Gage said, with a slight nod toward the ceiling. "People usually built them for the view. They could stand up there and see for miles in every direction."

"It was the perfect way to keep an eye on the plantation," Aunt Teeta echoed. "In the case of Belle Chandelle, they could see their whole property, plus the bayou and the road."

Miranda was trying hard to be patient. "The third floor, Aunt Teeta?" she pressed. "Was that all it was—just an attic?"

"Yes, darlin', used for storage. But on some plantations, that's where the house servants would have slept. And when guests came to stay, then *their* personal servants would have slept up there too."

Miranda gave a tight nod. She glanced up to see Etienne watching her.

"Oh, Miss Teeta," Ashley begged, "please tell us about all the rooms."

"Well, in a house like this, there might have been drawing rooms, sitting rooms, maybe double parlors, and most definitely a dining room on the main floor. Some houses had fancy ballrooms and music rooms and libraries. The kitchen was always separate, of course—to guard against fire."

She paused to survey her rapt audience. When no questions came, she smiled and continued on.

"Upstairs there were bedrooms and nurseries, naturally—and in some cases, there might have been little half rooms attached to the bedrooms. These would have been used for dressing rooms, or—if there weren't servants' quarters in the attic—this is where the guests' personal servants would have stayed."

Ashley's mouth opened, incredulous. "I can't believe they only had six bedrooms. I mean . . . there must have been so many people living here—how could they fit all their stuff in just six bedrooms?"

"Musta been plenty crowded, yeah?" Etienne kept a straight face. "All those big dresses and no closets?"

"They didn't have closets?"

He'd been propped on one shoulder, arms folded over his chest. Now he stretched himself away from the wall.

"These plantation houses, there were a lotta different designs. In some of them, people didn't even live on the main floor. Like where we are now, this woulda been an aboveground basement. And the rooms here woulda been used for stuff like wine cellars and laundry and storage."

"So then there would have been only six rooms total?" Again, Ashley was shocked. "Did they double up in their bedrooms? I can't even stand the thought of sharing a room with Roo."

Parker grimaced. "Who could?"

"But sons didn't usually live in the main house, did they?" Gage commented. "When they got older, they lived in garconnieres."

"In what?"

"Garconnieres."

"Gesundheit."

"That's true," Aunt Teeta smiled at Gage. "Garconnieres were small, separate buildings, often octagon-shaped, two stories high, and they usually stood at each end of the main house. A plantation this size would certainly have had at least one."

Parker was finally intrigued. "So . . . it was like a bachelor pad?"

"Something like that, yes. Boys were considered men at a much younger age back then. When they reached their teens, they'd move into the garconniere."

"Typical." Roo's disdain was obvious. "They had freedom. And privacy. And privileges. That the women didn't have—"

"But the real question is," Parker broke in, "did they have sneak stairs?"

"Sneak back doors," Etienne said.

"Sneak windows," Gage added.

Amused at their own cleverness, the guys continued to crack jokes, though Miranda was only half listening. Once more her eyes swept slowly up the walls, across the ceiling, back to her aunt's face.

"Aunt Teeta, you keep saying 'might have' or 'would have'—does that mean you don't actually *know* what was here?"

"We don't, darlin'." Aunt Teeta sighed. "The *miracle* of this place is that it finally has a future. The *tragedy* of this place is that it doesn't have a past."

"Oh, but it *does* have a past, Miss Teeta," Ashley insisted. "It has a past with us."

The guys had recovered themselves. Now Gage shifted his weight, realigned his crutches, and fixed Aunt Teeta with a slight frown. "So . . . you can't make this an *exact* replica of how it was. You don't even know what it looked like."

"Unfortunately, yes, that's what I'm saying." Pausing once more, Aunt Teeta made an all-inclusive gesture of the room. "Belle Chandelle sat empty for such a long, long time—way too long without anybody keeping track of it. When some buyers finally came along about twenty or so years ago, the house was nothing but a rotted shell—four crumbled walls and a collapsed ceiling. There wasn't really any interior to speak of; the place was pretty much gutted. From what little bit was salvaged back then, we know it went through floods and at least one fire—transients, probably, smoking or trying to keep warm. Or both."

"Smoking," Gage said, glancing pointedly at Roo.

Roo ignored him.

"We know there was a lot of vandalism—major parts of the original structure had been stripped and torn down. And for what wasn't stolen, time and Mother Nature did the rest."

"Oh, that's so sad." Ashley's voice faltered, teary. "This poor house has suffered so much."

As though some silent signal had been given, Parker, Gage, and Etienne all checked their watches. Smirking, Parker thrust his palm out toward the other guys.

"Pay up. I said twenty minutes; it took her nineteen."

Muttering good-naturedly, Etienne and Gage each dug into their jeans' pockets, relinquishing a five-dollar bill. The girls looked on in dismay.

"Parker Wilmington," Ashley demanded, "what on earth are you doing?"

Parker wasn't the least bit contrite. "We made bets on when you'd get all weepy about this house. And I won."

"Y'all are *not funny!*" Ashley protested, though the guys clearly thought they were. Roo looked at Miranda and rolled her eyes. And Aunt Teeta, trying desperately not to laugh, slipped a protective arm around Ashley.

"Shame on you, boys! Ashley, darlin', I feel the same way. My heart just *aches* for this sweet ole house."

Collecting the money, Parker jammed it into his shirt pocket, then winked at Gage and Etienne. "How well do I know my girl, huh?"

Roo shot him a dark-ringed glance. "How well do you know Kurt Fuller?"

Miranda saw the color change on Ashley's face. She felt her own expression freeze.

"Streak?" Parker asked, confused. "What the hell does he have to do with anything?"

But Roo was watching Ashley now, her expression genuinely puzzled. "What?" she mumbled. Then louder, "What'd I say?"

"You were saying about the house, Aunt Teeta," Miranda said quickly, while Gage and Etienne shrugged at Parker, the three of them completely lost. "What about those people who bought it? Did they do any renovation?"

Back on track again, Aunt Teeta shook her head. "Not that anybody could tell. They kept it awhile, then moved away and just let it sit there. And then some new folks bought it and worked on it a little bit, but they ended up selling, too. A place like this is overwhelming . . . time consuming—not to mention expensive. But the last owner *did* manage a partial reconstruction of the first and second floors—pretty much what you're seeing. You know, hon, I think they meant well, and I think they *tried* to base it all on facts, and I truly think they did their very best with what money they had—but it ended up being sort of a big ole hodgepodge. A *lot* of mistakes, and a lot of things *not* historically accurate."

"So the reconstruction you're doing now—don't you at least have pictures to go by?"

"One. Only one photograph of the original house, the exterior. Nothing at all of the inside. We're basing all the exterior and interior renovations purely on research—other plantation homes of that period."

"You'd think there'd be some sort of record," Gage mused. "A written description somewhere. A deed or a journal or something."

"What little information we have was discovered with a packet of notes and letters—and a few other personal belongings—written by a Yankee soldier. A scout, we think."

"Where'd you get it?"

"Parker's mama had it on file at the Historical Society."

Normally, Parker would have voiced a few negative comments at this. Instead, he was still staring at Ashley and Roo. "What about Streak?"

"The soldier's letter does mention a name," Aunt Teeta continued. "He talks about riding up to a sign on the road, that it's all overgrown with weeds and vines. The name on the sign is Belle Chandelle. And he thinks the plantation should be easy to take, because there doesn't seem to be anybody living there."

Ashley gave a visible shudder. "So . . . the whole place was just empty? Like . . . a ghost town?"

"Nobody knows, hon."

Frowning, Gage stroked a hand along his chin. "They would've known the Yankees were coming; they would've had some time to get out of there."

"What about slaves?" Roo asked. "Wouldn't there have been servants or workers around?"

"Maybe they were hiding and hoping the Yankees would go away," Ashley offered.

"I guess it's possible." Aunt Teeta's brow furrowed in thought. "Unfortunately, there's no more information on Belle Chandelle after that. And believe me, we've checked out every possible source."

But Gage wasn't ready to give up. "You said there's a picture?"

"Yes. It's taken from the bayou side. We know when the house was built. We think we know the name of the original owner. And we have a few items that were discovered on the property years ago. But other than that—"

"So . . . *what* about Streak?" Parker repeated, but Ashley gave a delighted little squeal.

"Miss Teeta, Miranda said Belle Chandelle's going to be a bed and breakfast! We're just thrilled to pieces, aren't we, y'all?"

Hardly, Miranda thought, surveying the group reaction. Parker couldn't have cared less. Gage didn't seem one bit surprised at the news. And while Roo at least nodded, Etienne just rubbed his eyes and looked tired.

"Gage," Ashley scolded, noting his reaction. "You already knew, didn't you. Etienne already told you—and you didn't tell me!"

Gage offered an apologetic shrug, the matter of bed and breakfasts clearly not high on his priority list. As Ashley aimed a punch at his stomach, he swiftly caught her hand in his while Etienne watched them, amused.

"But this isn't going to be just *any* bed and breakfast," Aunt Teeta emphasized, chuckling at Gage and Ashley. "The owners intend it to be *the* best bed and breakfast in this *entire* part of the South."

"With just twelve rooms?" Ashley fretted, pulling free from Gage. "I don't see how they can make it the *best* bed and breakfast with just twelve rooms."

"*Mon Dieu*, Ashley . . ." Mumbling, Etienne shook his head and walked past her, ruffling her hair on the way. The others followed him into the adjoining room, where he stopped beside the large set of blueprints, then began pointing things out as he talked.

"This layout here—what we think was the original—we're already taking those six rooms upstairs, breaking them down into smaller ones. Each guest room still has its own door out to the gallery. And each one has its own bathroom."

"Hey," Parker half raised his hand. "Speaking of bathrooms—"

Again Gage jerked his thumb toward outside.

"What about the main floor?" Miranda asked.

"Leaving it pretty much as-is." Etienne continued to slide his finger across the plans; he glanced back over his shoulder to see if the others had questions. "The entrance'll be here, in this middle room—pocket doors open on each side, closed at the rear. A nice big reception area, yeah? Sitting room, dining room, library, stuff like that. The rooms at the back are for extra—you got your ballroom, your space for banquets and weddings and whatever."

"What about storage?" Gage wanted to know.

"Outbuildings. And the kitchen, it stays separate—all the meals will be cooked there. Except for easy things—snacks, fast food, microwave."

"The owners are sure about what they want." Nodding at Etienne, Aunt Teeta received an affirmative nod in return. "Which is *great*. They're very specific. They want this place to be beautiful, top-quality, and completely authentic with modern conveniences. They want to attract tourists, not just from around the country, but from around the world. And they're even hoping to list it with the National Register of Historic Places."

Aunt Teeta stopped to take a breath. As her eyes moved from Etienne to the French doors at the front of the room, she let out a gasp.

"Oh mercy, it's getting dark, and I *swore* to myself I wouldn't rattle on! Why didn't y'all stop me? Etienne, do we have any flashlights around here, hon?"

Laughing at herself, Aunt Teeta grabbed Etienne's arm, playfully shook him, and shooed everyone out to the verandah. Etienne headed off in another direction, but the rest of the group turned left, making their way to the exterior stairs at the end, then up to the second-floor gallery, none of them even noticing when Miranda stepped aside and hung back.

She stood alone on the verandah now, listening to the strange and sudden quiet.

An unnerving quiet. *Unnatural quiet . . .*

The wind had died, not one hint of breeze. Thunderclouds hung low in the sky, bleeding dark into dusk; it was impossible to distinguish late day from early night. The thunder itself had silenced. Not a single sound drifted from the bayou. Miranda realized that she was holding her breath.

Calm before the storm. That's all it is. Just the calm before the storm . . .

She gazed off across the lawn, beneath the trees.

And saw the wooden swing . . . swinging.

It took her a moment to actually absorb what was happening . . . how the swing could be swinging without a breath of air to move it . . . and how it was moving so easily . . . not like a breeze might be stirring it, but a slow, deliberate rhythm, *up . . . back . . . up . . . back . . .*

She knew that the others were exploring the gallery above her—she knew that if she turned around, she would see them, she would hear them, all noisy and laughing and loud. . . .

But she didn't turn around.

Instead she began walking toward the swing.

Up . . . back . . . up . . . back . . . invisible legs pumping . . . invisible arms pushing . . . and if she squinted just right through the gloom, she could almost convince herself that there really *was* someone in that swing, a very *small* someone in that swing, even though she knew it was only shadows gathered there beneath the branches and leaves and moss, out there in the twilight. . . .

The swing stopped.

Stopped abruptly and hung perfectly still.

As Miranda stared at it, her heart froze. For she could see it now, that very small shadow drifting away from the swing, floating toward her, *deliberately* toward her, while all she could do was stand there and watch it, helpless, unable to move—

It was close now.

Close enough to touch.

"Oh God . . ."

A shadow—no, two shadows!*—silent footsteps on wet grass damp leaves soggy ground running straight at me two small quick busy feet—no,* four *feet!—*

Something took her hand.

Her body jerked at the sudden contact—*tiny fingers clutching mine shy curious fingers squeezing mine . . .*

So deathly cold now . . . quiet as the grave . . .

Miranda thought she might have called Etienne's name.

But the quiet was turning into a roar, and she fell deep . . . deep . . . down an endless spiral of centuries.

7

"**MIRANDA**."

She couldn't wake up.

"*Miranda.*"

Couldn't wake up, couldn't breathe, couldn't get warm—

"*Miranda, look at me, cher. Open your eyes.*"

Gasping, she tried to move. Her eyelids fluttered, lungs gulping air, but something was keeping her down—

"Breathe. That's right . . . nice and deep—"

"Etienne?"

"Try to focus. Here. On my face."

"What . . . happened?"

"I was kinda hoping you'd tell me."

Her eyes were wide now; his words calm and clear. She realized that she was lying on the ground and that he was kneeling over her, one arm cradling her head, his other hand patting her cheek. Full night was falling around them. The whole world teemed with shadows.

"I must have tripped," she murmured. "Can't . . . remember."

"Don't talk yet. Just keep breathing."

"No, I *have* to talk. What are you doing here? Did I yell or something?"

Etienne shook his head. "If you did, nobody heard you. They're pretty busy upstairs, taking the tour."

"Then how did you—"

"I just had me this . . . feeling."

"You came to find me? How long have you been here?"

"Not long. Just keep yourself quiet now, and—"

"And you didn't see anything? Not that you *could* have seen anything . . . and I don't even know how long I was—" She broke off, biting her lower lip. "What *was* I, anyway? Unconscious? Asleep?"

"I'm thinking you probably fainted. But you were trying to talk the whole time . . . somewhere way back in your head. Things I sure wasn't understanding."

Puzzled, Miranda considered a moment. "You couldn't make out *anything*?"

"Just . . . well . . . a couple times, you called for your mama."

"My *mom*?" she cringed. "That's so embarrassing."

"You seemed plenty scared. Only makes sense you'd be wanting your mama."

Miranda had no chance to respond. From out of nowhere, a chill stabbed through her, worming along her spine and into her limbs, leaving her trembling and light-headed. At once, Etienne eased her into a sitting position. He wrapped both arms around her and held her close.

"It's like summer out here," he mumbled, "and you're ice cold."

Darkness engulfed her. The darkness of nightfall, the darkness of Etienne. His eyes, his voice, his . . . *presence*. The smells that clung to him—dirt and sweat and windblown hair; worn leather and work-stained denim; blazing sunshine and autumn rain; moss and mud, wet grass and bayou breezes; the musky heat of his skin; his blisters, calluses, and scars. High cheekbones, chiseled features pressed close and hard . . . day-old stubble, rough against her forehead . . .

"So what do they want?" he finally asked. And then, when Miranda didn't answer, "The spirits, *cher*. The ones trying to reach you."

He ran his hands slowly down the length of her arms. Miranda tried to shut out the sound of him, the scent of him, the sight of him, but he only pulled her tighter.

"What are they needing, Miranda?"

Silence fell heavy between them. It was several long moments before Miranda could finally answer.

"How did you know?" she whispered.

"Hmmm . . . let's see. I get me this feeling something's wrong . . . I find you passed out here on the ground . . . you're half frozen and talking right outta your head . . ." Pausing, he gave an exaggerated shrug. "I'm just a lucky guesser."

"Etienne—"

"Listen, now. Your *grandpère* and me, we were friends for a long time. I saw what he went through; I understood him pretty well. And I understand *you* pretty well too. *Real* well, in fact. Probably even more than you want me to."

"No, you—"

"Yeah. I do. Your *grandpère*, he wanted to protect you from the tough things, the scary things. He never wanted you to be going through all that—but he knew you'd *have* to. 'Cause it's all part of the gift he passed you. The good and the bad of it."

"Well, I don't like the bad of it. But you're right—they are trying to reach me." In spite of herself, Miranda's voice trembled. "I think they've been trying to reach me all day, only I don't know what they want or who they are or—"

"Shh . . . calm yourself down. We'll just sit here awhile."

"But the others . . ."

"Your aunt Teeta, she's keeping them entertained. We got us a little bit of time."

Reluctantly, Miranda nodded. Everything was too fast, too mixed-up. She still wasn't sure what had happened by the swing; neither was she exactly sure what she was doing here in Etienne's arms. For a second, both situations seemed equally dangerous.

"So . . ." Etienne spoke at last. "You wanna start with the roof?"

"Roof?"

"What you were staring at on the roof earlier. When y'all first got here." Not getting any reply, he traced a fingertip slowly down her spine.

Another shiver went through her . . . but fluttery warm, not cold. "I just thought . . . I saw something," she admitted.

"Where?"

"In that window, right above where you were standing."

"What'd you see?"

"It could have been shadows, but—"

"It coulda been a *lotta* things, but—"

"It looked like a hand. A tiny hand . . . like a child, maybe . . . on the windowpane. Only there *wasn't* a windowpane. And it just made me feel . . ."

Etienne nodded. Waited for her to go on.

"Made me feel so *sad*. Like it was reaching for help, maybe . . . trying to get out." Frowning, Miranda pulled away a little, tilted her face to peer up at him. "Isn't this the part where you tell me there wasn't anyone inside?"

A not-quite-smile tugged at one corner of his mouth. "That's the attic you were seeing. The floor's not finished yet, and it's too dangerous to be walking around—so just the work crews go up there. And I'm the only crew here tonight. So . . . yeah. This is where I tell you there wasn't anybody inside." He paused, arched an eyebrow. "Nobody *alive*, anyhow."

"So you believe me."

"I always have. Always will. So . . . why don't you tell me what happened out here just now?" He stretched and shifted position. With knees drawn up and spread apart, he settled Miranda snugly between his thighs, drew her back against his chest. "Okay. From the beginning."

Miranda did so. From breaking the mirror in her bathroom that morning . . . to the vision at her locker . . . her uneasiness on the road to Belle Chandelle . . . her distorted view of the house . . . her glimpse of that shadowy hand at the attic window . . . the whisper of childish laughter on the lawn . . . the mysteriously moving swing . . . the ghostly feet running, the ghostly hands touching . . . till the moment she'd woken up, disoriented, on the ground.

Throughout every detail, Etienne said nothing, offered no comment. And though he did gently rock her from time to time, it wasn't till she'd finished that he finally spoke up, his voice tight.

"I'm sorry, *cher*. That's a hell of a lotta stuff to be dealing with—and especially in just one day. Whatever's going on—"

"*Wasn't* a dream," she insisted firmly. "*Or* a hallucination. It was powerful, and it was *real*. Like you said, someone—some spirit—is trying to reach me. And needs me to help them."

Etienne seemed to be pondering this. His eyes shifted to the oak tree, where the wooden swing hung, perfectly still.

"Listen to yourself," he said at last. "How far you've come in just a few weeks. Talking about all this, so natural—and how you fit into it."

"Well . . . do I have a choice?"

"You know you do. You can accept this gift of yours and do good things with it . . . or you can shut it out and pretend it doesn't exist."

"Honestly?" Miranda sounded almost wistful. "I don't think it's possible for me to shut it out. And I know Grandpa wouldn't want me pretending like it doesn't exist."

"I'm proud of you, *cher*."

"Don't be. This doesn't mean I'm still not scared out of my mind."

"Yeah, well that's why you got *me*, remember?"

She sensed his face lowering to her hair. Felt the light touch of his lips . . . the quickening of her pulse.

"Etienne?"

"Hmmm."

"I'm feeling too much in this place."

She was suddenly so aware of his heartbeat, hard against her back. Strong, solid, steady—not skipping like her own.

"This place?" he mumbled, his lips on the curve of her neck now, his arms tightening around her.

Instinctively, she tried to steel herself, but her insides were already beginning to melt, going weak and soft and helpless. She gathered her defenses . . . determined to stay focused on the matter at hand.

"This place?" Etienne asked again, his whisper warm and soft along her ear.

"Belle Chandelle," she murmured. "Etienne, are you listening to me?"

"Um-hmm."

Miranda caught her breath, steeled herself even more. "On the drive over . . . and when I got on the property . . . all these sensations started hitting me—sounds and smells and scenes in my mind, coming from every direction. But this place is so huge . . . and I'm only one person. I can't take it all in."

"And you shouldn't." Though he still held her close, Etienne finally lifted his head. His tone was thoughtful now; she had his full attention. "You shouldn't even be *trying* to take it all in."

"But—"

"Remember when we talked about this, me and you? When all this first started happening, when you first found out about your gift? Your *grandpère*, he had *years* of practice—you, you've only had a few weeks. You've hardly even *started* knowing what you need to know. It took him a lifetime to learn what to shut out, what to let in. You'll learn too."

A wave of emotions washed over her. Even though she knew it was just because of the crazy day she'd had . . . the things she'd been through . . . *Etienne* . . .

Get a grip, Miranda.

But she heard herself saying, "It's just that when things like this happen . . . I wish I could talk to Grandpa and get his advice. I wish he were still here."

"Your *grandpère*, he'll *always* be here with you. *Always*. And sure, you still miss him—you miss all those yesterdays you never had, all those tomorrows you got cheated out of. There's no rules about when you gotta stop missing somebody. Just talk to him, *cher*. Just think about him. Jonas, he'll help you. He'll show you the way."

Jonas Hayes. My grandfather. The reason all this got started in the first place . . .

Not wanting to cry, Miranda quickly changed the subject. "There's one more thing I need to tell you."

"Uh-oh. This sounds serious." His black eyes narrowed, teasing.

Shaking her head, Miranda laughed. "Please don't tell the others yet about . . ." She gestured vaguely toward the swing, the lawn, the house. "About . . . what's happened. I promise I'll tell them as soon as it's the right time. But not tonight, okay? I'm tired. I'm exhausted. It's been a long, awful day, and I just don't want to have to go through it all again."

Before Etienne could answer, there was a commotion from the gallery above.

"Hey!" Parker shouted. "Check out the action on the ground! I see you two rolling around down there!"

But Etienne was already standing, taking Miranda's hands, pulling her to her feet. There was an enthusiastic chorus of cheers and whistles as the others gathered at the upstairs railing, and Aunt Teeta roared with laughter.

"Etienne Boucher!" she called. "Hanky panky is most definitely *not* allowed till you take my niece out on a proper first date!"

Etienne feigned innocence. "But Miss Teeta, this *is* our first date."

More cheers, even louder. While Miranda concentrated on brushing herself off, Parker leaned over the baluster and shook his head.

"Perfect spot for that beautiful, old-fashioned romance, huh, Miranda? Mud . . . weeds . . . spiders . . . mosquitoes—"

"Trust me," Roo broke in, "she didn't notice."

The applause went wild; Miranda's cheeks went hot. Clearly unbothered by the teasing, Etienne steered her onto the verandah, where they waited for the others to join them.

"So . . . how was the tour?" Miranda asked, ignoring a sly nudge from Roo. "What did I miss?"

Parker did a droll rendition of enthusiasm. "Wow. Now, let me think. *Galleries*. All four of them. And . . . *French doors*. All . . . many of them. And *rooms*. All empty and boring and torn up. You should have been there, Miranda—the excitement was overwhelming."

"That's okay. I can explore another time."

"Okay, I guess we're done here!" Trailing Gage down the stairs, Aunt Teeta paused for a last backward glance. "We've seen all there is to see—for now, anyway. Etienne, did you find the problem with my electricity?"

"Yes ma'am, but I can't do much about it tonight."

"See there? That boy can fix anything." Aunt Teeta smiled at Ashley now, apologetic. "I just wish more of the house was finished, darlin'. And I wish there was more I could tell y'all about it."

"Me too." Ashley's sigh was wistful. "I'd love to know about the people who lived here . . . listen to their stories."

"Well, the only stories *I've* ever heard through the years are the spooky ones."

Miranda was instantly alert. "What do you mean? What spooky ones?"

"*No* spooky ones," Parker blurted, though Aunt Teeta kept chattering on.

"Oh mercy, you know—the ones we've all grown up hearing. Ghost stories and such like—"

"Stories!" This time Parker forced a laugh. "Yeah . . . but . . . see . . . that's just it. What *are* stories anyway? Just dumb rumors, right?"

Miranda ignored him. "What kinds of stories? What kinds of ghosts?" She was feeling cold again, colder by the second. No one was answering her questions, and Aunt Teeta was still talking.

"Well, Parker, I guess you're right about that. And we all know how small towns are. They need their own local haunted houses to talk about. And *brag* about!"

"People *always* think old houses are haunted if they've been abandoned for a while," Gage added smoothly. "And especially if they're in really bad shape."

But Parker's tone wasn't casual now. In fact, he was beginning to sound slightly panicked. "Hey . . . come on. No ghosts, okay? That ghost tour we did is *over*. We did our project, we all got A's. So no more ghosts. No more ghost *stories*, no more ghost *research*, no more ghost—*anything*. We're *all* done with ghosts. No more ghosts *ever*."

"Well, hon, I can't truly say if I believe in ghosts or not," Aunt Teeta conceded good-naturedly. "But I sure do love to hear tales about them. And I *do* know these new owners would be thrilled to *pieces* if there ended up being some nice, interesting ghosts here. Having a ghost or two on the premises is a major tourist attraction—and there's a whole lot of competition in this business. As a matter of fact, Miranda's mama and I were just talking about that this morning. Don't you think ghosts would be a good tourist draw, Miranda?"

"I . . ." Miranda's mouth had gone dry. She could feel her friends watching her, sympathy in every gaze but one. "Ghosts are sure . . . fascinating," she finished lamely.

"That's it." Spinning on his heel, Parker stepped off the verandah, his hands in the air. "I'm gone. Good night."

"Yeah, we better hit the road," Gage said quickly. "Thanks, Miss Teeta."

"Now, you boys wait a second." Aunt Teeta motioned them to stay put. "I don't want these girls walking back to their car by themselves."

"I'll lock up," Etienne offered, but she shook her head.

"Darlin', I've got plenty of good lanterns and lamps inside, and I need to look over a few more things before I leave. Now, y'all take these flashlights, and be careful where y'all step."

"Mom's frying chicken—she said everybody could come eat at our house!" Ashley announced, which brought hungry grunts of approval from the boys. "Miss Teeta, wouldn't you like to come too?"

"Bless your heart, hon, but when I finish up here, I'm heading home to a hot bath, some TV, and a nice, soft bed."

Linking arms, Miranda gave her aunt a hug. "I'll wait for you, okay? So you don't have to drive home alone."

The truth was, she didn't want to be with people tonight. Despite having talked with Etienne, been comforted by Etienne, suddenly she didn't feel reassured at all. And Aunt Teeta's idea of going home to a bath, TV, and a nice, soft bed seemed too tempting to pass up.

"Nonsense, darlin', I'm not one bit afraid to drive home by myself." Returning the hug, Aunt Teeta pushed Miranda toward the others. "Besides that, I'll be awhile. You just go on without me and have a good time. Can you get a ride home?"

"I'll bring her," Etienne promised. "It's a school night—we won't be late."

With Etienne and Parker holding flashlights, the six of them started back across the grounds to the parking lot. It was total dark out here now, that blacker-than-black-darkness found only in the countryside, made worse by thick canopies of moss overhead. A sluggish breeze blew off the bayou. Mist hung in the air, curling through the trees, glowing a fuzzy halo around the beams of the flashlights. While Ashley chattered to Gage and Parker, Roo lit up a cigarette, inhaled deeply, handed it to Etienne. Without breaking stride, he took a long drag and passed it back.

Shivering, Miranda couldn't help looking back over her shoulder. For one brief second, a breath of wind fluttered through the moss, sweeping it aside, offering her a view of the house. One small section of the roof . . . that dormer on the third floor . . .

And the pale glow of light moving past the window . . . flickering faintly beyond the broken glass . . .

"You sure your aunt's okay in there?"

Startled, she whirled around, saw that Parker had caught up with her. She didn't realize that she'd stopped walking or that he was staring in the same direction as she was, through those rippling curtains of moss.

"I'd be nervous about her being up in the attic like that." He frowned. "Especially now, with just that lantern or whatever it is she has. And all those sneaky stairs."

"Sneak stairs," Miranda whispered. "Parker . . . you *see* that?"

But the wind had died, and the moss was settling softly back into place.

And the attic window was empty and black as the night.

8

"MIRANDA, WHAT THE HELL WERE YOU THINKING?" Parker muttered.

He wasn't looking at the window anymore, he was scowling at her. Miranda realized that Gage and Ashley had caught up, and were practically on her heels.

"Thinking about what?" She didn't have a clue what Parker was talking about. Her thoughts were jumping back and forth between the house, the attic window, and what might possibly be inside. . . .

"I tried to save your ass back there about the whole ghost thing. *Which*, by the way, *Ashley* started with her stories-about-dead-people crap."

"I did," Ashley admitted guiltily. "I'm sorry, Miranda. Sometimes I forget to think."

Choked laughs all around. Ashley looked mildly offended.

"Well, I can't help it," she insisted. "It's not like I do it on purpose."

"We know," Gage managed a straight face. "We know you would never deliberately try to not think."

"It takes a lot of talent to do what you do, Ash," Roo added seriously.

Hesitating, Ashley smiled. "Well . . . thank you."

"So, as I was saying," Parker went on, "about saving Miranda's ass"—he broke off, pulled back a step, gave her rear end a quick once-over—"not that I minded so much, as it's a pretty nice ass, but all the same—"

Miranda walked faster. "I know you meant to help, Parker. But I *want* to hear about the ghost stories. I *should* hear about the ghost stories—"

"Why?" He still sounded slightly incredulous. "Haven't you heard enough about ghosts for a while? Or do you *enjoy* being terrorized on a regular basis?"

"It's not that, it's—"

"And did I mention that Gage *also* tried to save your ass?"

"Worth saving." Gage winked. "My pleasure."

Flustered, Miranda stammered on. "I know he did. I'm— I'm sorry, Gage. I just . . . look, you don't have to protect me. I appreciate it, I really do, but—"

"He's not trying to protect you," Roo said calmly. "He's scared of ghosts, and he still thinks we don't know."

Parker instantly snorted a laugh. "Right. Like I could be scared of *anything*, seeing you every day."

"I *appreciate* it," Miranda repeated, more firmly this time. "But I'm pretty sure ghosts are going to find me, even if you . . ."

Her mind was weaving back and forth. She could feel Etienne's eyes on her, and the silent message they were sending: *Tell the others what's going on.* But she wasn't ready, she had to think, sort things out, *and that light in the window, Parker saw it too, though he doesn't even realize what he saw. . . .*

"If we . . ." Parker prompted.

"Even if you"—Miranda snapped back to the present—"pretend ghosts aren't real."

Parker's expression went numb. "Oh my God. Listen to her. It's Ashley logic."

"What's that?" Ashley asked.

"Never mind. Miranda . . . you're trying to ruin my life."

For a long moment there was silence.

Then Parker drew a deep, slow breath.

"I'm throwing you in the bayou." Without warning, he lunged for her, catching her around the waist. Miranda never saw it coming. As Parker grabbed her, she jumped, let out a squeal, and twisted free from his grasp.

The minute it happened, Etienne swung the flashlight on them. Miranda saw the slow, sly dawn of surprise go across Parker's face. Her heart immediately sank.

"Why, Miranda Barnes!" He feigned shock. "Are you ticklish?"

"No," she said, a little too quickly. "No! Definitely not."

But Parker grabbed her again, before she could get away. Only this time he held on to her till she was helpless with laughter, "Why yes, I think you *are*! I most definitely think you are ticklish."

Everyone else seemed to be laughing now too, plus whistles and catcalls from the guys. It was Ashley who ran over to save the day.

"Parker, you let her go right this instant!"

Parker's hands flew up in the air while Miranda scurried out of reach. "Hey, it was an accident! All I wanted to do was throw her in the bayou—I didn't know she was going to be so *sensitive*." Then, cupping one hand around his mouth, he turned and gave an exaggerated stage whisper. "She's so little—*no contest*. Gage? Etienne? Have fun."

"Big bully," Ashley scolded, linking arms with Miranda. "You should be ashamed of yourself, Parker Wilmington."

But Parker couldn't resist one last taunt. "Surprise attack," he warned Miranda. Kung-fu style, he flung out his arms as though he might grab her again. "Perfect ambush. You'll never see it coming."

The group started moving again, getting near the parking lot. Miranda kept close to Ashley and as far as she could from Parker.

"Parker tried to tickle Roo once," Ashley recalled, "and she knocked him out."

"Knocked me out?" he blurted, indignant. "She almost *killed* me!"

Roo merely shrugged. "I didn't mean to. And I didn't knock you *all* the way out. Just stunned you."

"You hit me with a damn board!"

"It was lying there. How was I supposed to know how heavy it was?"

Grumbling, Parker joined ranks with Gage and Etienne while the girls brought up the rear.

"Oh, stop whining!" Ashley pointed her finger at Parker. "We'll just see y'all at the house."

Within minutes, everyone was on the road. Having flatly refused to let Ashley drive, Roo was behind the steering wheel this time, and Ashley in the backseat—while Miranda, resting her head against the window, felt numb, exhausted, and emotionally drained. She'd hoped for a quiet ride back to town, but Ashley's sudden outburst brought her up straight.

"Roo! I cannot *believe* you said what you did back there in front of Parker!"

The glance Roo flicked her was totally baffled. "And that would be . . ."

"*Kurt Fuller!*"

"You've been waiting all this time to yell at me about *that*?"

"What do you know, and how did you hear about it?"

"About him asking you out? It's no big secret, Ash. Your little cheerleader pals have been very busy spreading the news."

"Oh my God . . ."

"They saw you and Streak talking after practice." Lighting a cigarette, Roo held it out the open window. "They said he hung around for a long time, and he smiled a lot. And he was touching your thigh—"

"A bug! There was a bug on my leg, and he got it off!"

"And now that he's broken up with Delphine . . ."

"Oh . . . my . . . God . . ." Ashley covered her face with her hands. "Parker doesn't know, Roo."

"Well, he will by tomorrow. No, make that tonight."

"This is horrible."

"Why is it horrible? Did you tell Kurt you'd go out with him?"

"Of course not. But I suppose you want me to, right? Just to upset Parker?"

"Why, no. That would be shallow of me."

Ashley peeked out through her fingers. "I just don't want Parker to get mad and do something stupid." Even as Roo opened her mouth, Ashley cut her off. "Don't. Don't *even* say it."

Roo closed her mouth. Ashley lowered her hands again and looked miserable. And Miranda, thinking wishfully of her nice bed at home, resumed leaning on the windowpane, her gaze intent on the flowing darkness beyond.

Eventually the car swung into a wide, smooth curve . . . trundled over the old drawbridge . . . passed a moss-shrouded cemetery, bone-white tombs, a high-steepled stone church. Through the heavy downpour, buildings and streetlamps of St. Yvette came into bleary focus, and after several more turnoffs and a maze of quaint, crowded neighborhoods, Miranda realized that they had finally reached their destination.

She'd never been to Roo and Ashley's house before. Large and rambling, it stood on the very last lot—a double lot, at least—of a dead-end street, with curtains open and light streaming out from every window. Like so many homes in town, it looked old and well-kept—yet with a certain distinctiveness that set it apart from the others Miranda had seen. As though this eccentric, outdated, randomly-added-onto, four-story farmhouse had defiantly stood its ground while the rich land around it had continued to disappear and more modern houses had sprung up in place of cotton fields. A faded picket fence lined the front, where Parker's borrowed station wagon was angled onto the curb. And what might once have been a small barn—now rather lopsided and painted garishly orange—stood toward the back of an enormous tree-shaded yard, illuminated by strings of fairy lights dangling from its eaves.

A dog was barking close by; as Roo pulled into the driveway, Miranda turned to look. Next door, to the left of the house, stood a charming Victorian—pale blue with dark blue shutters, a wrap-around porch and gingerbread trim, fanciful gables and a three-story tower facing the street. Etienne's truck was parked at the side. Miranda could see a golden retriever racing back and forth behind the porch railing, and the silhouette of a woman in the front doorway, motioning the dog to come in.

Gage's house, she immediately thought, and couldn't help smiling. Soon after she'd met them, the girls had told her about being childhood neighbors with Gage. They'd also told her about Gage and Etienne being first cousins—another discovery that had surprised her.

"Etienne must have stopped for a shower," Roo said, indicating the pickup. Ashley, noting Miranda's curiosity, went on to explain.

"Yes, that's where Gage lives, if you're wondering. Oh, and that's Jazz on the porch—he's such a big goof—he adores everybody in the world. You'd *love* their house, Miranda. It's really old; they've done a whole lot of fixing up."

"I like the way *yours* looks," Miranda said truthfully. "It's old too, right?"

Roo slowed down, gestured vaguely toward the newly mowed lawn and the field of wildflowers that bordered it. "Older than Gage's. The story goes, that the farmer who lived here built the house next door as a wedding present for his daughter."

"I think that's so sweet," Ashley sighed.

"Yeah. If you want your parents spying on you for the rest of your life."

The garage was already open when they pulled around back. Feeling suddenly shy, Miranda got out of the car, then followed Roo and Ashley through a connecting door into a huge, country-style kitchen that was warm and fragrant and full of activity.

"Come on, Miranda." Ashley laughed. "Welcome to our zoo."

But Miranda stopped. She stopped just over the threshold and stood beside an antique pie safe that hid her from view.

There were dogs—*cocker spaniels, two; no, three*—running in and out of the room at breakneck speed; there was a mynah bird on top of a wooden hutch in the corner, yelling something that sounded suspiciously like "Roo's a bad girl!" Gage, minus crutches, had balanced himself against the sink and was rinsing silverware; Ashley immediately went over to help. A gang of cats—*five? you're kidding me . . . six?*—had surrounded Parker, rubbing against his legs while he muttered and swore and tried to maneuver his way to the refrigerator. And the two grown-ups in the room, cheerfully oblivious to the chaos around them, were Roo's and Ashley's parents.

Though Miranda knew that the two girls were stepsisters, she'd never been able to figure out who actually belonged to which biological mom or dad. As with the rest of the group's parents, Miranda had met Miss Voncile and Mr. Sonny at the hospital that night of Gage's accident—and her reaction now was the same as it had been then. She'd never seen such an odd couple—but odd in a cute and quirky way. Miss Voncile, an admired and respected artist. Crinkly eyes and smile; close-cropped spiky white hair; dangly feather earrings to her shoulders; tall, skinny body dressed tonight in jeans, raggedy moccasins, and an oversized work shirt—her clothes, face, hands, and hair streaked with all colors of paint. And Mr. Sonny, famous for his "Sonny Slim the Singin' Used Car Salesman" local dealership and commercials. Lanky as his wife; squinty blue eyes behind wire-rimmed spectacles; toothy grin and long handlebar mustache; and his customary Wild West attire—black snap-button Western shirt (this one with identical red stagecoaches across the chest and back), black jeans, black cowboy hat and boots. Right now Miss Voncile was at the stove, while Mr. Sonny—perched atop a tall stool—strummed a guitar and sang a country song.

"Oh, God, he's doing it." Roo groaned deep in her throat. "Somebody please shoot me."

Parker instantly brightened. "I volunteer."

"Is that a new song, Daddy?" Ashley asked.

Pausing mid-strum, Mr. Sonny touched a finger to his hat brim. "Just wrote it this afternoon, princess!"

"*This* is why I have no friends," Roo mumbled to herself, and walked past her dad while he winked at Ashley.

"He looks tired." Miss Voncile was fussing. "Gage, you look tired."

"I'm fine," Gage said.

"He's fine," Mr. Sonny echoed, breaking off the song. "Look at him, he's strong and healthy. Good exercise for that pitching arm—right, Gage? Hauling that crutch around for six weeks, working up those muscles for spring ball?"

Gage smiled, but Miss Voncile rushed on. "I don't care. His cast comes off soon, and I don't want to jinx it. I don't want him overdoing."

"If you're so worried about him overdoing, then why do you have him washing dishes?" Roo grumbled. "Does that even make sense?"

"Because *somebody* here didn't load the dishwasher before she left for school this morning, and we have no forks to eat potato salad. Does *that* make sense?"

"Where's Miranda?" Gage asked.

"And anyway, how can he overdo?" Roo grumbled again, heading straight for the refrigerator, bumping Parker out of the way so she could grab a soda. "He's got a whole harem around him every single minute of the day."

"What are you talking about?" Her mother held up a gigantic platter of golden fried chicken. "What is she talking about, Gage—this harem?"

"Nothing," Gage answered.

"Your entourage at school?" Roo mimicked a high, girlie voice: "Oh Gage, let me carry your books . . . oh Gage, let me open the door for you . . . oh Gage, let me help you up the stairs . . . oh Gage, that cast makes you look *so sexy*—"

"Oh Roo, you're just jealous," Parker mimicked back at her.

"Oh Gage, let me help you get dressed—"

"Nobody says that," Gage protested, flushing slightly.

Leaning over Gage's shoulder, Parker nudged him in the side

and did a falsetto of his own. "Oh Gage, let me help you get *un*dressed—"

Gage shook his head and continued rinsing.

"Exactly," Roo echoed. "And they're writing their *bra* sizes on his cast now."

Mr. Sonny tried to keep a straight face. "Is that true, Gage? Their *bra* sizes? Hey, let's see that cast. We might have us a good idea for a song there, buddy."

Laughing, Ashley hugged Gage, yanked a dishtowel from the oven door, and began drying the forks that he handed her.

"It was so beautiful out at Belle Chandelle today, Mama. Just one of the most *beautiful* places I've ever seen!"

"I'm *sure* it was for *you*, Ashley," Miss Voncile agreed, catching a bored glance from Roo.

"It was old and romantic and wonderful and just—just—in my heart, you know?"

"I'm sure, sweetie."

"Where's Miranda?" Gage asked again, louder this time. "I thought she was riding with you two."

"Miranda? Oh, I'm so glad! Did you bring Miranda?" Miss Voncile looked in every direction. "Roo, what on earth have you done with Miranda?"

"Maybe she's in the bathroom," Roo suggested. "Gage, go see."

Gage stayed where he was. "How can she be in the bathroom? We would've seen her go by."

"And," Ashley said solemnly, "she's never been here before, so she doesn't even know where it is."

"Maybe she talks to dead plumbing, and it told her where

to find the toilets," Parker mumbled, then winced as Ashley punched him on the shoulder.

"She was right behind me." Ashley sounded puzzled now. "Miranda?"

But Miranda's head was spinning; she couldn't move. All this confusion and noise and commotion . . . *all this closeness and family and love.* Suddenly she felt completely overwhelmed—*too much to handle, too much for one day.* In a split-second glance, she spotted a door on the side wall of the garage; at the same time she saw Parker turn from the refrigerator and stare directly at her. He stood there a moment, Coke in hand, a half grin on his face. Then, to her surprise, he cleared his throat and went back to the others, leaving her undetected there on the threshold.

"Do you smell smoke?" Miss Voncile sounded distressed. "I smell smoke. Ashley, I hope Roo wasn't smoking in my car."

"Maybe something's burning," Ashley said smoothly, exchanging amused glances with Gage. "Maybe something's boiling over on the stove."

"There's nothing boiling, and it's not that kind of smoke."

Roo retreated to the walk-in pantry. Her mother, with a stern shake of her head, lifted her voice disapprovingly.

"Roo, I hope you weren't smoking in my car!"

"No," came the voice from the pantry.

"Roo's a bad girl!" cawed the mynah bird.

"Hey, what about that game on TV last night!" Mr. Sonny exclaimed.

The guys immediately lapsed into sports babble. Two kittens tumbled out of the pantry. A door slammed somewhere, and

Etienne walked into the kitchen from an adjoining room, his hair wet, his jeans and T-shirt changed and clean.

"Where's Miranda?" he asked.

"Here." Taking a deep breath, Miranda stepped forward, miserably conscious of every eye upon her. "Sorry. I had . . . mud on my shoes. I didn't want to track it in."

This brought a general round of laughter. Miss Voncile, obviously sensing Miranda's awkwardness, swept over to greet her with a big hug.

"Honey, bless your heart for being so polite—but there is nothing in the world you could do to mess up this house. It's made to live in and feel comfortable in—we don't worry about nasty little things like mud and dirt."

"Or Roo," Parker added, which brought an even bigger round of laughter. As Roo emerged indifferently from the pantry, he handed Miranda a Coke and used his foot to drag out a chair for her at the table, while the free-for-all resumed around them.

"Now, Dad and I already ate, so y'all kids fill up your plates and go on in the den—there's chicken and baked beans and potato salad and biscuits and—and Roo, I should *not* have to remind you about the dishwasher. How many times do I need to remind you about the dishwasher? Please tell me you'll remember next time."

"I'll remember next time."

"Good. Now, see that you do. By the way, Ashley, did you have any trouble with the car?"

"Don't ask her that, Mom," Roo answered. "And don't ever give her the keys again."

"Why? Did something happen? Etienne, come over here. How's your mama? Ashley, don't you dare give him that dishtowel to dry his hair! You know better than that—"

"I didn't give it to him, he just took it."

"Shame on you. Y'all act like you were raised in a barn."

"We were," Roo said under her breath, while Mr. Sonny started singing again.

Amidst much shoving, laughing, and teasing, Miranda soon found herself in the cozy den off the kitchen, seated on the sofa beside Gage, with a huge plate of food on her lap. Old, well-worn furniture cluttered the room. Covering the wall next to Gage was an eclectic assortment of artwork—Miss Voncile's, she guessed—sketches and paintings; woven tapestries; designs in feathers and beads, cloth and metal; a round mosaic of silvery glass; arrangements of dried leaves and pressed flowers.

"Hey, eat up." Gage nudged her gently. "Before Parker comes over here and steals it."

"I will, too," Parker insisted. "I'm starving."

Grinning, he took the easy chair across from her while Ashley perched on the armrest. Roo sat on the floor, leaning against Gage's cast. And Etienne, standing comfortably in one corner, nodded at Miranda over a spoonful of beans.

"Whatcha thinking so hard about, *cher*?"

It came out before she could stop it. "You guys said there were spooky stories about Belle Chandelle—"

"God, Miranda," Parker groaned. "You haven't even swallowed one bite yet, and you're already talking about that damn house! Gage—just grab her right now."

"Yeah, Gage, grab her," Roo echoed under her breath. "You know you want to."

Gage moved his leg. Roo fell backward into the coffee table.

"I'm serious," Miranda said firmly. "I want to hear them. So tell me."

But Parker kept scarfing down fried chicken. "There's nothing to tell. Haunted Houses 101. Flickering lights. Clanking chains. Screams and moans and . . . gosh, come to think of it . . . Belle Chandelle's ghosts are really boring. And not very original, either."

"Actually, he's right," Gage agreed. "Everything I've ever heard is general stuff, pretty much stereotyped. And it's usually from kids who sneak out there on a dare, either to get drunk or make out."

"Or *both*." Roo flicked Parker a meaningful glance. She sat up again. She frowned at Gage and rubbed the back of her head.

"Not exactly credible witnesses," Gage concluded, ignoring her.

"I'd like to see that photograph of the house," Miranda decided. "And read that letter."

Parker's eyes rolled back. He moaned dramatically and flopped sideways in his chair.

"I've seen the picture." Pulling himself from the corner, Etienne chewed . . . swallowed . . . wiped one hand absently on his T-shirt. "Miss Teeta, she's got a copy of it—so does your mama."

Miranda couldn't help but feel a quick stab of guilt. If she'd shown an interest sooner in Mom's job, she'd have already known something about the house.

"So what does it look like?" she asked him.

He pondered a second . . . frowned. "Like Miss Teeta said. The house, it's in the distance, at an angle—all that's showing is most of the front and part of one side. I'm thinking you *should* see it for yourself, *cher*. See what you get out of it."

"Anybody for seconds?" Eagerly, Parker raised his hand, but all attention was on Etienne.

"So what *do* we actually know about the house?" Gage spoke up.

Etienne rested his fork on his plate, dark eyes sweeping the group. "Like Miss Teeta said, not that much. The original house they figure was built sometime late eighteenth, early nineteenth century. Later on from that, it became one of the biggest sugarcane plantations around here."

"How big? I mean, what kind of operation are we talking about?"

"Around thirty outbuildings—maybe more—plus the slave cabins."

"Wow." Even Parker looked reluctantly impressed. "And with all those sugarcane fields? There must have been hundreds of acres. Thousands, even."

"That'd be my guess."

"Seems like a spread that size would have been pretty famous."

Gage gave a slight shrug. "A plantation that big would've been almost totally self-sufficient. Practically like its own little town. They wouldn't have needed much at all from the outside world."

"Wait, wait—" Ashley was so intrigued, she could hardly sit still. "But Parker's right—that doesn't make sense. If it was that big, then why wouldn't there be anything more written about it? There should be *tons* of history about Belle Chandelle."

"Maybe not so unusual," Gage said quietly. "I mean, think about it. So many plantations were looted and burned during the War—and never rebuilt. And when towns were occupied by Union armies, there were probably lots of records stolen or destroyed . . . or just plain lost. There's no telling how many local histories disappeared."

"And what you said about the plantation," Etienne nodded in Gage's direction. "If it really *was* that independent, then maybe it really *didn't* have that much contact with the outside world. At least not on any regular basis."

Scooting to the edge of the couch, Miranda set her plate of half-eaten food on the coffee table. "That makes sense. Remember when we were trying to find out about Hayes House—Aunt Teeta's house? Traveling was such a big deal back then . . . not like it is now. People in the country were pretty isolated; it took a long time to get from one place to another."

"And Belle Chandelle *is* kind of far from town—even today, by car," Ashley echoed. "And all those woods, and being hidden there on the bayou. Back then, it probably would have taken *forever* to get there."

"Especially if *you'd* been driving," Roo noted.

But Parker was still stuck on the outbuildings. "Thirty-plus outbuildings? So these new owners—they're not planning to rebuild every single one of them, are they?"

Etienne looked mildly pained. "That's what I'm hearing."

"Just for some storybook bed and breakfast? That's crazy!"

"Why is it crazy?" Gage asked, shrugging. "Miss Teeta said they want it to be authentic. You can't have an authentic plantation without all those other buildings that go with it. Otherwise, it's just a house."

"He's right," Etienne affirmed. "Lots of people, when they hear the word 'plantation,' they just think of a house. But a plantation, it was really the whole farm, the whole estate. So yeah, the new owners, they're wanting every single outbuilding just like it was back then."

"Ooh, I love it!" Clapping her hands, Ashley almost toppled her dinner into Parker's lap. "And it's so smart, too! This way the whole thing will be historically accurate *and* it'll last forever, because it'll be done right. Because . . . you know . . . today's building materials will hold up a whole lot longer."

Parker smacked his palm against his forehead. "You're right! Damn! If only they'd put seamless siding on all those castles over in England."

"I'm ignoring you. This chair is an empty chair."

Finishing his plate of food, Gage stacked it on Miranda's. Etienne set his own empty plate on top.

"Unbelievable." Parker muttered, leveling a frown at the group. "Can you even imagine how much this whole thing is going to *cost*? These new owners must be richer than God. Who the hell are they anyway?"

Etienne slowly shook his head. "*Mais*, I don't know, I've never met them. I don't think Miranda's mama has either. Miss Teeta, she's been driving over to New Orleans when they call her for meetings; they always stay at one of those fancy hotels in the French Quarter."

"Don't they ever come here?" Surprised, Ashley let this sink in. "I mean . . . don't they ever come to Belle Chandelle?"

"From what Miss Teeta says, they've never seen the place at all."

"Then maybe they're celebrities! Or . . . or a royal family from some rich foreign country! And they don't want anybody to know it's them, because then they'd be mobbed when they come to St. Yvette!"

"Right," Parker agreed dryly. "All those wild paparazzi hanging out at Hank's Hardware and the Snowball Shack."

"What about that stuff on the property?" Miranda remembered suddenly.

Conversation stopped. All stares shifted to her.

"You mean the outbuildings?" Etienne raised an eyebrow.

"No, I mean . . . didn't Aunt Teeta say there was some stuff found on the property years ago?"

"Miranda?" Parker warned. "Stop."

But Etienne was nodding at her, angling back against the wall again, folding his arms over his chest. "Yeah, I know what you're talking about. I'm thinking there were some things from the house . . . like, *parts* of the house . . . mantels . . . doorknobs . . . things like that. But I'm not sure what else. You'll have to ask her."

"I just . . . well, you never know. It wouldn't hurt to see those things from the house. I mean . . . as long as we're looking at the letter and the picture anyway."

"Hey. *We're* not looking at the letter and the picture, okay?" Frowning harder, Parker leaned forward in his chair. "Gage. Help me out here. Do something. *Anything* so she can't talk. This is war, man."

But before Gage could react, the pillow came out of nowhere. A ruffled throw pillow sailing past Miranda's head, bouncing off the back of the cushions, knocking over a lamp, and landing on the floor beside Gage's end of the couch. For a long moment, Parker stared at what he'd done. Then tried his best to look contrite.

"Oops."

"Parker, for heaven's sake!" Ashley scolded as the room erupted in laughter. "You could have hurt Miranda. What on earth is wrong with you?"

"If we could figure *that* out," Roo replied solemnly, "world peace would be no problem."

Gazing at Parker, Etienne kept a perfectly straight face. "What, is that some kinda secret pass you been workin' on? No wonder y'all nearly lost your last game—"

"Win 'Em All Wilmington," Gage broke in. "I hear he was *awesome* in his glory days."

A sheepish grin tugged at Parker's mouth. He pointed his finger at Gage. "Meet me outside, Hopalong. I'll race you."

Another round of laughter—Miranda included. As both Ashley and Etienne started toward the fallen lamp, Miranda shook her head at them, jumped up, and circled around the couch. Luckily, nothing was broken. It only took a minute to reattach the lampshade, untangle the cord, and toss the pillow back to Parker—but as she set the lamp on the end table, an unexpected chill shot through her.

Someone's watching me.

Miranda froze. With one hand clasping the lamp, she stood there in sudden, inexplicable terror while the laughter and chatter of her friends faded into a distant roar.

Of course someone's watching you, Miranda—you're in this room with five other people. . . .

Yet she knew that wasn't it. Deep down in her soul, she knew that this was different, *something wrong, something close, something* here. . . .

The hairs prickled at the back of her neck. Her chest squeezed tight, breath trapped in her lungs as she finally lifted her hand, as she raised her eyes to the wall. . . .

The beautiful handmade art on the wall . . . feathers and beads . . . leaves and flowers . . . metal and cloth and glass—*no, not glass!*—the round mosaic of silvery glass—*not glass at all!*—staring at herself in those shiny little sections of mirror . . .

Miranda's reflection began to fade . . . go dark. Flickered softly again, in and out of focus.

She saw the horrified expression . . .

The dark eyes, wide with pain . . .

And the pale, mournful face gazing back at her.

The face of a woman . . .

A stranger whom she had never seen before.

9

IN THAT SPLIT SECOND, MIRANDA COULDN'T BE SURE—
sure if she'd dropped the lamp or tried to fling it against the wall.
She only knew that one minute she was holding it; the next
minute, Gage was stretching sideways over the arm of the
couch, catching the lamp before it hit the floor a second time.

"You okay?" he asked, puzzled.

"Clumsy," she mumbled, then wondered if she'd spoken aloud
or merely in her head. "Sorry."

But her hands were shaking, and she knew that Gage could
see. And even though Etienne was across the room, she felt
the piercing scrutiny of his eyes, glancing between her and the
wall.

"I . . . here, Gage. I'll take it," she mumbled again.

"You sure?"

"Yeah. Thanks."

As he passed her the lamp, his long fingers closed around
hers, strong and steady, warm against her ice-cold skin. For a
moment she wanted to cling to him, never let go, never look up
at that wall again, or into the silvery glass—*a woman's face there,
a young woman who's not me, staring straight into my eyes with
a terrible, silent desperation, as if I'm her reflection, as if I'm the
stranger in the mirror—*

"Isn't that pretty, Miranda?" Having forcefully taken away Parker's plate, Ashley was snuggling back against him. "That's what you were looking at, right? The glass thingy?"

Surprised, Miranda managed a nod. Focused on Ashley, not on the wall. "It's . . . fascinating. I've never seen anything like it."

"They're mirrors. Little pieces of mirrors. Mama put each one in by hand. Oh, and when the sun hits it, it's beautiful. It sparkles and makes colors all over the room."

"That's . . . really nice." Miranda set the lamp on the table, fiddled nervously with the shade.

"You can take it down if you want . . . if you'd like to see it up close."

"No!"

Was everyone staring at her? She couldn't tell, she just couldn't look at that wall. *But you have to, Miranda. You know you can't leave here till you do—*

"Miranda?" Gage's voice, concerned; Gage's hand, stroking her arm. Helplessly her eyes shot to the round mosaic, the glass, the mirrors, the reflection—

Me.

Just me, staring at me.

No woman. No stranger. No . . . whatever—whoever—that I wish to God I imagined but deep down I know I didn't. . . .

"Miranda?" Etienne's voice now, drifting through her confusion. She forced a quick, tight smile; felt Gage's touch slide away.

"You know what?" She laughed. Not a very convincing laugh, but a laugh all the same. "With school today, and the plantation, and all this great food—I am *so tired* all of a sudden. I think . . . Etienne, would you mind taking me home?"

Etienne didn't hesitate. "Yeah, I gotta get myself home too. Much as I hate to leave this wild party."

"Hey, no helping," Ashley ordered as Miranda began gathering plates, cutlery, and soda cans. "That's Roo's job, to clean up tonight."

Secretly, Miranda was glad. The urge to get home was stronger than ever now; she wanted to be in her own room, in her own bed, where she felt safe. She followed the others to the kitchen, joined in the chorus of compliments, thank-yous, and good-nights. When Etienne closed the truck door behind her, the last of her reserve gave out. She was vaguely aware of his cell phone going off, his voice muffled in a brief one-way conversation while he stood on the curb. Her whole body was tense. She leaned stiffly against the window, but she was trembling again and couldn't stop. All she wanted was to forget. Forget about the woman in the mirror, forget about every creepy experience she'd had today . . .

There's a mirror in my bedroom . . . will I see something in that, too?

She jumped as the driver's door opened and Etienne climbed inside. He shoved the key in the ignition but didn't turn it; instead, he sat there regarding her with a long, pensive stare.

"That was Mama," he said at last, tapping his cell. "I'm picking her up at your house."

"My house? What's she doing there?"

"Went with your mama to some meeting tonight. Guess you heard she's got herself a job cooking at Belle Chandelle."

"Aunt Teeta told me this morning. I think it's great."

"Yeah . . ." His black eyes narrowed, intent on her face. "But *you're* not feeling too great . . . not since you looked at that thing on the wall back there."

Miranda propped her elbow on the window ledge. She pressed one hand to her forehead, rubbed at the ache along her brow. Quietly, Etienne kept on.

"What, you think I can't tell the difference between clumsy and scared?"

Of course he'd realized. She'd known right away that he hadn't missed a thing. "That obvious?" she murmured.

"I don't think anybody there caught it. Well . . . except for Gage." Etienne paused . . . frowned . . . angled back against his door. "What'd you see, *cher*?"

"A reflection." Drawing a deep, shaky breath, she focused on being calm. "When I looked in that mirror, I saw a reflection. Only it . . . wasn't me."

He'd been ready for just about anything—but not this, she could tell. And though there was only a brief hint of surprise on his face, she saw it all the same.

"Who was it?" he asked bluntly, but Miranda could only shake her head.

"I have no idea. A woman . . . no one I've ever seen before."

"Can't you remember anything about her?"

Shaking her head again, she closed her eyes. It had begun to rain again, a light drizzle pattering the roof and misting over the windshield. After a few more seconds, Etienne squeezed her hand, started the engine, and headed for Hayes House.

It never took long to get anywhere in St. Yvette—not even clear across town to Aunt Teeta's. They made the drive in silence, though Miranda's mind was in full turmoil. She didn't want to think about what she'd seen, yet that was impossible. The mirror-woman's face was still seared into her brain, and she couldn't get rid of it, couldn't shut it out, even though she was desperately trying to.

Hang on . . . you can do it . . . you're almost home. . . .

The pickup slowed to make a turn. They were starting onto the Brickway now—the quaint, brick-paved road that wound through the town's historical district—and when Miranda opened her eyes, her own street corner was just coming into view. In another couple minutes she could escape to her room, lock the door, and have a private little breakdown. *Except Miss Nell's going to be there, remember?* Miranda didn't know if she could hold it together that long. As Etienne stopped in the driveway, she sat for a moment, trying to compose herself.

"You never have to go back, *cher.*" His voice lowered, unmistakably protective. "You never have to see that mirror again, if you don't want to."

Oh, why can't it be that simple?

But if Miranda had learned anything from her experiences, it was this one bitter truth—that even if she *didn't* ever see that mirror again, the haunting wouldn't stop. That woman—whoever she was—would find some other way to reach her. Again and again . . . till Miranda finally figured it out.

"You know that won't help," she whispered now, even as Etienne nodded.

"Yeah. I know."

Somewhat distantly, she heard her door open and felt his hand on her shoulder, coaxing her out; then his hand on her back, guiding her to the porch. The second they were inside, Aunt Teeta hurried from the kitchen to greet them.

"Here y'all are!" Throwing her arms around each of them in turn, Aunt Teeta couldn't have looked more delighted. "Come on in and have some carrot cake. Why, us three girls are just having ourselves the best visit!"

"I . . . I'm really tired, Aunt Teeta—" Miranda began, but the woman quickly cut her off.

"Just for a few minutes, hon—Nell's been waiting to see you, and your mama hasn't talked to you all day. And I'll put on some hot milk to help you sleep. Come on now."

There was no way out of it. Receiving a shrug from Etienne, Miranda reluctantly followed her aunt.

The kitchen, as usual, was a delicious haven—strong black coffee, sugar and cream, homemade cake, sweet tea, and stale cinnamon rolls left over from an early breakfast. Mom and Miss Nell were deep in conversation at the table, and from all the crumpled napkins, spilled crumbs, and used coffee filters heaped in the sink, it was obvious that the girl-talk had been going on for quite a while.

It was Miss Nell who looked up first. Miranda hadn't seen her since the night of Gage's accident—six weeks ago at the Falls— but she hadn't forgotten her. Small and delicate, almost frail; hair and eyes like Etienne's; dimples in her pale cheeks; and a brave smile that defied her most recent brush with cancer. As

Etienne winked at her and mumbled in French, she stood up, walked straight to Miranda, and gave her a hug.

Miranda didn't expect it. She barely managed to return the hug before Miss Nell stepped away, held Miranda at arm's length, and gave her a swift appraisal.

"I'm sorry you've been sick, Miranda." The woman's glance shot between Miranda and Etienne. "Maybe *some* people will be easier to get along with, now that you're back again."

Everyone laughed. Except for Etienne, who looked vaguely embarrassed and raked a hand back through his rain-damp hair.

"How are you, Etienne?" Miranda's mom spoke up cheerfully as Miss Nell returned to her chair. "You know, Teeta's been telling me how you used to come by here all the time to help out our dad."

Etienne paused, cleared his throat. "Yes ma'am. I helped out a little."

"Oh, don't be so modest!" Aunt Teeta fussed. "Listen to him! Why, he certainly helped out more than a little—he practically *rebuilt* this old house. And I *miss* having him around!"

"Well then," Mom smiled, "maybe he should start coming by more often."

"Maybe I should," Etienne agreed, nodding at the floor.

"Hon, you know there's always stuff around here that needs some special attention," Aunt Teeta reminded him sweetly.

Miranda shot daggers at both her mother and her aunt. Neither seemed to notice, though Miss Nell definitely seemed amused.

"But you know, it is so *funny* that y'all came in when you did—we were just talking about you two." Puttering at the counter, Aunt Teeta fixed Etienne and Miranda with an innocent smile. "Just look at y'all! I swear, y'all look so cute together! Don't you ladies think they just look so cute together?"

While the women laughed in agreement, Miranda cringed all the way to her toes. She couldn't even face Etienne; she had no idea how he was reacting. *I'm going to kill them. Mom and Aunt Teeta both.*

Luckily, Miss Nell stood up again and slung her purse over one shoulder. "Okay, Casanova, why don't you take your poor old mother home, hmm? I'm beat."

While the three women exchanged hugs and good-nights, Miranda walked with Etienne to the door.

"I'm so sorry," she mumbled, still flustered. "They just—Aunt Teeta—I didn't expect them to—"

His lips brushed hers with a kiss. She never saw it coming, never even saw him lean down.

"Don't be worrying tonight, *cher*. Get some sleep. We'll find the answers, yeah? We'll figure it out."

Slightly breathless, Miranda managed a nod. "I really want to believe that."

Amusement flickered in his eyes . . . faded slowly to genuine concern. Lightly he traced a fingertip over the spot where he'd kissed her. "Believe it."

"But—"

"Believe it 'cause I said so."

Miss Nell was there now, with Mom and Aunt Teeta behind her. And Etienne was already running to open the door of the truck. And her skin felt so warm, and her heart was pounding so hard, that she almost felt faint. . . .

Fear, of course. *Fear of the unknown.*

She watched till the pickup backed all the way down the driveway . . . honked its horn . . . disappeared into the pouring rain.

Fear of the unknown spirits, Miranda?

Or fear of the unknown Etienne?

10

SHE LAY AWAKE FOR HOURS.

Tossing . . . turning . . . trying not to remember, but remembering too much . . .

She didn't want to think of Belle Chandelle, yet the place kept pulling her back to an overwhelming sense of sorrow . . . a shadow at an empty window . . . a swing moving in motionless air. . . . She'd been so certain of those footsteps approaching, running straight toward her. . . .

And what about the mirror in my locker and the one on the wall at Roo and Ashley's house?

The shock, the terror when she'd looked up to see a stranger's face where her own should have been. The reflection of a woman she didn't know . . .

That woman . . .

And now, for the first time, Miranda began to separate the face from the fear. *That woman . . . a young woman.* She hadn't allowed herself to think about the mirror-woman before; all she really recalled were the eyes. But now, here in the calm and safety of her room . . . she slowly, reluctantly, let her mind open and her memory unfold. . . .

Blackness. Only blackness at first, deep and silent as death. But then . . . as the face of the woman began to materialize, small bits of color began to emerge with her . . . not bright or vivid, but faded . . . unnatural yellows and browns . . . like a distorted old photograph slowly being developed. . . .

A young woman, though she doesn't look it. Her skin is yellow, a picture yellowed with age—her face is worried and gaunt, making her seem older than she is, but she's no more than twenty-two. . . .

Miranda paused, stiff on her back, gazing sightlessly up at the ceiling. The images were coming faster now—soon she wouldn't be able to stop them. She pressed her hands over her eyes and drew a deep breath.

Dark hair pulled back, but messy, untended . . . a bun, maybe at the back of her neck, but strands hanging around her face, she's tired, so very tired, she hasn't brushed her hair in a while, hasn't fixed her hair in a while, she's tried many times to tuck it back but it keeps falling. And something on top . . . a cap?—a cap of dark lace and dark ribbons . . . and her collar is dark, too, the collar of her dress is dark, dark material and very dirty—

But her eyes! What is it about her eyes? So scared, no—more than scared—terrified panicky desperate pleading praying but God isn't answering! And something else, something else, something's wrong with her eyes, the color, it's not natural, the color of her eyes—what's wrong with that woman's eyes—

With a cry, Miranda bolted upright. She was shaking all over, and as she huddled back into her pillows, she could scarcely catch her breath. She knew that those details she'd seen just now—clothes, hair, even the woman's face—were far more than anyone could *possibly* see in a handmade design of tiny mirror fragments. Yet she *had* seen them—*known* them—with absolute certainty.

Were the things she'd experienced today all separate events? Or were they each somehow connected with Belle Chandelle?

"What does it mean, Grandpa?" she whispered into the darkness. "Can you hear me? Can you help me?"

God, how she wished she could talk to him again. Learn from him. Hear his wisdom and his guidance, face-to-face. And yet, here in the quiet of her room, she almost felt as if she *could* hear him, a little. And the promises he'd asked her to keep.

"Don't turn them away," he'd said. *"They'll come to you because they know you can see them. They'll speak to you because they know you'll hear."*

Jonas Hayes hadn't been afraid of the spirits. He'd spoken of them as if they were every bit as real as the living; he'd accepted them just as matter-of-factly as he'd accepted his own purpose of being their mediator.

"Don't turn them away. . . ."

And now, for whatever reason, desperate spirits had come to Miranda for help—had purposely sought her out, knowing that she'd be able to see and to hear. . . .

I can't turn my back on them. . . . I can't turn them away, these spirits who need me. . . .

A weight seemed to settle around her heart. Feeling more restless than ever, she flung back the covers, climbed out of bed, and went quickly down the stairs. On the second-floor landing, she could hear Aunt Teeta's faint snores and soft music playing behind the closed door of Mom's room. Good, they were both asleep. She didn't want either of them fussing over her right now, worrying about her being up at this hour. She needed to think but didn't want to . . . needed to calm her brain, but didn't know how. When she slipped out the front door, the warm, balmy air felt soothing against her skin, and she stood for a moment, breathing it in.

The rain was still falling, hard and steady, muffling out the world. From time to time it sprayed in beneath the eaves, but not onto the porch swing, where Miranda chose to sit. Curling up, she drew her knees to her chest, rested her chin on her knees. The swing rocked gently with every gust of wind. She let her eyes drift shut and her thoughts drift free. . . .

"Miranda?"

The voice was familiar and very close. As Miranda gasped and jerked upright, Etienne reached out for her, catching her shoulders and holding her in place.

"Whoa, take it easy—"

"Oh my God, you scared me to death!" All the strength rushed out of her. Shaking violently, she grabbed for his hands . . . started to shove them away . . . held on to them instead. "What are you doing here? Do you have any idea what time it is?"

"Around three in the morning, last I checked."

"Don't you have a curfew like normal people? Doesn't your mom ever wonder where you go?"

Both questions seemed to amuse him. As Miranda's grip finally loosened, he pulled free and stepped back. "I been parked over there for a while." He jerked his thumb toward the street. "Trying to decide if I should come up to your room. Just . . . wanting to check you're okay."

Miranda stared at him. Wet clothes clinging to his body . . .

Black eyes skimming over the porch . . . front door . . . swing . . . her. Shaking his head, shoving back his hair, lifting his T-shirt to mop off his face—unsuccessfully.

She looked down at her own T-shirt—last minute nightwear of choice. She'd forgotten about what she was wearing—just an oversized shirt and underwear, not much. Sitting up straight, she tried to yank her shirt down over her thighs, and nearly fell off the swing.

Etienne waited while she rearranged herself. Then he leaned casually against the porch railing. "So. Bad night, yeah?"

"I'm okay."

"Which is why you're sitting out here in the rain at three in the morning?"

Miranda almost smiled at that. "You could have come up," she said quietly. "Everyone's asleep."

"Hmmm. And how come you always got me sneaking up the back way?" Voice teasing, expression serious. "I'm starting to feel like a pervert."

In spite of herself, she laughed. "You're perfectly welcome at any door, day or night, and you know it. But then Aunt Teeta fusses over you—"

"Me, I like being fussed over—"

"And she embarrasses me—"

"That's always fun—"

"And you *know* I can't talk about ghosts and spirits and—and my *job*—in front of her and Mom and—"

"And you want me all to yourself, I get it."

Miranda tried to sound stern. "That is *not* what I meant—"

"Oh, I'm not complaining. It *is* a pretty small room. Not much space to outrun me."

More sternness—a look this time. He didn't seem at all intimidated.

"If you remember," Miranda scolded him, "the very *few* times you've been up there were emergencies. You talked me out of being terrified. You saved me from . . . from ghostly stalkers. You . . . you helped me figure out what to do. . . ."

Her words trailed off. All seriousness now, Etienne walked to the swing, nudged her over, and sat down.

"I *was* coming up. I was on my way to the back steps when I saw you walk out. And I was damn right to be checking on you." Again his eyes slid over her in cool, quick appraisal. "You haven't slept one minute tonight, I can tell. And you got that too-much-to-worry-about look on your face. Which means you been doing a lotta thinking and being scared since I left here with Mama."

Reality had returned, and Miranda said nothing. Seconds passed into minutes. Distractedly, she chewed on a fingernail but still didn't talk. When Etienne finally slipped his arms around her shoulders, she resisted at first, though her willpower didn't last long.

"You had yourself one hell of a day," he murmured. "You shouldn't be alone with it. And I'm staying right here—if you wanna talk, if you don't wanna talk—I'm staying till you tell me to leave."

She knew that he meant it. And that she didn't *really* want to be alone with it after all.

"I started remembering what she looked like," Miranda spoke so quietly that he had to bend closer. "But what I keep wondering is how she . . . *found* me. I didn't feel her anywhere at the plantation, and that mirror at Ashley's house doesn't even belong to me—I've never even seen it. This almost seems more personal than spirits I dealt with before. More . . . I don't know . . . intrusive. Like the barriers between me and them are getting thinner. Except I don't know how they *could* be getting thinner, because I haven't been doing it that long."

"So maybe they've always *been* thinner, and you didn't know," Etienne mused. "Maybe it's just you having to realize it on your own." Pausing, he gazed out at the rain. "So . . . what'd she look like, this woman?"

Miranda began to describe her. The yellowish overtones, like an old photograph; the woman's face and hair, the cap and collar; the inexplicable shock of those eyes; the feelings of panic and despair. Then, when she'd told Etienne all she could remember, she regarded him with a troubled frown.

"But I'm not getting it all," she murmured.

"What you mean, *cher*?"

"There's more. So much more she's trying to tell me—but I'm not getting it. Why can't it all just be simple? Why can't these . . . these ghosts, these spirits, follow a rule book? So I can be prepared when it happens? Not caught totally off guard?"

Etienne's voice softened. His gaze was firm, but not unkind. "It's life, *cher*. And whether it's *this* life or the *afterlife*—you can't be preparing yourself for every little thing that might come along. None of us have all the answers. And those people on the other side—they don't have the answers either, or they wouldn't be needing your help."

"Grandpa always knew what to do, didn't he?" She sighed, surprised when Etienne adamantly shook his head.

"No, your *grandpère*, he made *lotsa* mistakes. *Plenty* mistakes. What, you think he had everything perfect? Listen to me—he had to start over every single time. Feel his way, learn how to help them, trial and error. 'Cause each one was different—had a different problem, a different need. What worked for one didn't mean it worked for another one."

"You're making that up."

"Not me, I swear."

"How do you know that?"

"Your *grandpère*, he told me." Despite Miranda's obvious doubt, Etienne added an afterthought. "Maybe there's stuff you need to be learning about while you're helping them."

"Learning about what?"

"Yourself."

It was an answer she didn't expect—an answer she'd never considered. Puzzled, she reflected on Etienne's words, then relaxed a little and leaned into him.

"You know what's weird? Ever since I met Grandpa . . . and ever since he died . . . I've had this image in my mind of how perfect he was. Even if people *did* think he was crazy—I just knew that he *saw* things perfect, *did* things perfect, with his gift." She paused, her sigh almost wistful. "I hardly knew him . . . but I really miss him."

Etienne said nothing. His head was lowered, jaw clenched

tight, dark eyes fixed in a pensive stare—but Miranda wasn't fooled.

You miss him too, don't you, Etienne? That special bond you had with Grandpa, the one I still don't understand—you miss him too, even more than I do. . . .

"The thing is," she went on quietly, "when I found out I had his gift . . . *I* wanted to be perfect too. Just like him."

Etienne's eyes remained downward. "You don't need to be like anybody else. You're already perfect, *cher*. Just the way you are."

She smiled at that. Her fingers gently touched his shoulder . . . stroked down the strong, lean muscles of his arm. Though he was slouched back, she felt the slow tensing of his body, the ever-so-subtle catch of his breath, the heat of his skin, as she worked her hand beneath his wet T-shirt and over the tightness of his belly.

Scars here . . .

Without warning, her eyes filled with tears, and a surge of injustice shot through her. *Scars here and on your arms and God only knows where else your horrible father beat you—*

"Grandpa must have known, Etienne," she murmured, not even stopping to think. "Grandpa must have tried to protect you from him. . . ."

She knew at once that she'd crossed the line. Even before her words were out, even before the dark, steely look on Etienne's face, Miranda knew that she'd gone way too far.

"What the hell are you talking about?" His voice was deep, hoarse, almost threatening. His hand clamped hard around hers, making her wince before he pushed it aside. "I don't need anybody protecting me."

More startled than hurt, Miranda watched a whole range of emotions struggle over his face, while another range of emotions struggled through her heart.

"I'm sorry," she whispered. "I shouldn't have—"

"Don't ever ask me about that again."

He'd turned loose of her now . . . his body angled away, muscles so tense she could practically feel him quivering. Miranda realized that *she* was shaking. Shaking and sad and scared, all at once. For one crazy second she thought of wild animals—the ones people always try to tame—*only you can't ever trust those wild animals . . . their instincts, their true nature, always win out in the end.*

"I'm so sorry," she said again, choking through tears. "I didn't mean to hurt—"

"You didn't," he muttered, glancing down at one arm. "I've had these scars a long time. And believe me . . . they don't hurt."

Maybe not on the outside, Miranda longed to say, but didn't.

She couldn't see his face. He was still turned away from her, their bodies not even touching. Staring at his shadowy profile, she drew a deep breath and made an impulsive decision. Then pulled his arm slowly around her shoulders and nestled against him.

She was relieved—and a little surprised—that he didn't fight her.

"When I broke that mirror?" she went on, as if everything

were perfectly normal, "when I cut my hand on the broken glass? I think that's what started everything . . . you know, opened up some doorway. I had such a weird feeling about it, like I sensed something was about to happen. So maybe *that's* the connection."

"Could be, I guess." His tone was belligerent, his stare just as fierce, but at least he was looking at her again. "Did the mirror have anything to do with Belle Chandelle?"

"No. It was Aunt Teeta's."

"Then maybe it's something about *breaking* the mirror. Or cutting your *hand*."

"Or maybe they're all related. And I still have more pieces of the puzzle to find before I can put everything together." When he didn't respond, she made a show of yawning and rubbing wearily at her forehead. "We're not going to put it all together tonight. And you . . . you probably need to go home now."

"I told you, I'm not going anywhere till—"

"Till I tell you to leave, I know. Which is what I'm doing. Look"—Miranda was firm— "we're both really tired. We'll both think better after we get some sleep."

She could see the hesitation in his eyes and another silent battle of emotions. *You want to go, don't you, Etienne? You felt trapped and betrayed, and I caused it, and now you want to go. . . .*

At last he nodded. Releasing her, he slid to the edge of the swing.

"You sure?" A faint shrug, apathetic at best. "You sure you don't want me staying?"

"I'm sure." *Of course I want you to stay. Just as much as I know you should go, and as much as I want to know you, Etienne Boucher—all of you—the good and bad, the right and wrong, and all the places that hurt—*

"Last chance." Finally, a lame attempt at humor. Pretending—just like she was doing—that the whole unpleasant incident had never occurred.

As Miranda managed a weak smile, she noticed him reaching toward her lap. With all the other distractions to deal with, she'd completely forgotten about her T-shirt. Now, to her embarrassment, she saw that it had twisted up around her waist.

Cheeks flaming, she fumbled to untangle it, but Etienne was smoother. Grasping the bottom of her shirt, he eased it slowly down over her thighs while her whole body flushed hot.

He didn't seem to notice.

Instead he stood up and walked to the porch steps . . . paused there and gazed steadily out at the night.

"Just worry about your ghosts, *cher*. They're the ones you can help."

Miranda watched him disappear into the rain.

He didn't hurry, and he didn't say good-bye.

And he never once turned back to look at her.

11

"So what's happened since yesterday?" Mom teased. "Why the sudden interest in Belle Chandelle?"

Staring out the car window, Miranda was barely listening. Bad enough to have hauntings on her mind—now Etienne's visit had left her with a whole different set of questions and emotions that she'd grappled with till the alarm went off.

I should never have asked him about that stuff—about any *of that stuff—not Grandpa, or his father, or the scars. . . .*

Miranda gave an inward groan.

Could you have been any nosier? Brought up memories any more upsetting to him? He'd come by to check on her, and she'd blown it. She only hoped he'd forget about it and not hate her for the rest of her natural life.

"Miranda?" Mom asked gently.

But Miranda, deep in troubling thoughts, scarcely heard. Though some of Etienne's comments had stung, he *had* been right about one thing. It was the spirits—whoever they were— that she could help right now. Her own problems—including Etienne—would have to wait.

"Miranda?" Mom's voice again, more insistent this time. "You okay, honey?"

"Sorry, Mom. I was up late studying."

She'd been relieved when Mom offered to drive her to school. Usually Mom was gone when she got up, already at work on the grand resurrection of Belle Chandelle. *Things turn out weird sometimes,* she couldn't help thinking. *Now Mom and I are* both *connected to the plantation, but in totally different ways.*

Of course, Mom didn't know that. And even if she did, Miranda knew her mother would never understand. Ghosts and ghostly experiences just weren't in her mother's realm of believability.

"It's different seeing Belle Chandelle in person." Fumbling for an explanation, Miranda kept her tone casual. "I mean, once I was actually *there*, it really intrigued me."

"The *house* intrigued you? Or a certain *worker* out there intrigued you?" Mom teased.

His damp hair and warm skin . . . fingers gliding over my T-shirt . . . body tense . . .

"Come on, Mom," Miranda said quickly. "You're getting to be as bad as Aunt Teeta. I've told you before—Etienne and I are just friends. That's all."

Nodding, her mother laughed. "Well, *whatever* the reason, I'm really glad you like the place. Do you know, I remember it when I was a little girl? Going out there with Daddy, and how fascinated he always was with it? Of course, it was still in pretty bad shape then. And to think I'm going to have a part in bringing it back to life! It's . . ." Her face softened, nostalgic. "Well, it's . . . a *privilege*, really."

Smiling at her mother, Miranda felt an unexpected glow of happiness. It was rare these days for them to spend much time together, to have close and special talks. Not that she was complaining—Mom had a job she loved, and living with Aunt Teeta was a total joy, and Miranda was busy with her own life. But sometimes their schedules were so different that they seemed more like roommates coming and going. And Miranda forgot how nice it could be, she and Mom, just the two of them.

"Honey, you're always welcome to bring your friends out to the plantation," Mom offered. They were pulling up in front of school now, and once again, Miranda forced herself to pay attention. "Teeta and I don't even have to be there—I can give you an extra set of keys. And Etienne has a set, of course. Just don't go wandering around where it's dangerous."

The car was stopped, but Miranda made no move to get out. "Mom, Aunt Teeta said something about a picture of the house. And a letter written by a Yankee soldier. Any chance I could see them?"

"Sure, I know what you're talking about. The originals are in the museum at the Historical Society, but Mrs. Wilmington had some copies made for us. I can find those for you, if you like. Another school project?"

Miranda shrugged, evasive. "Maybe. Right now I'm . . . trying to decide on a topic."

"I'll be glad to help however I can. I just wish we knew more about the house. I keep thinking it probably has this whole dramatic saga going on that none of us will ever find out—or can even begin to imagine."

I'm sure it does too, Mom. Only I'm *going to find out what that saga is.*

"I'll pick you up here this afternoon. Have a great day, honey."

"Thanks, Mom. You too."

Hurrying up the front steps, Miranda wondered how she would ever keep her mind on school for the next seven hours. She wished she could just skip classes altogether, go out to Belle Chandelle instead, and start exploring the place in daylight. Things always seemed safer in daylight. More rational, less scary. Lots of construction workers would be around. Mom, too . . . maybe Aunt Teeta. Probably Etienne . . .

"You're perfect, cher. Just the way you are."

"Right," Miranda mumbled to herself, though her heart melted all over again. *And how many millions of girls have you said* that *to, Etienne Boucher? Danger signs, Miranda. Danger signs all over the place.*

Annoyed with herself, she maneuvered her way through the packed hallways. As she turned a corner, she saw Parker, Gage, and Roo in front of Ashley's locker—and even from a distance, she could tell that something was wrong.

"He asked you out, Ashley?" Parker was scowling when Miranda walked up. "He actually said that. He actually asked you out on a date."

For a minute, Ashley didn't answer, only met his accusation with a tight-lipped frown. Then she turned her back and shoved some notebooks into her locker. "It's no big deal."

"No big deal?"

"Maybe you two should talk louder." Glancing around, Roo defiantly met the stares of curious onlookers. "I hear people are putting big money on this fight."

"We're not fighting," Ashley said primly.

"One of you is."

Suspicious, Gage leaned close to Roo's ear. "Have you been taking *bets* on this?"

"No."

"I better not find out you're lying."

"You won't."

Ashley slammed her locker door. Parker's scowl deepened. "So what'd you say?" he demanded.

"What do you think I said?" Ashley's sigh was loud and impatient. "I said no."

"And you were going to tell me . . . *when*?"

"Oh, Parker, for heaven's sake. There's nothing to tell."

"Yeah? Then how come the whole school seems to know about it?"

"The whole school *does* know about it," Roo corrected.

Gage quickly stepped in. "Come on, you know how rumors spread around here. Streak's buddies are probably just trying to stir up some drama. And what do you care anyway?"

"Did you know about it?" Parker accused Miranda as she stopped beside Gage. But before she could respond, Parker turned his anger on Roo. "How did *you* know about it?"

"I am all-knowing," Roo replied solemnly. "I and God."

Gage elbowed her in the back.

"Plus the fact," Roo grudgingly relented, "that some of the cheerleaders heard Kurt talking to Ashley after practice. Apparently, he thinks she's hot."

Miranda caught Ashley's quick look of panic—and the angry

desperation that she shot at Roo. Thankfully, Parker didn't seem to notice.

"It's just what I heard." Relenting a little, Roo shrugged. "That definitely—"

"He thinks she's hot?" Parker broke in, incredulous. "He *said* that?"

"Definitely doesn't mean it's true," Gage finished diplomatically.

Roo stared at him "*What's* true? That Streak said it, or that Ashley's hot?"

"Everybody knows Ashley's hot!" Parker exploded. "That's the whole damn problem!"

"Okay. Hold that thought." Gage jerked his chin toward the classroom door. "Let's go, we're gonna be late."

"Parker, just drop it," Ashley said coldly. "It's stupid, and you're being silly."

"Oh. Now I'm silly. Do you think *Streak* is silly?"

"I'm not talking about this anymore."

"What's going on?" Etienne asked, sauntering up, books under one arm. His eyes slid over the group with lightning-speed perception.

"Well, look who decided to grace us with his sexiness," Roo greeted him. "What are you doing here?"

"Slumming." Nudging Roo with one shoulder, he held up a notebook. "Test."

"Did you study?" Ashley asked him, obviously concerned.

"Some."

"Come on, then, I can quiz you in study hall."

But Parker was still grumbling at Roo. "I suppose you're loving this. I suppose you think Ashley should go out with him."

"With me?" Etienne looked at Ashley. "*Mais*, yeah, I definitely think she should go out with me."

"No. Streak Fuller."

"You think Streak *Fuller* should go out with me?" Etienne raised an eyebrow. "He's not really my type, but . . ."

"Cut the jokes," Parker muttered. "He asked Ashley out."

"Streak asked *Ashley* out?"

"Oh, y'all!" With a cry of exasperation, Ashley spun and flounced off down the hall. Parker immediately glared at Roo.

"So *did* you? Come on, I want to know. Did you tell her to go out with him? Just to piss me off?"

"As much as I love pissing you off," Roo replied calmly, "I did *not* tell her to go out with Kurt. He's way too nice and polite and considerate. She wouldn't know how to act."

The bell rang before anyone could say more. Watching the rest of them leave, Miranda lingered a moment with Parker, falling into step beside him. Though he kept his eyes lowered, she could feel his anger and total frustration.

"Parker," she soothed gently, "you're the only one Ashley cares about. Don't you know that? Just trust her. Let it go."

Though obviously more confused than convinced, he managed a nod and walked with her to class.

By noon Miranda realized that this school wasn't so different from her old one when it came to gossip. In just those few hours, text-message rumors had it that Ashley had asked Kurt Fuller for a date, that Ashley was planning to break up with Parker, and that Parker had secretly been dating Delphine for months. When Ashley and Roo found Miranda in the library right before lunchtime, Ashley was visibly upset.

"You'll never guess what happened," she groaned.

Miranda immediately looked at Roo, who only shrugged. "Oh no, Ashley. What now?"

"You know I'm in the Tutor Group," Ashley reminded her.

Miranda nodded. She'd heard of it—a group of excellent students chosen by the faculty and appointed to help other kids with their studying. She knew that Ashley belonged, and as Ashley gazed at her miserably, she guessed what was coming next.

"You're . . . supposed to tutor Kurt Fuller?"

"I just found out. He has to pull up his grades, or he's off the football team."

"Well, first of all, do you *want* to? And second, can you get out of it?"

"No. And no. Everybody else is already working with somebody. And Mrs. Hayden specifically assigned me. I'm absolutely stuck. And anyway, how would it look if I said, 'I can't do this, my boyfriend won't like it.' I mean . . . it's for school. It's . . . business." She drew a long breath. "Parker will just have to understand."

"Good luck with that," Roo mumbled.

"Roo!"

"And don't be surprised if Kurt tries something."

"What would he try?"

"Hey. They don't call him Streak because he moves *slow*."

"Roo!"

"And I don't imagine you're very high on *Delphine's* popularity list right now either."

"Roo, stop it! Oh, this is just getting worse and worse. I don't even want to have lunch."

"Sure you do. You have to act like everything's normal. You haven't done anything wrong."

For a split second, Ashley's eyes misted. Her voice went sad and soft. "Parker thinks I have."

"Parker's a moron. A jealous moron. A jealous, insecure moron. A jealous, insecure, possessive—"

"Moron who loves her," Miranda broke in quickly.

Roo rolled her eyes. Ashley gave Miranda a grateful smile.

"I don't want people staring at me. Or talking about me." Ashley's sigh had gone miserable once more. "I wish Kurt had never said anything. I wish he'd never broken up with Delphine. I just want him to leave me alone."

The three headed outside to eat. While Ashley walked between them, Miranda scanned the lunch crowds scattered across campus, ignoring the occasional snickers and stares and whispered comments. Roo seemed oblivious. Linking her arm through Ashley's, she tilted her head back and squinted up into a warm, cloudy sky.

"Hey. It's getting cooler."

"Is it?" Miranda asked. "How can you tell?"

"I can feel it. Like a nip in the air."

"A very hidden nip."

"Maybe it'll be cold for Halloween tomorrow," Ashley said

halfheartedly. "That always used to ruin it for us, remember? It'd be so hot, and then suddenly it would get really cold, and then we'd have to wear coats over our costumes, and nobody could see them. After Mama and Daddy spent all that time making them for us."

Roo nodded. "Yeah, it was really hard duct-taping those sparkly little fairy wings to your jacket."

They'd reached their usual table now. Etienne was leaning comfortably against it, drinking a Coke, while Gage lounged back on one of the benches. Parker sat on the bench across from Gage, guzzling orange juice from a bottle. The three were obviously having an intense conversation, which abruptly broke off as the girls walked up. Miranda could only conclude that their guy-talk had been centered around Ashley and her new admirer.

"Hi, what's going on?" Miranda greeted them, but the three kept unusually quiet. Parker looked away. Gage slid over to make room for her. Ashley and Roo squeezed onto the bench beside Parker while Etienne, always casually detached, seemed even more distant than usual. Miranda had hoped to tell everyone about her latest ghostly experiences—but now was most definitely not a good time.

It was Parker who finally broke the awkward silence. Shouting a snap count, he aimed his empty bottle at the trash can and let it fly. The bottle hit . . . bounced—and unlike last night's pillow toss—landed perfectly on target. After a round of forced cheers, everyone relaxed a little and began talking again.

Teasing, Miranda bent to examine Gage's cast. "Any more intimate information since Babette LeBlanc?"

"Yeah, Gage." Parker kicked at him under the table. "I hope you're writing everything down for future reference."

"He's gonna need it," Etienne nodded. "Once that cast is off, all those girls feeling sorry for him are gonna forget who he is."

"No way!" Stretching over the table, Ashley pinched both of Gage's cheeks before he could dodge her attack. "How could any girl forget these dimples? These big brown eyes? This—"

Gage pulled free, scooted to the end of the bench, and resumed eating his sandwich. Laughing, Miranda scooted next to him and leaned against his side.

"This really cute blushing thing he does?"

Gage shook his head, a smile of good-natured surrender.

"Well, I won't forget you, Gage—cast or no cast. So it really comes off tomorrow, huh?"

"Tomorrow afternoon. I'll be free."

"And then what?"

"Rehab. Rehab. And . . . rehab."

Roo propped her elbows on the table . . . leveled him a solemn stare. "When they take off your cast, your leg will be all shriveled up. And totally pasty white. And rotten and smelly. And there won't be any hair on it."

Parker shrugged. "And she'll love you even more."

Shaking his head again, Gage took another bite of ham and Swiss. As Roo suddenly tugged at his arm, the sandwich dropped onto the table.

"Nice going," he began, but Roo was motioning across campus.

"Hey," she observed curiously, "is Kurt Fuller actually coming over here?"

Parker followed the direction of Roo's gaze. Etienne straightened up and narrowed his eyes. Miranda and Ashley looked at the same time. And then, as the six of them continued to watch, Kurt Fuller strolled past their table, taking his time, his handsome smile pinned on Ashley.

"Hey, Ashley," he said. "You look nice today."

"Hey. Thank you." Unnerved, Ashley nodded politely but kept eating her yogurt. Her cheeks went a ladylike pink. Kurt passed on by.

As Parker started to get up, Ashley's hand shot out to stop him. Roo pulled the ham from Gage's sandwich and popped it into her mouth.

"One thing you gotta say for him," Etienne mumbled. "He's got balls."

"Humongous ones," Roo said. "According to Delphine."

"*I* think you look nice," Parker blurted to Ashley. "I *always* think you look nice."

"Thanks." Gathering up her mostly uneaten lunch, Ashley paused to hand Etienne some notes. "Do you want to study a little bit more? I can quiz you on a few more things before that test."

"Ashley's tutoring Kurt in math," Roo announced.

"What?" This time Parker fairly sprang to his feet. His arms flew up in the air. "And when did *this* happen?"

"It's nothing," Ashley said tightly. "Roo, will you just keep quiet?"

"I'm helping you," Roo defended herself. "He's going to hear about it sooner or later—better he hears it from a friend."

"Since when have you and I been friends?" Parker shot back at her.

"Parker, I just found out last period," Ashley explained. "I hadn't even had a chance to tell you yet."

"So tell me now."

"And don't act like I'm trying to hide something from you. Mrs. Hayden assigned me to tutor him. If he doesn't get his grades up, he's off the team."

"No surprise there. The guy's dumb as a stump."

"But big as a tree," Roo added. "According to Delphine."

"I have an idea." Gage frowned at her, then at his two empty slices of bread. "Why don't you try making things worse?"

"Parker, it's nothing," Ashley insisted, but she was wringing her hands now, anger replacing embarrassment. "I'm helping him with schoolwork—that's *all*. As for that other thing, he broke up with his girlfriend, and he's looking for somebody to go out with—like *most* people do when they break up. Only *I'm not interested*. I told him *no, and he didn't push it. There is no drama here. End of story.*"

"Except that he's coming on to you," Parker snapped back at her. "And he knows you belong to *me*."

The silence that fell was icy cold. Parker gave a noticeable cringe and looked slightly ill.

"Oh, man." Etienne raised an eyebrow. "You must be tired of living, yeah?"

Taking a step toward Parker, Ashley clamped both hands on her hips. Her eyes were wide and seething, her voice like steel. "I do *not* belong to you, Parker Wilmington."

"That's not what I meant. I meant . . ." Parker glanced helplessly at Gage. "Tell her what I meant."

Gage opened his mouth. Closed it. Opened it. "What he meant was—"

Ashley cut him off. "I do not belong to *anybody*. This whole thing is stupid and ridiculous, and I'm *not* going to discuss it *anymore*. And if I want to go out with Kurt Fuller—then—then—I'll go *out* with him! And maybe I just *will*!"

Grabbing her things, she stuck her nose in the air and marched off toward the building, leaving Parker to stare morosely after her. Etienne regarded his study notes with a mixture of amusement and apprehension.

"I'm not sure if she's gonna be quizzing me or killing me. *Merde*, she's sure got a mad on."

Gage nodded and gave Parker a sympathetic shrug. "Not one of your brightest moves."

"No shit." Looking completely put out with himself, Parker reached over and shoved Roo, who nearly fell off the bench.

She caught herself just in time. Then glowered at him. "Excuse me?"

"Excuse my ass! See what you did?"

"What *I* did? You're just taking everything out on *me* because you know *Kurt* would pulverize you. And if you shove me again, *I'm* gonna pulverize you."

Etienne's chin jerked toward Roo. "My bet's on her."

"Forget Streak," Parker muttered. "I could take him in half a second."

"Do it then," Roo challenged. "Just let me get a shovel first, so we can scoop you up off the grass."

"Parker, it's not Ashley's fault." Once again Miranda tried to soothe him. "She doesn't even *want* to tutor Kurt. The teacher decides who Ashley gets stuck with—she doesn't have a choice."

But Parker didn't seem to be listening. "I need to stop by the gym," he muttered, and started off across the lawn. After only a few steps though, he turned and glared back at them.

"Gage!" he yelled irritably.

"Oookaay." Giving a low whistle, Gage hoisted himself up and grabbed his crutches. "Guess that's my cue for an exit."

Roo and Miranda got up as well, trailing the guys at a distance. Miranda was in no hurry to get back to class. She was worried about Ashley, frustrated about Etienne, and in a complete quandary over yesterday's supernatural happenings. From time to time she saw Roo casting her a sideways glance, but if the girl suspected what was going on—ghosts, Etienne, or otherwise—she didn't let on.

When Roo finally spoke, all she asked was, "What are you doing for Halloween?"

Miranda was glad for the distraction. "I haven't thought about it. Nothing, I guess. You?"

"What I always do. Make popcorn, sit in the dark, and have a horror-film marathon."

"Let me guess. And you can recite the entire dialogue from each one."

"Of course. Want to join me?"

"No, thanks. I think I just want a quiet night. What does everyone else do in this town?"

"We're pretty boring, actually. All the stores on the Brickway give out candy, but the sidewalks roll up before nine. Most of the kids from school go to parties."

Instantly Miranda's mind went back—to her life before, to her best friends. She and Marge and Joanie always went to at least one party on Halloween.

And I used to think Halloween was silly. I used to think that the supernatural was make-believe. I used to think that ghosts were just figments of crazy people's imaginations.

"Parties at their houses," Roo clarified. "Except Ashley always volunteers for some dumb Halloween program over at the preschool. And she's always totally worn out when she gets home."

"You mean she and Parker won't do something afterward?"

Roo shook her head. "Even if they *are* still speaking by then, there's a guys' night tomorrow." Then, when Miranda looked blank, Roo added, "At Belle Chandelle."

"What's that about?"

"The owners are nervous—with all the renovations going on, they think it's way more likely to be vandalized. So Etienne offered to keep an eye on the place. And he asked Gage and Parker to stay with him. I think they might be spending the night."

"How'd you find out?"

"I heard Gage and Etienne talking. Of course, they don't want *us* to know about it. They're probably afraid we'll go out there and crash their little get-together." Roo gave a sly half-smile. "Not that I haven't considered it. Sneaking out there. Giving them all heart attacks."

Picturing the scene, Miranda almost laughed. "I can't believe Parker's even going. Not after all his fuss about ghosts and Belle Chandelle."

"Point of honor, Miranda. He can't let the others know what a wimp he really is."

"Roo . . . he *did* save our lives at the Falls that night. Remember?"

Roo grimaced . . . gave a reluctant shrug. "Ugh. One night, then. I'll give him that, but absolutely no more."

They were going up the steps now, into the building. Roo paused on the threshold to scrape mud off the soles of her army boots.

"I wouldn't be surprised if something happens though," she added.

Miranda felt herself stiffen. "What do you mean?"

"Halloween night, Belle Chandelle—*any* night, Belle Chandelle." Another shrug, and a knowing glance at Miranda. "A place like that? That old, that much history? You know it must be swarming with all kinds of miserable spirits."

Roo planted both feet back on the floor. Her dark-ringed eyes pinned Miranda.

"But you know that better than anybody, right? Because you've probably already seen them."

12

"I DON'T KNOW WHAT'S HAPPENING OUT THERE." Mom frowned. As promised, she'd picked up Miranda after school, and now they were heading for Belle Chandelle. "Not a bit of trouble all this time, then suddenly this morning, four construction workers quit."

Miranda threw a quick glance at her mother's profile. A ripple of trepidation was already working its way up her spine.

"Did they say why?" she asked, trying to sound casual.

"Teeta was there; I wasn't. Oh, it was all nonsense. They said they felt weird. Like they were being watched. That the house has a funny feeling."

Miranda gave a vague nod.

"Now does that even make sense?" her mother asked irritably. "The house has sat there all these years. Renovation has started on it before. And nobody's ever had a problem with it."

"Well . . . I did hear rumors about it being the town's haunted house."

"Right. *Rumors.* Teeta and I were talking about it this morning. Rumors, but no actual proof. No reliable witnesses. It doesn't make sense. Why *now*?"

Growing quiet, Miranda redirected her gaze out the window. She didn't *want* to think what she was thinking, but it was there all the same. *Because of me? Because I went out to Belle Chandelle and disrupted something? Attracted someone?*

It was a frightening possibility—one she hated to even consider. That her mere presence somewhere could stir up spirits that had been quiet for hundreds of years . . .

"So what are you going to do?" she asked her mother.

"We found some replacements—that wasn't such a problem. I just hope these guys aren't as silly and superstitious as the others were."

It's not silly. Not superstitious. But again Miranda kept her eyes on the window and didn't answer. *You don't believe, Mom . . . and you're not helping.*

"Honey, I have a favor to ask," Mom went on, her mood lifting. "Would you mind taking some pictures for me at the plantation?"

Miranda winced, a new stab of dread shooting through her. "I don't know anything about taking pictures—"

"And I don't need anything professional. Just some before-and-after shots. Except these would be the *before* ones."

"Don't you and Aunt Teeta already spend enough time out there as it is? You need photos to remember it by?"

Mom obviously found this hilarious. "You know how Teeta and I are on that renovation committee? Well, the Harvest Festival's coming up, and the committee's decided to set up an information booth—right next to the Historical Society. People have been showing so much interest in Belle Chandelle, we thought this would be a good way to let the public know what's going on—along with some pictures to look at."

Miranda had learned about Harvest Festival just yesterday from the announcements in class. An annual November event when every business, organization, and club in town set up fun, tourist-friendly booths along the Brickway, and visitors came from miles around. Not to mention the local food and free samples, baking and cooking competitions, barbeques, picnics, and seafood boils—all of which St. Yvette was famous for.

Reluctantly, she nodded. "What kinds of pictures?"

"Details would be nice. Both insides and outsides of the buildings. It will certainly help with my research. We might even be able to use some later in a guidebook for the bed and breakfast."

"Okay. I'll give it a try."

"Honey, I really appreciate this; you have no idea how much time it will save me. The camera's right there in my tote bag—just go ahead and take it out."

Miranda did so, while trying to muster some enthusiasm. "Any new projects I should know about? And please don't tell me you're working till midnight."

"Well, I've got at least a million different decisions to make about the double parlors—but the main thing is, all the kitchen appliances are supposed to be delivered."

"Kitchen? You mean the one behind the house?"

"It's the first building we'll finish, and it's really starting to shape up."

"I thought none of the outbuildings were being renovated till after the house was done."

"They're not—but this one had a head start." Reaching over,

Mom rolled her window down and sniffed the air. "Is it my imagination, or is there a cool breeze out there? Anyway, the last owner rebuilt the kitchen so he could live in it while he was renovating the big house. Which is excellent for us."

"So it's a real kitchen? Or more like a cabin?"

"An authentic plantation kitchen. Walls, ceiling, floor, hearth, fireplace, the whole bit. What we've done is divide it so the old-fashioned part is what the tourists see. Then the other part—what the tourists *won't* see—is the actual working kitchen. And that's where all the cooking will be done for the bed and breakfast."

"Smart. Best of both worlds."

"Nell said she'd be here today too. Just to look things over . . . make sure they delivered the right orders."

Miranda couldn't help but smile. "I like her. I'm really glad she decided to take the job."

"From what Teeta's told me about her, she's a remarkable woman. And I guess Etienne is completely devoted to her."

"They've been through a lot together," Miranda said quietly, while her mother gave a sympathetic nod.

"Yes, honey. I believe they have."

A thoughtful silence fell between them. As the car began to slow down, Miranda recognized the turnoff to Belle Chandelle and knew they were getting close.

"So." Straightening in her seat, she tried to steel herself for the afternoon ahead. "Where should I start with the picture-taking?"

"Anywhere you like. Just don't wander off where you could get hurt."

"Which would be . . . ?"

"Didn't you get the whole tour yesterday? Including off-limits?"

Miranda thought fast. "Actually, I kind of got sidetracked. I started studying those blueprints and some of your sample catalogs—"

"Well, no wonder," Mom chuckled. "As for the house, there's still work that needs to be done on the roof and a few ceilings . . . and more plastering over the brick columns in front. Several wood floors still need to be put in, but the foundation is good and sound. All the rooms have pretty much been sectioned off, upstairs and down . . . but some of the windows—especially those dormers on the third floor—have to be replaced."

Just thinking about that dormer window, that shadowy hand, made Miranda shudder. She crossed her arms over her chest and hoped that Mom hadn't noticed.

"They still need to install all the ductwork for the central air and heat. And even though parts of the building have lights, not all the electricity or plumbing has been finished. Oh, and honey—the attic and the belvedere definitely aren't safe yet, so stay away from those."

On a whim, Miranda asked casually, "Mom . . . was the house yellow before you redid it?"

"Yellow?" Her mother looked perplexed. "No, I don't think so. Why?"

"I just . . . wondered."

"I can ask, but I've never heard that." Her mother thought a moment . . . gave a slight nod. "I guess it would make sense, though. 'Belle Chandelle' means beautiful candle . . . yellow for a candle flame?"

There was a half-empty delivery truck parked in the lot when they got there. While more appliances were being unloaded, Miranda grabbed the camera, then helped her mother carry boxes and shopping bags to the main house. She didn't see Etienne, but workers were crawling over the roof and moving along the galleries, filling the air with loud shouts, the noise of drills, hammers, and nail guns. As she and Mom neared the front entrance, a wild shriek stopped them in their tracks. Whirling around, they saw two little girls running at breakneck speed across the side lawn.

"Oh dear." Mom sighed. "I wish she wouldn't bring those kids here."

Miranda regarded her in surprise. "Who are they?"

"They belong to Coralee . . . she comes out here to help us clean," she explained as they went inside and deposited their stuff. "She's a single mom, and when she can't find a babysitter, she brings her little girls with her."

"They look . . . lively."

"Don't get me wrong, I love kids, and I admire a responsible parent—especially one on her own. But she can't watch them every minute, and there's just too much going on around here, too much for them to get into. I worry they'll get hurt."

Even as she spoke, the little girls ran to the doorway, peered in and waved, then took off again, squealing. Mom shook her head and looked distressed.

"Just do whatever you want, honey." Sighing again, she handed

Miranda a large metal ring full of keys. "Room angles would be helpful—locations of windows and doors—even though most of the upstairs bedrooms are all the same. Some long shots of the galleries. Some nice views of the grounds in front, with all those trees leading up. And any little details you notice? Like carvings or moldings . . . some of the ceilings have friezes . . . anything that looks really old . . . I'd love to have pictures of those. Oh, and take these keys. You can keep them—I made you a set."

"Aunt Teeta said there were a few things that probably came from the original house." Instinctively, Miranda glanced around the room, but saw nothing. "What are those, do you know?"

"I have a list of them . . . somewhere . . ." Rifling back and forth through a file folder, Mom paused, then frowned. "Honestly, even with my main office in town, I could sure use a *real* office here. Don't worry, I'll find it for you. Oh—and those other things you wanted. The house photo and the letter. I'm sure I'll remember where I put them by the time you come back. Right now I've got to go check on the kitchen."

"Okay, Mom. See you in a while."

"And be careful. Stay away from those dangerous spots."

"I will."

Taking the digital camera, she roamed leisurely through the downstairs, exploring rooms that she hadn't explored before. She still didn't see Etienne—she guessed he was probably helping his mom with the appliance deliveries—but from time to time various workmen strolled past, stopping to examine walls or floors or ceilings, greeting her with friendly smiles. This main level was even larger than it had appeared last night. As she wandered in and out of connecting doorways, she began to snap pictures and keep a sharp eye out for . . . *what?* She wasn't sure; she had only her instincts to guide her. She suddenly realized that she'd been guarding herself, holding herself in, ever since she and Mom had driven onto the property. But now . . . cautiously . . . she allowed her senses to open.

Anything. Anything that might give me some clue about this house . . .

The sadness was still here—that part hadn't changed. Hanging thick in every room, like a wet, black fog. *Wet with tears . . . black for death . . .* Closing her eyes, Miranda focused harder . . . reached farther. From some distant place, she could almost hear laughter—faint and tinny, like an old music box—fading even as she listened. *Joyful laughter, childish laughter.* Weaving its way through the mournful fog . . .

The present came back to her, veiled in past sorrow. Rubbing a chill from her arms, she went out to the verandah and stood for a moment, gazing off through the oak-lined alleyway, toward the bayou. She could see the swing hanging motionless from the tree limb. She snapped some photographs, then followed the verandah around the entire first story of the house, not finding much more of interest along the way. Massive, empty rooms, practically identical, bare of much décor . . . a chandelier here and there . . . wooden doors, banisters, and fireplace mantels in various stages of polishing, refinishing, and repair . . . Mom's requested friezes and crown moldings covered in layers of dust . . . one area rug, rolled up in canvas. Nothing that touched her, called to her. No whisper of long-dead secrets.

Frustrated, Miranda moved on. Up the staircase at one end of the verandah, up to the gallery above. She wasn't ready to tour all the bedrooms yet; she leaned on the baluster and tilted her face into the air. A breeze blew off the bayou, through the moss-laced trees, cooling her cheeks. It was bittersweet, standing where they must have stood, gazing where they must have gazed, those people who lived here once upon a time. *You could see for miles from up here. Past the driveway under the oaks, beyond the formal gardens, up and down the dirt road leading to town, over all your acres of land, clear across the bayou . . .*

You were happy once. Blessed.

What happened to you, Belle Chandelle? How could anyone have abandoned you?

So perfect, this spot, for some reason. This sheltered spot of calm and beauty, even though power tools hummed in the background and bulldozers crushed through the fields on all sides. The air grew thick around her. Thick and hot and suffocating, shutting out every sound of renovation . . . every sound of progress . . . *every sound of today . . .*

"Wait," Miranda whispered, "please wait . . ."

But she could already feel it happening—that strange but not unpleasant sensation of being removed to some different place. Some close but hidden place where she could watch herself frozen there, helpless on the gallery.

Where she could watch the tragic woman reaching out to her . . . a pale, misty hand passing cold through Miranda's heart, as if Miranda herself didn't even exist . . .

Dark hair pulled back, messy . . . strands limp around her haggard face; she's exhausted, empty, she hasn't slept in days, many days and nights, not for a very, very long time. The dark lace cap on top of her hair . . . and her dark collar, dark dress, black, smells sharp strong metallic rotted sour—

Eyes! Eyes full of horror, desperation—panicky pleading praying but still no one hears—unnatural eyes, brittle-yellow-photograph eyes, brittle-yellow-photograph skin, but the eyes are cloudy, foggy with despair—red coming through showing through red blurring her beautiful eyes, murky beautiful bloodshot eyes—

Miranda's breath came faster; she couldn't cry out, but she couldn't turn away. In a hazy rush, she heard carriage wheels trundling up the road—*why aren't they stopping?*—glass shaking, rattling, breaking—*look! For God's sake, look at the window!—and feet stumbling, walls smeared red—creaking, creaking, slow steady rhythm monotonous creaking on and on and on . . .* I'm here—I'll always be here—*soft muffled crying, innocent laughter, the high-pitched laughter of children—*

"Stop!"

Miranda brought herself back. As the present came sharply into focus, she felt the breeze on her face, saw her knuckles clutched white on the railing. A sick swirl of helplessness rose up from her heart, filling her head, bringing tears to her eyes. *I can't do it right now. . . . I can't figure it out.* She felt drained and unsteady. Holding tighter, she peered down onto the lawn below and suddenly realized that a small part of reality must have penetrated her vision.

Coralee's little girls were running across the lawn, laughing and squealing, playing hide-and-seek among the trees. As

Miranda watched, they turned and ran off, disappearing around the corner of the house.

Her knees were still shaking, her stomach still queasy. Every sense told her that the woman wasn't here anymore, yet her eyes scanned the wide gallery, the row of tall French doors along one side, the delicate tendrils of moss cascading onto the balusters. *Was this your favorite place to stand, where I'm standing now? On the original gallery, of the original house?* Miranda's grip slowly loosened. *Who are you? How am I supposed to find out about you? And what awful tragedy happened to you here?*

For a brief second, she could almost swear that she was being watched. By invisible eyes, from some invisible place. And that a faint glimmer of music drifted past her, carried gently on the breeze.

No, not music. Laughter.

Soft, giggling laughter. Children's laughter.

"Come and find us!"

Of course. Not ghostly laughter . . . Coralee's girls. With a sigh of relief, Miranda started walking to the far side of the gallery.

"Okay, you two! I hear you playing!"

The giggles came again, louder this time and more delighted.

"Come and *find* us!"

"How about I find you downstairs, okay? It's not safe to be running around up here."

They must have come up another stairway, she reasoned. There were four different sets of exterior stairs, one at each corner of the house—it would have been easy for the girls to slip up here unnoticed. *Especially in the zoned-out state I was in.*

But as she approached the end of the gallery, she saw no sign of the girls. She noticed only a pair of French doors standing halfway open, showing the dark, vacant room beyond.

"Girls?" Miranda called. A stab of uneasiness went through her. She was sure the voices had come from this direction, but maybe the kids had already retreated back to the first floor.

And then she heard the giggling again. Inside the empty room.

"Come on, I mean it." Hands on hips, Miranda planted herself in the doorway. Heavy shadows hung like black crepe, and dust motes thickened the stale, still air. "I mean it—it's not safe up here. Come out *now*, or I'm calling your mom."

The giggling stopped. Abruptly, chillingly. Miranda could hear time passing . . . could hear the wary beat of her own heart . . .

And the small, choked, frightened sob . . .

"Mama?"

"Is that you?" her voice asked, but it seemed to come from somewhere outside her, a voice in slow motion. "Girls, is that you? Tell me where you are."

The child was afraid—she could feel it in that cry, coming from somewhere inside the room, coming from somewhere inside the shadows, *somewhere no child should ever be—*

"Oh, God." Springing to action, Miranda began combing the guestroom—the walls, the floor, the fireplace—any area the girls might have gotten trapped. Because it *was* Coralee's girls, she kept telling herself, it *had* to be Coralee's girls, who else could it possibly be . . . ?

"Where are you?" she cried, half angry, half afraid. "Listen to me, girls—tell me where you are; I'm going to get you out of there!"

The cry came again. Muffled . . . just as frightened. And they were *both* crying now, she could hear their voices, two terrified little cries, only where *were* they, why couldn't she see them, there was nowhere else to search—

"Mama! Mama! Look at us!"

Miranda froze and stared. Impossible, she knew—yet the cries seemed to be coming from a spot against the wall, the back wall of the bedroom. Very slowly she ran her eyes over the surface, then noticed something she hadn't seen before. A wooden panel—a narrow door—concealed so cleverly in the woodwork that it was practically invisible. Hurrying over, she pounded on it and tried to pry it open.

"Hey!" she shouted. "Girls? Can you push from the other side? Just push the door if you can, okay?"

The crying grew worse. Heartbreaking sobs and whimpers. Pleas for their mother to save them. Despite her growing frustration, Miranda couldn't bear to hear those anguished cries.

"I'm here!" she reassured them. "Don't cry, I'm right here, I'm going to get you out!"

The panel moved a little. Putting her shoulder to the door, Miranda heard a groan of warped, damp wood giving way. And as the panel finally opened, she saw the narrow flight of stairs recessed in the wall behind it.

The sneak stairway.

The one Aunt Teeta had talked about, that ran from the main level all the way to the attic—

Oh my God. The attic.

It was obvious now, what had happened. The two little girls must have discovered the sneak stairs on the first floor, climbed inside to play, and then panicked when they couldn't get out again. And now they were still climbing . . . on their way to the attic and belvedere and certain danger.

Miranda wasted no time. Despite the close, winding passage, she raced up, shouting as she went. "Don't be scared, girls! I'm going to take you to your mom, okay?"

But it was so quiet. *Too* quiet. With a surge of panic, she reached the final step and the hidden door at the top of the stairwell.

A horrible stench washed over her. *Choking—suffocating—*dropping her to her knees while she gagged and fought desperately to breathe—*sweat urine vomit feces blood infection flies oozing sores rotting flesh baking heat festering heat—*

Miranda dragged herself to her feet. She pounded the door with her fists, but it wouldn't budge.

"Damn!" Even shoving as hard as she could, Miranda had no luck. It was as if the weight of the world were on the other side of that door, and her own strength couldn't begin to break it down. *What have those kids wedged up against that door?*

"Come out of there, you two! Open up!"

She remembered the keys. Yanking them from her pocket, she tried each of them in the lock, but to no avail. It was clear to her now that she wasn't going to get in this way. That the attic could mean only serious accidents; the belvedere, fatal falls. Not knowing what else to try, Miranda dashed back down the stairs all the way to the first floor, where she shoved open the camouflaged panel and fell out into one of the parlors, nearly scaring her mother to death.

"Good Lord, Miranda! What on earth are you doing—"

"Mom, Coralee's daughters, they were upstairs playing hide-and-seek—and I heard them in the stairwell—"

"Miranda—"

"And I tried to get them out, but they couldn't open the door, and I think an animal must have died up there—"

"Honey—"

"Is there another key or something? Or maybe we could use one of the ladders—"

"Stop." Squeezing Miranda's shoulders, Mom gave her a little shake. "Honey, stop. Calm down . . . take it easy."

"But Mom—"

"Miranda, I don't know what you heard, but it wasn't Coralee's girls."

"Yes! Mom, it was! Please, we have to hurry and get them—"

"Look. Just look."

Before Miranda could answer, her mother led her firmly across the room. Then, stopping at the open French doors, she pointed outside.

One of the little girls was on Etienne's shoulders; the other he was swinging around and around, by her hands, in a circle.

"But . . ." Miranda's throat closed up. She took a step back, suddenly weak. "They couldn't have gotten past me. It's impossible. They must have come down some other way."

"I guess they must have." Mom gave a puzzled smile. "Because they've been right out here all this time, playing with Etienne."

13

"**Miranda, are you all right?**"

"I . . ." Miranda's mind was racing. She braced herself against the wall, hugged herself tightly, tried to think.

"Honey, you're white as a sheet. Sit down; let me get you some water."

"I'm . . ." *Careful, Miranda. Pull yourself together; don't give anything away.* "I was just so scared, you know . . . that those kids might get to the attic."

"Well, of course you were. That attic is supposed to be kept locked, but you just never know."

"Mom, have you been here in the house the whole time?"

"I just got back here. I've been out in the kitchen."

"So . . ." It *could* be possible, she supposed. Panic, terror, a cramped, dark stairwell—time might easily have a way of getting distorted. And she *had* zoned out earlier, hadn't she? Those two little girls *could* have been playing hide-and-seek, playing a trick on her. *Yes, it* could *be possible.* Anything's *possible. . . .*

"Don't you want to sit down?" Mom worried. She forced a cup of water into Miranda's hand. "Drink this. I want to make sure you don't faint."

"I won't faint." Sipping her water, Miranda continued to gaze at Etienne. Coralee's girls were playing a new game now—

clinging to him, one on each side, squealing and trying to pull him in opposite directions. He was grubby and disheveled from work; his hair fell stubbornly over his cheeks and into his eyes. For several long minutes, he patiently endured the tug-of-war, then without warning, grabbed both girls in his arms and gave them a fierce tickling. Laughing and screaming at the top of their lungs, the two of them took off on a merry chase across the lawn and down the alleyway of oak trees.

Stretching, Etienne shoved his hair back from his face, and saw Miranda watching him.

"How long have you children been having fun out here?" she asked him. Though the matter was serious, she couldn't resist teasing him a little.

Etienne seemed faintly embarrassed. "Why? You gonna dock my pay?"

"I was just wondering." Pausing, she could sense his swift, keen appraisal. "When you started playing with the kids . . . did they come out of the house?"

"*Mais*, I don't know. They ambushed me behind those trees over there."

She wanted so much to believe it—that the little girls had somehow tricked her and run back down the sneak stairway. That the pitiful crying that she'd heard had come from real, live, flesh-and-blood children . . .

But she knew it wasn't true.

Deep down inside, she knew it wasn't true. And in that terrible, dark place where no child should ever go, two lost children were waiting for her to find them.

"Why you so interested in those kids, *cher*?"

Miranda wiped quickly at a blur of tears. "No reason."

"Don't be lying to me now. You got that look on your face."

"What look?"

"The one that says you just saw or heard something nobody else can see or hear."

He stepped close, strong fingers gripping her elbows, body brushing lightly against hers. No hint of awkwardness now, their argument apparently forgotten. Miranda stared at the front of his T-shirt; the damp trails of sweat; the long, dirty streaks where he'd carelessly wiped his hands.

"I saw the woman again," she told him softly. "On the gallery this time, not in a mirror. And I heard some children. Laughing at first, then scared and crying. I thought it was Coralee's girls, that they'd gotten lost on the sneak stairs."

Listening intently, Etienne gave her an encouraging nod. Then shot a curious, sidelong glance at the house.

"But maybe," Miranda went on, "maybe they're connected somehow—the woman and the children. And maybe those poor kids are lost in a different place. A dark, empty place where they're all alone."

"And you think something mighta happened to them here? Something bad happened to the kids?"

Miranda shook her head. "I don't know. The feelings I had . . . those heartbreaking cries . . . it was all really, really intense. And the smell—"

"What smell?"

"I almost threw up, it was so awful. Like something died in the attic—"

"No smell, *cher*," he murmured. "No smell—"

"Are you absolutely sure?"

"I was up there just a while ago. I think I woulda smelled something that bad, yeah?"

Miranda gave a reluctant nod. "I was *sure* Coralee's girls were trapped behind that wall . . . that they were headed straight for trouble in the attic."

"You actually heard them going up there?"

"I followed them. Well . . . I followed the *voices*. But I couldn't get the panel open. I couldn't figure out how they'd managed to drag something so heavy up against the door."

"But you were hearing them *inside* the attic?"

Frowning, Miranda thought back. A flicker of uncertainty went across her face. "No. When I got to the attic, it was totally quiet. Which scared me even more. That's when I figured they'd come back downstairs . . . except there's no way they could have gotten past me."

For a long moment neither of them spoke. Then Etienne broke the silence.

"So what about the woman? Why you thinking she's connected with those kids?"

"I don't know. It's just . . ." Miranda gave him a wry smile. "I *feel* it."

"Can't argue with that."

"If you'd seen the expression on her face—how frantic she

was. It's obvious she's begging for help." As thoroughly as she could, Miranda recalled the details of her vision. "She's worn out by something, Etienne . . . beaten down by something. I can feel her panic, but I can feel her helplessness, too. It's like she doesn't have any strength left. No . . . no will. Nothing left inside her."

"Maybe that's how come she couldn't touch you, *cher*—why her hand passed on through."

"What do you mean?"

"Maybe it's more than just being a ghost. Maybe her spirit died a long time before *she* died."

Miranda blinked away fresh tears. "After that, is when I heard the children playing."

"Well, yeah, that does seem connected."

"But also—when I first heard the kids' voices—they were saying, 'Come and find us.' And I didn't think about it then, because I just assumed it was Coralee's girls playing hide-and-seek, you know? But now . . ."

"Now," Etienne said quietly, "you're thinking maybe those kids were calling for *you*? *You* specifically . . . for help?"

"I think . . . they were terrified and needed their mother. And they couldn't find her. And . . . maybe they were trying to get *my* attention because—"

"'Cause they knew they could."

"Yes. Because—somehow—they knew they could."

"So . . . maybe they got something to do with that swing yesterday?"

Miranda nodded. His hands, still resting on her arms, began

a slow ascent to her shoulders . . . slid reassuringly over her back. A warm, shivery feeling went through her.

"Damn." Tilting his head, Etienne gazed up thoughtfully through the trees. "You been busy, *cher*."

In spite of everything, Miranda had to laugh. "Yes. Welcome to my wild, busy, exciting life." Then, solemn once more, she tugged on his shirt, forcing his attention back. "I've been thinking about something else, too."

"Me?"

She frowned him a look.

"Uh-oh." He winced. "Not Gage, I hope."

"I'm serious."

"So am I."

"Mom said some workers quit this morning."

"Yeah, I heard that—"

"Because they had a weird feeling about the house. And Mom said that's never really happened before. And I can't help thinking it's because of me. That because I came out here, other spirits who've never . . . I don't know . . . had a way out for all these years, have sort of . . . woken up."

"What I keep telling you, *cher*? You're not even *close* to tapping those powers of yours—you're gonna be *way* stronger than your *grandpère* ever was."

"Hey. Even though I'm all into helping unhappy spirits, I do *not* like the idea of walking around being a constant ghost magnet."

He stared down at her. The flicker of amusement in his eyes narrowed to shrewd intensity. "How many more times I gotta say it, then? That's why you got *me*. And no, before you even start thinking it, *not* just 'cause I promised your *grandpère*—"

"Hey, you two!" As her mom shouted from the open doorway, Miranda stumbled back out of Etienne's reach. "Sorry to interrupt, but I could sure use some help taking stuff to my car! And I'm talking *heavy* stuff!"

"I'm on it!" Lifting one hand in acknowledgment, Etienne winked at Miranda and strode off toward the house. Miranda started to follow, then suddenly remembered her mom's camera. At some point during her panicky experience on the gallery, she'd dropped it and left it behind. Now she wasn't at all sure that she wanted to go up there again and retrieve it.

She needn't have worried. The camera was lying just where she thought it would be, right where she'd had her vision. Still unsettled, she glanced nervously down the length of the gallery, then beat a hasty retreat and headed off behind the house to the kitchen.

Apparently, all the deliveries had been made. There wasn't a soul around that Miranda could see, but as she walked across the old tiles; around the long, functional trestle table; beside the wide brick hearth and big iron cooking pots, she heard an awful clanging and clattering from behind the rear wall.

"Miss Nell?" she called, though now there was only silence. "Miss Nell, are you here?"

Miranda peered through the connecting doorway. At once she spotted Miss Nell leaning forward against the counter, pots and pans scattered around her feet.

"Oh my God—Miss Nell, are you—"

"Fine." Instantly the woman turned, coming to greet her, taking Miranda's hands, squeezing them tightly in her own. "I'm just fine, honey. You know, I've had so much caffeine today, and then I skipped lunch—I *know* better. Made me totally light-headed for a second."

"Are you sure?"

"Yes! Of course."

But Miranda wasn't convinced. The woman's face was totally drained of color, her forehead shone with sweat. Her touch was too cold, and though she always appeared frail when Miranda saw her, she seemed even frailer now, her dark eyes unusually bright.

"Miranda, I'm so glad you stopped by." Miss Nell was pulling her gently, guiding her to a tall wooden stool in the corner. "Sit down, honey, while I clean up this mess I made—"

"Miss Nell, do you want some water—"

"No, don't you budge. It'll only take me a second."

Quickly, she gathered the pots and pans. After stacking them at the end of the counter, she reached down into a cooler on the floor, took out two soft drinks, and handed one to Miranda.

"No air-conditioning in here yet—Etienne swears it'll be in by the weekend. But isn't this wonderful? All these pretty things?" The woman spread her arms, indicating the shiny, new appliances surrounding them. Despite her wan appearance, her voice was excited and happy. "By tomorrow, we'll have cold drinks in the fridge. And hot food in the oven and on the stove."

"That's great," Miranda agreed. Despite her concern, she began to relax a little; at least Miss Nell didn't seem quite so shaky as she had a few minutes ago. "But I especially like that other part of the kitchen—the reproduction. It looks real. Like the servants are going to walk in any second and start fixing dinner."

"That's exactly what we're hoping guests will think too. Once it's finished, we'd like to do cooking demonstrations out there. Fix recipes that would have been served back then. Show how to cook in the fireplace. Bake in the brick ovens. How to grow herbs and use a real kitchen garden."

Miranda couldn't help but be fascinated; Miss Nell's quiet enthusiasm was contagious.

"What about recipes?" Miranda prompted, and was glad when the woman smiled. *A sweet smile, a determined smile— determined to be brave, to be happy—but sad, too . . . old beyond her years . . . very, very tired . . .*

You're scared of something, Miss Nell. Something you've hidden very well but not quite deep enough, because I can sense it, right down here—

"My own recipes, when we had our restaurant," Miss Nell was saying, and Miranda snapped back to attention.

"Aunt Teeta told me about that. You had a really great restaurant here in St. Yvette—a long time ago, right?"

"It was pretty popular, and customers had their own personal favorites. I need to get back in shape, though." Pulling up another stool, Miss Nell sank down and perched on the edge. She gave an exaggerated shudder. "It's been a long time since I cooked for that many people. Though come to think of it, that's probably not so different from cooking for two teenage boys."

"You mean Gage and Etienne," Miranda said, and the

woman's smile widened. "You and Gage's mom are really close, aren't you? I mean, being sisters and all."

"Extremely close. Jules and I are twins, though we don't look alike." Miss Nell paused, went thoughtful. "That's one reason Jules and Frank decided to move here, you know. When the boys were small. We wanted them to have each other . . . to grow up together and experience some of that closeness."

Miranda considered this. "Gage told me once that Etienne's not close to anyone . . . but that if he were, he'd probably be closest to Gage. And I know—we *all* know—he's close to you."

"Close to making me crazy, is what you mean." Chuckling, she slowly shook her head. "Etienne *is* closest to Gage, and vice versa. Even when they were little, they always had each other's backs."

The image made Miranda smile. "So how old was Gage when he came to St. Yvette?"

"They moved here from Natchez when Gage was five. And Etienne was six."

"Really?" Miranda was only mildly surprised. "I didn't know that . . . but Etienne *always* seems older to me."

"He got held back a grade. He . . ." A quick, dark cloud passed over Miss Nell's face. "He missed too much school. He was . . . sick a lot."

Because of those scars on his arms . . . those beatings from his father . . .

"So," Miranda redirected, "I guess it's like Gage and Etienne have always had two families?"

"Absolutely. And it's good for them. Keeps them both in line."

Miranda found the concept hilarious. The thought of this tiny woman keeping Gage and Etienne in line. Though she had no doubt that Miss Nell could do it—and did it often.

"When our boys were little, if Etienne needed a firm hand, Jules and Frank had my full cooperation—not to mention my blessing. And the same went for Gage, when *he* needed correcting." Miss Nell paused, raised an eyebrow. "Though I don't recall Gage needing *nearly* as much correcting as Etienne."

"Those big, brown eyes," Miranda stated.

"Dimples!" They both laughed.

"Or," Miss Nell speculated, "maybe he was just sneakier at not getting caught."

"I don't know . . . Etienne's pretty sneaky, if you ask me."

Miss Nell was clearly amused. "And you seem to know him pretty well."

Miranda could feel her cheeks warming. "Not that well," she said quickly—too quickly. "Just . . . just a little well. Like I know Gage. Just sort of . . . well." *Great, Miranda. Nothing like being obvious.*

Miss Nell hadn't missed it, of course. She was still trying to keep a straight face. "So you think a lot of our boys, do you?"

"Gage and Etienne?" Miranda fumbled. "What I think of them?"

Again Miss Nell burst out laughing. "Not such a hard question, Miranda. One or two words will do."

"They . . . they . . ."

"They sure think a lot of you." A secret twinkled in the woman's eyes. "And *about* you."

Miranda didn't know what to say. For a split second, two distinct images flashed through her mind—Etienne's night-black stare, Gage's melt-your-heart smile. The two equally irresistible, just in different ways.

"And I could be all wrong about this," Miss Nell went on casually, getting up from her chair. "But my guess is, you like *them*, too." Pausing, she shot Miranda a knowing glance. "Both of them."

Blushing again, Miranda was at a loss. She watched silently as Miss Nell picked up a damp sponge, ran it over the countertop, then tossed it into the sink.

"Quite the catch, our boys." A dimple flashed in Miss Nell's cheek. "Either one of them."

"What, is this all girl talk going on in here?" As Etienne appeared in the doorway, Miranda avoided his eyes. She had no idea how long he'd been in the building, no idea how much of the conversation he'd heard. His face, of course, told her nothing. His mother only shrugged at him and dug down into the cooler for another soda.

"That's for us to know," she replied. Handing him the can, she pulled back and stared hard into his face. "And don't look so smug. You don't have a clue what important matters Miranda and I have been discussing."

She reached up to wipe dirt from his cheek. Clearly amused, Etienne ducked out of reach.

"Your mama, she's ready to leave," he informed Miranda. "Or I can bring you on home later, if you want."

"No, I better leave now." *Too much to think over . . . too much to sort out.* "Thanks, Miss Nell. I love your kitchen. And I hope I see you again soon."

"You can count on it." The woman gave her a quick hug. "I'm sure we'll find lots to talk about."

Etienne's eyes narrowed suspiciously. "Like what?"

"Like it doesn't concern you." Miss Nell turned back to her new refrigerator. Muttering under his breath, Etienne shepherded Miranda outside.

"I love your mom," Miranda told him. "I'm so glad she's going to be here."

Nodding, he squatted down to retie one of his boots. "Yeah, this is gonna be good for her. It's making her happy. She's just loving to be busy in the kitchen again."

"Listen . . . will you do me a favor?"

"Sure, I'll come up to your room tonight."

"I'm serious."

"So am I."

"That's *not* what I was going to ask you."

She swung at him as he stood up. Catching her fist, he jerked her against him and steadied her in his arms.

"I mean it!" she scolded, though she couldn't help laughing. "I need to tell the others what's going on. And I've really been trying to, but it's never been a good time."

For just a moment, she surrendered. Let herself relax against him; her body fit with his.

"Miranda?" a voice called.

Jumping, she tried to disentangle herself while Etienne

deliberately held her closer. Miss Nell was standing right outside the kitchen door, assessing things with a split-second glance.

"Honey, why don't you come for Sunday dinner?" Miss Nell asked, expression perfectly composed.

"I—I—" Miranda twisted, but to no avail. Etienne glanced from her to his mother with a carefully hidden smile.

"Etienne can pick you up," Miss Nell went on smoothly. "How about six? Okay, good."

She raised an eyebrow at Etienne. Shook her finger. He replied with an innocent shrug.

"I can't believe you just did that to me!" Miranda railed, though he only held her tighter.

"You were saying . . . about the meeting, *cher*," he reminded her, all business.

Miranda made an exasperated sound in her throat. "Just be there. Be there with me when I tell them."

"And where is this gonna be happening?"

"A public place," Miranda grimaced. "So Parker can't kill me."

14

"MIRANDA, I'M GOING TO KILL YOU," PARKER SAID. Rising halfway from the bench, he made a sweeping gesture of the schoolyard. "It doesn't even matter if there are people around. No sane jury in the world would convict me."

Miranda had the grace to look sheepish. "Sorry, Parker. It's not like I have a choice."

Sometime during the night, autumn had finally arrived, gusting all the hot weather away. The air was cool now, and fresh—the mood across campus, noticeably lighter. A few kids had thrown on ridiculous Halloween costumes. A few more were running and laughing, tossing candy. As a shower of candy corn rained down on Parker's head, he yelled out his opinion and plopped back down on the bench.

"So how come you waited to tell us?" Roo asked Miranda. Opening a small plastic container, she peered down at the wet glob of food inside. "It just makes sense to tell us from the beginning. That way, we don't miss any good stuff. Or waste any time."

"I tried to," Miranda assured her. "I wanted to. But there were too many other things going on."

As Roo placed her lunch on the table, Parker instantly recoiled. "What the *hell* is that?"

Roo tipped the container on edge. Set it back down again. "Some kind of casserole, I think."

"You think? Don't you know?"

Leaning sideways, Gage gave the meal a cursory glance. "How long has that been in your refrigerator? It's black."

"So?" Roo's stare was mildly irritated. "What are you, a food critic?"

"No, and I'm not a paramedic, either. So don't eat it."

"Oh, Miranda, you should always tell us," Ashley insisted, reaching across the table, squeezing Miranda's hand. "You should always tell us *anything!* And . . . *everything!*"

Despite Parker, Miranda felt that her announcement had gone well. She'd waited till they were all gathered outside for lunch. She'd waited for a lull in the conversation. And then, after an encouraging nod from Etienne, she'd dropped her bombshell.

The reactions had been varied. And predictable.

Ashley had gotten emotional over the children on the stairs; Gage had once again volunteered his time and research skills. Parker, looking stubborn, had pulled back and not offered anything at all. Roo's comment had been wise and matter-of-fact—"See? I knew you were picking up spirit vibes that day in the car." And Etienne, silently observing, had seemed amused.

"Please don't do this again, Miranda," Ashley pleaded. "You don't have to go through these things by yourself. It's too hard, and we want to help you. In fact, we *like* helping you."

Parker's reply was muffled by a large bite of taco. Gage offered Miranda a heartening smile.

"She's right, you know. We all have different ideas, different perspectives—"

"Different talents," Etienne broke in.

Roo leveled him a stare. "I like *your* talent best. I hear you win first prize in every contest you enter."

Etienne winked. Roo smiled slyly and turned back to her lunch.

"Different information about stuff," Gage went on, as though he'd never been interrupted.

"Thanks, you guys." Miranda smiled at each of them in turn. "*Thank you*, Parker."

Parker's snort was derisive. "Don't thank *me*, *I'm* not helping. Did you even *hear* me say I'm helping? Because . . . you know . . . I'm *not.*"

"So the woman you saw in the mirror," Gage prompted Miranda, "do you think she's connected to the children somehow?"

"I don't know," Miranda answered truthfully. "But that look on her face . . . in her eyes . . . it's so intense. It goes right through me. I think that's the kind of desperation only a mother would feel for her kids."

Ashley was starting to look weepy again. "You said they were calling for their mom. And they sounded scared."

"At first they didn't." Miranda frowned, thinking back. "At first they were just playing . . . well, it *sounded* like playing. Like some game—"

"Like the swing that night," Etienne broke in. "Little kids having fun, not being scared."

Again, Miranda let her mind go back. "Whatever—whoever—it was, didn't *seem* scared. The footsteps were light and quick, definitely not grown-up. And they came right to me."

"Maybe you surprised them," Roo suggested. "And they ran into you because they didn't realize you were there."

"Or maybe they *did* realize," Gage added quietly. "When they first saw you . . . or sensed you . . . maybe that's when they realized you could help them."

Remembering the ghostly touch on her hand, Miranda shivered. "It's like they're leaving me this weird trail of clues, you know? First the games . . . and then afterwards on the stairs—that's when they sounded so lost. Really frightened and sad."

"And calling for their mother," Ashley whispered, still upset.

Parker kept a straight face. "Maybe they got stuck in the wall and died."

"Parker Wilmington, that is a terrible thing to say!"

"Why is that terrible? Miranda just got through saying she heard them hollering in the wall—"

"They were crying," Miranda corrected. "And calling for her, but not loud. They sounded . . . faraway."

"Afterlife far enough away for you?"

Ashley clapped her hand over his mouth. Parker pulled it away, grinned, and kissed her fingers. It seemed that Ashley had forgiven him for his behavior the day before.

"Even if they *had* gotten stuck inside the wall"—Miranda gave Parker a scolding look—"which seems *very* unlikely—someone would have found them."

"Maybe not." Parker shrugged. "If nobody else was there."

"Well, of course someone else was there—someone else was *always* there. The house servants used those stairs all the time. And their mother probably knew all their hiding places."

"They were rich," Roo pointed out. "They would have had a nanny."

Parker's reaction was immediate—and disdainful. "Then trust me. Their mom was totally clueless about what they did each day."

An uncomfortable silence fell. As knowing glances criss-crossed the table—*Parker's childhood, Parker's too-busy-to-be-bothered parents*—Ashley tried to keep the discussion going.

"Maybe it's just that they were happy there . . . and then they *weren't* happy there. I mean . . . something happened to make them *not* happy there."

"Ashley logic." Parker patted her head. "That's my girl."

Amused, Gage twirled his soft drink can between his fingers. "It sort of . . . makes sense. If the kids were really happy, the house would've held on to that happiness. But if they were also really sad . . . the house would've held on to that, too."

"Two major reasons for ghosts to be hanging around, yeah?" Etienne shot a glance at Miranda. "Deep happiness and deep sadness."

Ashley squirmed excitedly in her seat. "So maybe it's just their emotions you're supposed to pay attention to! And the game on the stairs is more like a . . . a symbol! Just a symbol of their happiness, not an honest-to-goodness clue!"

"I'm not sure." Miranda mulled this over. "The way they kept calling for me to come and find them, while Coralee's girls were outside playing hide-and-seek. It just seems like too much of a coincidence. But I also don't see how a game—even if they *did* get lost for a while—has anything to do with their mother and how frantic she looked."

"Tell us about her again," Roo said, and Miranda did so. Listening intently, Roo was so focused on Parker's last taco that he nervously moved it to the far edge of the table. "Her eyes," Roo stated, when Miranda had finished. "You said her eyes were red?"

"Forget it, Roo," Etienne teased. "I'm sure she wasn't a vampire."

Miranda almost smiled at that. "Bloodshot. They looked really bloodshot. I kept thinking how exhausted she was. Just . . . if I could have seen her move, I'm sure she'd have been weak and staggering around—"

"Dead on her feet?" Parker looked pleased with himself while everyone else groaned.

"I think you're right," Roo assured Miranda. "From the description, it sounds like she was sick. And that cap on her head . . . with her hair pulled back . . . she was probably married. Single girls wore their hair down."

"Where do you get this stuff?" Parker asked, both curious and annoyed.

"Louisiana History, eighth grade. Gage and I had the mother of all term papers."

"Which *Gage and I* wrote," Ashley couldn't help reminding her.

Roo merely shrugged. Nibbling halfheartedly on a pretzel,

Miranda watched dead leaves and stray bits of litter somersault over the grass.

"Her clothes," Miranda mumbled. "When I saw the woman this time, her clothes were a lot more real somehow. A lot more detailed."

Parker offered a sage nod. "Right. Real clothes on a not-real person. Makes sense to me."

"Parker, if you don't shush—" Ashley warned.

Miranda tried to concentrate. "They were all so black . . . *more* than black. Her dress, her collar, her cap, every button and piece of lace—I know this sounds weird, but it's like her clothes were a color . . . and a *feeling*."

Miranda didn't realize that she was shivering. Not till Gage leaned toward her and began to gently rub the chill from her arms. And then . . .

"Those are funeral clothes," Miranda murmured, the truth slowly dawning. "She's in mourning."

An uneasy quiet settled over the table. Almost at once, Parker began attacking his lunch, rustling paper, rattling plastic cutlery.

"Oh, Miranda." Ashley seemed dangerously close to tears again. "Do you think her children died? And she wants you to find them?"

"But they're all in the same place, yeah?" Etienne frowned. "The mama, her kids—Miranda's seen all of them at the house already."

"But the first time she saw the woman wasn't at Belle Chandelle, right Miranda? It was on the wall in our den!"

"And what's that about, anyway?" Parker unexpectedly spoke

up. "If she belongs out there at the plantation, what the hell's she doing at Ashley's?"

Ashley's face instantly lost color. "You don't think she's coming to our house again, do you? Looking for Miranda or--"

"She was in that mosaic," Roo cut in dryly. "She could have been anywhere, so why there?"

"The mirrors." Satisfied that Miranda had stopped shaking, Gage settled back in place. "It's made of all those little mirror pieces—"

"But what does that have to do with anything?" Miranda frowned, even as Etienne gestured toward the school.

"You had that weird thing going at your locker, remember?"

"But that wasn't her. I mean, I didn't actually *see* anyone."

"Then it *coulda* been. You can't be sure."

"There just doesn't seem to be any connection. This whole mirror thing doesn't make sense."

"You broke a mirror that morning," Roo said ominously.

Gage pointed at Miranda's palm. "And cut your hand."

"People cut their hands every day," Miranda grumbled, but Gage only smiled.

"Maybe you're not supposed to know any significance yet, Miranda. Maybe right now, it's just the way your ghost got in. The . . . open door between you and her."

"And what about that little ghost hand you felt by the swing?" Ashley piped up. "Maybe *that's* what connected you with those children."

"It . . . sort of makes sense, I guess," Miranda admitted grudgingly. "Even though I wish it didn't."

Lounging back against the edge of the table, Etienne crossed his arms, stretched out his legs, and focused on Roo. "You're looking awful serious, *cher.*"

"Forget serious," Parker corrected. "She just looks awful. As usual."

Roo grazed him with a stare. Then nodded at Etienne. "So we're pretty sure the ghost woman's in mourning. And she's also sick. With those shadows under her eyes, and the way her cheeks are kind of sunken—"

"I look like that when I've had too much beer," Parker scoffed. "Maybe she's really drunk."

"Maybe you're really dead."

Before Parker could respond, Miranda intervened. "My feeling was so strong about her being sick. And that maybe she'd been sick for a while. You know how sometimes when people are sick for a long time, you can see it in their faces? They have this certain look. Like . . ."

As she caught sight of Etienne's stoic face, her voice trailed away. She'd been thinking about her own bout with the flu; she hadn't meant to bring up any reminders of Miss Nell's cancer. *Oh my God . . . first Etienne's scars, and now this.* Horrified at her slip of the tongue, she sat there, miserably aware of everyone else trying to ignore what she'd done.

"Like . . . when you had the flu," Gage suddenly announced, way too casual. "You probably had bed hair."

"Yeah!" Parker jumped right on it. "Did the woman in the mirror have bed hair? Or maybe . . . bed cap?"

"Pillow face," Roo added, and Ashley burst out laughing.

Miranda shot Gage a grateful smile. Etienne, seeming all too aware of her discomfort, shrugged and shook his head: no big deal.

Not sure *what* to say now, Miranda chose her words more carefully. "And even though she *looked* sick, how could I know for sure? That first time, she was more like an old photograph. The way old photographs are shaded."

"That's right," Ashley recalled. "You said she looked more like an old *picture* than an actual *reflection*."

"Those old-fashioned tints, like old photographs have . . . and the way papery things always turn yellow and sort of brittle with age? It made her skin look yellow. So . . . maybe in a different light, *true* light . . . she wouldn't look so unhealthy."

"But still scared?"

"Yes, still scared. No colors could *ever* hide how panicky she was."

Frowning slightly, Gage shifted his leg to a more comfortable position. "Speaking of photographs," he reminded Miranda. "What about that letter and photograph your aunt Teeta was talking about? Have you seen them yet?"

"Mom made copies for me. I looked at them last night, but they seem pretty obvious—just like Aunt Teeta told us."

Roo jabbed a fork at her mystery lunch. "Refresh me on the letter and photo."

"The letter's written by a Yankee soldier—he talks about the Battle of St. Yvette and how his scouts have spotted this big plantation about a mile away, and they're going to see if there's anything left to raid. But they're not going to burn the house, they're going to stay in it instead."

"So how do you know it's the same place?" Parker stole Ashley's napkin, wiped salsa from his upper lip. "How do you know he's even talking about Belle Chandelle?"

"Because he says something about a sign, they see a sign on the property . . . you know, quite a ways from the house."

"Well, they probably would have had a beautiful sign," Ashley imagined. "Or maybe one of those big arbor things curved over the driveway to the house." Resting her head on Parker's shoulder, she lapsed into dreaminess. "It probably would have been close to the road, don't you think? Right at the front of the property. To welcome everybody who passed by. And let everybody know the name of the plantation."

"They find the name Belle Chandelle written on the sign— but the soldier says it's all overgrown with weeds and stuff. That the sign is so camouflaged, they almost missed it."

"Maybe the plantation had already fallen on hard times." Parker's shrug was dismissive. "Slaves off fighting or run away . . . no crops . . . no money . . ."

"Maybe. The soldier *does* say the whole place looks quiet and deserted, that they shouldn't have much trouble taking it."

"That wouldn't be so unusual," Gage noted. "Some families took off when they heard the Yankees were coming. Just left everything behind."

"But some of them didn't have anywhere else to go." Ashley's tone went sad. "Just think of all the ones who stayed. And tried to hang on to their homes. And be there when their husbands came back. And their sons came back. And their brothers came back. And their uncles—"

"We get it, Ash." Parker finished his taco. Wadded his napkin. Tossed it into Roo's half-empty container. "So did you bring these great pieces of history with you today?" he grumbled at Miranda, seeming resigned to his fate.

"They're in my locker."

"Could I borrow them?" Pushing aside his unfinished lunch, Gage reached for his crutches, hoisted himself to his feet. "I've got to leave early for the doctor . . . but I'm always in the waiting room forever. And I'm really tired of those twenty-year-old magazines."

"Sure. I'll grab them when we go in."

"What about the pictures?" Roo asked suddenly.

Everyone looked at her, puzzled. Roo looked back at them, unfazed.

"The camera you used yesterday," she told Miranda. "At the plantation. What about the pictures you took?"

Miranda still didn't get it. "Mom said she was going to get them printed after she brought me to school this morning."

"There could be something on that memory card, you know. Ghosts. Some kind of spirit activity."

"Are you kidding?"

"You could have photographed a ghost and not even realized. You could have surprised him . . . caught him off guard."

"I hope he wasn't naked." Parker shot Miranda a reproachful glance. "Shame on you, Miranda. Taking porno shots of ghosts—"

"Parker," Ashley broke in sternly, "this is serious."

"Hey, we could start our own website. The Paranormal Peeping Tom. Or would that be Peeping Miranda—"

"*Parker!*"

But Miranda's attention had stayed on Roo. "There wasn't anything weird about the pictures I was taking. It's a digital camera—I saw all the images while I was shooting. And there wasn't anything there that shouldn't have been there."

"That's just it." Roo solemnly returned her gaze. "Just because you didn't see anything weird *then*—or any ghosts *then*—doesn't mean they won't show up when the pictures get printed. God, Miranda, don't you ever watch that stuff on TV?"

"Roo's right," Gage agreed. "As intense as your visions were yesterday, there's no telling *what* you might've picked up on camera."

"I do *not* want to hear this." Fidgeting anxiously in her seat, Miranda appealed to Etienne. "If there really *is* something there, I don't want Mom seeing—"

"I'll take care of it," Etienne assured her. "Where'd she drop off the memory card?"

"I . . . the drugstore, I think."

Etienne nodded. Shoving off from the table, he gave a long, leisurely stretch. "Just call and tell her I was stopping off there on my way to work. If we're lucky, she hasn't been by to get them yet."

"She's picking me up at two thirty. She wants me to have one last check-up at the doctor."

"Me, I'll be gone by then, *cher*. No problem."

"I just wonder what kinds of great pictures you could take out there after dark." Roo seemed slightly stunned at the prospect. "Can you imagine? Or during a storm? The conditions would be a million times better."

Parker reared back, regarded her with cool disbelief. "You'd actually go out there to that big dead house. And wander around with a camera. And go into those pitch-black rooms to take pictures. Of nothing."

"Oh, don't worry—we know y'all are having your fun little guys' sleepover out there tonight. We wouldn't *dream* of crashing your party."

"They are?" Ashley asked, surprised. "Is this like, a celebrate-Gage's-leg party or something?"

"Okay. Who's the spy? As if I didn't know." Parker frowned at Roo. "And yeah, Ash. We're honoring Gage's leg. With a special welcome-home celebration."

"But don't say anything," Gage echoed, managing a straight face. "It's a surprise. My leg doesn't know."

"There's a cake with its name on it," Etienne added. "And balloons."

"And *no girls allowed*," Parker finished.

"And like we'd even want to." Roo's tone was as patronizing as her stare. "But as long as you're there, why don't you big brave heroes do some serious investigating on your own?"

"Maybe we will," Parker threw back at her. "In fact, maybe we'll solve the whole Belle Chandelle mystery tonight."

The three girls exchanged glances. And began to laugh.

"Right." Roo nodded. "And maybe I'll be wearing a bikini to school tomorrow."

Parker immediately grimaced. "Jesus, Roo. That's even scarier than Halloween."

Miranda was glad to be staying home that night.

While Mom worked late at the office, Aunt Teeta made a big batch of blueberry pancakes, country ham, and buttery grits for the two of them, then they ate together in the kitchen, talking and laughing and enjoying each other's company. Afterward, Miranda gave out candy to a steady stream of little trick-or-treaters while Aunt Teeta watched her favorite TV shows. Etienne called around nine to confirm that he'd picked up the photos—and that they were perfectly normal. Relieved, Miranda headed upstairs to her room to finish up the small bit of homework she had.

She was surprised when Aunt Teeta knocked on her door about eleven o'clock; even more surprised when Aunt Teeta asked if she could run an errand.

"Now?" Miranda was puzzled. "Does Mom need something?"

"No, but Etienne does."

"Etienne?"

Laughing heartily, Aunt Teeta nearly shook the curlers off her head. She already had on her nightgown and robe and favorite kitty slippers.

"Those boys, bless their hearts! You know, darlin', I asked Etienne to go out to Belle Chandelle tonight and kind of keep an eye on the place? With it being Halloween and all, and you just never know about kids playing pranks. Well, I just called his cell phone to check on him, and guess what? Gage and Parker offered to go out there too, and keep him company! Now, wasn't that sweet?"

Miranda didn't think *sweet* quite described it. God only knew what sort of stupid guy-things the three of them were doing out there. But she humored Aunt Teeta with a smile. Then tried to focus back on her studying.

"I just feel so sorry for them." Aunt Teeta clucked her tongue sympathetically. "I told them the least I could do was bring them some food."

Uh-oh, this can't be good. And though Aunt Teeta didn't say anything for several long seconds, Miranda had a sneaking suspicion where this was headed.

"Now, I know this is an imposition, darlin'—and I wouldn't ask you to do it otherwise—it's just that I can't see worth a darn to drive at night, and that ole road out there is so dark . . ."

"Just have it delivered," Miranda interrupted. "Just call some pizza place and have it delivered."

"It's almost midnight—this is St. Yvette, hon. There's nothing open this late on a weeknight. But I've got all kinds of fixin's for po-boys and there's plenty of that carrot cake left over. Oh, and what about the macaroni salad—"

"Aunt Teeta, Miss Nell probably left them tons of stuff in the fridge. I really don't think you need to worry—"

"Well, actually." Cupping one hand around her mouth, Aunt Teeta gave an exaggerated whisper, "I wouldn't be a bit surprised if those hungry, growin' boys already ate everything in Nell's fridge *and* pantry. Now . . . I really hate to ask, but . . ."

Oh no, Aunt Teeta—do not *do this to me.* "Why can't one of the guys just come here and pick it up?"

"Because I just don't feel right, asking them to drive all the way back *here*, when they're out *there* doing me a favor! That wouldn't be polite. Now, you're still dressed—I'll hurry with those sandwiches, and you take my car. And put on a jacket. It's actually feeling cold out there!"

Miranda couldn't believe it. Here she was, tucked in all safe and warm and happy, and of all the places she *didn't* want to go, it was Belle Chandelle. She wished she had the nerve to just refuse—but what could she say? By the time the food was ready, she was more agitated than ever. She grabbed a jacket and Aunt Teeta's keys, and stood there frowning with an overloaded picnic basket in her arms.

"Now, be sure and hold it from the bottom," Aunt Teeta instructed her. "It's mighty heavy. And I boxed up a couple big jugs of tea in the trunk—and a couple thermoses of hot cocoa. And some cider. Oh, and a few other little things I thought the boys would like. That should just about cover it, I think."

"Why don't I just take the whole kitchen?"

"Darlin', this is such a nice thing the boys are doing for us."

Miranda grunted. "Will the gate be locked? You better show me which key to use."

"I'll call the boys as soon as you leave, so they can be waiting for you in the parking lot. And take a flashlight—there's one in the backseat!"

Miranda was still grumbling to herself when she drove off.

The country road seemed even longer tonight, even blacker—a bottomless-well black that pressed too close around her. The sky was starless, and the chilly breeze that had finally blown in whipped ragged clouds across the moon, keeping it mostly hidden, snuffing out its pale gray light . . . Miranda turned on the heater, but still shivered. It was silly, she kept telling herself— but there was a sad sense of foreboding hanging over her. *No, not hanging over me . . . deep inside my bones . . .*

At last she reached the parking lot and pulled inside. Twisted shadows writhed across the ground, macabre distortions of empty construction equipment. The sky seemed to shrink into itself . . . grow darker. The wind felt raw. Where were the guys? Why weren't they out here to meet her?

She sat there for a while, trying to decide what to do. *Wait till someone comes? Turn around and go home? She wished Aunt Teeta hadn't crammed so much food into the car;* the smells were making her sick. *I'm going to kill those guys!* It would serve them right if she left, but Aunt Teeta would be so disappointed. And anyway, she couldn't very well drive all the way back in a reeking car, could she? Great, Miranda. Won't this be fun, lugging a two-ton basket and a big flashlight, and trying to keep an eye out for . . .

For what?

She was beginning to learn that the people who stalked her were invisible and silent. Protected from flashlights and the sharpest of ears. *So what do you expect could be out here tonight? The woman in the mirror? The children on the stairs?*

Countless other spirits trapped there in the house, in the fields, in the memories of Belle Chandelle?

"Well, I haven't got all night," she muttered, and got out of the car. Fumbling with the basket, she balanced it in her arms and clutched the flashlight in her right hand. It was awkward, but manageable. *If something scares me, I'll attack it with macaroni salad and run.*

That made her smile, a little. But *damn* that Etienne. And *Gage*! She'd expected at least *one* of them to show up. She made her way from the empty lot to the pathway. And started walking.

This world was shrouded in darkness and moss. As Miranda kept cautiously to the path, she could almost believe that the house didn't exist at all . . . perhaps had *never* existed. Or if it did, if it had . . . it was now faded helplessly into a fragile netherworld. Caught between the living and the dead . . . rooms empty and silent . . . longing to be filled with hope.

Stop. Quit scaring yourself.

She could feel herself getting annoyed again—angry, even. Good. That was a lot better than being scared.

She kept her eyes deliberately focused, gazing straight ahead over the heavy basket. She knew that if she glanced to either the left or the right, she might see things she didn't want to see, things she didn't want to know about. Because from the corner of her left eye, she could *already* make out the image of flames sputtering from outdoor fires, cooking fires outside the slave quarters, and long curls of smoke, black against black, from the chimneys of their cabins. And from the corner of her right eye, more images danced in light—lanterns bobbing through the shadows of the bayou; carriage lamps bouncing along the road, turning into the long driveway, sparkling through the oak trees, up the alley to the house . . .

And the house!

At last Miranda saw it; she was there.

And the sight was so spectacular that she stopped in her tracks and let out a cry of wonder.

The whole house was ablaze with light. Like one magnificent candle, as lovely as its name—*Belle Chandelle, Beautiful Candle*—every window glowing, every gallery flickering like stars, golden warmth and hospitality flowing from every welcome-wide French door . . .

Oh my God . . .

Tears filled her eyes.

Her heart ached; she couldn't breathe—

None of you knew, none of you realized that these were your last bright moments of happiness here—

And then it was gone.

One last sputter. One desperate burst of radiance. Fading . . . fading . . . to a deep, eternal sorrow . . .

Miranda's picnic basket was on the ground.

The flashlight shook in her hand.

Completely unnerved, she stood there on the path, probing the dark with her senses, hoping for one more spark of light.

But Belle Chandelle was glorious no longer . . .

Barely even a memory in the shadows.

15

MIRANDA WAS FURIOUS BY THE TIME SHE REACHED THE MAIN HOUSE.

Still badly shaken from her vision and angry that no one had met her in the parking lot, she lugged the basket as quickly as she could, muttering the entire way. She could see doors standing open off the verandah; light glowed out across the threshold, while voices laughed and argued from the room beyond.

Slipping to the doorway, Miranda peered in.

An intense poker game seemed to be in progress, the three contenders slouched in folding chairs around one of Mom's cleared-off worktables. Parker was laughing, elbows propped on the table edge, drinking a beer and holding a fan of cards. Etienne was hunched forward, one eyebrow raised as he slid a stack of chips toward the center pile. And Gage, minus his cast, was balanced comfortably in a tipped-back chair, baseball cap turned backward, shaggy hair tucked behind his ears.

In spite of her anger, Miranda couldn't resist watching them. *The past-five-o'clock shadow on Gage's jaw and upper lip . . . the chiseled angles of Etienne's face . . . the cocky charm of Parker's grin.* Music was blaring from an iPod and portable speakers. There were coolers scattered around, along with bags and boxes of snacks, and a growing heap of trash in one corner.

Without warning, Etienne let loose with something in French; Gage answered back in kind. Parker was immediately indignant.

"Hey, if y'all are going to cheat, at least cheat so I can understand you!"

An amused response from Gage; laughter and swearing from the other two. Miranda, doing her best to look intimidating, cleared her throat and stepped in.

"Where have you been?" she demanded.

The three boys nearly fell off their chairs.

"Christ, Miranda!" Parker yelped. "Why don't you warn a guy when you're sneaking up on him?"

"You were supposed to meet me!"

"*I* was?" Parker looked mystified.

"I was waiting in the parking lot!"

"*You* were? Are we having an affair?"

Miranda shoved the basket out in front of her. "You were supposed to come and get all this food! And don't bother hiding that beer—I've already seen it. Wait. You're *all* drinking beer?"

Quick, covert looks passed one to another—too late to hide the evidence. Parker offered a sheepish grin; Gage, a reluctant but guilty shrug. Etienne, gulping the mouthful he'd just taken, was on his feet and moving toward her, but Miranda wasn't ready to be appeased.

"Does Aunt Teeta know you're drinking out here?"

"Well—we—it's just—"

"Does my mom?"

"Aw, come on now—it's not like we're hurting any—"

"Does the renovation committee?"

"You mean the prohibition committee?" Beer aloft, Parker gave her a toast.

"Look, *cher*," Etienne insisted, "I can explain."

But Miranda was finding immense pleasure in this. "Hmm. Looks like grounds for blackmail to me."

"Wait now. You're not even supposed to be out here, yeah? So how come—"

"Macaroni salad." Again she shoved out the basket. "I'm pretty sure the lid came off, so you'll have to scrape it all back together."

"And I'm still not understanding this . . . what about macaroni salad?"

"Aunt Teeta sent food, Etienne. Didn't she call?"

A quick flinch went over his face. "*Mais* no. The last time I talked to her, she told me she was going to bed—so I turned off my phone. I'm really sorry—"

Miranda's sound of exasperation said it all. She started to leave, but he reached out and caught her arm.

"Why don't you sit yourself down and eat with us."

"No thanks."

"At least take something to drink."

"We've got Cokes!" Parker announced, yanking open a cooler. "See? Ice cold and ready for fun. Cokes for the little lady."

Miranda gave him a scowl. "No, I want to go home. You guys just enjoy your little slumber party."

"At least have a look at Gage's leg."

"It looks just like my other leg." Gage quickly assured her. "When you've seen one of my legs, you've seen them all."

As tempting as it was to embarrass Gage, Miranda kept her eyes on Etienne.

"So you're supposed to be guarding this place tonight?"

"That's the plan, yeah."

"Uh-huh. And you do realize the gate was open when I got here?"

Another round of glances, sheepish this time.

"Kind of defeats the purpose, don't you think?" Miranda couldn't help adding, but now Etienne was starting to look amused.

"Kids are gonna be climbing the fence whether that gate's locked or not. And folks don't usually try to steal bulldozers, *cher*. They'd rather be sneaking around up here by the house."

"Yeah," Parker frowned at her. "Like you."

"Pretty quiet tonight, though," Etienne went on. "Nothing much going on."

"See, Miranda?" Parker shrugged. "No big bad ghosts. Or . . . should I say . . . no little bitty kiddie ghosts."

She considered slamming the basket over his head. Instead she suggested, "Well . . . maybe you haven't been looking in the right places."

It was hard to tell who actually caught on first—Gage or Etienne. Both their expressions changed simultaneously, furtive glances sweeping the shadows, then returning to Miranda's face. Parker either didn't notice—or didn't want to.

"Something happened, didn't it?" Gage asked her quietly. "After you got here. And we weren't with you."

He sounded so sorry for it that a little of her anger began to fade. Etienne was gazing down at her with a half-stern, half-apologetic frown.

"Mon Dieu, *cher*," he mumbled. "Tell us. What happened?"

"Yeah, tell us," Parker echoed. "This will be perfect entertainment, right guys? Halloween stories while we eat." He was rummaging through the basket, unwrapping po-boys, examining containers. He pulled out a lidless one, turned it upside down, then scowled. "Hey, Miranda. This one's empty. And there's . . . like . . . slimy shit everywhere."

Miranda glared. Parker, oblivious, began picking out macaroni, piece by piece, and popping them into his mouth.

"It's good, you know? But it's stuck to everything. You should be more careful next time."

As Miranda stepped toward him, Etienne blocked her path and put both hands on her shoulders. "That contest at school." He was speaking so low, from one side of his mouth, that she could barely make out what he was saying. "That Win a Date with a Cheerleader thing?"

Miranda was completely in the dark. "So?"

"Streak, he won a date with Ashley."

"*What?*" Miranda actually felt her jaw drop. "Are you . . . are you *sure*?"

Etienne nodded. Glancing around him, Miranda saw Gage give another shrug, sympathetic this time.

"How do you know that?" She was whispering now too,

though Parker, still searching for macaroni, didn't seem aware of their discussion.

"They had the drawing at the end of the day," Etienne explained.

"When you and I weren't there? Oh, poor . . ." She hesitated, gave Etienne a bewildered frown. "Actually, I don't know *who* to feel worse for. Parker or Ashley."

Etienne jerked his chin in Parker's direction. "He's got a game tomorrow night. He can't be drinking."

"Oh, no. And he's been doing so much better about that. I was hoping—"

"Yeah, I know. He was pretty bad off when he got here. But me and Gage, we been watering everything down, pouring everything out as much as we can. Keeping him distracted."

"Trust me," Gage added. "It's been easy. He hasn't noticed."

Miranda hadn't heard Gage approaching. Turning, she saw him standing close behind her, while Parker continued to dig through the food.

"What about Ashley?" she asked softly. "How did she take the news?"

"Ashley's fine with it." Lifting his head, Parker chewed thoughtfully on a slice of roast beef. He considered a moment, glanced at the three of them, then gave a philosophical shrug. "It's all for a good cause. She's doing it as a . . . *business* arrangement. I don't have *anything* to worry about. In fact, I'm being *stupid* for worrying."

"Parker," Miranda said seriously, "listen to Ashley. She's telling you the truth."

"I didn't try hard enough," he sighed.

As the others watched, he sat down on the floor, unwrapped a wedge of cake, and gazed morosely at a clump of icing on his finger. Miranda, Gage, and Etienne exchanged hidden smiles.

"Didn't try hard enough," he sighed again. "Should have tried harder."

"At what?" Gage asked.

"I bought a hundred tickets."

Gage's eyes flew wide. Etienne snorted a laugh.

"*Merde*, a hundred damn tickets?"

"And I lost," Parker grumbled. "What does that tell you?"

"It tells me the drawing could've been rigged," Gage concluded, while Miranda nodded agreement.

"So is it fate?" Parker sighed. "Should we really be together?"

Etienne could no longer take the drama. Squatting down beside Parker, he clapped a hand on his shoulder and gave him a shove. "Hey. Ashley, she's been crazy for you all these years, yeah? But when she finds out you spent a hundred dollars just to win a date—"

"No, no. *Hell* no. She can't find out."

"How come?"

"Hey!" Indignantly, Parker drew himself up. "I've got my pride, haven't I?"

Another silent exchange of amusement among the other three; Parker, fumbling for a fresh beer, didn't catch on.

As Miranda watched Parker lift the can to his lips, Gage mouthed, "I'll get that one. I hope."

"Look, there's more stuff in the car," she informed them.

"Aunt Teeta sent tea and cocoa and cider and another whole box of food. I just couldn't carry it all."

Squeezing her shoulder, Gage nodded. "We can handle that. But first, you need to tell us what happened tonight."

Miranda really didn't want to talk about it now. What she really wanted to do was go home—but she realized that neither of them would ever consent to that. Gage pulled out his chair for her to sit. Etienne stood pensively by, eyes narrowed. And even Parker, who was doing his best to look uninterested, sat down and leaned over the table, resting his chin on folded arms.

Miranda described her experience in detail—the ghostly splendor of Belle Chandelle. By the time she was finished, Etienne was doing his usual pacing, and Gage had lowered himself into the seat beside her, his gaze thoughtful.

"So," Gage mused, "you don't really know if what you saw has anything to do with those children. Or the woman in the mirror."

Miranda's reply was weary. "That's just it. I've been getting hit with so many images since I first stepped on the property, I don't know how to sort it all out. This place has way too much history going on."

No one seemed to have any ideas. As the silence stretched out, Parker buried his face in his arms, and Etienne finally motioned to the door. "I'm gonna get that stuff from your car, *cher*. You got the keys?"

"I left it unlocked."

"I'll be right back."

Nodding, she and Gage watched him go. Then after several quiet moments, Miranda sighed and leaned back in her chair.

"So how's your leg?" she asked Gage. "I really did mean to ask you when I got here. I was just . . . upset."

"Understandable. It's good."

"I noticed you're still limping."

"Just a little. The doctor says it'll go away eventually. Especially once I start rehab."

Miranda couldn't help herself. "So I guess the girls at school are still going to feel sorry for you after all, with that limp."

"Stop."

"And you still won't be able to outrun Babette LeBlanc and her bra size for a while."

"Okay, that's enough."

Hiding a smile, Miranda reached over and lightly touched his thigh. "I bet your leg's really cute."

"Not as cute as yours," he mumbled, glancing away.

Parker's head instantly came up. "Rehab," he announced, having missed their last few seconds of talking. "You have to be ready for spring ball, hotshot."

A little flushed herself now, Miranda pulled back from Gage. "What about spring ball?" she asked innocently.

"He's starting pitcher for our baseball team," Parker explained. "Pitcher. That's what you were saying, right? 'Pitcher'? Or 'pictures'?"

Miranda looked at Gage. He was leaning sideways, elbow propped on the table, cheek resting against his palm. He shrugged, smiling.

"Speaking of pictures," he said agreeably, "those things you loaned me? The picture and the letter? I was looking at them this afternoon."

"And?" Intrigued, Miranda straightened in her seat, senses sharpening.

"Something . . . I don't know, exactly. *Maybe* something."

But Miranda had seen Gage's instincts in action before. And trusted them. "Tell me."

"In the letter—which he dated—the Yankee soldier says they're going to seize Belle Chandelle. That they don't anticipate trouble, because it already looks deserted—in fact, he says it looks like a place where only the dead would stay."

Nodding, Miranda recalled those words from the letter. Words that hadn't affected her till now, listening to Gage repeat them. "Go on."

"He says they're going to use the house for their headquarters. They know there's going to be heavy fighting, there's already been some pretty bloody skirmishes. Now . . . we know the date of the Battle of St. Yvette, and we know when the town was occupied. And it's been pretty well documented—a timeline of less important battles—raiding parties and smaller attacks around the area."

Miranda didn't have a clue where this was headed. But she nodded encouragement anyway.

"When you look at the photograph," Gage's voice dropped, more intense now. "You see Belle Chandelle at a distance, in the background. And you can tell just by the landscape that at least one battle's already been fought there. I mean . . . everything's burned and bloody and torn up. But . . . the house still looks the same."

Again she didn't get it. Staring at Gage, she frowned and shook her head. "Sorry, but I—"

"It doesn't look like there's anybody there. It's after the time of the letter, but there's nobody around the house. No horses, no officers. There's no flag. The house still looks totally empty and deserted. Like the Yankees never even stayed there."

"But . . . why wouldn't they?"

"That's just it—*why wouldn't they*? It was free and clear; they didn't have to fight anybody for it. That whole, big house, and they planned to stay there, but I don't think they did. It just doesn't make sense."

But something was stirring in Miranda's brain. Something deep inside . . . something gnawing and nagging, just at the edge of her consciousness. Gage, noting her sudden restlessness, gave a concerned frown.

"What?" he asked. "What is it?"

"What the soldier said about the house."

"You mean, a place where only the dead would stay?"

"Hey, maybe the Yankees were afraid of ghosts." More alert now, Parker allowed himself a stretch, then swigged from his beer. "They didn't have Miranda around back then—they were probably afraid of the ghosts in Belle Chandelle."

"Oh my God." Miranda's eyes widened. Leaning across the table, she grabbed Parker's arm and shook it so hard that the beer can went sailing to the floor. "That's it! Parker, honestly, sometimes when I least expect it, your genius still amazes me."

"Me too," he grumbled, wiping a spill off the front of his shirt. "What the hell did I do?"

"Maybe it was the *ghosts*," she said excitedly to Gage. "Maybe Belle Chandelle was *already haunted* when the Yankees got there. Maybe they were afraid—maybe there was a bad feeling they got, or maybe something happened, they saw something, heard something, that scared them off."

Gage straightened slowly in his chair. Pushed his cap higher up his forehead. "Wow. You never think about there being a haunting back *then*. You always think of back *then* as being what caused the haunting. But . . . it makes sense. Which means—"

"Which means, whatever happened here—to the woman and the children—must have happened before the War."

"And sometime between then and the siege of St. Yvette, the plantation was totally abandoned?"

"Or . . . what if the thing that happened, and the plantation being abandoned, took place at the same time?"

"Jesus," Parker mumbled, and lowered his head onto his arms once more.

"When the Yankee soldiers came, Belle Chandelle could have been sitting empty for years." Gage lounged back more comfortably in his chair. "Still . . . you'd think somebody would've bought it in the meantime."

"Not if it was haunted," Parker's voice was muffled *and* annoyed. "How many times do I have to say it?"

Gage and Miranda shrugged.

"He's right," Miranda conceded. "Definitely a possibility."

"So what about the woman and the little kids?" Gage asked.

Frustrated, she let out a sigh. "*That* I haven't figured out yet."

"Figured *what* out yet?" Etienne stood in the doorway, boxes clutched in both arms, expression curious. "What'd I miss?"

"These two playing touchy-feely under the table." Parker didn't even bother to look up. "Other than that, not much."

Etienne's glance slid between Miranda and Gage. Miranda looked innocent; Gage motioned dismissively in Parker's direction.

"He's been asleep," Gage said.

"No, I haven't," Parker replied.

Shaking his head, Etienne jerked his chin toward the verandah. "I'm gonna go put this stuff in the kitchen. And for sure, we need to be making some coffee."

"Do you even know how to use the coffee maker?" Miranda spoke up, relieved to change the subject.

Three pairs of eyes aimed in her direction.

"Guys don't make coffee." Parker stated. "It's a law."

"I think I can figure it out, *cher*," Etienne assured her. "You need to be going on home. Your aunt Teeta, she just called me . . . worrying about you."

"Oh. So your phone's back on."

"And gonna stay on till morning. Who knows? Maybe we'll get us another nice surprise like you."

"Doubtful," Gage said, matter-of-fact.

Etienne nodded agreement. "I'll walk you to your car. And you can be filling me in on all those theories y'all came up with while I was gone."

"Well . . . how about *Parker* walks me to my car?" she asked, surprising all of them—especially Parker. Then, lowering her voice, she added, "Nice fresh air. Might make him feel better."

"Ah. Good idea."

"And actually . . . I can even drive him home, if you want."

Blocking Parker's view, Etienne dangled a set of BMW keys between his fingers. "I think we can keep us a better eye on him here, yeah? Thanks, though."

Miranda had to laugh. "Come on, Parker." Standing up, she tugged on him, ignoring his moans of protest, forcing him to his feet. "Be a gentleman and walk me to my car."

"I'll tell you one thing," Parker grumbled, following her to the door. "I'm never buying this kind of beer again. I swear to God, it tastes like Coke."

"If he's not back in a little while, you better come look for him," Miranda warned.

"No way," Gage deadpanned.

"He sleeps where he falls," Etienne insisted.

Smiling, Miranda turned on her flashlight and led Parker away from the house, still hearing Gage and Etienne in the background, their voices back and forth.

"So you gonna tell me what was happening while I was gone?" *Etienne.*

"We talked." *Gage.* "We came up with some great theories."

"I mean, everything."

"That is everything."

"Even the touchy-feely parts?"

"Stop."

"I can't even be trusting you for a few damn minutes. . . ."

Their voices faded into the night. A stark, stygian night that swallowed the house and all its secrets, like a curtain drawing shut between worlds. Miranda was thankful that Parker was with her. To her relief, he seemed to have no trouble maneuvering the path.

"Here," he said, and unexpectedly reached for the flashlight, aiming the beam higher and farther. "You . . . you're okay about driving home alone?"

Surprised, she glanced at him, but his eyes were fixed straight ahead. "Sure. Small town, right? Even the hitchhikers are safe?"

"That's not what I meant. I meant . . ." In typical Parker fashion, he grew irritated at his own show of concern. "Driving on this road. Kind of a long stretch till you hit town."

Miranda's heart softened. "You mean . . . because of the visions and things?"

"I heard you tonight. Watched you tonight." The flashlight bobbed and weaved, vague patterns over moss-shrouded trees. Parker's voice lowered, mumbling. "You could give it up. You could *turn your back* on it. You could . . . *ignore* it."

"Ignore it?" An ironic smile worked over her lips. "Right. I've got visions coming out of nowhere, like miniseries inside my head, till I don't even know what world I'm living in. I've got invisible strangers talking to me about their problems and expecting me to solve them. It's like . . . like the worst sort of intrusion. Like I'm being . . . violated." She paused, drew a deep breath. "So no, even though I really *want* to and I really *wish* I could—no, I don't think it's possible to just ignore it."

"Yeah, well. I guess some people think it's totally great, what you do." Though Parker's tone was neutral, Miranda heard the underlying disdain. "Helping spirits. Wow. Big, noble calling. But I don't see it that way. As a matter of fact, it doesn't make sense to me at all. Putting yourself through fear and pain. Opening yourself up to every weird, creepy, dangerous thing floating around out there."

Jokingly, he clawed the air with his hands. Moaned a spooky sound . . . held the flashlight beneath his chin, made a spooky face. Then glanced at her and shrugged his shoulders.

"To me, that's just . . . *hell*. And a whole hell of a lot . . . *unfair*. But hey . . . what do I know about noble callings, anyway." Waving the flashlight, he curved a great arc over their heads through the sky. "You're a weird kid, Miranda Barnes."

"How's that?"

"Dead people don't scare you. But you were hiding behind the pie safe in Ashley's kitchen the other night."

As her mind scrambled to refocus, Parker leaned over and snapped his fingers in front of her face.

"Hey, listen up. Pie safe. Ashley's kitchen. Ring a bell?"

Annoyed, she grabbed his fingers and held on. "I was . . . I told you. Wiping mud off my shoes."

"Lie. You looked like a deer in headlights. You were scared shitless."

"Oh, all right," she conceded grudgingly. "I was . . . observing."

"You were overwhelmed. Just like I was, the first time I went to their house."

"*You* were?"

"It took me a long time to get used to that crazy family. And by the way, if you want to hold on to me, I have lots of other parts you'd like better."

Miranda turned loose his fingers. As Parker gave her a suggestive half-grin, she ignored it and kept talking.

"I wanted to go in," she admitted. "It was just so wonderful, and everyone was so comfortable with each other. Like one big happy family. And I wanted to be part of it, but . . ."

Her excuse trailed off. This was getting too personal, and she didn't understand why she was feeling so anxious all of a sudden, so edgy and sentimental. Besides that, she knew Parker would just make fun of her if she said any more.

"But I'm *not* part of it." The words were out before she could stop them. "Not really. I mean, I actually *had* those things in my old life, but they're gone now. Like they never even happened. And I hear you all talking about when you were kids, and I hear all the memories you share with each other. The five of you have a history together. You have all these private jokes and little rituals. You know each other better than anyone else ever will. Who wouldn't want that? To be a part of that?"

But Parker didn't joke. For a split instant, Miranda sensed a heaviness about him—a deep, sudden plunge into troubling thoughts. And when he finally *did* speak again, his voice was low and very serious.

"My family was never like Ashley's," he explained hesitantly. "No jokes . . . no pets . . . forget the noise and laughing. No happy, old-fashioned family dinners . . . though Imogene—our cook—*does* make some pretty great jambalaya once in a while. And God forbid anybody should ever hug." He gave a mock shudder. "The first time I went home with Ashley, I wanted to turn and run like hell, just like you wanted to. It was, like, totally foreign to me. I thought they were all insane. Almost made me not want to ask her out."

"You never went over there till you asked Ashley out? Never in all those years?"

"I wasn't here all those years, Miranda. My folks lived in St. Yvette, but I was stuck away in boarding schools. Which I consistently got thrown out of." He paused, looking proud of himself. "I didn't start school here till eighth grade."

"So when did you get together with Ashley?"

"Two years ago." Another wink, more sly this time. Back to his usual self. "She wanted me. Bad."

"Uh-huh."

"Yeah," he insisted, puffing out his chest, "she did. She chased me for months, but I kept playing hard to get. Finally, I felt sorry for her and let her catch me."

As Miranda reached over and shoved him, a wide grin spread across his face. "Yeah, she's lucky, all right. But *major* pressure on *me*."

"What do you mean?"

"Are you kidding? If I ever hurt Ashley, don't you think Gage and Etienne would come after me and hunt me down? Hell, they'd cut me up in little pieces and throw me in the bayou. And that's not even *half* the suffering Roo would put me through."

A look of extreme horror before his grin began to fade.

And then unexpectedly, his features went still once more, and thoughtful, and he gazed full into Miranda's face.

"It's this thing between them, you know. The four of them. This bond they have. Growing up together like they did . . . that history you were talking about."

For a while, both of them were quiet. And a question was forming in Miranda's mind—a possibility that she'd never even considered before now.

"Parker," she mumbled at last, "are you saying that *you* still feel like an outsider sometimes?"

He stopped abruptly. In the drawn-out silence, Miranda felt his embarrassed discomfort, those defensive walls going up again, that cocky irreverence slamming back into place. He leaned toward her with deliberate slowness, his eyes narrowed, his face perfectly deadpan.

"I'm saying that if you tell Ashley *one word* about the beers I had tonight, there will be *no* place in the universe you can hide from me. Got it? Now, where's your damn car?"

It *did* seem like they'd been walking quite a distance. . . that they should have reached the parking lot by now. Unconsciously, Miranda sped up, trying to match Parker's long strides. He was going faster, and she began to have the oddest feeling that the two of them had passed this way already, just moments ago. Nervously, she scanned the edges of the pathway, where thick shadows drew back from the light. If she didn't know better, she could almost swear that even those shadows looked familiar. . . .

That's stupid . . . doesn't even make sense. . . .

A ripple of fear crept up her spine.

"What the hell . . ." Parker muttered under his breath, then sliced the darkness right to left with his flashlight beam.

Miranda hadn't noticed any fog out here before—yet a thin, gray mist had materialized out of nowhere . . . swirling softly, seductively, along the path . . . enclosing them all around.

The fear inside her was turning cold. Instinctively, she reached out and touched Parker's arm. "Are we lost?"

"Lost? Of course we're not lost, how the hell could we be lost? Come on."

But the forced confidence in his voice wasn't convincing, and once more Miranda hurried to keep up with him. *He's right— there's absolutely no way we could be lost—the path only goes in one direction, between the parking lot and the house; there's no possible way we could have wandered off track without knowing—*

And yet she had the distinct sensation of going in circles . . . winding back and forth . . . retracing their own steps over and over again. An endless loop outside of time and space and—

"Shit!" Parker stopped so abruptly that Miranda ran into him from behind. She didn't even notice when he reached back to steady her, then drew her quickly, protectively to his side. "No way," he croaked. "That's impossible."

She could see now what he was gawking at. Through the rapidly vanishing fog, through the swiftly opening curtains of moss—*oh my God, we're right back where we started!*—Belle Chandelle looming high above them, silent and watchful, cold and black as the night . . .

No . . . not *quite* black.

That window . . . that window in the attic . . .

It should have been empty, Miranda told herself. That third-story dormer window should have been empty, as empty as the room locked up tight on the other side of it. And yet something was moving beyond it. Something flickering beyond it . . . gliding slowly, deliberately from side to side . . . a candle carried by an unseen hand . . .

"You see that," Miranda whispered. "My God, Parker . . ."

For one brief instant, the movement stopped. And then . . . without warning . . . a vague silhouette appeared within the window frame. Invisible eyes watching them from the dark. Invisible eyes, brimming with purpose and pain and terror . . .

As Parker squeezed her shoulders, Miranda clutched tightly at his hand.

The window went blank.

The moss settled softly back into place . . . the night went eerily still.

"Parker," she whispered again. "She knows. She knows we're here—"

Her words broke off as he grabbed her. As he grabbed her arm and began dragging her down the path, even while Miranda stubbornly kept talking.

"Parker, you saw her too—"

"You're crazy," he grumbled, yanking her harder, though Miranda tried to twist free.

"Don't pretend you didn't just see that! Just like you saw something out here the other night—in the very same window! Except you thought Aunt Teeta was up there, you thought she had a lantern, but it wasn't her at all—"

"Knock it off, Miranda. You don't know what I saw or didn't see—what, are you communicating with my eyeballs now?"

"I *asked* her, Parker. *Aunt Teeta wasn't up there.* Nobody goes up there except the workmen; it's too dangerous—"

"Christ, what's with this stupid path? If you hadn't been babbling forever, and if that damn fog hadn't come—"

"Well, do you see any fog now? No! Admit it, you can't explain what we just experienced! So tell me what's going on with you—"

"Nothing's going on with me. Besides the fact that I can't *think* because *you* won't shut *up!*"

"You know I won't say anything to anyone. And—"

"Holy crap—look." As Parker halted midstride, Miranda was finally able to break loose. She saw the lurch of his flashlight beam and the roof of Aunt Teeta's car illuminated beneath it.

"The parking lot," she murmured. "We're back at the parking lot."

"Get in the car."

"But—"

"Get in your damn car, Miranda."

He had her elbow in a viselike grip. He snatched her keys from her hand, then opened the door and thrust her behind the steering wheel.

"Go on." Reaching in, he started the engine. He slammed the door and jerked his thumb at the gate. "Go home."

But Miranda couldn't give up now—she had to know. Before he could back completely away, she got the window down and clamped her fingers around his wrist.

"Please, Parker," she begged him. "I know you're upset about what just happened—"

"Upset? I'm not upset. There's nothing to be upset about, because nothing happened, so I'm definitely not upset—"

"You're the only one who sees some of the things I see. I need to know why—don't you understand how much it would help me? How much it would help both of us—"

"I don't need help. *You're* the one who needs help. I don't even know why we're arguing—"

"Parker, please talk about this with me, please tell me what's going on!"

Silence plunged between them. For an endless moment, Parker's eyes lowered, his features tense, his body rigid. And then he looked at her again. And slowly, methodically, began to uncurl each of her fingers from his arm.

"Jesus, Miranda, you ever consider pro wrestling? You got a hell of a grip there—"

"Parker—"

"I'm drunk tonight, remember? And the whole world is beer." Backing away, he made a mock bow, swept his arm in a grand gesture toward the road. "That's what I saw, Miranda. And by morning, it'll be just another hangover."

16

FOR THE SECOND TIME THAT WEEK, MIRANDA OVERSLEPT—
which meant catching a ride with Aunt Teeta and being late for
school. The whole campus was abuzz with the news of Ashley
and Kurt Fuller's date. Once again, there were underground
wagers being made on Parker's temper, but when Miranda saw
him in first period, he seemed resigned, almost quiet. Though
a few jokes were tossed his way, he deflected them with his
usual wit, and—best of all, Miranda noted—he also seemed
completely sober. Maybe he and Ashley had discussed the whole
Win-a-Date matter earlier. She certainly hoped so.

At lunchtime—and with Gage's help—she filled the others in
on the latest happenings and theories regarding Belle Chandelle.
Etienne wasn't at school, and Parker offered no comments about
visions, speculations, or anything else. Roo listened intently
while pinching the batter off her French-fried onion rings. And
Ashley, despite her usual enthusiasm for the plantation, had a
hint of sadness in her smile.

"Is Ashley upset about the contest?" Miranda asked Roo on
their way back to class.

"Kind of. She wouldn't talk to anybody yesterday after she
found out."

"Not even you?"

Roo shook her head. "She locked herself in her room after cheerleading practice. I think she really dreads this stupid date, but she doesn't want to upset Parker. So she's trying to make the best of it."

"And Parker's trying to make the best of it for her?"

"Since when do I know what Parker's trying to do?"

"What about the game tonight? Do you think there's going to be trouble?"

"I'm sure the coach knows exactly what's going on. He'll probably threaten Parker and Kurt at practice."

Sighing, Miranda shifted her books to her other arm. "So when's the date, do you know?"

"Tomorrow night. He's taking her to an outdoor concert." Then, when Miranda drew a blank, Roo added, "Not here. In Moss Bridge—it's about an hour away."

"Well, that seems pretty platonic, doesn't it? Music, fresh air, lots of people around?"

Roo's tone was flat. "Hello? An hour away? If she wants to come home in a hurry, she can't."

"Why would you even say that? Are you *expecting* she'll want to come home in a hurry?"

"Look. Everybody says how nice Streak is. And nice guys are usually really boring on dates. Would you want to be stuck for hours and hours with some totally nice, boring guy, and you can't escape?"

"*Gage* is nice. And *he's* not boring."

A knowing glance from Roo. "So you'd like to be stuck with Gage for hours and hours, and you can't escape?"

"Roo, that is *not* what I said, and you know it."

"Gage might surprise you, Miranda. You might not *want* to escape."

Flustered, Miranda steered the conversation back on track. "Well, I hope you're right about Kurt being boring. The situation's already tense enough without him making macho moves on Ashley."

"He won't," Roo assured her. "Not if he wants to live long enough to graduate."

The afternoon seemed to drag forever; Miranda couldn't wait for the day to be over with. By last period, she was so tired, she could hardly keep her eyes open, and she could hardly talk without yawning. Luckily, Miss Dupree's class always seemed to fly—mainly because the others were there with her.

She saw Roo come in and walk over to her place near the middle row, just opposite Gage's seat. Ashley sat directly across from Miranda, Parker closer to the front of the room. As Gage maneuvered toward his desk by the window, he tossed a small packet casually on top of Miranda's book.

"Etienne forgot to give you these."

"Oh, thanks. The stuff Mom asked me to take pictures of."

"Ghosts?" Roo asked loudly while Miranda tried to ignore a few curious glances. Gage smacked Roo on the head with his notebook.

"He said not," Miranda murmured.

Ashley peered over her shoulder. "That's disappointing," she whispered. "I was really hoping something would show up in there to help us."

Before Miranda could answer, Miss Dupree clapped her hands for attention.

"Okay, people, let's get started. Well, Gage, this is certainly wonderful—I see you've finally got that cast off."

Gage dropped into his seat as all eyes turned to him. He nodded politely and mumbled a reply.

"And how does it feel?" Miss Dupree asked.

"That's what we'd all like to know," Roo declared. "Let's all line up and touch it."

"Oh, me first!" Ashley waved her hand, winking at him.

The room exploded in laughter as Gage slid lower in his seat. Miss Dupree struggled to hold back a smile.

"All right, class, tempting as it is, Gage and his leg will *not* be the focus of our discussion today."

Boos from the girls now, cheers and insults from the guys. Looking relieved, Gage immediately opened his notebook.

Luckily, everyone's focus quickly switched to Miss Dupree and the handing out of study guides. But Miranda couldn't concentrate—just like the night before, her mind kept going back over the strange occurrences at Belle Chandelle. She tried her best to block it; she couldn't afford to fall further behind in class. The woman in the mirror . . . the children on the stairs . . . the faded glory of that long-ago house . . . *go away . . . leave me alone. . . .*

It was happening more and more, these intrusive images and questions. She could hardly think about anything else. She chewed on her pen, scribbled patterns through her notes. She glanced up to see Gage watching her. *He knows . . . he knows where my mind is.* She doubled her efforts to concentrate, but it didn't do any good. *Thank God it's Friday. Maybe this weekend I'll figure something out, find the right clues, end this once and for all.*

Growing more agitated, she shielded the photographs with her textbook and began flipping through them again. *Boring. Really boring. Boring to me, but just what Mom wanted—mantels, ceilings, tiles, floors, marks on walls, carvings, doors and windows, and—*

Miranda heard herself gasp.

A loud, audible sound, a sharp wheeze of cold air catching hard in her throat.

Her hand fluttered to her neck as though she might dislodge that gasp, push it back down. She wondered if anyone else had noticed, but then she saw Gage. Gage straightening in his desk, clear across the room, but stretching, as though he were trying to reach her. And the others, too: Ashley, face worried, hand already touching Miranda's arm; Parker frowning, puzzled; Roo swiveling around in her chair, that dark stare, not surprised—

"Oh God . . ." Miranda choked. "Oh my God . . ."

But how could they have known, she wondered—none of the other students seemed to have heard her, or seemed to have seen—just the group, just her friends, frozen in their places, while she gazed down at the photo that was trembling in her hand.

"You said no ghosts," she whispered, even though Etienne wasn't there to hear her. "That was what you said. *No ghosts.*"

But there *was* a ghost.

A ghost standing by the fireplace.

His body nearly transparent, part of the shadows, part of the fireplace he was next to, part of the wall above it, features pale and hazy and half-formed, yet she could see them all the same . . . and she *knew* that face, that spectral face, with eyes looking straight into the camera, and out of the photograph, and into her own—

"Grandpa . . ."

"I'm sorry, Miranda." Ashley was genuinely distressed. "I can't see him."

Gathered outside their classroom door, the others peered over Miranda's shoulder, scrutinizing the ghostly photograph.

Gage touched it lightly with his fingertip, sounding almost apologetic. "And he's here by the mantel?"

"Yes," Miranda insisted. "He's looking straight at the camera. He's standing right in front of the fireplace."

Roo's frown was puzzled. "Where in the house *is* that fireplace?"

"I don't know. I mean, there are so many rooms, and I went into all of them. I think each one had its own fireplace, and some of those bigger rooms had two or three. I'll have to go through the whole house and look again."

Ashley gave her a consoling hug. "Maybe Etienne will recognize it. Or your mom or aunt Teeta."

"Yeah, maybe." But even to herself, Miranda wasn't convincing. Once more she stared down at the photo; once more she racked her brain, trying to recall where that fireplace might be. "I need to find it. I *have* to find it. He's trying to tell me something, I know. Either about that mantel, or about the room it was in."

"He wanted you to see him, Miranda," Ashley said quietly. "Even if we can't."

"But think about what this means," Roo said matter-of-factly, taking the picture from Miranda, squinting at it through her bangs. "The intelligence this shows. The awareness—not just of *his* world, but *yours*. Your grandfather knew you were there, knew you were taking the picture. He knew the exact second you shot the photo."

"And that ability to transpose," Gage murmured. "Stepping back and forth between his world and ours . . . with no effort at all."

In spite of herself, Miranda teared up. "Ever since he died, I've wondered. I mean, I know he helped me before with the spirits of Nathan and Ellena, but I hadn't felt him around me since then. And now . . . with this . . . I do think maybe he's watching over me."

"He is," Gage's hand slid to her shoulder, gently squeezed. "Sure, he is."

"See?" Catching Parker off guard, Ashley, jabbed him in the stomach. Parker woofed out a startled breath.

"See what? Damn, Ashley!"

"There is *no* way you can deny now that ghosts exist, Parker Wilmington. After *not* seeing Miranda's grandpa in this picture."

As Parker's brow furrowed, he shot a bewildered look at Gage. Gage hid a smile and shrugged.

"So there," Gage told him.

"Perfect logic, as usual," Roo mumbled.

"Thank you," Ashley said. "I have to go to practice."

"Yeah, me, too." Still looking slightly befuddled, Parker followed Ashley down the corridor, while Miranda turned back to Roo.

"Are you going to the football game tonight?" Miranda asked her.

Roo's tone was derisive. "I don't do football games." Then pausing, she considered. "Though it might actually be worth it to see Parker and Kurt annihilate each other."

"Are you kidding, they'll be on their best behavior," Gage assured them.

"How do you know?"

"First, Coach will be watching them like a hawk. And second—if I know Parker, he's saving up everything till *after* Ashley's date."

"Good point. So where are you off to now?"

"Locker. Meet you outside."

As Gage went in the opposite direction, the two girls headed for the exit. There weren't many students lingering this afternoon; with no school tomorrow, the hallways and campus had already cleared out. Digging into the top of her boot, Roo immediately withdrew a crumpled pack of cigarettes and an even more crumpled book of matches. She shifted her backpack to her other shoulder, barely breaking stride.

"Miss Nell invited me for Sunday dinner," Miranda blurted. She hadn't planned to; it just popped out before she realized.

Roo, however, looked anything but surprised. "Wow. I can't believe you kept it in this long."

"You knew?"

Rolling her eyes, the girl shot Miranda a sidelong glance. "Don't be nervous. She'll make you feel right at home."

"I'm not nervous—"

"And this is a really good thing you're doing, by the way. Seeing where he lives . . . where he grew up . . . what he's all about." She pursed her lips, seemed to be carefully choosing her words. "I'm not sure I can even explain it—Etienne's world. But I think you'll realize, once you're out there. I think you'll get it."

"You mean . . . sort of like Etienne's territory?"

Roo gave a snort of amusement. "Wherever Etienne happens to *be*, that's his territory. Don't worry, you'll figure it out. Oh . . . and did I happen to mention—don't be nervous?"

"Yes, you did, and I'm not."

"If you say so."

"Just . . . kind of surprised, that's all."

"Miss Nell likes you, Miranda."

"She doesn't even know me. I've only talked to her three times in my whole life." Then, when Roo didn't answer, Miranda added softly, "I like *her*, too."

"Yeah, she's special." A smile played over Roo's mouth. "I remember the very first time I ever met her. She'd brought Etienne over to Gage's house, and we were all out playing in the wading pool, and she sprayed us with the hose. Etienne tried to drown Gage, and then she took us to get ice cream."

"Etienne tried to drown Gage?" Miranda chuckled.

"No . . . wait. I think that was *me* trying to drown Gage."

"That sounds a lot more accurate."

Roo shrugged, clearly untroubled by her homicidal past. "We must have been about five. That's when Gage moved in next door."

"Really? I thought you and Etienne were friends way before then."

"No, he never went to preschool or kindergarten—Ashley and I didn't even know him. But after Gage moved here from Mississippi, Etienne started coming over to their house, so that's when we really got to be friends. Ash and I were so excited to have this new kid next door to play with—and then it was even better, because his cousin would be there too. We had so much fun . . . all of us running and screaming and rolling around in the backyard."

Miranda lapsed into silence. It was easy to picture younger versions of Roo and Ashley and Gage—the three of them roughhousing, teasing, playing games. But not Etienne . . . *so hard to envision Etienne as a carefree child . . .*

"Was he ever happy?" she asked Roo now. "Etienne, I mean. I've never even seen him smile. And I certainly can't imagine him laughing."

"He used to laugh. He still does sometimes."

"I bet it's a nice laugh."

"Deep . . . sexy . . . kind of hoarse. Definitely worth waiting for." Slowing down, Roo pulled out the very last cigarette, stuffed the empty packet in her boot. "I remember I got this detective kit once for my birthday—it had these very cool handcuffs, strong for a toy, you know? They looked really authentic."

"Uh-oh." Miranda braced herself. "Do I even want to hear this?"

But Roo kept right on, her expression perfectly composed. "So I put the handcuffs on Etienne, and he could *not* get out of those things. Gage and Ash and I tickled him till he was totally exhausted. He couldn't move. He couldn't even *breathe.*"

"Etienne playing, laughing, *and* ticklish? No way, you're making it up."

"Ash thought Etienne was dead. She started crying and ran in the house to get Mom." Despite her solemn tone, Roo's dark eyes had begun to sparkle. "Naturally, I figured I'd get in trouble, so I told Mom I'd lost the key. That made Etienne mad, and he swung at me, so I punched him and tickled him harder."

Miranda burst out laughing. As Roo paused to light up, there was a sly hint of mischief on her face.

"Mom was fussing, Gage and Ashley were trying to pull me off, and Etienne was cursing in French at the top of his lungs."

"Poor Etienne! What happened to him?"

"Dad finally ended up cutting those handcuffs off."

"So did you ever figure out where you lost the key?"

"I didn't lose it." Roo took a long drag on her cigarette. "I put it down the front of Etienne's pants."

"You didn't!"

"Yeah." Roo was looking more and more smug at the memory. "Etienne's ticklish, all right. And in some really . . . *fun* . . . places."

"*Roo!*"

"I sure wish I still had those handcuffs."

Both girls dissolved into laughter. As they neared the gate by the parking lot, Roo plopped down on a wooden bench, crossed her legs, and seemed immensely pleased with herself. Groaning, Miranda leaned against the fence and tried to catch her breath.

"You'll see him," Roo said suddenly, seriously, as Miranda regarded her in confusion.

"See who?"

"Etienne. You're worried about him being happy. He's happy sometimes. One of these days you'll see it."

The mood had changed so quickly that Miranda was caught off guard. Roo took another deep puff on her cigarette, held it in the V of her fingers, studied it thoughtfully.

"I watch them sometimes, him and Gage. I can see them from my bedroom window, when they don't know I'm there. Just hanging out, the two of them. Shooting hoops or playing with Jazz . . . working on Etienne's truck. They're so cute, you know? Laughing and goofing around like two kids."

Another long drag. Another moment of reflection.

"Etienne's relaxed then, just being himself. His guard's down. Like . . . he's free."

Miranda's eyes stung with tears. Surprised at Roo's sentimentality. Surprised at her own reaction.

"It's nice," Roo said quietly.

"What's nice?"

Startled, the girls saw Gage approaching, just a few feet away. Neither had noticed him coming. As Miranda straightened and waved, Roo drew herself up, bland expression resumed.

"You," she informed him, "when you loan me money for cigarettes."

"Forget it."

"We were just talking about childhood," Miranda said quickly. "Well . . . your childhood."

"Mine?"

"Ours," Roo clarified. "When we were all little. Miranda thinks it's hilarious, for some weird reason."

The girls exchanged glances, hid smiles.

"Just dumb stuff," Miranda added.

Shrugging, Gage lifted his can of root beer and took a swig. "Dumb stuff, huh? Then it must have been about Roo."

"Actually, we were talking about games." Roo looked up at him, innocent. "Why don't you tell Miranda how we all used to hold you down and—"

"There's Etienne." Whatever memory Roo had triggered, it was clearly not one that Gage wanted to share. "Come on."

"Why don't you tell her how we *still* hold you down and—"

Roo's words gasped off. As Miranda watched in stunned silence, Gage poured a slow stream of root beer over the top of Roo's head.

"Hurry up," Gage said, his tone now as innocent as Roo's. "Etienne's waiting." Crumpling the can in his fist, he pitched it into the exact center of the trash barrel, then left through the gate. "See you, Miranda."

Roo blinked a few times. Ran her palm slowly across her forehead . . . shoved her wet bangs from her eyes. As Gage climbed into the truck, Etienne leaned out the window and shook his head at Roo, a smile tugging one corner of his mouth.

"Be sure and get yourself cleaned up, *cher*. I don't want you dripping all over my fancy seats in here."

The sound of Gage's laughter. The radio turning up loud.

"Oh, Roo." Trying desperately to be sympathetic, Miranda was already digging in her bag. "I think I have some tissues in here somewhere—"

"I don't need tissues. Tissues would be admitting defeat." Shaking her head, Roo gazed at her fizzled cigarette. With complete dignity, she got to her feet, then stomped her cigarette under her boot. "I will track him down. Slowly and methodically. He will never see me coming; the ambush will be swift, silent, and complete. I am . . . *Anaconda Woman*."

Try as she might, Miranda could no longer keep from grinning. She could see Aunt Teeta's car now, pulling up in the driveway, so she followed Roo out to the parking lot.

"By the way," she called, before Roo quite reached the truck. "About that handcuffs thing."

It worked, obviously—just the distraction Roo needed. Even from where she stood, Miranda saw her friend's shoulders move with stifled laughter.

"What about it?" Roo called back.

"I was just wondering . . . have you ever tortured him since?"

"In my deepest, darkest fantasies."

"Only there?"

Roo stared at her. Arched an eyebrow. Gave a slow, catlike smile. "Wouldn't you like to know."

17

MIRANDA HADN'T TOLD ANYONE THAT SHE WAS GOING OUT to Belle Chandelle again after school. She planned to go through the house with a fine-tooth comb, if necessary—and discover the truth about the photograph. All this time, the mysterious and frightening things that had happened to her had left her feeling confused and frustrated and helpless. But now, thanks to Grandpa, she felt strengthened. She hadn't been sure where to start before, she'd felt sabotaged by dead ends—but now she had hope. Direction. Jonas Hayes, her grandfather, had shown up in the photograph with wisdom in his eyes, *conviction* in his eyes, looking straight into her mind and her heart. Miranda *knew* that he had a message for her. Something crucial, something that would help *her* help those poor, tormented *others*.

Remember this, Miranda. The next time you doubt that Grandpa is with you, remember this—how he's contacting you, how he's guiding you.

It gave her a new sense of purpose. Even on the boring trip, while Aunt Teeta drove and chatted the entire way, Miranda was deep in her own thoughts, trying to tune in to her grandfather's message. *What is it, Grandpa? What are you trying to tell me?* When they finally got to the house, she cautiously showed the photo to Mom and Aunt Teeta, asking them if there was anything about it that they recognized. Luckily, neither of them noticed the spirit of Jonas Hayes—*unluckily*, neither of them could quite remember the fireplace.

"I'm sorry, honey," Mom told her. "There are so many around here, and memorizing them all just hasn't been high on my priority list. Is this one important for some reason?"

"I just . . . really like the carving along the top."

"That's odd," Lifting her glasses, Aunt Teeta peered more closely at the picture. "I can't recall a single mantelpiece around here being this clean. Everything we've seen so far is in terrible shape. Layers and layers of gunk to scrape through."

"All these photos you took are great." Mom was sincerely delighted. As she pulled them from Miranda's hand, Miranda grabbed the one photo back again.

"Okay if I hang onto this awhile? I'd like to find that fireplace, if I can."

"Well, you really captured those details I wanted, honey. While you're going back through the house, maybe you'll notice something else interesting . . . take some more pictures for me."

Yes, I might find something interesting, Mom—but I doubt if you'd want to see it. . . .

"I'm leaving pretty soon, darlin'." Aunt Teeta gave Miranda a hug. "So be sure and catch a ride home with your mama. Or Etienne, if you can find him. I don't think he's working here today, but Nell is, so he might be around somewhere. And take a flashlight when you go off exploring. The sun's setting earlier now—when dark comes, it comes fast."

Miranda had no desire to be crawling through Belle

Chandelle after sunset. For the next few hours, she worked her way along the upstairs galleries as quickly as she could, checking every room, trying to finish before nightfall. Like the changing weather outside, the rooms felt damp and wind-chilled. She soon realized that Aunt Teeta's observation was true—the details of the fireplace in the photograph were sharp and clear, while the other fireplaces in the house were sadly inconspicuous due to years of neglect. Mantels lay shrouded in dust, their intricate carvings plastered over with grime. Many had been damaged, chipped, gouged, worn down, burnt by careless fires and flying embers. Inspecting each one, comparing it to her photograph, was a slow and painstaking process. When she finally stopped long enough to check her watch, she couldn't believe how late it was.

Tired, thirsty, and covered with dirt, she decided to make a trip to the kitchen. The place was empty when she arrived, though it looked as if Miss Nell had been there most of the day. Curious, Miranda decided to explore —she found sweet tea in the fridge, poured herself a big glass, and started looking around, poking through cupboards and drawers, examining bins and canisters and cabinets, flipping through the growing stack of cookbooks that Miss Nell must have brought. On one wall was a neatly camouflaged walk-in freezer that she hadn't noticed before; on another wall, the door to a pantry stood open, revealing row upon row of shelves and extra storage space. Miranda stepped into the pantry. And as she heard the door swinging shut behind her, she also heard voices coming into the kitchen.

She realized at once who it was—Miss Nell, Gage, and

Etienne. The boys had probably come to take Miss Nell home, Miranda figured—and they were obviously giving her a hard time about something. Miss Nell was fussing at them and laughing. The refrigerator opened and closed. Ice was dispensed, drinks were poured, food was unwrapped. More teasing then, more fussing.

Very cautiously, Miranda inched the door forward and peered out through the crack. She felt silly hiding in here, but she felt even more awkward announcing herself to the little group out there. From this vantage point, she could see one wide angle of the kitchen—Miss Nell busy at the sink; Gage sitting on the counter, legs dangling, hands tucked beneath his thighs; Etienne lazily straddling backward on a chair. There was a plate of cookies on the table behind him, a huge bowl of chips beside Gage.

"How many times I gotta tell you, Mama," Etienne was saying. "Me and Gage, we got everything under control."

"He's right, Aunt Nell," Gage insisted. "I've done those swamp tours a million times—I can do them in my sleep. I can do them anytime y'all need me to. So stop worrying."

"These aren't good months for business anyway. Not like the phone's ringing off the hook."

"And when tourist season rolls around again, we'll both be out of school."

"Let it go, Mama. You got all this new fun stuff going on in your life—you should be enjoying it."

For the first time, his mother turned slightly, shot him a mild frown over her shoulder. "I just don't think my being here is fair.

You work way too much as it is. You won't cook for yourself, you hardly eat . . . just look at you."

Etienne angled back, spread his arms wide, ran his eyes down to his feet. "I'm looking. Damn, it's a pretty sight."

"Pretty unimpressive," Gage said.

"Oh, yeah? I hear you were almost Miss Dupree's special class project today."

"What's that?" Miss Nell asked.

But before Gage could protest, Etienne quickly cut him off. "All the girls, they're still fussing over that leg of his. 'Oh, poor Gage . . . here, let me make it all better.'"

Gage shook his head. Tossed some chips into his mouth. Spoke around a mouthful of crunch. "When did Roo tell you that?"

"How you know it was Roo?"

"Who else would it be?"

"Maybe it was Miranda." Standing in one smooth motion, Etienne sidled up close to his cousin, leaned down to speak into his ear. "Umm, and I bet she could make it feel all better."

Gage reached out to shove him. As Etienne neatly sidestepped, he bumped into Miss Nell, who good-naturedly pushed him off and resumed adding sudsy water to her dishpan. Even with her back turned, the woman wasn't missing anything, Miranda suspected. Not a single movement or facial expression or under-breath comment from either of her two boys.

"See, Mama, he always goes ten shades of red when I talk about Miranda. I'm thinking he's in love."

"You don't know anything," Gage grumbled.

"Me, I know everything. Why you getting so defensive on me, anyhow?"

"You're the one who's always coming on to her. You and all your 'Me, I'm this big hot stud, yeah' bullshit."

Etienne was all innocence. He planted his feet wide apart, then once more swept his arms out to his sides. "Me, I'm just proud of my heritage, yeah?"

"Yeah." With a derisive snort, Gage nodded at the front of Etienne's jeans. "Proud of your heritage. Right."

Etienne aimed a punch at Gage's abdomen; Gage blocked it with his elbow. Miss Nell, moving back and forth around them to wipe the countertops, looked amused and acted as if this sort of behavior happened on a regular basis.

"Just tell her, Gage," Etienne persisted.

"Tell who what?"

"Miranda." Casually, Etienne wandered back to the table . . . studied the plateful of cookies. He chose the biggest one and stuffed it in his mouth, chewing thoughtfully. "Just tell her how you're feeling. Get it off your . . . chest. And . . . other places."

"Shut up."

"You boys better mind the way you treat Miranda," Miss Nell said. Her admonishment was firm—and obviously unexpected—judging from the guys' startled reactions.

Etienne was the first to recover. "Aw, Mama, we're just kidding—"

"I'm not kidding. I'm serious. She's a sweet girl. And she has a tender heart."

"But—"

"No buts. I don't want her hurt, you understand? She deserves . . . gentleness and . . . respect."

Gage and Etienne grew sober now . . . exchanged puzzled glances.

"Miranda's special. She—" Breaking off, Miss Nell stared down at her hands, at her fingers clasped tightly in front of her, twisted in the folds of the dishtowel.

"Mama . . ." Etienne murmured, but the woman quickly shook her head.

"Nothing." Lifting her eyes, Miss Nell stared at each of the boys in turn. Then her voice went quiet . . . almost sad. "She just reminds me of someone, that's all."

"Who, Mama?"

The awkward moment was gone. Miss Nell drew herself up, gave her dishtowel a dismissive flap. "Just someone I used to know- -it doesn't matter."

"Aunt Nell—"

"The point is, and as I was saying," she continued, forcing a laugh, "I can just tell that Miranda is a very special girl. And that she deserves the very best. Like the two of you, God help me."

Tears burned in Miranda's eyes. All the while she'd been eavesdropping, her feelings had been in turmoil—surprise and embarrassment, excitement and happiness, shyness and confusion—from the things Gage and Etienne had said about her, to their gentle reprimand from Miss Nell. Miranda had never expected to hear herself being talked about; she didn't understand why Miss Nell had even brought it up. She only knew that the woman's emotions were sincere, and that Gage and Etienne had listened. And that she was deeply touched by what she'd just overheard.

With Miss Nell's lecture concluded, the mood lightened once again. Good-natured banter, jokes flying, cousins doing their best to one-up the other. The next time Miranda peeped out, both guys were leaning against the counter, propped back on their elbows, long legs stretched out and crossed. With Miss Nell wedged in between them, they slyly squeezed in tighter, exchanging winks over the top of her head.

Startling, the two boys' resemblance—it never failed to amaze Miranda when she saw them up close, side by side. Those high cheekbones, lanky frames, and dark good looks. Yet what was even more apparent was the stark contrast in their eyes—one soulful and sensitive, the other suspicious and blatantly defiant. Two different childhoods . . . two different worlds . . . As their bodies finally nudged Miss Nell out of place, the woman gave Etienne a playful swat on his backside; she lay one hand gently on Gage's hair. And watching them, Miranda could almost swear that Etienne's expression grew troubled.

"You feel okay, Mama?" he said seriously. "You're looking kinda tired."

"I'm no such thing." Stepping back, his mother motioned vaguely toward the outside door. "I need to run in the house for a second. Honey, are y'all in a hurry to leave?"

Gage shook his head. "Take your time."

"I won't be long, I promise. Why don't y'all take a walk or something." A suggestive wink. "Go and find Miranda."

The boys shrugged at each other, mock dismay. And stayed where they were.

The change in Etienne was almost immediate when Miss Nell left the room. Gage, staring solemnly at him, seemed to already know what he was going to say.

"Mama keeps saying she likes it," Etienne began. "She keeps on saying she's really liking it here—"

"She does," Gage assured him. "I heard her talking to Mom. She has energy. She feels good. She's doing something she really loves. Truth? I think she's happier than she's been in a long time."

"I don't know, Gage . . . I just . . ."

Gage pushed himself away from the counter. Stood in front of Etienne and peered intently into his face.

"Are you worried you're doing something wrong by letting her work here? It's a hell of a lot better than the tours . . . and so what if she spends long hours on her feet or at the stove? It's something she's passionate about. And you . . ." Gage paused, thought a moment, chose his words carefully. "You've got to let her live some kind of life. You've got to . . . let her have some kind of purpose to it . . . while . . ."

While she can. The words hung silent between them, so palpable that Miranda felt them too. *While she can . . . while there's time . . .*

What happened that day, Miss Nell? When I came in here to the kitchen, when you looked so sick and pretended like nothing was wrong?

"She's in remission," Etienne mumbled, averting his eyes. Gage gave an agreeable shrug.

"I know that."

"She's feeling okay. She's doing really well."

"I know."

But Etienne's brow was creased in thought, and he seemed to be studying something on the kitchen floor.

"Hey, you're taking good care of her," Gage told him firmly. "Nobody could take better care of her than you do. Than you've always done. She knows that. We all know that."

The long silence was almost painful. At last Etienne ran a hand back through his hair; Gage jerked his chin in an "okay?" nod. Then the two of them turned and left the room.

Miranda waited awhile to make sure they weren't coming back. As touching as that first overheard conversation had been, this one between Gage and Etienne had affected her even more, reaching deep, deep into her heart. She felt strangely troubled by it, both moved and depressed, as she slipped from the pantry and went outside, systematically moving along the rear verandah, searching what rooms she could. Dusk had already fallen; she was glad she'd examined the upstairs first. Since some of the rooms were still without power, she knew it would be even harder to explore by flashlight—but she couldn't wait for tomorrow, she had to know now.

It's got to be the answer, Grandpa. The answer to what the spirits need. It must be, or you wouldn't have tried to show me.

But her luck down here was no better. Room by room, inspecting each fireplace, scraping away more grime, comparing it to the photograph. Feeling more frustrated by the minute, more lost and more bewildered. *Surely it's in this house—it has to be in this house, Grandpa's standing right here, right beside it, clear as day—damn, why can't I find it?*

But the house was shrouded in darkness now. She'd looked everywhere that she could think of; there were no more rooms to search.

Except . . .

Except for the attic.

She'd forgotten about the attic. Never even considered it. Because she hadn't taken pictures up there . . . because of the dangerous conditions . . . because of the locked door . . .

But it's the only room left. The only room where that fireplace could possibly be.

Miranda paused, thoughts racing. She'd come full circle on her search, returning to one of the front parlors. Through the half-open pocket doors she could hear a radio playing, papers rustling, and the soft humming of her mother's voice. *I'm almost sure this is where I came out that day, out of the hidden staircase.*

She moved as quietly as she could. But as she tried to sneak past the doorway, her mother's head came up, and the volume came down.

"Oh, Miranda, you scared me! I wondered where you were."

"Sorry, Mom. Still . . . exploring."

"Well, I'm trying to finish up here, so we can go home."

"Great." Forcing a smile, Miranda moved on past the threshold and out of sight, straight to the back of the room. "Let me know when you're ready."

"Oh—Gage and Etienne were here earlier. Picking up Nell. They were looking for you."

"Really?" *Over on this wall, I think . . . a hidden panel . . .*

"Nell certainly seems to like you a lot."

"She does?" *Right about here, if I remember . . .* "I like her a lot, too."

"What are you doing in there?"

"Just . . . finding more stuff to take pictures of."

"Wonderful! I can't wait to see everything!"

"Uh-huh." *Yes . . . here it is.*

Miranda's fingers worked quickly at the panel. After waiting for Mom's radio to turn up again, she opened the door and slipped cautiously inside.

Instant blackness. The passageway was so narrow that she stood for a moment, gathering her resolve. She switched on her flashlight, played it over the walls . . . steps . . . ceiling. Dust and cobwebs. Spiders. Water stains and wood rot and mildew. Mice had been here recently . . . and rats.

She hadn't remembered it being this bad before . . . *But I was trying to save those children and didn't notice . . .*

Shuddering violently, she started up.

Up and up the close, cramped stairwell . . . up to the very top floor. Her hand slid into her pocket, pulled out her set of keys. Her mouth had gone dry, and her heart was racing—she had no idea what she'd find on the other side of that attic door.

So far, so good. No children laughing . . . no awful smells . . .

Yet it looked just like it had the last time she'd seen it, was locked just as tight. She had to fumble through half a dozen keys before she finally found the right one. Then, hand trembling, she heard the latch click free and the door creaking inward . . . inch by painstaking inch . . .

Just an attic.

As the flashlight made another thorough sweep, she felt a wave of disappointment.

Nothing special . . . just a plain old attic.

And nothing in here at all.

She wasn't sure what she'd expected, exactly—certainly more than this enormous space; low-sloped ceilings; gaping holes in sections of the floor; broken windows covered with boards and tarps; more spiderwebs and animal droppings; trash and dampness and years of dirt. Tools lay everywhere; a set of unpainted French doors leaned against one wall. But no keepsakes or memories, no trunks or boxes or furniture left behind, not a single clue from a long-forgotten past.

And no fireplace.

Miranda felt a curious mixture of disappointment and relief.

She'd been so hopeful that she'd find that mantel in here, but instead there were only shadows and emptiness and strange echoes. . . .

Soft, distant echoes . . . my breathing . . . my heartbeat . . .

The attic was so hot. Too hot for the season, too hot for this time of night. *It wasn't this hot when I came in, I would have noticed.* She suddenly realized that she was moving across the floor. Her hands had begun to tremble, yet the beam from her flashlight held steady, fixed on those carelessly propped French doors. She set her flashlight down on the floorboards. She dragged the doors away from the wall. And when she saw what was there, it was hardly even visible, shrouded so thickly in dust and webs and mold, and just beyond reach of the light.

But Miranda recognized it.

She would have known it anywhere.

Pulse racing, she stood in front of the fireplace, running her hands gently across the mantel, over the stains and scars and soot, along the carved edges and intricate designs.

Reaching up . . . reaching higher . . .

Hands pressed flat now against the wall—*no, not a wall!*

Her fingers dragged through mats of cobwebs, thick as moss, tearing them down . . . and something moving there—*moving like I'm moving*—like a shadow-person, not real . . .

A silent scream froze on her lips. With shocked eyes, she gazed at herself in a dingy mirror and saw a pale light glowing behind her, though she knew the room was dark.

The smell came out of nowhere. Thick and foul, washing over her, drowning her, the swarming of flies, the stifling heat. In the mirror Miranda saw an iron bedstead against the wall, shadows licking across two little faces—terrified! so terrified!—tearstained, dark eyes dark hair so much the same, holding hands, soiled nightgowns, sweat-drenched covers—and the eyes of the woman, staring eyes, imploring eyes—*I know those eyes*—black dress black hair black cap . . . back and forth, in and out of flickering candlelight, in and out of shadows creaking, so quiet in her rocking chair, back and forth creaking, back and forth on the floorboards creaking, slower and slower and silent.

Oh God! bloodshot eyes, yellow skin—the stench of sickness, the stench of decay—

"Mama"—the little ones weeping, the little ones pleading—*"Mama, look at us. . . ."*

And the whole time, the mantel in the sickroom, the mirror over the mantelpiece, she could see herself, Miranda could see herself there, her own reflection, staring back at herself in horror—

But the smell was too much now, smothering her, choking deep in her throat. She couldn't breathe, couldn't move, couldn't even cry out—*"Mama, Mama,"* the children sobbing, barely above a whisper now, baby cries, dying cries . . . *"Look at us, Mama, we're right here—"*

Miranda fell to her knees.

She watched her own reflection reach for the two little children . . .

But the candle went out . . .

And the crying stopped.

18

"**Miranda!**" *Mom's voice.* "Miranda, honey, can you hear me?"

"What happened?" *Etienne?*

"I don't know! Honey, are you all right? Please answer me!" *Mom distraught.* "Maybe we should call 911—"

"No 911," Miranda mumbled. Opening her eyes, she immediately closed them again and turned her head away. "I thought there weren't any lights up here."

"What's she talking about?" *Mom.*

"I saw the fireplace . . . but they were all so sick."

"Oh my God. She's delirious."

"She's probably just confused." *Gage?* "I'll get some water."

"Yes, yes, in there. On my desk, there's some."

"Good idea," Etienne murmured.

No, bad *idea.* Miranda felt totally sick. Sick at heart, sick to her stomach, sick in her thoughts. She was afraid that if she opened her eyes again, she'd throw up—so she decided to lie there and keep them closed.

"I'm okay," she said at last, so they wouldn't think she'd died.

"You don't look okay." Etienne's tone was half teasing, half concerned. "Do you know where you are, *cher*?"

"The . . . attic?"

"The parlor. Do you know what happened?"

Yes . . . yes . . . I know, but it was so horrible, I don't want *to think about it. . . .*

"Here," Gage said gently. His hand on the back of her neck, the rim of a cup at her lips, cool liquid in her parched throat. She prayed that the water would stay down.

But Mom wasn't ready to be reassured. "Do you remember anything? Did you feel sick all of a sudden? Are you in pain anywhere?"

"No . . . I . . ." *What do you want me to say, Mom? Certainly not the truth, not when the truth is so unbelievable.* "I must have passed out or something." *But how did I end up in the parlor? And how did I get downstairs?*

This time Miranda did open her eyes. Embarrassed, she saw Gage and Etienne staring down at her. A look passed among the three of them, which her mother didn't catch and wouldn't have understood if she had.

"Tell her I'm okay," Miranda begged them.

"She's okay," the guys echoed.

Miranda promptly sat up, Gage holding one arm, Etienne the other. "See, Mom? Nothing to worry about. I was standing over by this wall and . . . and I . . . sort of felt dizzy and then . . . you know what? I bet it was the paint fumes."

"That's odd. I didn't notice any paint fumes." Shaking her head, Mom's expression grew tender. "Well, thank God you weren't in that stairwell. What if you'd passed out and fallen down all those steps? What if—"

"The steps aren't even straight, Mom. I'd have to be a stuntwoman to roll all the way down."

Again Miranda was embarrassed that the guys were watching all this. Etienne was standing to one side now, arms folded, left hand stroking the stubble on his chin. Gage was still squatting on the floor beside her, one arm draped across his knee, holding the cup just in case. Neither of them looked particularly eager to surrender her to Mom.

"No more work," Mom insisted firmly. "I'm taking you home."

"We can take her, if you like," Gage offered, but Mom was already heading for her makeshift office.

"No, I think I better take her. But maybe you two could help me get her to the car."

"Mom, for God's sake, I don't need any help," Miranda declared, face reddening. "I'm fine. Just let me sit here for a second."

Pausing, her mother let out a sigh of relief. "Thank you so much, boys. I can't believe you were here when this happened. Wasn't that lucky!"

"Aunt Nell forgot her purse," Gage explained. "We came back to get it."

"Now, honey, don't get up too fast," Mom warned, as Gage and Etienne reached down and hauled Miranda to her feet. "Don't want you passing out again."

Miranda was getting annoyed with all the fuss. She tried to push the guys away, but both of them held on to her till they were convinced that she could walk.

They knew, of course.

She could see it on their faces, read it in their eyes—both of them knew what had happened to her, and that it didn't have the slightest thing to do with dizziness or paint fumes. That she had just gone somewhere, heard things, seen people, that none of the rest of them could ever experience or begin to comprehend.

They all said good night in the parking lot. Miranda managed to hold it together during the ride back to town, and even keep up appearances after she and Mom got home. It wasn't till after she went upstairs and closed the door to her room that she finally broke down.

The tragic memory still clung to her. The memory of that awful room, the stink of sweat and urine and vomit and blood . . . the endlessly creaking rocking chair . . . the plaintive sobs of the two little girls, clinging to each other in their bed . . .

Over and over, she tried to shut them out, force them away. Over and over, they crept stealthily back, into the dark, shadowy recesses of her mind, into the raw, tender places of her heart. . . .

Is this really what you wanted me to see, Grandpa? For this scene was so horrific that she almost felt betrayed. *You're supposed to be protecting me. Looking after me. Why did you let me walk into that?*

The pain of it was too deep, too overwhelming. The helplessness she felt, the outrage—even though she still didn't know the story behind what she'd witnessed, even though she still didn't know the truth. *Or what I'm supposed to do about it*, she reminded herself grudgingly.

She lay facedown on her pillows and cried. Unaware when she drifted . . . unaware when the stealthy figure slipped across the sunporch and through the door . . . pausing beside her bed . . . standing there to watch her. From some faraway realm of slumber, she felt the bedsprings give as he sat down . . . felt his hand, strong and protective, on her back.

"Etienne?" she murmured.

He whispered to her. Words in his soft, magical language that she didn't understand but loved hearing, *needed* hearing. His hands moved in slow, calming circles over her back. After her first trembling intake of breath, she felt herself warm and relax beneath his touch.

"So why didn't you wait for us, *cher*?" he finally asked. "Why didn't you wait for me or Gage to be with you?"

"Because I didn't know it was going to happen," she said truthfully. She paused as his hands slid gently to her waist. "And I certainly didn't *plan* for it to happen. I mean . . . I thought of the attic, I thought maybe the fireplace might be there, but the woman and—" Breaking off, she gave a humorless laugh. "You don't even know what I'm talking about, do you?"

"You'd be surprised what I know." A smile in his voice, as gentle tonight as his touch. "Gage, he told me about the picture. So your *grandpère*, he's looking after you, yeah? You can't be doubting that now."

"Looking after me? By making me go into the hell where I went tonight?"

"Guiding you, then. So you can be looking after all those other ones . . . all those spirits depending on you."

Miranda made a sound of disgust deep in her throat. She shifted slightly beneath his fingertips. "Why can't any of the scenarios be nice ones?"

"'Cause I'm guessing if they were nice, those spirits wouldn't be stuck here, needing your help."

"I guess not." Then, after a long silence, she murmured, "I knew you'd come tonight."

"Yeah? Guess I'll have to work on that, then—I'm getting a little too predictable."

"Can you . . . will you . . . hold me?"

"That's what I'm here for."

He stretched out beside her, wrapping her in his arms, his touch cautious, his body still. No intensity tonight—none of the longing that he could so effortlessly make her feel. Instead, he knew instinctively what she needed. The two of them lay silently side-by-side, pressed close. Miranda rested her cheek against him, traced her fingertips back and forth across his chest. His heart beat strong and slow. From time to time he reached over and smoothed her hair back from her face . . . lingered a kiss on her forehead. Miranda snuggled closer.

They stayed like that for a long time while the TV blared from downstairs and the sound of Aunt Teeta's snoring drifted up from the second floor. And gradually Miranda told him everything about the experience she'd had tonight, the horrifying scene she'd witnessed in the attic. Etienne stayed quiet, thinking, listening, staring at the ceiling. Then at last he turned his head and frowned at her.

"But it didn't happen right away, yeah? Just when you looked in the mirror?"

Hesitating, Miranda tried to remember. "That's right. After I found the fireplace and the mirror."

"And you were right there with them . . . in the room with them?"

"Not exactly. I was in the room, but I was seeing a *reflection* of the room. Like everything was happening behind me. You know . . . backward."

"And you didn't find out what they need? What you're supposed to do for them?"

"No. Or how I ended up downstairs again from the attic."

Another thoughtful pause. Then, "Maybe next time you will."

"Next time?" When she shuddered, he pulled her tighter, rubbed her arms, tried to warm her up. "Well, obviously I'm supposed to do *something*. So as much as I even hate to think about it, I'm pretty sure there *has* to be a next time."

"But not when your mama's around." Another hint of a smile. "You're scaring her way too much."

In spite of herself, Miranda chuckled. "Poor Mom. Totally clueless."

"That's good. Better keep her that way."

"Well, it's not like I passed out for the fun of it." And then, as the humor suddenly faded again, Miranda's mood went dark. "The children were dying, Etienne."

He didn't say anything this time, though his expression turned grim.

"Crying for their mother, but I knew they wouldn't live long. And she was in the rocking chair, not going to them. Staring at the room, but not going to them."

"Too painful, maybe? 'Cause she knew she couldn't help them?"

"Worn out? Remember I told you how worn out she looked in the mirror? Just exhausted . . . nothing left to give."

"And she'd have been plenty sad, yeah? Knowing she couldn't help them, that no matter what she did, they were gonna die anyway."

"But the room was a pigsty. I could smell blood and urine and vomit . . . it was hot, there were flies. Even if she knew they were going to die, she'd have kept the room clean for them."

Etienne considered this. "Unless she couldn't. Maybe she didn't have anybody to help her."

"She had the whole house. Servants."

"Maybe not. Maybe all the slaves were gone. Sold? Run away?"

"But why? That doesn't make sense—if the servants were gone, then why weren't she and the children gone too?"

Too sad, too depressing to think about. Closing her eyes, Miranda burrowed against Etienne, yet the unanswered questions kept nagging at her. They both heard the shrill ring of the telephone. As her mother called from the kitchen, Etienne jumped to his feet and prepared to flee.

"She won't come up," Miranda assured him. "Just stay here; I'll be right back."

She took the phone on the landing. She was all too aware of

Mom watching from the bottom of the steps, clutching a cup of coffee, and giving her a curious once-over.

"Look at you, honey—you should get your pajamas on. You look like you've been tossing and turning in those clothes."

"Good idea, Mom." Grimacing, Miranda picked up the phone. "Hello?"

"Hey, Miranda, it's Gage. Hope I wasn't interrupting anything."

"No. Of course not." Her face instantly flamed. Gage *couldn't* know Etienne was here—*could he*?

But Gage, as usual, was concerned and sincere. "I just wanted to make sure you're okay."

"I'm fine. Totally embarrassed, but fine."

"Come on, don't be. I think it's called an occupational hazard." He laughed softly, teasing her. Then his voice went serious once more. "Well . . . if you need anything. Anything at all. You've still got my number, right—and Etienne's?"

A twinge of guilt. No . . . *more* than a twinge of guilt, though she didn't want to address it at the moment. "Yes. Both."

"And whatever happened tonight . . . you're probably tired of hearing this by now, but you really *don't* need to go through it alone. I'm . . . you know . . . here. Always here."

Super guilt, and Miranda instantly melted. "I know. Thanks, Gage."

A brief pause before he cleared his throat. "Look, Roo and I were thinking, maybe breakfast Sunday morning? We can all meet and put our heads together—see what six great minds can come up with about Belle Chandelle."

"Where and what time?"

"The Tavern, as usual? Roo says she'll think a lot better with waffles."

"I love it there." Miranda chuckled. "And Roo's right—perfect food, perfect ideas."

"Okay if I come by for you about nine?"

"I'll be ready."

"Great. See you."

She hung up, imagining those soft brown eyes, that shy smile. *Not fair. Why do Gage and Etienne both have to be so perfect? And what the hell are you doing, Miranda?*

Hurrying upstairs, she slipped into her room and shut the door behind her.

"Etienne?"

But the bed was empty, and Etienne had gone.

Saturday was blissfully slow . . . wonderfully normal. Miranda declined her mom's offer to go out to the plantation—instead she stuck close to home. Caught up on all her missed schoolwork. Watched TV and ate a whole pan of brownies. Made a run to the grocery store, helped Aunt Teeta in the yard. She wondered about Ashley's date with Kurt. She wondered what she'd wear to Miss Nell's for Sunday dinner.

Ordinary things . . . routine things . . . *distracting things.*

Knowing the whole time that she needed to solve the mystery of Belle Chandelle, but not quite ready to face it yet.

Better to wait for the others' input . . . get the consensus of the whole group. Give her mind time to clear and calm down. Give her senses time to gear up again.

And stay away from mirrors. . . .

By evening she felt much better. Mom got home early, and they rented movies—the three of them in their jammies, sprawled comfortably around the den, having popcorn fights and laughing their heads off at old comedies. Miranda loved the being-togetherness of it all. She finally called it a night when both Mom and Aunt Teeta fell asleep—on the couch and easy chair respectively—and the last movie credits scrolled to the very end.

The phone rang on her way upstairs. Surprised, Miranda grabbed it, then glanced at the hallway clock. Midnight. *No, please . . . I can't take any more bad news. . . .*

But to her relief, it was Ashley. Sounding quiet and secretive and mildly upset.

"What happened?" Miranda immediately asked. Hurrying to her room, she shut the door and curled up in her bed. "You don't sound happy—did something happen on your date?"

A long silence. Miranda realized that she was holding her breath . . . fearing the worst. *Oh God, if Kurt tried something with Ashley, the guys are going to murder him.*

"Ashley? Tell me . . . what's wrong?"

"Nothing!" Ashley burst out. "That's just it! Nothing's wrong!"

"I . . . I don't—"

"It was *wonderful*, Miranda. I had a wonderful time . . . he was wonderful to me . . . it was just a wonderful, wonderful date."

Miranda groaned. Fell back into her pillows. "Tell me. Everything. Don't leave out a single detail."

"Can you hear me?" Ashley's voice had lowered again, nearly to a whisper. "I don't want Roo listening in."

"I thought you had separate rooms."

"We do. But you know how Roo is—she *knows* things. I don't want her hearing *any* of this."

"My lips are sealed. And I've got on my hearing aid."

Satisfied, Ashley recounted her entire evening. Kurt picking her up, bringing her flowers. Kurt opening her car door, helping her in. The nice things Kurt already knew about her, and Kurt wanting to know even *more* about her—showing interest and asking considerate questions. The things they both liked and didn't like, and "*Can you believe it, Miranda, we have so much in common!*" The outdoor concert, Kurt finding the perfect spot, Kurt bringing a blanket and picnic, Kurt so attentive, so smart, so sweet, so funny, so . . .

Miranda lay there with her eyes closed, letting it all sink in. And not missing the miserable confusion in Ashley's voice.

"Wow, Ashley. You really like him, don't you?" she finally said.

"I—I don't know. I don't think so." A long pause. A groan, even more miserable. "Yes, Miranda. I *like* him. I really like him a *lot.*"

"Well . . . it's . . ." Miranda fumbled to console her. "It's all new, you know? A whole new person, a whole new experience. It's normal to feel . . . interested . . . in a brand-new experience. And person." Then, when Ashley didn't respond, "Are you planning on . . . having more new experiences with Kurt?"

This time the silence seemed to last forever.

"Ashley? You there?"

"I'm here. I want to go out with him again."

"You do?" Miranda flung one arm across her eyes. *Oh God . . . poor Parker.* "Well . . . did he ask you?"

"Yes."

"What'd you say?"

"I said . . . no."

A surge of relief shot through Miranda. Though she wasn't exactly sure why she felt so defensive about Parker all of a sudden.

"And then I said yes," Ashley added.

"You . . . you said yes?"

"Yes. I said yes."

"Ashley—what in the world are you—?"

"I don't know." Ashley's voice rose, genuinely distraught. "That's just it, Miranda—I don't *know* what in the world I'm going to do. I can't go out with Kurt while I'm with Parker. And I don't want to hurt Parker. I just want to . . . you know . . . go out with Kurt. *And* Parker. Is that horrible of me?"

You're asking me *that?* Miranda's head was reeling. *You're asking* me *that, when I'm madly in love with both Gage and Etienne?*

"Okay," Miranda took a deep breath. "Okay . . . so . . . how did this end, exactly? *Are* you going out with Kurt again?"

"I told him yes, I wanted to go out with him again. But that I couldn't. Well . . . not like a *date* date. More like . . . I could . . ."

"Ashley?" Miranda did her best to sound stern.

"Like I could maybe tutor him at the coffee shop sometime.

Or the . . . you know . . . park. Nothing romantic. Just science, plain and simple."

"Yeah . . . right. And which science are you tutoring him in?"

"Well . . . biology. Well . . . human anatomy."

"Very smart, Ashley. Tutoring him in a crowded public place."

"Oh, Miranda. I had such a good time tonight. He treated me like I was . . . special."

Miranda's heart gave a curious ache. *None of your business; stay out of it.* Yet Ashley hadn't seen Parker's face the other night, hadn't seen how dejected he was after learning about Kurt winning the date. And Ashley didn't know how Parker had bought a hundred tickets—spent a hundred whole dollars on her—just so he could win the raffle. *And why am I still sticking up for Parker anyway? Parker can be a jerk. And Parker can take care of himself. . . .*

"I'll have to lie," Ashley sighed, snapping Miranda back to attention.

"You will?"

"Of course. When everyone asks me about my date, I'll have to lie and be very polite. I'll have to say it was nice and I enjoyed it, but thank goodness it's over and done with." Another sigh, more dramatic this time. "A sacrifice I had to make for the cheerleading squad."

Miranda held back a laugh. "So . . . is he a good kisser?"

"Shh . . . I have to go."

"Ashley! Hold on! You can't just hang up without telling me how he—"

"I know Roo's listening—I can *feel* her listening. I'll have to tell you later. Bye!"

Dial tone.

And the soft, still night sounds settling comfortably over the house.

Miranda stretched under the covers. Plumped her pillows. Rested her head on folded arms and gazed thoughtfully up at the ceiling.

Ashley would be dreaming sweet dreams tonight . . . about Kurt . . . and concerts . . . and probably passionate kisses.

Not dreams about attics and mirrors and children about to die . . .

I used to be like that . . . have dreams like that . . .

Normal . . . simple . . . innocent . . .

She suddenly realized that her pillow was damp.

She suddenly realized that she was crying.

Crying for that normal, simple, innocent Miranda . . . who would never be like that again.

19

SHE WAS WAITING OUT ON THE VERANDAH WHEN GAGE came by the next morning. The air was brisk, a definite touch of fall in the air, and some of Aunt Teeta's trees in the front yard had begun shedding leaves overnight. Miranda had put on jeans and a sweatshirt, opted for pockets instead of a purse. As Gage started up the walkway, she hurried to meet him.

"You look a lot better," he greeted her, and she immediately felt better. It was always that way with Gage—just seeing his face, hearing his voice, could lift her spirits like nothing else could. Today his jersey was the same chocolate brown as his eyes and hair. He was—to put it mildly—drop-dead gorgeous. "No scary visitors last night, I hope."

She flicked him a look of uncertainty. *Maybe he really does know Etienne was here last night, and maybe he knows about all the other times too.* It was naïve of her to think otherwise, she told herself grimly—but Gage merely stared at her, all innocence. Ducking his head, half smiling, he led the way back to the sidewalk, where they ambled up the street and turned onto the Brickway, following its loop to the top of the hill.

He didn't press her about what had happened Friday at Belle Chandelle—didn't even mention it. As they made their way past

St. Yvette's historic homes and buildings, Miranda was the one who suddenly found herself opening to him, naturally, easily, the way she always seemed to do with Gage. She took him through the whole experience, her reflection in the mirror and into the past. Gage listened intently, breaking in with a question from time to time, giving her his undivided attention.

"It was just so real," she finished. "Like actually being there, but watching a movie at the same time."

Considering a second, he shot her a sidelong glance. "And you're sure it's the same fireplace. The one where your grandpa was standing in the picture?"

"Positive. The thing is, I was never in the attic before. I never took that picture."

"But you said you dropped your camera on the gallery that day. And you didn't go back for it till later, right?"

Miranda couldn't suppress a shudder. "Grandpa wanted me to find that fireplace."

"And the mirror, too, obviously."

"And I think he must have guided me back downstairs, because I don't remember how I got there." Another shiver worked through her. "And I wish I couldn't remember anything about that attic, either. Their faces . . . that smell. Oh, Gage, what happened to those poor people?"

Still lost in thought, Gage absently shook his hair back from his forehead.

"Maybe this will help you," he said quietly. His voice had gone somber now, his dark eyes genuinely concerned. "I did some research last night. In 1853, there was a yellow fever epidemic here. Well . . . not just here, but all around here. Hundreds of people died. And a lot of places were quarantined."

Miranda stopped walking. As something suddenly struck her, she reached out and caught Gage's arm. "The woman's face . . . not just an old yellowed photograph? But maybe the real color of her skin?"

"It starts with an infected mosquito," Gage explained. "Once a person's bitten, symptoms usually develop in three to six days."

Miranda nodded, stunned. "And the vision of Belle Chandelle I saw that day. The house was yellow. . . ."

"The disease goes through three stages. In the first stage, her skin would've been jaundiced—that lemon-yellow color. She ached all over . . . fever, vomiting. She couldn't eat." Gage paused, clearly disturbed by his own narrative. "And you talked about her eyes, remember? You thought they were bloodshot from being so tired. But other symptoms were red eyes . . . even a red face or tongue."

Again she nodded. Turned loose of Gage's arm. "Yes. That all makes sense. The horrible smells in there . . ."

"It gets worse, though. After about three or four days, sometimes there's a remission. And a lot of people actually recover at this stage, but others go into a *third* stage, the most *dangerous* stage." Thrusting his hands in his pockets, Gage stared off into the distance with a troubled frown. "Liver and kidney failure. Hemorrhage. Delirium and seizures. Then coma . . . shock . . . and death."

For a long moment, neither of them spoke. Feeling weak, Miranda stopped abruptly on the pavement, and Gage stopped with her.

"Gage . . . they *all* must have died of yellow fever. And nobody came to help them. That's why I sensed prayers that weren't answered . . . the terrible panic and desperation . . . they all died, and nobody came."

Such tragic imaginings on such a beautiful morning. Depressed and angry, Miranda kicked at some rocks, swallowed a cry, forced back helpless tears. *Dying there, alone, the three of them, without anyone to help* . . . Her whole body was shaking now. She felt Gage's hands on her shoulders and looked up.

"Come here," he murmured, arms going around her, drawing her close. "I'm sorry, Miranda. I'm sorry you had to go through that the other night."

Her tears spilled over. She realized that she was hugging him back, hugging him tighter and tighter, her face to his chest— and she could feel the lean curves and ridges and muscles of his body. He was surprisingly strong, and there was nothing the least bit shy about the way he was holding her. . . .

"I'll always have to go through it." Her voice caught. "For the rest of my life, I'll always have to go through it—and what if it always gets worse—"

"You'll never have to go through it by yourself. I promise I'll never let that happen."

"Gage–"

"Shh. Don't cry."

She wasn't sure how long they stood there on the Brickway,

pressed together without speaking, while she struggled to get herself under control. That night in the attic had been bad enough—but now, knowing about the yellow fever and what the three victims in that room must have suffered was too painful to even think about.

"No wonder she was so desperate," Miranda whispered at last. Slowly, reluctantly, she pulled back from Gage and stared up into his warm, gentle eyes. "Knowing her children were sick, and there wasn't anything she could do for them."

"So what can *you* do for them?" he asked softly.

"God, I wish I knew. Right now I'm not even sure I can go back there."

"And I'm not even sure you *should* go back there. But . . . there's also the thing with your grandfather. Do you have any idea yet what he wants?"

"I found the fireplace that was in his picture, so at least I know *that's* right. From there, I don't have a clue. Only . . . I'm supposed to help somehow."

Hesitating, Gage seemed to be carefully choosing his words. And seemed to already know what Miranda's response would be. "Are you upset with him? Because of this?"

Oh Gage . . . you always understand. "Yes," she replied truthfully. "More than upset. Hurt, too, I think."

"It's a normal way to feel, Miranda."

"It's just that . . . why would he show me such a tragedy? These are . . . little girls. Sweet little girls crying for their mother. Can't you just imagine how she must have felt, hearing them cry and not being able to make them better? And having to watch them die?"

"No, I can't imagine. It's got to be a mother's worst nightmare." Shaking his head at the prospect, he only grew more serious. "Miranda . . . I don't know what plans your grandfather has for you. And I don't know if what I'm going to say will help. But some spirits are always going to be stuck because they're unhappy. Because they're suffering, because they were part of some terrible tragedy . . ."

He ran a hand back slowly through his hair. A slight frown settled between his brows.

"It's okay," Miranda encouraged. "You can tell me."

"And I know this doesn't seem fair, but . . ." He drew a deep breath. "Maybe so you can empathize with why they're here, *you* have to feel it yourself. Maybe when you take on some of their pain, it allows them to let go and move on."

Again Miranda stared into his eyes. Those liquid brown eyes so full of compassion, of wisdom beyond their years. Cautiously, he reached out and brushed a lingering tear from her lashes.

"Your grandfather wouldn't have given you that responsibility—as painful as it is—if he didn't think you could do it," Gage assured her. "Because . . . you know . . . not just anybody could."

Miranda hadn't taken her gaze from his face. His hand was resting on her forehead now; she laid her own hand on his and pressed it to her cheek.

"Gage?

"Yeah?"

"You know what I love about you?"

A brief flash of dimples as he smiled. "Everything?"

"Yes. Everything." Playfully, she touched a fingertip to each side of his mouth. "Especially this . . . and this."

Color rose in his cheeks. Before she could pull away, he caught her wrist and once more pulled her against him. They were both laughing now, playfully wrestling, and as Gage's arms locked around her, a horn blared loudly, close by.

"Hey, y'all need a ride?"

Heads jerking up, they saw Etienne's truck idling at the curb. He was leaning out his window, and as his glance flicked from Gage to Miranda, she could swear that one corner of his mouth twitched.

"No, thanks," she said, embarrassed. "We . . . need the exercise."

"Yeah." Etienne gave a solemn nod. "It sure looks like y'all are exercising. I swear to God, Gage—what is it about those dimples of yours?"

Gage's flush deepened. As he turned away, Miranda latched on to his arm and steered him up the sidewalk.

"Come on," she said, wanting to laugh, knowing it would only make things worse. "We should probably hurry."

Gage cast a frown back over his shoulder; Etienne, driving slowly past them, responded with an innocent shrug.

Always a favorite hangout, the Tavern was crowded when they got there, but Miranda spotted the others at their regular table near the back. Ashley looked uncharacteristically subdued— Parker, seated next to her, seemed edgy. Whether the two had discussed Ashley's date last night Miranda could only guess, but neither looked particularly happy. Roo slumped in her chair, glancing between Ashley and Parker, then shifting to Gage and Miranda as they made their way over. When Etienne walked in a few minutes later, they all got down to business.

Once again Miranda related the events of Friday night, her discovery of the fireplace, her tragic observation in the mirror. She recounted everything, described everything—sights, smells, sounds—and when she was done, Gage filled them in on his research about the yellow fever epidemic. Between her narrative, general comments, curious questions, and emotional exclamations, they all scanned their menus, ordered their food, and started in on their coffees, juices, cappuccinos, and—in Roo's case—peanut butter milkshake. Parker, sitting next to her, looked seriously close to gagging.

"I can't stand it," Ashley choked, dabbing a napkin at her eyes. "Having to watch your children die. Knowing there's nothing you can do. And that nobody's coming to help."

"And listening to them call for you." Miranda couldn't shake the memory. "It was like she was in shock. Completely empty. Just sitting there, rocking and rocking in her chair."

"And there wasn't anybody else there? Not even any servants?"

"All I saw were the two little girls. They were huddled on the bed, absolutely scared to death and holding on to each other."

Again Ashley's eyes brimmed. "Tell us again, what they looked like."

Miranda didn't need to think back—their faces were engraved on her memory. *Engraved there forever, probably.* "They looked alike, but one was older. I'm not sure how I know that . . . just an impression I had. They both had dark hair and dark eyes; the younger one had a softer, sweeter, more babyish face; the older one was holding her hand. They were crying so hard. And . . . and *pleading*. And their little nightgowns . . ."

Her voice trailed away. *Just a dream, it's not real, just a glimpse through time, it's not real—*

"Their little nightgowns were filthy, soiled. Their hair was matted, their little faces were wet, streaked with tears . . ." Like Ashley, Miranda grabbed for her napkin, wished she could escape, from the table, the restaurant, her purpose, and the past. "Sorry," she whispered, "I know it's not real—"

"Yes, it is." Roo gave Miranda a somber frown "It *is* real, it *was* real. Look, I know the whole thing sucks, but that's why they're here. And why you're here. And why you have to help them."

"Don't sugarcoat it," Parker said coolly. "Tell us what you really think."

"It *does* suck." Keeping her stare on Parker, Roo demonstrated, sucking noisily on her straw. Parker groaned and turned away.

But Miranda was together now; taking a deep breath, she willed herself to continue. "They were practically babies. Both of them just little kids. And Roo *is* right. I've got to help them. But how?"

Their meals arrived. There was a short break while everyone passed around syrup, jam, hot sauce, ketchup, butter, salt and pepper, sugar and cream. Cups were refilled; water glasses refreshed. Then, enjoying their breakfasts, they all picked up the conversation.

"Okay," Gage began, "we know they were alone there . . .

abandoned there for some reason. And we know they had yellow fever. That the mother couldn't save her kids, and they died—"

"Quarantined," Roo announced flatly. "Or . . . the doctor just wouldn't come."

"A lot of doctors died during those epidemics. Slaves, too, if they stayed."

"And the plantation *was* pretty isolated."

Nodding, Gage rested his knife and fork on his plate. "So . . . what's the actual point?"

"Main objective: free the spirits so they can move on." Finishing off her milkshake, Roo started in on peanut-butter-whipped-cream waffles. Parker immediately stood up.

"Somebody trade places with me? Please? I'll give you my car."

In grave unison, everyone shook their heads. Parker groaned again and sat back down.

"Okay . . . so . . . why are they not free?" Miranda asked, still trying to focus. "What's holding them back?"

"Something about that room," Roo answered.

"But Miranda heard the children outside," Ashley reminded Roo. "And on the stairs—"

"Maybe the stairs and the swing were just ways to get my attention," Miranda guessed.

"Gotta be the room," Etienne agreed, splashing hot sauce over his biscuits. "That's where Jonas was standing—by the fireplace—so that's where he wanted Miranda to look."

Exchanging glances, Gage nodded at his cousin. "I think so too. That seems to be the source of the tragedy."

"Death usually *is* the source of the tragedy." Parker stated. "Hello? No death? No ghosts?"

"It's more than the room," Miranda insisted stubbornly. "With all the weird experiences I've had, there's got to be something about the mirror, too."

Ashley pondered a moment . . . picked listlessly at her fruit plate. "Maybe just a reflection of the past. Like I said before . . . a symbol."

"Everything happened with the mirror, yeah?" Etienne offered. "That was pretty intense stuff, what Miranda was seeing. Like everything was coming together, when she looked in that mirror."

"Eww." Ashley shivered. "Y'all make it sound like it was alive or something."

Miranda's senses honed in. "But it *did* seem almost alive. I can't explain it . . . it was just a mirror, like any mirror. But then—when I looked into it—there were . . . people and . . . sounds . . . and emotions and smells . . . and it was like . . . it really *did* come to life."

"Miranda, that's so scary. I would have died of fright right then and there." As Ashley's voice sank to a whisper, she pressed against Parker's side. Instinctively he reached for her, then stopped, paused, and leaned slightly away.

Roo didn't miss it. And neither did anyone else.

"There's a connection," Gage said quickly. "Only we're not getting it."

"Try again, *cher*," Etienne urged, dark eyes fixed on Miranda. "Everything you can remember about that room—and that mirror. I know how hard this must be, reliving it over and over again—but maybe there's something else, yeah? Some tiny little detail you missed."

"I don't think so." Miranda sighed. "But . . . okay."

She squared her shoulders. Wiped her hands nervously on the napkin in her lap. Took a deep breath . . . coaxed her mind to that different, distant place . . . "The awful smells of sickness . . . and the flies . . . the heat. The little girls crying . . . their mother in the rocking chair . . . rocking back and forth . . . that awful creaking sound, back and forth and—"

A frown brushed her lips.

"What is it, *cher*?"

"The creaking," she realized. "It was so loud and annoying, so *irritating*, back and forth, the rhythm of it, the sound of it. And then"—clutching her napkin, Miranda wiped her damp palms—"the creaking stopped."

"You're sure?"

"Yes." Eagerly she bobbed her head. "It stopped. That awful sound, and then suddenly it *stopped*. And the silence, when it stopped, the silence was so much louder than the creaking."

"So . . ."

"Her face." Miranda choked now, fingertips at her own cheeks. "Her face, in the candlelight, back and forth in the candlelight . . . and the way her eyes were so big and staring."

"Miranda, don't do any more," Ashley begged, alarmed. "If it's too much, you don't have to do any more—"

"You said she was in shock," Gage prompted gently. "About her children."

"No. I was wrong." Miranda could hardly speak. "I think . . . I think she was dead."

"What?" Ashley burst out, close to tears herself. "Their mother was dead?"

Miranda was thoroughly shaken now. She could sense customers glancing over, curious stares, even from the servers; and Ashley making soft, whimpering sounds in her throat; and her own tears welling up and running over . . .

"She was dead. Oh, God, she was dead, and . . . and her little girls were still alive."

It was as if the restaurant receded around her, the noise, the activity, the crowds, even the smell of food vanished into the past. For one brief second, she was there again, standing at the mirror, watching that pathetic scene, the children crying for their mother, their mother dead in the rocking chair. . . .

"They were there alone," Miranda murmured. "They cried for her, but they were there alone. Sick and alone. Dying and alone."

The restaurant was back. Every fork at their table had lowered, every head lowered as well. Ashley was crying. Gage's eyes were endlessly sad. A muscle tightened in Etienne's jaw. Roo gazed solemnly at her plate. Even Parker looked grim and upset.

"She must have known," Miranda said at last. "She must have known she was dying. And that her children would be there alone."

"Oh my God." Ashley covered her face with her hands. "I can't even stand to think about it. It's too much for a mother to bear."

"Not bad enough that she suffered from yellow fever," Gage reflected quietly. "Then she had to suffer even more, knowing her kids would die all alone."

"How can life be that cruel?" Ashley whispered. Again she leaned toward Parker; this time he slid his arm around her shoulders.

Roo, glancing around at curious onlookers, boldly stared them down.

"Their mama, maybe she never knew till the end." Etienne sounded hopeful. "I mean . . . she woulda known her kids were dying—but maybe she really thought she'd live long enough to be there for them."

Ashley, however, was practically inconsolable. "But there *had* to come a point when she realized. When she realized what was happening. And then that anguish she must have gone through."

None of them had expected it to be this tragic. None of them wanted to imagine what those last days, those last hours had been like for that desperate mother. Trying to nurse and protect her children. Knowing that despite her love and best efforts, she couldn't save them from dying. And then—after all that heartbreak—to realize that she would die before them and leave them totally alone.

"And what the children went through," Ashley couldn't stop agonizing. "What they must have thought. Crying for their mother . . . seeing her in that rocking chair . . . wondering why she didn't come to them or comfort them—"

"Do we really have to talk about this now?" Parker, growing

irritated, began to fidget. "Can't we just eat our breakfast and talk about something nice and normal for a change? Which, of course, means we can't talk about Roo."

"It would have been a bad way to die, too," Roo said philosophically. "A horrible way to die."

More silence around the table. Though everyone toyed with their food, there wasn't much interest in eating anymore. Except for Roo, who kept digging away at her gooey layers of waffles.

Frustrated, Miranda glanced at each of them in turn. "But . . . that still doesn't tell me what I'm supposed to do."

"No, it doesn't." Ashley's sniffles had eased a bit. "So let's all put on our thinking caps."

Parker viciously attacked his steak and eggs.

"It's there, I know it is," Miranda persisted. "Right in front of us. Something I should be tuning in to, but I'm not. In fact, it's probably so obvious that's why we're missing it."

Gage answered with a distrait nod. Picked up his hot coffee . . . blew carefully over the rim of his cup. "What about you?" he asked Etienne.

"What *about* me?" Etienne met the stare, unflinching.

"You've been working in the attic, right?"

"Sometimes, yeah."

"Did you ever notice any weird stuff going on up there?"

"Me, I didn't even notice the mirror." Etienne seemed genuinely annoyed with himself. "I didn't even know that fireplace was there."

"Are you serious? How could you not have—"

"It was covered up," Miranda explained, before Etienne had

the chance. "It had stuff leaned against it—some big French doors. I wouldn't have found it either if I hadn't . . . you know . . . sensed something."

"As in *good* sense?" Parker did mock surprise. "Oh . . . no. My mistake."

Aiming him a fierce kick, Ashley scooted forward and propped both elbows on her placemat. "So you pulled all that stuff away, and the fireplace was just there? And you realized it was the same one in the photograph?"

"Not right away." In her mind, Miranda could see the whole scene again, clearer than any movie. "I had to scrape all the dust and spiderwebs off—they were hanging everywhere, like big sheets of them. On the mirror, too. It was totally covered, and—"

Breaking off, she looked over at Gage. She could see him straightening slowly in his chair, his lips moving ever so slightly, the strange expression on his face as he set his cup down on the table and pointed vaguely to some invisible revelation in the air.

"Covered," he mumbled.

"Right." Parker pointed back at him. "You got me covered; I got you covered, amigo."

But Gage wasn't in the mood for jokes. Instead he fixed Miranda with a calm, troubled gaze. "The mirror in the attic, Miranda. It was covered when you found it—but what if it *wasn't* covered when they died?"

Perplexed glances passed from Miranda to Etienne to Parker. "Meaning? . . ."

"He's right," Ashley echoed, almost reverently. "Back then, when somebody passed, all the mirrors in the house were covered. Draped with some sort of cloth."

"My *grandmère*, I think I remember her talking about that," Etienne admitted. "She heard stories from *her grandmère*." Pausing a moment, he frowned. "I never really thought about it though . . . she had herself a lotta superstitions like that."

"Which obviously are *not* superstitions." Roo couldn't help sounding smug. "People believed if they didn't cover up the mirrors, then the dead souls would be trapped inside there forever. And wouldn't be able to move on."

Miranda's heart was beginning to race. As a sense of expectancy stirred through the group, she leaned forward, her voice tight.

"So, Roo . . . if the mirrors weren't covered . . ."

"She and her little girls are trapped there. Inside the mirror."

Once more the room seemed to fade, the present swirling into the past, the past beckoning through a sorrowful, gray haze. Miranda could only sit there and try to focus, dimly aware of voices speaking around her, the faint smell of restaurant food, the way she was clamping her fingers together, a vague, alarming awareness of where she had been two nights ago—and where she was destined to return. . . .

"I have to go back," she murmured. "I have to go back there and get them out."

Roo was touching her arm. Frowning at her, mildly incredulous. "Miranda, do you even realize what you're saying?"

"Yes, I'll have to go into the mirror."

"And *then* what?"

"Cover it. From the other side."

Silence descended, heavy and charged with emotions. Miranda felt the weight of five grave stares.

It was Parker who finally broke the stillness, though his laugh was forced and loud. "That's insane! Listen to yourselves—mirrors and walking through glass and covering up dead—what?"

"Parker, stop." Ashley's tone was no-nonsense. "I know you don't want those little girls to be in torment forever, do you?"

"No. Shit no, of course not. You mean, the little girls—*ghosts*—whatever—that *aren't real*?"

"You always do this when you're nervous. You always do this when you're scared."

"Scared? Oh, right, Ash. That's a good one." Indignant now, he started talking faster. "If it was worth being scared over, well, okay, great. But since it's *not* real, then I'm not *scared*. And I'm certainly not *nervous*. In fact, I'm not even halfway—"

"Intelligent?" Roo finished.

But Ashley persisted. "What is wrong with you, Parker? You don't have to do anything about *anything* at Belle Chandelle. Everybody knows how you feel—and nobody needs your help."

"So what do you want from me, Ash?" Parker snapped back at her. "You've been on my case all morning—maybe I should take you over to Streak's house, huh? Maybe you should have breakfast with *him*."

"Now, now, children," Roo began, wagging her finger, "if you two can't get along, we'll have to separate you."

Gage jabbed her sharply in the ribs. "Great choice of words. See? They look happier already."

For a brief moment Etienne observed the furious couple—Ashley close to tears again, Parker hurt and sullen. Then, clearing his throat, Etienne smoothly stepped in.

"But *something's* really bothering you." he confronted Parker. "Something besides Kurt Fuller, yeah?"

Parker's outburst was sudden, angry, and completely unexpected. "Hey—fine if y'all don't need my help. Like I could give a crap. But if Miranda covers the damn mirror—then how is she going to come *out* again?"

Shocked, everyone stared. Parker, flustered at having given himself away, ravaged his leftovers with a vengeance. He kept his eyes on his plate. He refused to look at any of them. His whole body was practically quivering.

For an endless moment, Miranda watched him hacking away at his steak. Then, trying to break the tension, she caught his eyes and gave him a wink. "Hey, are you actually worried about me, Parker? Just a little?"

"No." A quick glower in her direction. "I'm worried about my food. Why the hell did we come this morning anyway? Nobody's eating. Everybody's too *grossed out* to eat—yellow fever and vomit and blood coming out of people's eyes, for Christ's sake. Oh, excuse me. Everybody's too grossed out to eat *except* for Miss Weird Cuisine here. And why the hell do my eggs taste like peanut butter?"

The strain began to ease a bit . . . into amusement . . . relief . . . yet lingering concern.

"Is that possible, what Parker said?" Ashley's glance flicked nervously from Gage to Etienne. "Could Miranda not come out again?"

"I'll be fine, Ashley," Miranda soothed her before the two boys could answer. She hadn't missed the looks passed between them—thoughts unspoken but obviously understood. "The spirits want my help, they don't want to hurt me."

"But . . . what about the mirror?"

"I can't get trapped in the mirror. I'm not dead." *And listen to yourself, Miranda Barnes—you might as well be discussing the weather.* She was startled by her own show of confidence. Startled and somewhat reassured, though the fear was definitely still there. *I wouldn't have sounded nearly this positive two months ago. . . . I just hope I know what I'm talking about now.*

"So when will you do it, Miranda?" Ashley broke cautiously into her thoughts. "When are you going into the mirror?"

Eyes downcast, Miranda shook her head. To be honest, a part of her wished that she could put it off forever. Not because she *didn't* want to help them—but because of what she'd have to face *before* she could help them. That foul room again . . . the incessant creaking of that rocking chair . . . the dead woman . . . the terrified faces and pleading sobs of those dying children. *So maybe I have made great strides in accepting and using my gift. That still doesn't make my job any less painful or heartbreaking.*

"So when, Miranda?" Ashley asked again, more quietly.

"No rush," Parker quipped. "Once you've been in torment for eternity, a few more days won't matter."

Ashley landed another kick under the table. Yet Parker's words were just what Miranda needed to hear. The thought of those children being in torment for even *one* more day—no matter how much she longed to put it off—was suddenly unbearable.

"Now," Miranda decided. "The sooner the—"

"Hold on now, *cher*," Quickly Etienne stopped her. "I know you're wanting to take care of this right away, but your mama needs that electricity fixed—she's got an emergency crew working out there all afternoon." He paused . . . frowned . . . checked his watch. "Damn, and I'm late. You're gonna have to put it off a little, yeah? At least till tomorrow."

He hadn't said anything about dinner at his mom's. Miranda glanced at Roo. Roo glanced back, then shot a shrewd look between Etienne and Gage. Both boys glanced at Roo but not at each other.

"Etienne's right." Noting Miranda's disappointment, Ashley tried to bolster her with a smile. "You can't concentrate on helping those spirits with people coming in and out, and all that mess and noise."

Miranda knew her friend was right—there was no way she could reach those spirits again without some privacy and uninterrupted time. Distantly, she felt a comforting touch . . . realized that Gage's hand was resting on her shoulder.

"Tomorrow, then?" he asked, scanning each face in the group. "I know y'all have stuff after school—and there's no way Mom's gonna let me miss physical therapy. So later's better anyway. Everything—and everybody—will be a whole lot calmer."

Ashley was the first to nod. "And we *all* go. Miranda, you do *not* go by yourself."

"'That's an order." Etienne's expression was as unrelenting as his tone. "Don't even be thinking about it."

Pinning Miranda with a stare, Roo joined the consensus. "It's for your own good—and theirs. Think about it. If anything happens to you, then who else is going to get those kids out of the attic?"

They were all standing now, pushing back chairs, tossing money onto the table, turning to leave. Throughout their final discussion, Parker had kept silent, turned away from the conversation, seemingly lost in thought. Not looking at anyone—not even Ashley—as they headed for the front of the restaurant and out the door.

Miranda was the last in line. She saw Gage step aside to hold the door open, but Parker grabbed it first. He caught her arm before she could walk through; he leaned down quickly and put his mouth close to her ear.

"Don't do it," he whispered tightly.

"Parker, I—what?"

"This whole mirror thing. Just . . . don't do it."

She couldn't ask him anything else.

One second he had a hold of her . . .

Then next second, he had a hold of Ashley, walking rapidly away down the street.

20

SHE SPENT THE AFTERNOON WORRYING. About Belle Chandelle, the long-ago tragedy in the attic . . . Parker's warning . . . and what she was going to wear for dinner.

Come on, Miranda, it's just dinner, don't be so paranoid. It's not like you've never had dinner at someone's house before.

"True," she muttered to herself, digging through her clothes, systematically tossing them on the bed. She'd had dinner at hundreds of people's houses before. *Just not Etienne's.*

It didn't even count as a real date. After all, Etienne hadn't invited her to come, his *mom* had. Not that she had ever *considered* it a date to begin with. *And why can't I stop thinking about Gage?*

Miranda, you are completely hopeless. You are so going to get your heart broken.

In the end, she decided on her favorite jeans, her blue flats, her favorite knit top—also blue—with the tapered sleeves and tiny buttons down the front. She'd always liked this outfit; it was flattering but not showy; it was comfortable, but made her feel confident. When she saw Etienne's truck pull into the driveway, she thanked God that Mom and Aunt Teeta weren't home to embarrass her.

She climbed into the passenger side before Etienne even

had time to get out. He looked as if he'd come straight from work—hadn't even stopped to change—torn jeans and work boots all grimy, ripped T-shirt all stained. His thick, black hair was straighter than usual, hanging longer in back, falling limply over his cheeks and brow. Telltale furrows there, Miranda noted, where his long fingers had raked back through it many times. There was a light trace of windburn on his narrow cheeks. The day was pale sunshine and turning more chilly, but his skin was deep summer, and he wasn't wearing a jacket.

"You thinking how handsome I am?" he asked suddenly as they headed out of town.

"No, I'm thinking how smelly you are." She couldn't resist picking on him. "Are there any more windows we can open?"

He reached over and grabbed her. Hooked his arm around her side and dragged her against him, never once taking his eyes from the road.

"Now . . . what was it Parker was saying about you being so little and so much fun to—oh yeah, now I remember."

Miranda squealed as his fingers dug into her ribs. Laughing helplessly she twisted in his grasp but couldn't get away. Etienne was obviously enjoying himself—though he did ease up for a few seconds to let her catch her breath.

"That Parker, he sure knows what he's talking about." Etienne's shrug was innocent. "Especially with that cute little laugh you got going on there, and—"

"Stop! It's not funny!"

"And *damn*, you're looking good today, *cher*."

"No, I'm not," she insisted, trying to sound stern despite the flush on her cheeks. "And even if I *did*, then I certainly don't *now*—not with all your dirt and sweat on me."

Once more his fingers threatened lightly against her ribs. Renewing her efforts to escape, she glimpsed a hidden smile teasing at one corner of his mouth, and she realized that struggling was useless.

"You're going to run us off the road," she warned, opting for a different approach.

"Me? No, I'm a good driver."

"I'll tell your mom," she threw back at him.

That not-quite smile grew more amused, though he gave a dramatic groan.

"Uh-oh, now I *really* gotta be on my best behavior."

Finally relenting, he let her scramble into the safety of her corner. Then he glanced at her and winked.

Not a date, she thought firmly. *Just a visit, Sunday dinner, not a real date . . .*

And what *would* a real date with Etienne be like, anyway, she wondered—she couldn't even imagine such a thing. The kind of normal, typical, boring high-school date like everyone else went on? No, Etienne was . . . *beyond* that somehow. *Above* that somehow. A whole, secret, mysterious world away from everything and everyone else . . .

"Miranda?"

How long had he been watching her? She'd been so deep in thought that she hadn't even noticed, but now she jumped and met his eyes.

"Hey," he said casually, "I didn't mean to upset you—"

"No. You didn't. It's not you."

"What, then?"

Yes—what *then, Miranda?* She'd been halfway confident earlier, getting ready in the security of her room—but now she was starting to feel nervous and uncertain. Being here in the truck with him, and his closeness and his touch and the playing around, and staying in the Boucher house for an entire evening with no Roo or Ashley for backup—

God, Miranda, you're embarrassing yourself.

Her stomach fluttered; she ran the tip of her tongue slowly between her lips.

Could you possibly act any more immature?

"You thinking about the plantation, *cher*?"

Miranda nodded, though she could tell that Etienne didn't believe her. "Did you get the electricity fixed?"

"No. And one of the guys got himself hurt pretty bad, so that didn't help any."

"You mean electrocuted? Is he okay?"

"Gonna be. But they're shutting down work for a few days. Till they can figure out what's going on."

Good, Miranda thought. *Easier for me to do what I need to do.* Then she instantly felt guilty because of the injured worker.

"What you looking so upset for?" Noting her frown, Etienne tried to reassure her. "I told you, the guys's gonna be okay."

"Do Mom and Aunt Teeta know?"

"I already called Miss Teeta. She said they're driving to New Orleans tomorrow. Meeting with the owners."

"Oh. Right. Mom told me, I think. But I'd forgotten."

She could feel his stare, his suspicion, his concern—but he didn't press her.

"Hey." He shrugged, gaze back on the windshield. "Try and forget about Belle Chandelle for just one night. Try to have yourself a good time for a change."

"I will."

"And don't be nervous about coming to my house."

"Why would I be nervous?"

"I can't think of a single reason."

He shot a quick glance at the rearview mirror . . . shifted gears . . . veered off the main route. With St. Yvette far behind them now, Miranda turned her attention to the open window and the bayou country beyond.

Almost immediately, the woods closed ranks around them. Trees crowded tight in all directions, leaving practically no space between one massive trunk and the next. From both sides of the road, branches arched and knotted together, weaving an overhead canopy, obliterating the sky. She couldn't even see the ground anymore—just an unbroken tangle of leaves and vines and snaking roots, layered in shadows. Like long gray tears, moss wept from every limb. And the farther they drove, the darker it grew.

Miranda shivered. She didn't even realize that she'd reached for Etienne's hand . . . not till his strong fingers closed tightly around her own.

"The bayou's that way," he said, gesturing vaguely toward his window. "If we keep ourselves here on this road, we'll end up at the office, where we run the tours."

But he didn't stay; he took yet another turnoff, onto yet another track of crushed oyster shells. The forest was denser then ever, squeezing the road to half its width. And though the day had been cool back in town, the air here hung warm and still and perpetually damp.

Despite her best intentions, she was still uneasy. *More* uneasy, she realized, with every mile and minute that passed. She had no idea how far they'd come or how long they'd been traveling; she had absolutely no idea how Etienne or anyone else could *ever* find their way around this godforsaken place—

"This is it," Etienne announced, though Miranda saw only wilderness in every direction. "I told you not to be nervous, yeah?"

"I'm—I'm not, but—"

"What, you think I was kidnapping you? Or maybe I forgot where I live?"

Just ahead of them, the trees were finally thinning, the road widening again and straightening out. To Miranda's surprise, the branches suddenly parted to reveal a clearing on the other side, and as the pickup drove in and rolled to a stop, she sat forward and stared.

And instantly fell in love with the place.

Built mostly of wood, the Boucher house perched modestly on raised concrete blocks, protected against the floodwaters of the bayou. A red front door—the same cheery shade as the trim and shutters—stood open in welcome, and birds sang noisily atop a chimney of faded red bricks. Bordered by flowers, a neat picket fence enclosed the small front yard while even more flowers lined the path to the steps. There was a wide front porch and a screened one in back on the bayou side, its view overlooking a large wooden pier at the water's edge. The driveway angled off to the right, toward a big garage and several wooden sheds. And though everything was surrounded by moss-drenched trees, soft patches of afternoon sunlight still managed to break through, dappling the rooftops and roses and recently mowed grass.

"It's beautiful," Miranda murmured, and realized that Etienne had been watching her again. Quickly he turned his eyes away and cut the engine.

"Maybe you'd like to see the bayou while you're here?" He shrugged. "I could take you on the tour, if you want."

Before she could answer, Miss Nell was already down the front steps, coming toward her, waving.

"Miranda! Come on in, honey, you need something cold to drink!"

Miranda got out before Etienne could help her. The nervousness was back again, but a sort-of-nice nervousness, she decided, not the sick-to-your-stomach kind. As Miss Nell greeted her with a hug, she suddenly felt shy, and caught Etienne's knowing glance from over his mom's shoulder.

"And my, my, just look at you." Turning Miranda loose, Miss Nell scrutinized Etienne with an unconvincing frown. "So glad you dressed for dinner."

Etienne was completely unfazed. "Miranda likes me in these clothes, Mama."

"Why, yes, I'm sure. She *looks* like the kind of girl who likes dirty laundry and a complete lack of personal hygiene."

"Manly smells, Mama." Etienne leaned down and kissed her on the cheek.

She jerked her thumb toward the house. "Go. Wash. Change clothes. I'm sure Miranda and I can find lots to talk about."

"Me, probably."

"Go. And use plenty of soap!"

Hiding a smile, he bounded easily up onto the porch, then turned back to face them.

"I thought I'd take her on the tour, Mama. We got time before dinner?"

Before Miranda could object, Miss Nell instantly brightened. "That's a wonderful idea—and yes, y'all should go now, while it's still light out."

"Oh. Hey. Listen," Miranda assured her, "really, I don't have to do that today. I can do it next time. *Anytime*, actually, so please don't go to any trouble—"

"Honey, it's no trouble at all—in fact, I think you'll really enjoy it. Lots of our tourists write back to us, saying how much fun they had and how they want to come back again. And—as much as I hate to admit it—you won't find a better guide *anywhere* than that one."

A hint of pride in Miss Nell's tone as she indicated her son. A fresh spark of apprehension in the pit of Miranda's stomach as she glanced toward the water. She'd already had a realistic glimpse of this wild bayou world, and that had been from the relative safety of the truck. But the thought of being thrust out there in the very middle of it, in a boat where anything could climb in—

"I think something might be wrong with the motor, though." Miss Nell's voice snapped her back. They were walking into the house, and Etienne stood aside, holding the door, allowing them to pass. "I tried it this morning, and it's acting up again. And none of the usual remedies seemed to work."

"How many times I gotta tell you, Mama. Let me be the one worrying about all that. Or call Gage or Uncle Frank."

His mother feigned indignation. "In case you've forgotten, I've been repairing boats and motors and cars and trucks for longer than you've been alive."

"Yeah, yeah, I know. I'll go have a look."

"And don't worry," Miranda assured him quickly. "Don't worry if you can't fix it."

"Jesus, *cher*, how many times I gotta tell you—I can fix anything."

He was right, of course; Miranda knew she was stuck. *No way I'm getting out of this stupid swamp tour if anyone here can help it.*

Yet it didn't take long for her nervousness to disappear. Enveloped by Miss Nell's hospitality and the genuine warmth of the house, Miranda soon started relaxing and enjoying herself. From the very beginning, she and Etienne's mother found dozens of things to talk about, sharing memories and experiences, personal feelings they had in common, like two longtime friends. Miranda adored the small, homey rooms; the old wooden floors and lace curtains and fresh flowers; the oversize brick fireplace and worn, comfortable furniture that she guessed was handmade.

"Etienne's father," Miss Nell admitted, when Miranda asked. Miranda could swear that the woman's voice tightened—a mixture of anger and sorrow—though her face was as kind as ever. "He built this house for me when we first married . . . but of course, it's been added on to through the years. Frank—Gage's dad—did some of it. But Etienne did the most."

A million questions yearned to be asked, but Miranda knew that this was neither the time nor place.

"The house and the fireplace and a lot of this furniture . . . all Lazare's work," Miss Nell volunteered. "He . . . he was the one who taught Etienne how to build things. How to work with his hands."

"He's great at that," Miranda agreed. "Working with his hands." Then, blushing, she stammered, "Building things and . . . making things, I mean."

Obviously amused, Miss Nell seemed to appreciate the distraction. "Lazare's side of the family is pretty traditional—somehow they've managed to hang on to their culture in this crazy modern world." A brief pause, her voice hardening once again. "I'm not close to them anymore, but Etienne stays in touch . . . sees them when he can. They care about him so . . . that's good."

They had settled in the kitchen at a large wooden table. Though the other rooms lacked nothing in coziness, this one was more spacious and clearly the heart of their family—shelves filled with cookbooks, dishes and teapots on display, pots and pans hanging from the rafters, potted plants and herbs crowded along the window ledges. A huge pot bubbled on the stove; the promise of stewed chicken and shrimp and peppery spices filled the air. Homemade bread was baking in the oven. Two sweet-potato pies cooled side-by-side on the countertop. As Miss Nell and Miranda refreshed their glasses from a pitcher of sweet tea, the girl talk continued.

Miss Nell's childhood in Natchez. Life with her twin sister, Jules. Her favorite grandmother, who had inspired her love of cooking. At one point, Miranda worried about being too nosy, but the woman quickly laughed and dismissed it. She was enjoying herself, she assured Miranda—and in turn began asking about Miranda's years in Florida, her friends, her school, and how the hurricane had changed her life. When Miranda teared up at one point, Miss Nell reached over and squeezed her hand.

"But you're here now," she insisted sweetly. "Everything happens for a reason, you know. And I'm so very glad you're here with us now."

"Thanks, Mama," Etienne broke in. "I knew y'all would be missing me."

Startled, Miranda got herself under control. Miss Nell simply stared at Etienne, who was propped lazily against the doorframe, barefoot. He cleaned his hands on a rag, then wiped his face on the sleeve of his T shirt, leaving a trail of grease across his left cheek. Miranda couldn't believe how sexy he looked, even with all the grime.

"There you are," his mom fussed. "Worse than ever."

"Here I am," Etienne responded. "Fixing that motor you told me to."

Miss Nell burst out laughing. Rising from the table, she nudged Miranda in his direction. "She's all yours, Etienne— I've monopolized her long enough. You two have fun. And *be careful*. We'll eat when you get back."

A hundred excuses whirled through Miranda's brain, but Etienne had her by the elbow, steering her outside. She remembered him mentioning some office where the tours were launched, but they obviously weren't taking his pickup to get there. Instead he guided her down a wide, crushed-shell path that led away from the house, a route winding scenically between bayou and woods.

They walked close, side-by-side, without speaking. The humor had faded from his expression, and his pace was leisurely, hands in pockets, eyes straight ahead. Miranda could feel her emotions stirring again—that subtle mix of excitement and shyness that she found so confusing . . . and annoying. A tentative silence hung between them, yet she didn't know what to say. Trying not to be obvious, she stole a swift glance at his profile. Startled, she saw him watching her.

"Here," she said. Impulsively, she grabbed his elbow and stopped him. Then she took the rag he was holding, found a clean spot at one edge, and gingerly rubbed at his cheek.

He hadn't expected it, she could tell. For a brief instant, something like surprise flickered in the black depths of his stare. She could almost swear that he was a little embarrassed.

"Guess I coulda cleaned up a little," he mumbled, and immediately ran his arm across that same dirty cheek, smudging it all over again. "But then we woulda had less time for the boat and—"

"You don't need to clean up. I like the way you look."

"*Mais*, yeah? Sweat and all?"

"Sweat and . . . and *everything* and all—"

Oh my God. Out before she could stop it, just like that. *And how many* more *ways are you going to humiliate yourself today, Miranda?* She could feel her cheeks turning pink, she could see the muscle moving in his jaw and that maddening almost smile playing at the corners of his mouth. She waited for him to tease her, but he didn't. Instead, he jerked his chin at the pathway, a signal to keep walking. It was several more minutes till he spoke again.

"I could hear Mama laughing when I came back to the house earlier. You and her musta been having a pretty good time? Going on and on about stuff?"

Miranda smiled . . . nodded. But before she could elaborate, Etienne kept on with his thoughts.

"That's just about the best sound—when she's happy like that. She . . . she really likes you."

Self-consciously, Miranda brushed it off. "Come on. I'm sure she really likes *all* the girls you bring home."

"I don't bring girls home."

This time he walked on without her, not even waiting while she hurried to catch up.

It didn't take long to get there. As a small wooden building came into view, Miranda noticed a wide covered deck in front, a dock and ramp and wooden posts on the bayou side. There was a large painted sign—BOUCHER SWAMP TOURS—some sheds, a workshop, a garage, and a boathouse. And tied to one of the posts, floating all by itself in the water, was what must be the—

"Tour boat?" Miranda stopped and stared. "I thought you said it was a tour boat!"

Etienne, already halfway along the dock, sounded amused. "This *is* our tour boat, *cher*. A Cajun fishing boat."

"It's . . . no, it's not. It's too small."

"I can go places in this boat where other boats can't even get to. And the motor's real quiet, so you can still hear the birds."

But Miranda was growing more and more skeptical. "And it's . . . open."

"Open? What, you mean like those Disney World kinda boats—"

"There's no top on it. Isn't it supposed to have a top?"

"What the hell you need a top for?"

"Snakes. They can fall out of the trees onto your head."

"Not my head."

"Etienne, I swear. I saw it on TV—"

"*Bon Dieu*, just get yourself in here."

Jumping into the boat, he reached for her hand. Miranda held her breath, stepped down to the wide, flat bottom, and glanced longingly at the shore.

"Don't we need lifejackets?"

"Naw. If we turn over, the gators'll have us before we got time to drown."

"That's not funny."

Yet despite her misgivings, Miranda reluctantly began to sightsee. And within minutes she was just like any other tourist, drawn with curious fascination to the wild, primal beauty of her surroundings.

"There won't be quite as much going on now, this time of year," Etienne explained, following the sluggish curve of the thickly wooded embankments. "Once fall and winter come, things start slowing down around here."

Leisurely, expertly, he began pointing out various highlights of nature along the way—rare plants and foliage, animals and birds, reptiles and insects and fish. The birdcalls were almost deafening—the chatter and singing, the patter of wings— Miranda guessed there had to be hundreds, maybe even thousands of different species. A nutria swam past them, totally uninterested; turtles basked on fallen logs in the last warm rays of sunlight. When Etienne's keen eyes honed in on a deer and a fox in the woods, Miranda couldn't see a thing; when he spotted an owl, a water snake, and a giant spider, too, she accused him of making it up.

"Be careful, now," he warned her. "I just saw about a hundred snakes up in those trees there. Better cover up your head."

Despite his teasing, she shuddered and made a face at him. He'd insisted she sit up front while he handled the motor, but she couldn't help glancing back from time to time. He was poised so confidently at the stern, lean silhouette against the backdrop of the sky, eyes narrowed, hair streaming back from his chiseled face. Yet his face grew hard when he talked about losing the bayou, the modern threats to its survival, the possible extinction of its wildlife. And though his voice went cold, his eyes burned with rage.

They turned down another, narrower waterway. More shadows here . . . more isolated. As Miranda gazed at some fallen trees near the shoreline, she could swear that one of them was moving. . . .

"You *were* kidding about the alligators, right?" she asked suddenly, suspiciously, and wondered why Etienne seemed to be steering them toward that one weird log. "Oh my God—"

"Now, don't be getting all Ashley on me, *cher.*"

"Oh my God," Miranda choked, frantically gauging the shallow sides of her seat. *No escape. None.* "It's a real alligator, isn't it—it's going to crawl in the boat—"

"Not in my boat. Watch, now."

There was no other choice *but* to watch. As Etienne reached down into a tackle box and scooped something into his hand, the massive alligator lifted its head, slid into the water, and glided toward them, invisible except for its eyes.

Miranda couldn't move.

With one smooth motion, Etienne flung what he'd been holding—a shower of little white pellets. The alligator immediately went to retrieve them and began to eat.

"You got yourself a real treat today," Etienne assured her, sounding almost proud. "It's still kinda warm outside, otherwise you mighta missed him."

But she still couldn't talk. All she could manage was a reproachful glare.

"Marshmallows," he explained, as though this were the

most natural thing in the world. "I'm telling you, he *loves* marshmallows."

"And is this the *only* alligator out here in this entire swamp?" she accused him.

Etienne feigned innocence. "Well . . . you *see* any more?"

"They're watching us, aren't they? Probably millions of them—"

"Aw, now don't be getting upset with me. You're from Florida—I thought you'd be plenty used to gators."

"Oh. Silly me. I forgot about all those alligators who used to lay out on the beach to get a tan."

Straight-faced, Etienne stretched over, ruffled her hair. "That gator there, he's old and blind in one eye—he's lost a whole lotta teeth. But me and him, we've grown up together, since I was a kid. Bubba, he's a good boy. And he sure does love the tourists."

"Really? For main course or dessert?"

Again the boat turned, a different inlet, shores even wilder and overgrown, a soft and fading quiet. The water lay still and shallow here; a golden-green mist hovered lightly in the air. Etienne guided their boat easily around an obstacle course of ancient trees, some rising ghostlike from the water, others shattered or fallen or half submerged, practically everything shrouded in moss. Only a few birdcalls now . . . echoing hollow . . . sounding sad . . . like phantoms lost and trapped in time. From the clotted underbrush of the banksides came the swift rustling of predator and prey, the sudden, sharp scream of inescapable death. . . .

"Miranda. You okay?"

She spun around, startled. He'd come up behind her, and

the boat wasn't moving—she couldn't tell if the motor was idling or simply stopped.

"Talk to me, now. What is it?"

But Miranda turned back, to the camouflaged patterns of the forest—foliage rotting, never quite dry; air like a wet sponge, never quite squeezed. As though no sunlight could ever break through to illuminate ancient secrets, to heal nature's wounds and battle scars; as though no breeze could ever penetrate deep enough to sweep away perpetual dampness, wild territorial scents, and the struggles of death.

"That animal crying," Etienne tried once more. "I know it's hard to listen to."

Miranda paused . . . nodded. Refocusing on him, she noted the flash of sympathy in his eyes, though his tone remained matter-of-fact.

"Survival, *cher*. The swamp here, it's got its own laws, its own way of doing things. It's cruel sometimes . . . but—"

"But that animal didn't want to die. It wanted to live."

"And some of them *don't* die. Some of them *do* live. Some of them get scars that make them stronger—"

"But not *that* animal, the one we heard. Not that one."

A long silence fell between them. When Etienne spoke again, his expression had softened.

"No. Not that one."

"And sometimes *people* try really hard to survive," she insisted stubbornly. "They fight and they hope and they pray and they do *all* the right things, and *they* don't deserve for bad things to happen to them, and they *don't* deserve to die. . . ."

Her voice trailed off, uncertain. She had no idea where that unexpected outburst had come from or why that sudden surge of emotions. She was feeling all mixed-up—she didn't want to be out here anymore, so far away from her own reality where she felt safer and more in control of things. She wanted to leave this untamable world—this unforgiving and unpredictable world—yet she felt helplessly, inexplicably drawn to it, stirred and strangely aroused by it, threatened and thrilled and terrified all at the same time. . . .

"Come here." Slipping his arms around her, Etienne pulled Miranda firmly back against him. "You can't save everybody and everything, *cher*. Alive *or* dead. You can only keep doing what you do best. Which is more than most people *ever* do."

Tears welled up in her throat. She managed to choke them back down. *If only things could always be like this,* she found herself thinking—*Etienne's warmth, Etienne's wisdom, whenever the world was too much to bear . . .*

"You really do love this place, don't you?" she murmured.

For one split second, his embrace seemed to tighten. "What's not to love?" he returned quietly.

His fingers stroked her sleeve. Taking his hand in hers, she found his wrist . . . lightly kissed his pulse. Two scars there beneath the ground-in dirt, jagged lines coursing past his elbow. Cautiously, she touched one of the narrow welts . . . traced its length slowly along a hard ridge of vein.

His body tensed. That same trapped reaction as he tried to pull free—only this time she clasped him more tightly.

"Stop it, Miranda."

Miranda kept going. "I don't care about your scars . . . you don't have to be afraid to show me—"

"I mean it—"

"You said scars make us stronger, and you're right. You're the strongest person I've ever known—"

"Don't!"

Etienne jerked away. Before Miranda realized what was happening, he climbed over the seat and stood there in front of her, feet planted wide apart, eyes stormy. On his face was a look she'd never seen before—a fierce struggle of embarrassment, shame, and defiance. He yanked his T-shirt off over his head. Shook back his hair. Fixed her with a cold, hard, unrelenting gaze.

"So look," he muttered. "Look at me."

She'd seen him without a shirt before, but never this close, in this much light. Now here were the marks of his childhood—the badly healed burns and welts, the faded cross-cuts and creases and furrows—all the sad, permanent memories etched deeply into his arms and shoulders, his back and chest. She observed them with no emotion; she kept her tears and her horror inside. She slid to her knees in the bottom of the boat. Strained and silent, Etienne followed, squatting back on his heels to watch her.

She knew he was watching, and she took her time—caressing these scars . . . kissing these scars. His skin was burning salt. His breath was raspy in the back of his throat. She could feel him trembling, though every muscle was locked in place. Without warning, he grabbed her wrists. Eased her onto her back. Gently . . . gently . . . she drew him down.

He was lying on top of her now. His black eyes narrowed, his jaw clenched. Miranda traced the angles of his cheekbones, the faint stubble of beard along his upper lip, down each side of his mouth, across the strong line of his chin. His piercing stare never wavered. His head began to lower . . . lips brushing lips . . . and as she closed her eyes, he covered her mouth with a deep, slow kiss.

They pressed tighter. Etienne's heart beat wildly against her own, strong and solid and sure. She was lost in him, consumed by him—*his heat and scent, the feel of him, body and voice, lips and touch, the irresistible need to surrender*—

His kisses grew more passionate. As she whispered his name, he caught her face between his hands . . . gazed endlessly into her soul.

"*Belle* Miranda," he murmured. "So beautiful, *ma cher*."

And then he smiled . . .

And there was no other time but this one perfect moment . . .

No other world but this bayou and Etienne.

21

"**MERDE.** Shit, Miranda, wake up."

As Miranda's eyelids fluttered open, she peered around in total bewilderment. Shadows lay thick as far as she could see, and for one split second, she had absolutely no clue where she was. *A boat?* Trees and moss and water and . . . *Etienne's bare skin beneath my cheek, Etienne's strong arms around me . . .*

"*Allons,*" he said, pulling free, instantly on his feet. "Get yourself dressed, *cher.* We need to go back."

Etienne's body, tall and lean in the last golden rays of sunset . . .

Reality slammed full force. As he threw on his jeans and T-shirt, Miranda's brain scrambled to make sense of what was happening. *Miss Nell's for dinner . . . we talked and drank tea . . . and then the bayou tour . . . and then . . .*

With lightning speed, Etienne gathered her clothes, helping her into them, fastening buttons, jerking everything into place, giving her hair a quick smooth-down. He was very good at it, she noted—he'd obviously done this sort of thing many times before.

Considering this, she began to feel paranoid.

"Your mom's going to know, isn't she?" Miranda asked suddenly. Drawing back from her, Etienne seemed half perplexed, half amused.

"What you talking about?"

"Coming back late like this . . . and I'm all wrinkled—"

"You're not wrinkled, you look fine. And Mama, she won't be thinking anything about it—she knows we got ourselves a late start. And folks, they always get themselves a little bit wrinkled when they ride in a boat, yeah?"

She knew he was teasing her, but she wanted to believe him. The day had been so perfect, what they'd shared had been so perfect—she'd expected a different follow-up, not the rush and panic going on now. She wished they could have drifted forever. But Etienne was busy with the motor, and she was feeling more agitated by the second.

Do I look different? Besides my rumpled clothes and messed up hair, do I look different? Is it obvious somehow, what just happened? Will everyone be able to tell?

God, Miranda, you are so lame.

Nervously, she smoothed her sweater. Smoothed it twice more. Adjusted the sleeves, noticed a smear of grease down the front. *Oh, great. Just great.* The boat was moving again, and Etienne was intent on their surroundings—thickening mist . . . murky water . . . shifting, distorted shadows . . .

Still huddled on the floor of the bow, Miranda tried not to watch. "How long were we asleep?" she asked him.

"Not long—we just dozed off. But Mama, she's gonna be plenty upset with me if dinner gets ruined."

"Are . . . are you sure you know where you're going?"

"What, you think I can't get around here with both eyes shut?"

Whether he was teasing again or not, Miranda soon realized that he was right. Swiftly now, just as expertly, he guided the boat all the way back, whistling softly, completely unconcerned about the encroaching night. She was almost limp with relief by the time they landed. After tying the boat, Etienne draped his arm around her shoulders and guided her along the pathway to the house. She could see bright lights glowing ahead of them—floodlights, she guessed—and right before they entered the clearing, he suddenly stopped, turned her to face him, and held her in a long, leisurely kiss.

Miranda's emotions went spinning. As Etienne finally released her, he stepped back, cocked his head, and regarded her with a frown.

"You got your buttons all wrong there," he mumbled.

"What!"

"No big deal. Here—let me help. . . ."

He was already solving the problem—long fingers opening her sweater, realigning buttons and holes, closing them up again.

Miranda's cheeks flamed crimson. "Wonderful. Just one look at my clothes and . . . and your mom's going to figure it out."

Though she tried to hang back, he nudged her forward, pushing her toward the yard.

"She's going to *know*," Miranda persisted.

"She's not gonna know."

"I bet *you'd* know."

"Well, yeah, if you and Gage did it, I'd know."

"See? Then Gage might know too."

Etienne groaned. "Okay, if Gage were here, then he might know. But Gage isn't here."

They could see the house now. A minivan was parked near the gate, and without any warning, Etienne froze midstride.

"What is it?" Miranda asked, stopping beside him.

"What the hell's Gage doing here?"

"Gage? Oh my God—"

"Hey." Before either of them could move, Gage appeared from the rear of the van, arms loaded with grocery sacks. "Hey, Miranda."

"What are you doing here?" Etienne frowned. And then, as his mother hurried past him to lend a hand, "What's Gage doing here?"

Miss Nell seemed genuinely puzzled. "What do you mean, 'What's Gage doing here'? He always comes for dinner when I fix gumbo. It's his favorite, you know that."

"I just didn't know you were inviting him, is all," Etienne grumbled.

Still pulling bags from the van, Gage shot his cousin a quick sidelong glance—definitely suspicious. Miranda's heart sank.

"I didn't invite him," Miss Nell scolded. "He's your cousin, he doesn't have to be invited. And I needed some things from the store, and he was sweet enough to pick them up on his way. As a matter of fact, I tried to call *you*, but your cell went straight to voice mail."

"I . . ." Frowning, Etienne ran a hand through his hair. "Wonder how that happened."

"Maybe you left it in your truck," Gage commented dryly.

"Yeah, maybe. Probably. Thanks for reminding me."

But there was no helpfulness on Gage's face, no humor in his expression. He'd walked away from the van, Miranda realized, and was only a few feet from her now. Miss Nell, oblivious to the sudden tension, took the last load of groceries into the house. And while Etienne wrestled the van door shut, Gage simply stood there and looked at her.

He knew, of course.

Those soft brown eyes sweeping over her, and in one split second he knew.

And it didn't really matter what gave it away—her clothes, her hair, the flush on her cheeks, though she did her best to hide it. She even crossed her arms tight over her chest, but it wasn't enough to keep him out.

That one instant glance of total awareness . . .

And hurt.

"You went out in the boat?" Gage asked, as though he already knew the answer.

"Yeah." Sauntering over, Etienne kept his voice casual . . . almost indifferent. "Showing her all the sights."

"I bet."

Miranda blushed to the roots of her hair. She tried to look away, *wanted* to look away, but all she could see was the wounded expression on Gage's face. A thousand regrets coursed through her. She knew she was being irrational, and she also knew that Etienne was watching her, just as intently as Gage.

"Y'all come eat!" Miss Nell called, breaking the mood, the awkward silence. But Gage turned and walked back to his van.

"I can't stay, Aunt Nell."

"What?" Standing on the porch, Miss Nell peered down at them, clearly disappointed. "But it's your favorite, honey. I thought—"

"Sorry. I have . . . I forgot I have to take Mom somewhere."

"Tonight? She never said anything to me—"

"Yeah, it . . . just came up. She just called on my cell."

"But I hung up with her about ten minutes ago. Etienne, why is he leaving?"

"You heard him, Mama," Etienne said crossly. "He's got stuff to do."

"What's going on? Something, I know."

There was a screech of tires, an explosion of gravel as Gage sped away.

Etienne promptly scowled. "Let's just eat, yeah?"

Miranda didn't know how she ever survived the evening. The whole mood, her state of mind, her entire life had done a complete one-eighty since Etienne had picked her up that afternoon. It took every ounce of effort to be a good guest— eating amazing food that she had no appetite for . . . making conversation that she couldn't concentrate on . . . forcing herself to smile and laugh when all she wanted to do was cry.

It's not supposed to be like this. Etienne and I were together today and it was so wonderful, more than wonderful. . . .

But Etienne was more quiet than usual—and it was obvious that his mother really *did* know that something was wrong, though she never once asked. Several times she covered Miranda's hand with her own, giving it a gentle squeeze. And several times Miranda caught Miss Nell staring at her—brief glimpses of sympathy and kindness and understanding—but she couldn't really be certain, and she was too embarrassed to meet the woman's eyes. When Etienne put her in his truck to take her home, Miss Nell called him back to the porch, and Miranda could hear their politely muffled voices, angry and arguing.

There was no talking on the way to town. Once they'd pulled up at the house, however, Etienne drew her into his arms and held her close, his chin resting lightly on top of her head.

"I'm sorry, *cher*," he murmured. "I'm sorry you were embarrassed tonight."

So maybe he *did* realize, maybe he *did* understand. Yet instead of feeling comforted, she only felt more unhappy.

"Gage knows, doesn't he?" she asked, and saw him nod. "And your mom?"

"Maybe. After tonight . . . probably, yeah."

Miranda blinked back tears, gazed out the windshield at the moonlit sky.

"It's just that . . . it's private, you know? It's like this really private, sacred thing, and I waited because I wanted to . . . and . . ."

Pulling away, she got out and slammed the door. And then, before Etienne could stop her, she hurried up the front porch steps and went inside.

Miranda was relieved to have the house to herself.

She took a shower and washed her hair and had a good, long cry. Luckily, Mom and Aunt Teeta were still out—and by the time they came home, she was already in bed, faking sleep and avoiding eager questions about her Sunday dinner experience. She knew they'd corner her eventually; in the meantime she needed to sort out her emotions. Practice looking innocent. The Mom Test would be the worst. Even as preoccupied as Mom was these days, this just might be major enough for her to pick up on.

Etienne didn't come back that night, and he didn't call her either. Not that she'd really expected him to—or even wanted him to. Still, a little confirmation would have been nice. A considerate follow-up to their evening together. *What did you expect, Miranda—for Etienne to show up on the sunporch with roses?*

I bet Gage would have brought roses.

Which had depressed her to tears all over again. Because she couldn't stop thinking about Gage.

She didn't even know why it upset her so much. They didn't have a commitment; Gage had never suggested it or made any kind of move. Yet she kept seeing him over and over in her mind—the way he'd looked at her with that sad sort of accusation, the betrayal and disappointment in his eyes. It killed her to think that she'd hurt him.

She dreaded going to school the next day. Though she was almost certain that Gage hadn't said anything, the group *always* seemed to know when something was going on. She'd have to face him sooner or later, get that first awkward moment over with. Still, that wouldn't be half as awkward as Etienne being there, watching her and acting as if nothing had ever happened.

She purposely dawdled the next morning—by the time she was finally ready, Mom and Aunt Teeta were too stressed about their business trip to spend much time being nosy. When they dropped her off, a pop quiz was already under way in first period. Parker barely acknowledged her as she walked in. Intent on his paper, he kept his head lowered while she sat down—though he did grin from time to time, trying to read her answers. To her relief, no rumors seemed to be circulating around school— not about her *or* Etienne—no gossip in the hallways, no smirks or whispered comments. Miranda's paranoia began to fade. In third period, Ashley subtly motioned to her, a secret "we need to talk" signal—then silently mouthed, "Kurt." Gage, sitting next to Ashley, was preoccupied with a book and a marking pen; he had nothing to say, and he kept his back turned for the entire hour. Deserved or not, it still hurt Miranda's feelings. And made her more determined than ever to patch things up with him.

She found her chance at lunchtime. As usual, the group was congregated around Ashley's locker before heading outside to eat, and when Miranda paused at the end of the corridor, Ashley gave her a halfhearted wave.

"Hey, Miranda. We were just talking about you."

Instant panic. *Cool, Miranda, stay cool.* "You were?"

"You and Belle Chandelle. Gage said it might not be a good idea to go out there tonight—something about the power being out? And somebody getting shocked?"

No answer from Gage, who was hidden behind the open door of his locker. *Okay, Gage—but you must have heard that from Etienne—which means he must be trying to talk to you, even if you're not talking back.*

"No goblins tonight, what a shame." Parker sighed.

Not looking particularly upset about it, he backed casually into the hall, bouncing a tennis ball off his bicep. Roo watched him, low tolerance level. No sign of Etienne.

"What do you think, Miranda?" Ashley persisted. "*I* really don't think we should go if it's dangerous; do you?"

But Miranda's attention had focused now, three lockers down from Ashley's. She could see Gage there, frustrated with an avalanche of papers and notebooks that kept sliding out as quickly as he stuffed them back in. She took one step, then halted. She thought about turning around and leaving, but mustered her courage instead.

"Hi, Gage."

It would have been better if he'd ignored her completely. So much kinder than the careless glance he shot her, the dismissive shrug of his shoulders.

"Uh-oh." Switching the ball to his other arm, Parker sidled closer to where Gage was standing. "Somebody got up on the wrong side of a wet dream this morning."

"Shut up," Gage grumbled.

"Well, you're certainly a Mr. Mopey," Ashley scolded him, shaking her finger. "He's never like this, Miranda—he's always so *sweet*. But he's been a Mr. Mopey *all morning long*."

"Maybe Mr. Mopey needs more sex," Parker suggested.

But Ashley was still in fuss mode. "What are you mad about, Gage? Whatever it is, there's no reason to take it out on Miranda."

Roo's shrewd glance went from Gage to Miranda, assessing

the tension in between. When it finally settled on Gage again, it had changed to a knowing stare.

"Actually," Roo offered, "there might be one very *good* reason. Who just happens not to be here today."

"Ah," Parker caught on at once. "*That* reason."

Ashley was completely bewildered. Miranda stood there miserably while Gage ignored Roo's innuendoes.

"Okay, I'm starved!" Parker announced, a little too loudly. "Anybody for lunch?"

But before anyone could move, Miranda walked past them, directly over to Gage. He'd finished reloading his locker now; he gave the contents one last shove. His eyes were lowered, avoiding hers—and his body was tense, muscles clenched tightly on both sides of his jaw.

"Gage," she whispered, and gently touched his arm. "Gage . . . I . . . I just—"

"Hey, I'm not your boyfriend, Miranda." Shrugging, he stepped back and slammed the door of his locker. "You can go screw whoever you want."

Silence plunged around them—a cold, shocked silence of disbelief. Tears rolled down Miranda's cheeks. Ashley gasped, and Roo's eyes widened in dark reproach. Parker froze where he stood, tennis ball dropping to the floor.

"Jesus, Gage," Parker muttered.

As Gage turned, he met Parker's stare head-on. "What the hell are you looking at?"

"Uh . . . an asshole?"

The four of them watched him go. Numbly, Miranda felt herself being hugged, then suddenly realized it was Parker.

"Hey, he's in a crappy mood," Parker shrugged, one arm clumsy around her shoulders. "Don't take it personally."

"Don't take it *personally*?" Ashley was horrified. "Didn't you hear what Gage just *said* to her?"

"I'm just glad the whole *school* didn't hear what Gage just said to her." Hesitating, Parker considered. "At least he was pretty quiet about it."

Roo seemed deep in thought. Sliding her hand to her forehead, she pushed distractedly at her bangs . . . cleared them away from her eyes. "I'll go," she said flatly.

Before anyone could react, she marched off along the corridor in the same direction that Gage had taken.

"Look at her." Parker grimaced. "A troll on a mission."

"No, it's good," Ashley insisted, brightening just a little. "Gage listens to Roo. Wait, Miranda . . . you'll see."

"Yeah," Parker agreed, hug ended. "In some . . . weird . . . creepy . . . Roo way, I'm sure she'll . . . do . . . whatever."

But Miranda didn't wait. She didn't wait, and she didn't care about figuring things out. She heard Ashley calling her, but she didn't stop or look back. Instead she hurried down the hallway and the stairs, through the side door and across the grounds, hoping that no one would see her, or report her, or get her suspended for leaving campus. Then she started to run, out the back gates and into the parking lot, and past shops and quiet neighborhoods, all the way home.

Aunt Teeta's hatchback was in the garage, keys in the ignition, as usual. She and Mom had driven Mom's car to New Orleans and wouldn't be back till late. The group would be in classes for the next few hours. Ashley and Parker had practices; Gage had rehab; Etienne was off working somewhere. And if Roo wasn't walking dogs at the animal shelter, then she'd probably be spending the rest of the day trying to cool Gage down.

And no work crews at Belle Chandelle.

The plantation would be deserted.

The rooms would be dark.

The afternoon, quiet and undisturbed.

Perfect for me, Miranda thought. *Perfect for what I need to do.*

She wasn't even afraid, she realized.

For the afterlife wasn't nearly as scary as her own life had become. . . .

And the dead were far less trouble than the living.

Belle Chandelle welcomed her like an old and dear friend.

Miranda felt strangely at home.

She made her way directly to the hidden staircase, her footsteps echoing endlessly through the dark, empty house. When she reached the third story, she hesitated only a moment before thrusting her key in the lock . . . turning the knob . . . and slowly pushing the door. Her heart began to beat faster. Standing there on the threshold, she swept her flashlight beam over the floors and rafters and walls. . . .

Don't wait. You know what you have to do.

The attic was cold . . . only blackness around her, thick and musty. A tarp flapped at one of the broken windows, sucking in and out through the broken glass, as if the room were breathing.

Do it now.

Unsteadily, the glow of her flashlight slid across the mantelpiece and up to the mirror—catching its own image in a sudden burst of brightness. For one instant, Miranda saw the room reflected there—the *past* reflected there—and her face in the midst of it, ghostly pale but resolved.

Get it over with. Before you lose your nerve.

Almost dreamlike, she moved to the fireplace and stopped directly in front of it. Stared into the depths of the mirror, into her own solemn eyes. As she pressed her hand to the dingy glass, she could feel her instincts begin to stir, a curious though not unpleasant detachment. What she needed now was to distance herself. To focus. To find that place within where she could open her mind and her senses . . . reach out in all directions . . . surrender . . .

And pass through to the Other Side . . .

The room was just as she remembered.

The smell washing over her in waves . . . the terrified sobbing from the shadows.

Same fireplace, same mantel, same mirror, and her eyes gazing steadily back at herself across an eternity of sorrow . . .

It's okay, Miranda. You're here . . . but you're not here. . . .

Flies rose up around her, swarms of flies, and the heat, she was already choking, suffocating, *can't breathe, need air can't breathe . . . little faces—terrified! So terrified! Tear-stained, dark eyes dark hair so much the same, holding hands, soiled nightgowns, sweat-drenched covers—and the eyes of the woman, staring eyes, imploring eyes—black dress black hair black cap with lace—back and forth, in and out of flickering candlelight, in and out of shadows creaking, so quiet in her rocking chair, back and forth creaking, back and forth on the floorboards creaking, slower and slower and silent* Oh God! *bloodshot eyes, yellow skin—the stink of sickness, the stench of decay—*

"Mama," *the little ones weeping, the little ones pleading . . . Mama, look at us . . .*

And the smell was too much, much worse than last time, smothering, choking deep in her throat—*can't breathe—can't move*—"Mama, Mama," *the children sobbing, barely above a whisper now, baby cries, dying cries . . .* "Help us, Mama, it hurts—"

"Shh," Miranda soothed. "Hush, now."

She was moving toward them across the threshold, across the filthy floor, pools of urine and blood, gagging, trying not to, moving around the woman with the sightless, staring eyes, eyes frozen in desperate mother love. "Shh," Miranda murmured, "don't be afraid."

Lifting the babies one by one, jaundiced little faces and red eyes, red from sick, red from crying . . . gently, tenderly, "I've got you, my darlings, I've got you . . ." Two little girls squeezed tight against her, tight against her heart . . .

Miranda held them as they sobbed. Smoothed their damp, stringy hair, rocked them, comforted them, hummed them childhood lullabies. And all the while, "Your mama loves you," she promised them, over and over again, tears streaming down her cheeks, silent sobs aching in her chest, "Shh . . . your mama's here, your mama loves you so very much."

And when at last they were quiet and still, even then, *even then*, she chose to believe that they were sleeping instead of dead. Even while she laid them in their mother's arms and tucked their mother's worn black shawl around them, binding them close to her, keeping them safe. *Sweet little girls . . . sweet little—*

Puzzled, Miranda drew back.

She traced a fingertip over each clammy forehead . . . each nose . . . each tiny chin . . .

No . . . not girls—

Feeling in some weird, distant way that they were almost familiar somehow—*dark hair, dark eyes so much the same—* that she might have seen them somewhere, long, long ago, in another place, in another world . . .

No! Not little girls, she suddenly realized, *but little boys!* And she should have known it sooner, thought of it before—their nightgowns, long nightgowns that little boys wore back then, their hair, long curls that little boys wore back then . . .

Motherless boys . . . little boys lost . . .

But you're not lost now . . . not now, not ever again.

For one last time, she kissed them.

Sleep angels . . . sleep loved in your mother's arms . . .

Through timeless shadows, Miranda walked to the mirror. She pulled some covers from the bed, then stood for a moment, clutching a blanket in her hands and staring deep into the murky glass.

The room pulsed softly, low burning candles. From far across a century, the mother gazed back at her, tears of gratitude in her tragic eyes, beloved sons held close. . . .

Understanding, Miranda nodded.

She carefully lifted the blanket and draped it over the mirror.

Your own time now, Miranda . . . your own world. This isn't your place anymore.

Centering herself, she drew a calming breath. Emptied her mind . . . opened her senses . . . willed herself to follow . . .

Something's wrong.

She knew it at once, that catching of her breath, that quickening of her heartbeat, that sudden terrible fear inside as every candle flame sputtered . . . dimmed . . . began to go out. She groped for her flashlight, but couldn't find it; she whirled around and stared at the room while a scream clawed silently at her throat.

The room was still there—walls, floors, furniture, everything just the same—just as before, nothing any different, nothing changed. Nothing except . . .

Oh God . . . God no—

The sickroom all around her—heat and filth . . . death and decay . . . pain and suffering . . . hopelessness, anguish, despair . . .

This can't be happening, it's not supposed to happen like this—
Because something was different, she realized. Something

that struck her just as the very last candle faded, and the room went completely black.

They're gone. . . .

The mother . . . her children . . . all of them vanished . . .

I'm the only one here.

22

DON'T PANIC, MIRANDA. *Stay right where you are, and be calm.*

It would be worse, she knew—*much* worse—if she panicked. She had to stay focused, had to gather her thoughts into some semblance of order. If she started screaming, she'd never stop. If she gave in to hysteria, every emotion would be exposed, and her senses would completely shut down, and she'd never get out. . . .

But you're not *really here, remember? You're only thinking this, it's only in your mind.*

Yet this room wasn't a dream or a thought—this room was *real*, just as the smell was real, as her terror was real, a primal terror, a childhood fear of the dark, *and things in the dark I can't see—*

"They're gone," Miranda kept telling herself, "The ghosts are gone now, there's nothing else in the dark, nothing else but me. . . ."

But there *were* things here, she could sense them. Other spirits suffering . . . and waiting . . . and watching . . . sizing her up, gauging her skills, waiting to make themselves known to her.

She couldn't breathe. So hot—so weak—so dizzy—her legs

wouldn't hold her, and she crumpled forward, hands clutching at the mantelpiece, tearing at the folds of the blanket, ripping it from the mirror—

No reflection there—no attic—no me—

"Help me!" she screamed. "Somebody please help me, I'm in here!"

But how could they help her, how could anybody help her? When this place she was trapped in was a world unknown to the living?

Yet over and over she tried. Clearing her mind, redirecting her focus, reaching out with her instincts. Over and over, determined and hopeful, till she was sick and shaking and utterly exhausted. With every failure, she grew more desperate. She'd been so confident, so sure of her abilities—she'd slipped through to this side so easily, it had never occurred to her that she might not be able to slip back.

Parker knew. Parker warned me. Parker, who hid his abilities from everyone, even Ashley, and most of all himself. *Why didn't I listen to him?* The very fact that he'd come to her with his warning should have been clue enough that something bad was going to happen.

"Oh, God, what am I going to do?"

Her panic was steadily mounting. No one knew she was here. They all had things to do this afternoon. After her confrontation with Gage, they'd all think she'd just run off to hide somewhere at school or maybe gone home. They'd made her promise not to come out here without them—why hadn't she waited? She didn't even know how long she'd been gone—

there was no concept of time in this lost place. *Hours? Days? A hundred years or more?*

None of this is real, Miranda, just will yourself back again, back the way you came, it's a dream, a fantasy, you're still in the attic, you're standing here at the mirror, and you're imagining all this, in your mind, in your thoughts, just open your eyes, and it will all vanish like the worst kind of nightmare. . . .

But the voice of reason was a voice she no longer recognized. And the darkness was growing steadily darker, and the silence even more silent . . .

"I'm here! I'm trapped, and I'm here!"

Her screams, soundless in the air. Her fingers sliding slowly down the mirror where nothing at all was reflected.

"I'm in the attic! Can anyone hear me?"

But no one heard, and no one came.

Only shadows and sorrowful memories.

"—*body!*"

Parker was dozing.

"—*ease . . . some . . .*"

Dozing just the way he always did in the library. It had the most comfortable chairs in the whole school, it was the only time all day he could do any real relaxing around here, and besides, Miss Callaway the librarian thought he was cute and let him do pretty much whatever he wanted, as long as he didn't snore.

"—*elp . . . please . . .*"

"Huh?" he mumbled. "What?"

A kid at the shelves gave him a funny look. Parker gave him the finger and settled back in the cushy, oversized chair.

"—*in here!*"

"What?" Parker asked, and realized once again that nobody was talking.

Dammit, what's going on? He was trying to sleep, he had important things to think about, like the game Friday and making sure Ashley got his English paper done on time and keeping an eye on that jerk Streak Fuller . . .

He wanted to believe that things were okay with Ashley.

After all the agonizing he'd done, and the money he'd spent on those stupid cheerleader tickets. And even if he did still think the raffle had been fixed.

And Ashley *had* been open about the whole date thing; she'd told him about her night at the concert—so he couldn't complain about that. She'd had fun, though, he could tell—so he sure as hell *could* complain about *that*. . . . And sometimes lately she had that weird look on her face—the look girls always got when they were thinking about some guy. Except suddenly he wasn't quite sure if *he* was the guy Ashley was thinking about, so there was one *more* thing he could complain—

"*Parker!*"

"Who is that?" he demanded, and got to his feet, turning in a slow, suspicious circle.

Miss Callaway was at her desk, politely frowning. So it didn't really make sense that somebody was playing a joke on him, rigging up voices, watching to see what he'd do so they could laugh. And Miss Callaway would never allow that in her library, anyway.

Maybe he'd fallen asleep, he reasoned—gone into one of those deep, eye-twitchy levels people always talked about. Whatever it was, it was really starting to piss him off. He looked forward to these little catnaps. And it creeped him out when things played with his head.

Parker sat again, slid down in his chair. Folded his arms over his chest. Lowered his chin . . . closed his eyes . . .

"Parker, please hear me!"

"Miranda?"

This time he bolted upright, brain spinning wildly. Not a dream, he was sure of it—he'd know her voice anywhere.

But where was it?

And how come he was the only one in the whole library who seemed to be picking it up?

She'd run away earlier, after Gage had acted like a total prick. Ashley had tried to stop her, but Miranda had been so upset, and actually he couldn't blame her. Damn that Gage. And Etienne, too, since it was pretty obvious what had happened. Parker hated seeing girls with hurt feelings, but especially girls he knew . . . and liked. Miranda was cool. She had balls. He didn't want to see her heart broken.

So what's going on?

He walked outside to the water fountain. Trying to calm himself down, trying to think. He'd assumed Miranda had gone home; under the circumstances, he'd have gone home. He would have gone after her too—but he couldn't afford a suspension for leaving school grounds. Luckily, Ash knew that chick in the office. After Miranda left, Ashley had told the girl that Miranda was sick, and so she'd marked it down, all legal. Ashley was upset for Miranda, and Parker didn't blame her. It had surprised him, how fast Miranda and Ashley became friends.

"*—help . . . in here—*"

Goosebumps shivered up his spine. He was totally freaked, hearing Miranda like that, being so sure it was her stuck up in his head with nowhere else to go. He gulped some water, then began to pace. Maybe she was just bored at home right now, testing out her stupid powers, using him for a guinea pig.

Damn you, Miranda. Damn you for making me face this—

"*Parker!*" Shit, was she crying? It sure *sounded* like she was crying—"*Parker, please find me!*"

"Jesus Christ . . ."

What's happening, Miranda? Can you hear my thoughts like I can hear yours? Can you tell me where you are?

"*Help me. . . .*"

There was terror in her voice . . . a sense of loss and emptiness . . . like a voice at the bottom of a well. A lonely place . . . a dark place . . .

And she was scared . . . and alone . . . and . . .

Trapped.

Parker bolted for the exit, fished his cell phone from his pocket, punched in an all-too-familiar number.

It rang once, twice, and then—

"Etienne? You need to find Miranda—*now.*"

*   *   *

Gage knew immediately that something was wrong.

The way Etienne's tires screeched right up next to the fence, the way he was out of the truck before it even had time to stop. From the top row of bleachers, Gage watched his cousin slip through the back gate, hurry toward him across one end of the playing field, then stop in front of him with a frown.

"Gage, Miranda's gone."

"Gone? What are you talking about?"

"Nobody can get a hold of her, they've all been trying to call. I'm thinking maybe she got herself in some kinda trouble over at Belle Chandelle. Parker said she was upset earlier—ran outta school in a hurry—"

"Well, you know Belle Chandelle better than anybody," Gage cut him off. "You should be able to handle it."

"And that mirror? The one she was talking about going into? I'm having a real bad feeling about that. You need to come."

For a long awkward moment, neither said a word. Then finally, unapologetically, Etienne sighed. "Look, Miranda and me—it just happened."

"It always just happens."

"I'm not gonna hurt her. I could never do that."

"You'll do it. This one won't be any different."

"Look, Gage, we can be having ourselves a pissing contest all day long . . . or we can go find Miranda. What's it gonna be?"

Etienne turned and headed back to his truck.

Gage silently watched him go.

*   *   *

Help . . . somebody . . . the attic . . . the mirror . . .

Miranda couldn't scream anymore. Not with her voice and not with her mind. Her throat felt raw, as raw as her hands felt from pounding on the mirror, from prying at the hidden-panel door. *But maybe there really is no pain, no screaming, no pounding or prying. Just this nightmare where I'm trapped, this imaginary place that I can't come back from.*

Reality had no meaning here; time had ceased to exist. She'd fought so desperately to hold out, but the fear and the dark and the sickroom smells had eventually worn her down—drifting her in and out of consciousness. After a while, she hadn't even tried to struggle anymore. She'd shut off her senses, her thoughts, her emotions—to block out the horrible truth. *To survive.*

Not real . . . not real . . . not real . . .

And then the shadows began to come.

Comforting her, caressing her, in soft, seductive whispers. *Stay, Miranda, stay here with us . . . stay at Belle Chandelle . . .*

She wondered if she really might be dying. And realized that she was already in her tomb.

She thought of Mom and Aunt Teeta. Of Roo and Ashley . . . Parker and Gage. Etienne.

She imagined him on the boat, in those last golden rays of sunlight, and his hands making her feel safe, and his heart beating strong against hers, and his voice calling her name, *Miranda . . .*

"Miranda!"

So sweet this imagining, so perfect in her memory, that she could almost believe it had happened once. . . .

"Miranda!"

But it never happened, and it's not real, and it's only in my head—

"Miranda, can you hear me? Wake up!"

Etienne?

The room began to grow smaller. Shadows stirred restlessly on every side. Shadows content to sleep, not wanting to be disturbed by intruders. *Stay with us, Miranda . . . no fears . . . no problems . . . no running away . . . nothing to cry over, ever again . . .*

"Miranda, where are you?"

Gage? "Oh, Gage, yes! Yes, I'm here!"

The room had disappeared now. Smothered in shadows, and only this mantelpiece remaining. Only this mantelpiece and mirror left behind.

Miranda reached out cautiously toward the glass . . . saw a faint shadow move on the other side. *A silhouette of a hand . . . the low murmur of voices . . . voices that I recognize . . .*

And then, like a fog slowly lifting, the mirror began to clear . . . lighten . . . and reflect.

An image of another attic . . . another time . . . another Miranda . . .

She could see herself lying there on the cold, dusty floor. Darkness lit eerily by lanterns and flashlights, friends gathered closely around. Gage and Etienne kneeling over her, one on each side, Etienne holding her hand. Ashley sobbing in the circle of Parker's arms. Roo standing somberly behind Gage.

Like dream people. Like people in a play.

No . . . no . . . I'm the dream person . . . and I'm trying so hard to wake up. . . .

"Wake up, Miranda," Etienne mumbled. "Come on, *cher*. Open your eyes."

"Is she dead?" Ashley sobbed, while Parker held her closer. "She looks dead, are you sure she's not—"

"She's not dead." Gage insisted quietly. "She's . . . just . . ."

"In another place," Roo finished. "An in-between place." Collecting jackets from everyone, she leaned over, covered Miranda, then lightly touched Etienne's shoulder. "Does she even know us? Does she even know we're here?"

Etienne frowned, his face half light, half shadow. "She can't stay like this. Not for much longer. She's hardly even breathing."

"Well, we can't take her to a hospital," Parker argued. "They sure as hell won't know what to do with her."

"Oh, and like, you do?" Roo challenged him.

Ashley held up her hands for peace. "We don't even know how long she's been like this. She's never done this before . . . this hasn't ever happened. Not *supposed* to happen."

"It's my fault," Gage said unhappily. "If I hadn't said what I did—"

"Your fault?" Etienne scowled. "I'm the one who got her all upset—"

"Does it even friggin' matter?" Parker was pacing, back and forth, the width of the room. "Just figure out a way to get her here. You can settle this other shit later."

Reaching out, Ashley stopped him midstride. "Parker's right. How do we get her back?"

"Same way she went in," Gage replied softly, "would be my guess."

"But she went in through her mind."

"But her mind went through the mirror."

Miranda could see Gage standing, moving toward the mirror. His face leaning in, his eyes and fingertips carefully scrutinizing every inch of the glass. He was so close, she could have touched him. He pressed his hand flat against the mirror; she placed hers against it. He stared at her, almost as if he sensed her presence, but obviously seeing nothing.

"Gage, I'm here. Please see me."

But instead, Gage turned on his heel and gazed at Etienne. "You'll have to bring her back."

A quick glance, startled. Etienne's hand tightened around Miranda's limp hand. "Me? How?"

"You're the one with the strongest connection. You're the one her spirit will be most drawn to. Especially if she's lost . . . or doesn't have the strength . . ."

"I'm not leaving her." Again his grip tightened on the unconscious Miranda's hand.

Gage took a step toward him. "Look. Suppose she *is* stuck in some alternate world. And because she went in through the mirror, that world is . . . backward. Everything reversed. I mean . . . it makes sense. The attic there would be switched around, opposite to this attic. We have the living on this side, they have the dead. And just because we can't see Miranda doesn't mean she can't see us. Right now. She could be watching us right now, even though our side of the mirror looks empty."

The attic was silent for several moments. It was Etienne who finally spoke.

"Look at her." His voice was rough, barely a whisper. "What if she's *not* over there, on the other side of that mirror? What if she's really in *here*? Really still in *here*, and she's not coming back, no matter what?"

Tears rolled down Ashley's face. Roo's eyes shone with undisguised emotion; Parker choked down a sudden lump in his throat.

"Miranda's not in there." Walking over to Etienne, Gage put a hand on his shoulder. "Etienne, it's not her lying here on the floor. Trust me. Let go of her hand . . . so you can get her back."

But mirror-Miranda could feel herself fading . . . fading like the ghosts of the mother and her children . . . fading like all the spirits who had passed this way before her. And when she finally heard Etienne's familiar voice, it seemed like some distant memory that she couldn't quite recall. . . .

"Miranda."

That voice . . . I've heard that voice before . . . but where?

"Touch my hand, *cher*. Can you hear me? Go the mirror, and touch my hand."

Another shadow . . . passing by the mirror . . . pausing on the other side of the glass. Glass hazy again, dusty with time, washed with the tears of many grieving hearts . . .

"I know you're there—you've *got* to be there. Just take my hand . . . just reach for it . . ."

Sharp silhouette, fingers splayed, palm flat . . . those hands that I held, that held me, caressed me, protected me, wanted me . . . warmth, purpose, strength, life—

Weakly, she stretched her own hand to the mirror. Fingertips sliding uselessly away . . .

"Miranda," Gage said sharply, "look at the mirror. Take Etienne's hand. Do it now."

That hand . . . yes . . . that hand that I know . . . that I love . . .

With her last ounce of strength, she touched the shadow on the mirror. And instantly felt the connection—

Etienne.

"Come on, *cher*. Reach out to me, that's right, I can feel you—"

"Let your heart go, Miranda," Gage said softly. "Hold Etienne's hand . . . let your heart go . . . and follow it."

The world went upside down.

Every century, every day, every second of Belle Chandelle rushing past her, around her, each bright and bitter moment filling the mirror with images of long ago. In a dizzying blur, Miranda swept through the shadows and the sorrows and the spirits. . . .

And returned from the Other Side

She was still clutching Etienne's hand.

She was lying on the floor, with her friends around her, a blur of laughter and jokes and tears. Unspoken words in Etienne's eyes. Ashley, Parker, and Roo all talking at once. And Gage standing apart; hands clasped together behind his neck; a relieved and weary smile.

Miranda rose up on her elbows. She saw Roo walk over to Gage, the grateful hug she gave him, the modest hug he gave back.

But as Roo turned away, Gage's eyes met Miranda's.

Holding her in a gentle gaze . . .

As he touched one hand to his heart.

23

"MISS NELL WANTS US TO COME OUT THERE AND EAT," Roo explained. "Some new recipe she's trying. You know, for a crowd?"

Yawning, Miranda ran a hand through her tangled hair. Switched the phone to her other hand. Sat down on the porch swing and pulled her snuggly robe tight around her.

"Well, I definitely think the six of us qualify as a crowd," she agreed. "Is Miss Nell out at Belle Chandelle now? What time is it anyway?"

"A little after three. How's your coma?"

"No coma. Just mirror-itis. Luckily, Mom still thinks it's just a flu relapse. Although I *have* been getting a lot of I-told-you-so's."

"You should take advantage of your sick-leave. Stay home longer."

"No, thanks. One day is plenty. I'm sick-leaved out."

"Watch more comedy reruns. Enjoy more pampering. I mean . . . going back and forth through time takes a lot out of a person."

Miranda had to laugh. "Tell me about it."

"Anyway, Miss Nell said to come any time after five-thirty You want Parker to give you a ride?"

"You know what?" Miranda said quickly. "I'm pretty sure I can borrow Mom's car. I'll just meet you out there."

"Okay."

The truth was, Miranda had her own agenda in mind. Something none of the others knew about, something she hadn't even been aware of herself till she'd slipped through that mirror for the final time, returning from the past to the present.

It had weighed on her mind ever since. With every memory of the attic and its occupants, a troubling insight had been forming in her mind, gathering substance and truth and reality. It had haunted her—not threatening this time, but with a strange sort of affection—murmuring into her dreams and then whispering her awake with gentle knowings.

She was right about it, she was certain.

The others weren't there yet when she got to Belle Chandelle; she'd purposely driven out early, after hanging up with Roo. Only Miss Nell's car was in the parking lot, and as Miranda walked toward the house, she could already smell the seafood boil—shrimp and crabs, potatoes and corn and onions, all boiled together with spices, outside in a giant cauldron. There was French bread baking too—butter being warmed, bread pudding in the oven, rum sauce gently simmering. When Miranda walked into the kitchen, Miss Nell was angled away from the door, leaning on the counter, poring eagerly over cookbooks. Miranda almost turned around and left. Maybe it was wrong to bring up this matter she wanted to discuss. Too intrusive. Too private . . . *too special*—

"Miranda! Come in! Has that flu finally run its course? I was so hoping you'd be here today."

Before Miranda could change her mind, Miss Nell had her wrapped in one of those perfect hugs. Maybe it was a sign, Miranda told herself—to go ahead with her mission.

"Are you here early for a sneak preview?" Miss Nell teased. "Did you notice the picnic tables? It's such perfect weather today, I thought we could eat outside. Plus, I think I'll be cooking for the work crews a few days a week from now on."

"That's great. No, I just decided to . . . see if I could help with anything."

"Honey, that's so sweet, but I think I have everything under control. Just some heavy stuff that can wait till the boys get here. Oh. And I brought something to show you." Clearing off a chair, she motioned Miranda to sit down. "Since you were telling me that day how much you like looking at old pictures . . ."

Miranda couldn't believe it. There couldn't have been a more perfect lead-in to what she had to say if she'd planned it herself. When Miss Nell placed the family album down on the table in front of her, Miranda immediately gave a squeal of delight.

"Gage? Oh my God, that *has* to be Gage—"

"It is," Miss Nell chuckled. "He looks like a little doll . . . those eyes and those dimples. See here, next to Etienne, he makes Etienne look like some criminal-in-training."

"He *is* a criminal-in-training," Miranda insisted. *He steals hearts, and batters down defenses, and sneaks in when and where you least expect him to.*

Miss Nell gave a knowing smile. As if all too aware of what Miranda was thinking.

Miranda was having so much fun. Family members and friends, summer vacations for Gage and his folks, pictures of Miss Nell's restaurant, historic images of St. Yvette and its charming transformation through the years. And on every page, snapshot after snapshot of Gage and Etienne.

The boys clowning around, competing, cutting up. School pictures and family holidays, the bayou in every season. And the rest of the group, of course—Ashley and Parker and Roo—keeping life interesting and entertaining through the years.

By the time Miss Nell closed the album, Miranda was sore from laughing. They'd gone through a whole pitcher of tea and finished off a bag of extra spicy pork rinds and talked till they were almost hoarse. But now, and unexpectedly, Miss Nell pulled a photograph from the album and passed it to her.

Miranda looked up in surprise. "What's this?"

"I was noticing how you looked at this one. As if you especially liked it."

Gage and Etienne side-by-side. Dark hair so much the same, but different; dark eyes so much the same, but different. The hard line of Etienne's jaw, the dimple in Gage's cheek. Miranda felt her throat tighten.

"Oh, Miss Nell . . . I mean—"

"It's my favorite too. I'd like you to have it."

"But—"

"Please. When they behave . . . irresponsibly—that picture will remind you of how good and wonderful they truly are."

Miranda ducked her head . . . felt a quick flush of embarrassment. Obviously, Miss Nell never missed much. And obviously, she knew her boys.

"I . . . need to ask you something, Miss Nell."

The woman's glance was totally open. "What is it, honey?"

Slowly, Miranda looked up. She gazed full into Miss Nell's black eyes, so very much like her son's.

"Gage and Etienne," Miranda murmured at last. "They're not . . . what I mean is . . ."

And she saw the expression on Miss Nell's face—a split second of acknowledgment, but no surprise . . . an instant of reflection, but no denial. Before Miranda could even say the words, Miss Nell's eyes told her everything that she needed to know. Immeasurable sadness . . . unbearable pain . . . and then finally . . . gently . . . surrender and relief.

"Gage and Etienne," Miranda could barely speak. "They're not cousins, are they?"

Straightening her shoulders, Miss Nell sat down again, directly across the table.

"No."

"They're both your sons. They're brothers."

Time crept by, and with it, a poignant silence. At last Miss Nell's mouth twisted into a brave, bitter smile. "Etienne's father didn't want another baby," she explained. "When I got pregnant with Gage, Lazare was drinking again, violent, the abuse worse than ever. I took Etienne and went to Jules and Frank's in Mississippi around my due date. And I had my baby there. I told Lazare it was stillborn—which was believable, actually, considering the beatings."

Now Miss Nell's eyes were tearing up. She hesitated a moment, got her emotions under control. Cleared her throat and continued.

"He didn't care, of course, and he didn't question it. In fact, I'm sure he was relieved. Jules and Frank arranged Gage's adoption. I didn't want Gage to go through all the torture and humiliation that Etienne had. No child should ever have to endure that."

"And Gage doesn't know."

Miss Nell shook her head, absolute resolution. "And neither does Etienne. And neither one of them must *ever* know."

Reaching across the table, Miranda took the woman's hand. "Of course, I won't say anything if—"

"I'm dying, Miranda."

Time stopped. Pain stabbed from nowhere. As Miranda stared through a haze of shock, the whole world turned dark around her. Her sorrow was spilling over now; she could scarcely see Miss Nell for the tears.

"The cancer's back," Miss Nell said softly. "It's just a matter of time."

"Oh my God . . . Miss Nell . . ."

"Etienne doesn't know about that, either. And that's another thing you have to *promise* me—*swear* to me—you'll never tell him."

"But—but what if he figures it out? He—"

"Yes, he's always had a way of knowing things. But this one's different. He *doesn't want* to figure this out, Miranda. He *doesn't want* to know. He wants to believe I'm in remission, so that's exactly what I'm going to let him think. For as long as possible. For as long as I can hide it. And for as long as he wants to believe it."

"And how long . . . how long do you—"

"Well, it's a battle between my body and my will now, isn't it?" Despite the grim topic, a dimple flashed in Miss Nell's cheek. "And my will hasn't failed me yet. I just might outlive Belle Chandelle, who knows?"

She laughed. A courageous laugh. A determined laugh. A laugh that warmed Miranda's heart, despite the troubling shadows.

"Miss Nell." Her voice trembled. "I'm so sorry."

"Don't be sorry, honey. All of us are dying every day . . . just like all of us are living every day." Laughter faded now, Miss Nell's tone grew solemn once more. "The thing is . . . I always thought I'd be here a long time, to watch my boys grow up. Protect them. Keep them safe. But life didn't work out that way. And I don't want whatever time I have left with my boys to be bitter or sad or . . ."

Miss Nell pressed her hand over her eyes . . . shook her head. Miranda's face was wet with tears.

"But," Miranda had to say it, "don't you think Gage would *want* to know? About you being his mother? Especially if you're going to . . . not going to be here someday?"

"Gage has a mom and dad who adore him; a wonderful,

loving home; a great life." Her hand lowered back to the table, her voice grew urgent. "What more could a mother ask for her son? Why would I go and ruin that for him—because of things he didn't have any control over? Then there would be regrets, and guilt, and all those other things I don't ever want Gage to go through. I love him so much . . . *so much*. I don't want to put the burden on him of who I am."

"Miss Nell . . . you're incredible."

"Shh." With eyes gleaming tears, Miss Nell reached across the table. She took Miranda's hand tightly in her own. "I know that what I'm asking you to do is a huge thing . . . an enormous responsibility. To keep these secrets from Gage and Etienne. But I *need* you to do this for me, Miranda . . . *and* for them."

"I swear."

"Thank you, honey." Stretching from her chair, Miss Nell leaned over and kissed Miranda's forehead. Then she wiped the tears gently from Miranda's cheeks. "You remind me of somebody, Miranda. Somebody I used to know."

"Who's that?"

Sliding her fingers under Miranda's chin, Miss Nell gazed deep into her eyes. "Me. And you're a whole lot stronger than you think. Don't ever forget that."

There were sounds outside now, banter and fussing, laughter and commotion. Kicking into high gear, Miss Nell started toward the stove, stopped, and looked back at Miranda with a puzzled frown.

"Just out of curiosity . . . how did you figure out I was Gage's mother?"

"Would you believe the dimples?" Miranda teased.

"No, I wouldn't." Miss Nell laughed. "There are lots of people in our family with dimples. They're the bane of Gage's existence, poor thing."

An ache of tenderness went through Miranda's heart. "Watching you with them. Watching you love them."

And watching a dark-eyed mother with her two dark-haired sons. A mother whose love lasts forever . . .

The door burst open without warning. Etienne strolled in with Gage and Roo at his heels.

"Uh-oh—looks like we got ourselves some serious girl talk going on in here." Etienne elbowed Roo in the side. "Maybe you wanna be joining them, huh *cher*?"

Roo leveled him a look. "I don't do girl talk."

"Then maybe," Miss Nell said smoothly, "y'all wouldn't mind chopping some of this stuff for salad?"

As the prep crew got to work, Miranda slipped out of the kitchen. She could see Parker sitting on one of the picnic tables, Ashley drawn back between his knees, his kisses lazy on the top of her head. But Parker couldn't see Ashley's expression . . . the faraway dreams in her eyes. *And what secrets do you have, Ashley? That could change two lives in a minute?*

Lost in her thoughts, Miranda sneaked past them and headed away from the house.

The weather was beautiful. Cloudless sky, crisp breeze, and leaves swirling in every direction. A golden, glorious Southern day, and she was thankful to be alive.

She didn't hear the footsteps coming up behind her. Didn't

see Etienne till he caught her by the shoulders and swung her around to face him.

Swamp black eyes pinned her in a stare. And her heart was already racing.

"I thought you were mad at me," he mumbled.

For a minute Miranda stared back at him, trying to figure out what he was talking about.

"That's how come I didn't call you that night," he mumbled again. "After the boat, after I took you home. I thought maybe you were sorry about what happened. And so . . . I just wanted to tell you."

His voice was gruff, he was holding her so tight. She'd never heard him talk this fast before.

"Why would I be sorry?" was all she could think of to say.

"For how you got all embarrassed. And . . . well . . . for Gage."

A long silence passed between them. When Miranda finally shook her head, it was in mild disbelief.

"When you didn't call, I thought maybe *you* wished it never happened."

"Me? Now, why would I be wishing that?"

"I thought I was just one more of your . . . your . . ."

That hint of amusement, playing over his mouth. "One more *what, cher*?"

"One more . . . victory!" Miranda looked highly indignant. "Among hundreds, I'm sure."

"Hundreds?" As Etienne's eyes widened, he made a faint sound in his throat. "*Bon Dieu*, you're flattering me, girl. But I'm liking the compliment, just the same."

He caught her face between his hands . . . covered her lips with a deep, slow kiss. When he spoke again, his expression was grave . . . and tender.

"I always thought I'd know what to do, how to keep you safe. But the other night, when I couldn't get you back . . ."

Shaking his head, Etienne looked away . . . fixed his gaze on the roof of Belle Chandelle.

"Gage . . . he saved your life, *cher.*"

"You both did," Miranda whispered. "You both saved me." *And Parker saved me too, though I swore I wouldn't tell.*

"Yeah, well, don't be getting used to this teamwork stuff. I work alone."

"I'll remember that."

Stepping back, Etienne folded his arms, cocked his head, cleared his throat. "So I was thinking . . . maybe you might wanna do something this weekend."

"Etienne Boucher, are you asking me out on a date?"

"I'm asking what you wanna do, that's all. Like, if I can get me some time off, what would you like?"

"To see you smile again."

She hadn't planned on saying it—and from Etienne's reaction, it was the last thing he'd ever expected to hear.

"What the hell you talking about, Miranda?"

"Well, it's not as adorable as Gage's, but it's pretty darn cute. And I'd like to see it again. As much as possible."

He glanced away, vaguely embarrassed. Miranda tried not to laugh.

"Now . . . you were asking me about a date?" she prompted.

Sighing, he hooked one arm around her neck, steered her onto the path. "Well, yeah. If you're not gonna be too busy—"

"Hmmm . . . I *might* be busy. I guess it just depends on who I'd rather be busy *with*."

"Gage," Etienne groaned. "I'm right, yeah? Always gonna be Gage—"

"I'm not saying. It's a secret."

And as they strolled the tangled grounds of Belle Chandelle, Miranda couldn't help marveling at the irony of it all.

Grandpa made a pact with Etienne. A secret he never told.

And now I've made a pact with Miss Nell. A secret I can never tell.

"Secrets," Miranda said again, but more to herself than to him.

"What's that, *cher*?"

"Nothing." She smiled. "Not important."

Yes, Belle Chandelle was full of them. Just like St. Yvette and the world right here around her and that Other World beyond . . .

But some secrets were *meant* to be discovered. Shared and healed and put to rest . . .

And that's why I'm here.

And today's secrets are just the beginning.

Turn the page to sample the first book in
RICHIE TANKERSLEY CUSICK'S
horror series . . .

Prologue

She had deceived him!

He realized now with a terrible certainty that she'd deceived him from the beginning—planned this whole thing from the very start.

And she knew everything about him—*everything!*—what he was and what he'd done and all he was capable of doing . . .

She'd sought him out and gained his trust, for one purpose and one purpose only.

To see him destroyed.

After he'd been so careful . . . so cunning all these years . . . concealing the very nature of his soul . . . the ageless secrets of his kind . . .

And he'd trusted her. Taken her. Loved her more than he'd ever loved anyone.

Tears clouded his vision.

As though he were seeing the future through a dark red haze, a veil of blood.

He glanced down at his hands.

His strong, gentle fingers, wielding the power of life and death.

He hadn't even realized he was gripping the dagger, the dagger of his ancestors, nor did he remember even drawing it from its sheath.

He was gripping the blade so tightly that a stream of his own blood seeped from his fist. He watched it, strangely mesmerized, as it dripped onto the cold stone floor and pooled around his feet.

He hadn't thought he could feel such pain.

Not from the knife, for he had borne far worse injuries than this in his lifetime, had suffered the ravages of a thousand tortures. But those scars had faded quickly, like shadows swallowed by night, and the few that remained were points of honor to him now, sacred testimonies to his very survival.

No, this pain was different.

This pain burned from deep within, filling him with rage and a craving for revenge.

A craving so intense, he could almost taste it.

1

She should never have come here.

Not into this deep, dark place, not in this miserable weather . . . and *especially* not at night.

"A graveyard," Lucy murmured. "What was I thinking?"

But that was just it—she *hadn't* been thinking, she hadn't had *time* to think, she'd only felt that sudden surge of fear through her veins, and then she'd started running.

Someone was following her.

Not at first, not when she'd first left the house and started walking, but blocks afterward, six or seven maybe, when the storm had suddenly broken and she'd cut through an alley behind a church and tried to find a shortcut home.

No, not home! The words exploded inside her head, angry and defensive. *Aunt Irene's house isn't home, it won't* ever *be home. I don't have a home anymore.*

The rain was cold. Even with her jacket Lucy felt chilled, and she hunched her shoulders against the downpour, pulled her hood close around her face. She hadn't even realized where she was going; there was no sign posted, no gate to mark the boundaries of this cemetery, just an unexpected gap through the trees. She'd heard the footsteps and she'd panicked, she'd bolted instinctively into the first cover of darkness she could find.

But this was a terrible darkness.

Almost as dark as her own pain.

She crouched down between two headstones, straining her ears through the night. It had taken her several minutes to become aware of those footsteps back there on the sidewalk, and at first she'd thought she was imagining them. She'd thought it was only the rain plopping down, big soft drops, faint at first, but then louder and faster, sharper and clearer. Until suddenly they seemed to be echoing. Until suddenly they

4

seemed to have some awful purpose, and she realized they were coming closer.

She'd stopped beneath a streetlamp, and the footsteps had stopped, too. She'd forced herself to look back, back along the pavement, across the shadowy lawns and thick, tangled hedges, but there hadn't been anyone behind her.

No one she could see, anyway.

But *someone* was there.

Someone . . .

She was sure of it.

And that's when she'd run . . .

"I'm afraid you'll find Pine Ridge very different from what you're used to." How many times had Irene told her that, just in the one agonizing week Lucy had been here? "We're right on the lake, of course, and the university's here, so there's plenty to do. And we're only a half-hour drive to the city. But our neighborhood is quiet . . . rather exclusive, actually. Peaceful and private, just the way residents like it. Not at all like that old apartment of yours in the middle of downtown."

But Lucy had loved her old apartment, the tiny, third-floor walk-up that she and her mother had filled with all their favorite things. And the sorrow she'd felt at leaving it only grew worse with each passing day.

She'd been too depressed on their ride from the airport that day to notice much about Pine Ridge; she had only the vaguest recollections of Aunt Irene pointing things out to her as they'd ridden through town. The college campus with its weathered brick buildings and stately oaks. The renovated historical district with its town square and gazebo; its bars, coffee shops and open-air cafés; its bookstores and art galleries and booths selling local crafts. They'd passed farms and fields to get here, and she'd caught occasional glimpses of the lake through dense, shadowy forests. And there'd been frost sheening the hillsides, and she remembered thinking that she'd never seen so many trees, so many vibrant autumn colors . . .

"And it's safe here in Pine Ridge," her aunt had assured her. "Unpleasant things don't happen."

You're wrong, Aunt Irene . . .

Lucy pressed a hand to her temple. That all-too-familiar pain was starting again, throbbing behind her eyes, stabbing through her head, that agony of unshed tears, of inconsolable sorrow . . .

You're wrong, because unpleasant things do *happen*—anywhere—horrible, bad things—*and just when you think they couldn't possibly ever happen to* you—

"Oh, Mom," Lucy whispered. "Why'd you have to die?"

For a split second reality threatened to crush her. Closing her eyes, she bent forward and clamped her knees tight against her chest. She willed herself to take deep, even breaths, but the smell of stagnant earth and rotting leaves sent a deep shiver of nausea through her.

Don't think about that now, you can't think about that now, Mom's gone and you have to get out of here!

Very slowly she lifted her head. Maybe the footsteps had followed her in here—maybe someone was waiting close by, hiding in the shadows, waiting for her to make the slightest move. Or maybe someone was coming closer and closer this very second, searching methodically behind every tombstone, and she'd never hear the footsteps now, not on the soggy ground, not with the sound of the rain, not until it was too late—

Come on, move! Run!

But where? Where could she go? She wasn't even sure where she was, much less which direction to run in.

"Unpleasant things don't happen . . ."

Lucy's heart hammered in her chest. She clung desperately to her aunt's words; she ordered herself to *believe* them. Maybe she really *had* imagined those footsteps back there. Maybe it *had* just been the rain and she'd panicked for nothing. After all, she hadn't really been herself since Mom's funeral. As mechanical as a robot and just as hollow inside, moving in slow motion through an endless gray fog of days and nights, confused by the long, empty lapses in her memory. But shock did that to a person, Aunt Irene had informed her, in that cool, detached tone Lucy was beginning to get used to—*shock and grief and the unbearable pain of losing someone you love . . .*

I can do this . . . I have to do this . . .

Lucy got to her feet. Steadying herself against one of the headstones, she pushed her long wet hair back from her face, then turned slowly, blue eyes squinting hard into the gloom. High above her the limbs of a giant elm flailed wildly in the wind, sending down a soggy shower of leaves. The sky gushed like a waterfall. As the moon flickered briefly through churning clouds, she saw nothing but graves in every direction.

Just dead people, Lucy.

And dead people can't hurt you.

The storm clouds shifted, swallowing the moonlight once more. Swearing softly, Lucy ducked her head and ran.

She didn't have a clue where she was going. She'd never had any real talent for directions, and now she ran blindly, stumbling across uneven ground, weaving between headstones, falling over half-buried markers on forgotten graves. She wondered if Aunt Irene or Angela would be missing her about now—or if they even realized she was gone.

"Or care," Lucy muttered to herself.

The truth was, she'd hardly seen Angela since their initial—and totally awkward—

introduction. Angela—with her perfectly flowing waves of jet-black hair and tall, willowy model's figure—had been slumped in the doorway of her walk-in closet, smoking a cigarette and surveying her extensive wardrobe with a petulant frown.

"Angela, for heaven's sake!" Irene had promptly shut off the CD player that was blasting rock music through the room. "This is your cousin Lucy!"

Angela's eyes had barely even glanced in Lucy's direction—huge, dark eyes ringed with even darker layers of mascara. "So?"

It hadn't been said in a rude way, exactly—more apathetic if anything—but Lucy had felt hurt all the same.

"And get rid of that disgusting cigarette," Irene had ordered, shoving an ashtray toward her daughter. "You know how I feel about smoke in the house. And would it kill you to be civil just once? On Lucy's first night here? After all, you two are the same age; you probably have a lot in common."

Angela hadn't flinched. "You're kidding, right?"